~~~~~~

ALMOST HUMAN

THE FIRST TRILOGY

VOLUME 3

EVOLVING ECSTASY

BY

MELANIE NOWAK

~~~~~~

Praise for Melanie Nowak's Venomous Vampire series
ALMOST HUMAN

"An emotional rollercoaster that will have you sitting in suspense one moment, laughing out loud the next, and then crying your eyes out. ALMOST HUMAN is definitely a book series that should be read slowly and savored."
– www.NightOwlReviews.com

"This intriguing story has lots of action, full of surprises for all the characters. There is a great twist and Nowak certainly knows how to bring the reader into battles of zombies and vampires, as well as torturous internal battles. I love the way the stories progressed and the ending was very satisfying. I look forward to the next series."
- Amy's Bookshelf Reviews

"As the plot thickens, this wonderful story becomes even more enticing. The ending has twists that might be painful to some, but overall is an uplifting, emotional read."
- www.ParanormalRomanceGuild.com

"Melanie Nowak has written her characters in such a way that they keep developing before your eyes, and she keeps you guessing as to what is going to happen next."
– www.2ReadOrNot2Read.com

"Evolving Ecstasy, had me on a rollercoaster ride of who I wanted with who, with a surprise ending I did not expect. I love how this author throws you curve balls that completely leave you hooked and wanting more."
– www.ParanormalRomance.org

"This series has continued to be consistently excellent. I am seriously impressed that the level has remained so outstanding with each book. If you aren't reading this series, you should be!"
- www.NerdGirlOfficial.com

*"I loved this story - such a moving read! Another 5*****stars from me!"*
- Strawberry Reads: The Almost Human Diary (YouTube review channel)

*ALMOST HUMAN - The First Series was originally published as a trilogy of novels, now broken into novellas as an alternate format. The story is told in a serial succession - not stand-alone books. Each novella is meant to be read in order, as the story unfolds chronologically. Each series will be contained enough to be read on its own, with a certain amount of main storyline closure with the last novella, but there will also be some story-ties leading from one series into the next.

If you enjoy this book, please take a moment to leave a review online, on your favorite book review website! Questions and comments can be directed to: WoodWitchDame@aol.com

You can join author/reader discussions about the series, and get updates on upcoming book releases for this series on the author's web site at:

www.MelanieNowak.com

Copyright 2004, 2018
Melanie Nowak, WoodWitchDame Publications
Cover Artwork, Book formatting/Editing: Melanie Nowak
Cover Photo/Model: Natalie Paquette
http://natalie-paquette.wix.com/photos
http://fetishfaerie-photos.deviantart.com/gallery

EVOLVING ECSTASY
ISBN: 978-9824102-7-1
ISBN-13: 978-0-9824102-7-1

~~~~~~~~~~~~~~~~~~~~~~~~~~~~~~~~~~

A Special Thanks to

~~~

My Mom & Step-Dad, Adele and David Weitzel
who have always given their love and support

~~~

My dearly departed brother, John,
who is loved, and missed each day

~~~

And to my wonderful and loving husband,
Scott,
and our sons, William & Eric,

who had patience when I was obsessed with writing,
gave me never-ending confidence and inspiration,
and for whom I am forever grateful
and blessed to have in my life.
I love you dearly.

~~~~~~~~~~~~~~~~~~~~~~~~~~~~~~~

ALMOST HUMAN was originally published as a series of novels, now also broken into novellas as an alternate format. These are not stand-alone books - they are meant to be read in order, as the story unfolds chronologically.

ALMOST HUMAN ~ The First Series

FATAL INFATUATION
Part 1: Captivating Vampires
Part 2: Tempting Transgressions
Part 3: Venomous Revelations

LOST REFLECTIONS
Part 1: Persistent Persuasion
Part 2: Telling Tales
Part 3: Battles and Bliss

EVOLVING ECSTASY
Part 1: Ecstasy Unleashed
Part 2: Stakes and Sunshine
Part 3: Evolution of Love

ALMOST HUMAN ~ The Second Series

BORN TO BLOOD
Part 1: Vampiress Rising
Part 2: Exceeding Expectations
Part 3: Coping with Chaos
Part 4: Vampire Vertigo

DESCENDENT OF DARKNESS
Part 1: Determining Desires
Part 2: Undying Devotion
Part 3: Emotional Maelstrom
Part 4: Crossing the Line

DESTINED FOR DIVINITY
Part 1: Home of the Bloodthirsty
Part 2: Enemies and Allies
Part 3: Vicious Survival
Part 4: Divining Destiny

ALMOST HUMAN ~ The Third Series

VAMPIRESS REIGNING
Part 1: Uniting Vampires
Part 2: Dreams and Schemes
Part 3: Moon Storm

ALMOST HUMAN ∽ THE FIRST TRILOGY

VOLUME 3 ∽ EVOLVING ECSTASY

Contents

Part 3: Evolution of Love

Part 1

Ecstasy Unleashed

Chapter 1 – You'd *better*

Felicity

Felicity's car
Friday, midnight

Felicity felt as though she were on autopilot driving back to Cain's house. Cain was sitting silently beside her. It had been a long night. After sending home their last 'customer', Felicity had quietly questioned Ben. "What are we going to tell Mr. Penten?"

Ben had surveyed the remains of the vampire attack on the store, and shrugged. "We were robbed…by a gang…they were probably on drugs."

"There's no money missing," Felicity had pointed out.

Ben smiled. "That's 'cause I fought them off."

That's when Alyson had started laughing again. "*You* did? You and Felicity, that's your story?"

"It could happen. Anyway, I guess *you* could have been here, but something tells me that *he* won't want to be involved in questioning," he'd said with a gesture towards Cain. Sindy had already slipped out the door.

Cain answered. "I can have been here if you'd like. I've got valid I.D., and you must admit, it would make your story a bit more credible," he'd added with a smirk.

Ben probably hadn't liked the insinuation that no one would believe that he could have done it alone, with only the help of two girls, but he kept quiet. Felicity had then brought up another problem. "So where do we say all of the ashes came from?"

After a thoughtful moment, Ben had asked, "Got a blow dryer?"

And so, Cain and Felicity had gone back to her room for her hair dryer. Upon leaving the store, they had been very surprised to find Sindy, sitting out front on the curb.

To Felicity, she had looked very frightened and alone, sitting on the edge of the parking lot, hugging her knees and looking out into the dark. It had been very odd to see Sindy that way. She got up immediately at their approach, trying to put on a brave face it had appeared. Felicity tried to picture how it would feel to have to walk out into that darkness alone, and actually felt sort of bad for her. "You need a ride somewhere?"

Both Sindy and Cain had looked very amazed that she would ask, but of course, Sindy hadn't accepted. "Na, I'm good." She'd quickly walked away and Cain hadn't said anything about it.

They'd gotten into the car and then Felicity had turned to Cain. "You have I.D., like a driver's license?"

"Mm-hmmm."

She'd just stared at him for a moment. "I can't really picture you standing in line at the D.M.V." He'd laughed and pulled his license out of his back pocket for her to inspect. She'd held it up in the light from the parking lot lamps. "Who is that?"

He'd laughed again. "It's supposed to be me. I paid someone to go get their picture taken for me. Tell me that there's some resemblance," he'd added hopefully.

She had studied his face and the picture in turns. "I guess. He does look a lot like you, but you're definitely the better looking of the two."

"Thanks." He'd given her a smile and a kiss, and then she looked at the card a moment longer. It was issued in New York, but listed his address as being in a town that she didn't know. The name read: Cain Herald VI, Sex: M, Eyes: Bl, Ht: 5' 11". He must have seen her looking a bit confused. "Something wrong?"

She'd looked up at him tentatively. "It says 'Cain'."

His eyes had turned downcast as he answered quietly, "*Christian* Herald has been dead for about two hundred and ninety years." She must have still looked confused. "Did you expect me to list my date of birth as December 25th, *1664* as well? It's not always easy, trying to live in the 'civilized' world but I've managed. In order to keep possession of the Manor and keep my bank accounts in order, I do have to *die* now and again, on paper that is."

"What's the VI?"

"That's the roman numeral for six. I am actually considered to be my own great, great, great, great grandson. It gets a bit confusing I know. I've figured out how to keep things going pretty smoothly now though.

Every thirty years or so, I have a fictional girlfriend 'give birth' to a new persona, my son and namesake, to whom I am given sole custody of course. I give him about twenty years to mature, then I die, and he takes over. It's just a bunch of paperwork really, but you'd be amazed what you can accomplish by giving the right amount of money to the right people. There's probably an easier way to go about it, but I prefer to keep things as legal as possible. I don't like to feel as though I'm hiding anything."

She'd glanced at it once more and then handed it back for him to put it away. It also read 'DOB: 12–25–64'. "According to that you're over forty."

He'd grinned. "I know. I look pretty good for my age, don't I? It'll be time for a new one soon. I start at twenty-one and usually let it go until fifty or so. Much past that and I start drawing odd looks. Of course, I try not to use it unless I have to. It serves."

Just then, Allie had startled them by rapping on the window. Cain had rolled it down for her. "You two haven't even left yet? Let's get this over with and then you can get a room." Cain had just shaken his head with a smile as Felicity started the car and Allie went to get into her own.

They had returned with a blow dryer, to find that Allie had gotten hers as well. They did their best to blow all of the ashes out the broken window and door, while Ben used the attachments on the vacuum cleaner to try and clean up behind the counter. They didn't want it to look 'too' cleaned up before they reported the incident, but at least the ashes were scattered around sufficiently, so as not to be noticeable. Then

Ben had called the police and Mr. Penten, trying to sound out of breath and distraught.

They spent a good deal of time answering questions and standing around waiting to be allowed to leave. They had all agreed ahead of time as to the exact events of the evening so that there had been no discrepancies when reporting to the authorities.

Since there was no money missing and only the windows were broken, they weren't very closely questioned anyway. Mr. Penten was none too pleased about having to close for repairs on a Saturday morning, but at least insurance would cover the windows.

They had finally been allowed to go their separate ways. Allie and Ben each left in their cars, as Cain and Felicity got into hers. She had been about to automatically drive to Cain's house, when he'd turned to her. "You'll probably want to go home, to shower and change. I can walk if it's easier."

Felicity had been behaving normally, cleaning up, answering questions; to everyone else, she must have seemed fine, but she felt as though she was in shock, doing things because she had too, but not really thinking about anything but what had happened and what it might mean for the future. Now that it was finally quiet, all she really wanted was to crawl into Cain's bed and be safe in his arms.

Once he'd mentioned it though, she'd realized that a shower would be a very welcome thing. She'd had little bits of slimy mud, and God knows what else smeared on her from her struggling with the last zombie. She had washed her arms in the sink at the DownTime before the police had arrived, but she'd still felt grossly soiled. She had turned to Cain slowly and asked, "Would you come with me...and wait? I wanna go to your house after."

He'd looked a little concerned, as though just realizing that she might be upset. He'd given her a little smile and said, "Of course luv, whatever you'd like."

She had driven back to her dorm and left Cain in the car while she went in. She had wanted to have him follow, but Maggie had been standing in the doorway, talking with someone. Felicity didn't feel like being questioned, as to Cain's presence.

She'd gone to her room and gathered her things for a shower. She'd come back to her room after, and found Cain sitting on her bed. He'd gestured to her open window. "I hope you don't mind. Didn't want people to think I was sitting out there casing the place."

She'd just smiled, giving her head a little shake. Cain had busied himself looking through her schoolbooks, as she'd changed into her sheep pajamas and thrown clothes for tomorrow into a bag. She'd then slipped on some socks and sneakers, put on a sweatshirt over her pajamas, and went to give him a kiss. As much as she wanted to just melt into his arms, she gave him only a quick peck on the lips. She didn't want to be here, Cain's felt safer. "See you at the car."

She'd planned to say she was going home for the weekend if asked, but Maggie was gone. Cain was already in the car when she got there. So now, they were driving back to his house. All was quiet, and she was glad. She couldn't talk anymore right now. She just stared at the road and wanted to be there already.

They entered the house and went straight downstairs. She

dropped her bag and unzipped her sweatshirt, dropping it to the floor, while eyeing his bed. Cain looked at her thoughtfully. "Tired?" She just nodded her head, took off her shoes and socks, and went to get in the bed. He took off his boots and followed her. He was gazing at her curiously, as she got beneath the covers. "Are you all right?"

She nodded again, but she could feel the tears welling up in her eyes. Cain must have seen them, because he instantly came to her and wrapped her in his arms. "Oh Felicity, it's all right. It's all right now, you're safe." She drew a deep breath and tried not to cry. He must think she was so weak. She didn't know what to say, until he spoke again. "It's all right, it's over now."

She looked up at him, through watery eyes. "No, it's not. You heard her. Chris wants *me*. He wants to kill me...or *worse*."

He seemed a little shaken by the 'worse', but still tried to comfort her. "You know that I will never let you fall into his hands. Don't be afraid, you're safe now."

"But there were so many of them, grabbing at me..."

He looked almost surprised at her. "You've fought far worse. You killed Luke, and that vampire in the cemetery. These tonight were nothing compared to them."

"But they were so, rotten...and awful."

"They may have seemed the stuff of nightmares, but you've seen them before. They are stupid, slow and easily defeated."

"Yeah, for you. I've seen you fight. You're so good at it."

"Unfortunately, I've had a lot of practice."

"Ben killed like four of them! Allie killed one. Even Sindy, did you see her? She was like, *ripping them apart.*"

7

"She killed two or three," he said with a little shrug.

"I didn't kill any. All I did was hide behind my vial and scream."

Cain leaned back to smile at her. "You are a gentle soul, who shouldn't be expected to engage in such pursuits, but you have a strong spirit, and have done remarkably well in these situations. You shouldn't reproach yourself for not fighting like the others. Ben seems to have 'hating vampires' in his blood, *that* fuels his efforts. Alyson does usually fight well, but she's had formal training, and still you've done just as well as her in the past. Sindy...well, against mindless zombies, she hasn't much to fear. They can scratch and bite at her all they like, but without a stake and the presence of mind to use it properly..." He shook his head. "They can't really hurt *her.*"

"I guess knowing that, would give a person confidence. They all have something to make them feel confident and strong. I don't have anything."

Cain tipped her chin to make her look at him. "You've got me." She tried to smile, but the phrase 'screaming horror flick chick' kept haunting her. She tucked her head back down into his chest for a hug. She loved the fact that Cain made her feel safe, but still, she didn't want to have to run to him, every time that danger threatened.

There was a simple solution. Go home. Go back home where danger wouldn't follow, just remove it from her life. It sounded so easy, but she wouldn't do it. If she left, she knew that she would never see Cain again. He was going to take care of all of this and then leave. Somehow, she just knew it. Felicity was unwilling to let him go, not yet.

Holding the vial out in front of her, to ward off that

zombie, had seemed so flimsy and stupid. She wished she'd had the confidence to fight them like Sindy. Sindy seemed to be unafraid of anything. Well, she was frightened of Chris and Marcus, but who could blame her for that? Chris may not be all that intelligent, but he was smart enough to kill her for real and to get Marcus to help him do it, but Sindy sure wasn't scared of much else. What must it be like, to have the assurance of immortality to fall back on?

Something else came to mind, a solution that she had been very carefully avoiding. She could let Cain mark her again. It wouldn't guarantee anything; Chris may still be able to work around it, but she was pretty sure that it would protect her from any lesser vampires he might make. They were driven by instinct. They should have an overwhelming desire to stay away from her, if she was marked.

In fact, she suddenly realized that Ben had that advantage. No wonder he had managed to kill an impressive three zombies and one real vampire, without getting hurt. They were unable to bite him!

Still, she had kept the experience of being marked by Cain, safely hidden away from her conscious mind. It was not something she had ever thought to consider again. It was so much easier to think of Cain as a man, and not someone capable of such strange things. He was just holding her quietly, trying to make her feel safe. She looked up at him again, trying to 'see' the vampire in him. It just wasn't there for her to see, not now. He smiled at her. "You needn't worry about Chris. I won't let him get to you."

"I know, but he had so many others."

"Whom we killed."

"He can make more."

Cain looked thoughtful. "I suppose it's possible that he kept a few in reserve, but I doubt it. As for making more, we won't give him the time. Creations such as his, take time to reawaken. Unless he uses a considerable amount of care in making more, they will take a week or two to come back. In fact, judging by the condition of some of them, I'd say he made them more than a month ago."

"Yeah, I guess, but he still has *Marcus*. Cain, no offense but I don't even think that *you* could take *him*."

Cain gave her a kiss on the forehead. "Don't you worry about it. For *you*, I'd fight Satan himself. Now get some rest. I'm going to go and take a shower of my own." He hugged her close for another minute and then got up from the bed. At least she felt safe here. She lay there, feeling very comforted just lying snuggled warm in his bed and watching him move about the room.

She admired his body as he undressed. She had to smile remembering that earlier, in her room, he had purposely *not* watched her as she disrobed to change. He was such a gentleman. She'd been glad at the time. He had seen her body often enough in the past week that she shouldn't be self-conscious, but she still *was* a little. Now she noted that he didn't even seem to notice or care if she watched him. Everyone she knew seemed so much more confident than she was, in every way. He shut all the lights, save those behind the bar, and disappeared into the bathroom. As she listened to the water begin to run in the shower, she drifted off to sleep.

~~~~~~~~~~~~~~~~~~~~~~~~~~~~~~~~~

Beep-beep-beep. Felicity awoke, thinking that her alarm clock sounded very odd. That's because it was the microwave. Oh yeah, she was at Cain's. She didn't feel as though she could have slept long. It must still be the middle of the night. She opened her eyes and found Cain in the dim light, coming out of the laundry room to go behind the bar. He'd already showered and his hair was mostly dry. He was dressed in a pair of blue pajama pants, nothing else.

He didn't seem to notice that she was awake. Her eyes lingered on his broad, muscular shoulders as he took his cup out of the microwave and turned to lean on the bar. He was reading the newspaper. She lay there, for what seemed like a very long time, just watching him drink from his mug and read. Even in that unassuming pose he seemed so strong and unshakable; handsome and robust, her protector. And yet, he seemed so incredibly normal, like any guy in his pajamas, reading the paper and drinking his morning coffee...only it wasn't coffee.

She knew that there must be blood in the cup. That seemed so strange to her. She realized that he never drank in front of her. He must purposely drink when she was not around. She wondered how much of it he actually had to drink. Where did he get it all from? How could he actually drink that? She could not imagine voluntarily drinking blood; it seemed so nauseating. It was true that his body had been changed to need it, but still. What did it taste like? He didn't actually *like* it, did he? Did it taste good to him now?

He finished what was in the cup, stood there for a moment finishing the page he was reading, and then put down the mug. Felicity closed her eyes. She wasn't sure why, but she knew he was going to look up at her, and she didn't want him to know that she was awake yet. She liked lying there cozy and sleepy, just watching him.

After a moment, she heard him moving around behind the bar again. She opened her eyes to see him take something from the refrigerator. It looked like a Ziploc bag…of blood. He began to pour it carefully into his mug. She leaned up a little on her elbow to see better. She just couldn't believe that he had *blood* in a bag like that, in the refrigerator. Surely it seemed perfectly normal to him, but it was just so odd.

He saw the movement and looked up to see her awake. He seemed a bit startled, and she was very glad that she hadn't made him spill it. He carefully finished pouring, and then closed the bag.

She was still openly watching him with morbid fascination. He just stood there for a moment, looking back at her. She sat up better on the bed. Finally, she had to ask. "Where do you get that?"

He furrowed his brow and seemed to think that she would already know. "The butcher."

Felicity sighed with realization and relief. "Oh, it's *cows'* blood."

Again, Cain seemed a bit confused at her response. "What did you think, that I robbed the red cross?" he asked with a little laugh. He turned and put the cup into the microwave, setting it for a minute. "Actually, this is pig's blood, but sometimes it's cow."

Felicity was looking at him very strangely. "You can tell the difference?"

Cain gave her an odd little smile. He seemed amused that

they should be having this conversation. "You'd be amazed." She just stared at him for a moment until the microwave beeped. Cain removed his cup, swirled it around a little, turned to face her and took a small sip. It almost seemed to Felicity, that he did it very intentionally, for her to watch; as though it were high time she faced the truth. He was not human, no matter how well he could pretend to be.

She watched him as he drank some more. "I guess it's a lot different from..." she forced herself to say it, *"human blood."*

Cain gave her a weary little smile. "Water and wine my dear. Water and wine."

So weird. How could the same thing taste so different, just because it came from a different source? "So do different people taste different too?" Felicity suddenly shook her head, becoming disgusted with herself. "Ech, why am I even asking you this? This is so morbid."

Cain gave her a sympathetic little laugh. "It's alright; you're allowed to be curious. I won't tell anyone," he added, conspiratorially. Felicity tried to regain her composure and think of something to change the subject, but before she'd the chance, he answered her question. "If you continue to think of it as 'wine', different people are like different vintages, if you will. Some are similar." He eyed her, a bit hesitantly. "Some are very unique." After a moment, he then gave a little laugh. "I suppose you could consider animal blood to be watered down grape juice in comparison."

Cain had never denied her any information that she'd asked after, but she still felt as though this were a very rare and privileged conversation; one only relegated to the middle of the night in a dimly lit room. It was a conversation that she would not have the courage to continue at another time. She decided that if she was going to satisfy her curiosities, she ought to do it now while she still had the courage. "What's it like for you, when you...feed, from a person I mean? Is it just...food?"

By the look on Cain's face, she could tell that he thought she already knew the answer to that. "What do you think?"

She looked away for a moment, biting her lip and remembering when he'd drunk from her. "I think it's...much more," she answered reluctantly.

He seemed glad that she would admit it. "Much, *much* more." Cain took another sip from his cup, but seemed to find it distasteful now.

Felicity nerved herself to repeat the real question. "So, what's it like, for you?"

He came out from behind the bar and leaned against it, in front of the bed. It seemed obvious that this was a topic that she had been avoiding all along. "Are you sure this is a can of worms you want opened, luv?"

Felicity's answer was quiet but insistent. "I want to know."

He sat down on the bed next to her, with his mug still in hand. Its content was so dark; it could almost be mistaken for black coffee...almost. Felicity raised her eyes from it to find him watching her inspect the cup with quiet amusement. She fidgeted a little and rested her hand on his leg.

Felicity was very interested in what he had to say, and yet even through that, she could not help but be very physically aware of his body. He was only half dressed and so close to her on the bed. The temptation was great to try and rebury her questions back into her subconscious mind in lieu of other pursuits. Damn but the man was sexy!

She kept her eyes on his face, and chased indecent thoughts from her mind. He had lost his little smile and seemed to exude an odd sense of anticipation, over the conversation of blood and his vampire experiences. As though these were things he had been waiting to discuss. Like he could hardly believe she would finally ask, and was unsure how to answer in a way that she would accept and not be frightened of. "It's kind of hard to explain." He took her hand and kissed it. "It's more the kind of thing you have to..." He then, in a bizarre gesture, dipped one of her fingers into the blood in his cup, "experience."

He was holding her hand in front of her. She looked at her bloody finger then back at him, thinking 'You're crazy if you think I'm going to taste that'. She moved her hand towards his mouth and looked away from him. Cain sucked the blood from her finger, almost as though it should be something seductive.

He leaned forward to make her meet his gaze. "Perhaps my experiences have caused me to view things differently than most, but it *is* only blood. 'Tis not something vile or distasteful really, just a natural thing. It's in all of us, in one way or another. And to both of us, it means life.

The experience of *drinking* it however, from a vampire's point of view, is something not easily relayed. Kind of like trying to describe sex to a virgin," he added with a grin.

Felicity pulled back her hand, trying to keep her mind from the remembrance of losing her virginity to him in the very bed she now sat upon. "Now you're just teasing me."

15

He stood up with a little laugh. "Good analogy though." He went to put his cup down on the bar. "You must realize that this is not something I have all that much recent experience in." He looked at her with a fond little smile. "But from what I remember from less enlightened days, most feeds were like...a one-night stand. An intense, erotic encounter with someone you barely knew, that culminated in brief, fleeting ecstasy... Then you left them, and moved on." She did not look very kindly upon that description; however accurate it may be.

He took on a gentler tone. "But then I learned to drink *not* to kill. And then I learned to drink *not* for food. Once I drank, for the *experience*... *That* was something entirely different. You know that I don't drink human blood any longer, not on a regular basis. You also should know that it is an experience like none other; for me, *and* for you.

To drink from a host, for a vampire, is the ultimate experience. Just as sex may be for a human being. Sex is *meant* to be pleasing for you. 'Tis procreation; vital to the continuation of human existence and so, the Lord made it enjoyable as well.

While physical love in the human sense, is enjoyable still to the vampire; blood, *that* is true ecstasy. Drinking blood is my ensured continuance, as well as being one half of the act of creating another, and so, acquiring blood is pleasurable to my body, as sex is to yours.

In order to assure cooperation from the one whom a vampire chooses to drink from, there is the venom. That ensures that *your* body will find it pleasurable as well.

Now, in the common order of things...in the world of

'predator' and 'prey', you may consider that a 'dirty rotten trick'," he said with a little laugh. He gently eased himself to sit back down on the bed next to her again. "But *ours* is not a *common* relationship, is it?"

Felicity gave him a shy smile and dropped her eyes to the bed sheets. "I think I see where this might be going."

Cain sighed. "It doesn't have to go anywhere, but I must submit that although it's a comparison that *you* haven't the perspective to fully appreciate...having sex without love, a 'one-night-stand' if you will, is like drinking from someone...for the blood. I can't say why there should be a difference, but drinking from someone that you truly care for...that experience is like the difference between *having sex, and making love.*"

He continued cautiously, as though he knew he was moving into tender territory. "Drinking from you, for your mark... Well, I didn't take much. I didn't want to weaken or overly frighten you more than necessary. I never would have hurt you, but...drinking from you..." his voice dropped to the barest whisper, "was beyond *divine.*

I thanked God for my self-control, because nothing less than iron will could have pulled me from *your* throat that night." He closed his eyes and seemed to breathe in her scent, to help recreate the moment in his mind. There was a moment of uneasy silence between them, as he recalled the experience.

She couldn't bring herself to speak, so *he* asked the unvoiced question that had always lain between them. "That night...we never have spoken of it, not really. *Your* thoughts, impressions, feelings...and fears. To be honest, I've been afraid to ask."

He seemed suddenly so vulnerable and frightened of her response. He was usually so confident, that those times when he did leave himself open to her, so obviously exposed emotionally, it melted her heart.

She gave a small smile and swallowed nervously. How could she possibly call up that memory again and then try to *describe it?* "I don't think I have the words." She took a deep breath and forced herself to dig out the experience from her memories. She closed her eyes and could feel it as though it were happening again. Her rapid pulse, the prick and penetration of his fangs into her throat, the swooning dream state, the waves of...

She raised her eyes to his. "It *was...divine.*" Her voice trembled with the whispered confession and she felt choked, tears rising to her eyes. She couldn't have said why, except that she had tried not to face it for so long, hidden it away, but she had known it all along of course.

She looked at him silently, her bottom lip slightly quivering. She knew what he wanted. Did she want it too? She would feel comforted to be marked, but that seemed almost an artificial reason. Part of her wanted to relive that experience, she did. She had just been loath to admit it to herself, until now, but another part of her was still afraid.

Not really afraid that he would hurt her. She trusted him, if he said he had sufficient control, she believed him, but she was frightened that to her mind, he would no longer be Cain, her safe and comforting rescuer. That he would become...something else. One of *them...a monster.*

Eventually, she made a decision. She knew how to decide

what she truly wanted, a way to see how she would feel about it. She told him in a quiet, little girl voice, what she needed him to do. "Change for me."

Cain clearly did not like this turn of things. He was obviously worried to frighten her from him. It seemed as though he worried that if she saw him that way, their relationship would not recover from the development. He answered her in a mumbling sort of voice, avoiding eye contact. "Oh, I don't have to. I can do it at the last second, you wouldn't even know...until you felt it."

Felicity smiled. "What, you're suddenly shy? I want to see."

He tried to shrug it off. "You've seen others."

"Not up close, not like this. And *they're not you,*" she insisted.

Cain looked very reluctant and still had trouble meeting her eyes. "Sure you can handle it?"

Felicity put one finger to his chin to tilt his head to look at her, as he so often did to her. "Guess we'll find out."

Cain fidgeted on the bed next to her. He'd obviously like to decline, but she was determined not to let him. "You sure?" he asked one last time.

She let out an exasperated huff. "Are we going to do this or not?" Without another word, she watched as Cain closed his eyes, seeming to prepare himself mentally, and brought forth...the vampire within.

He didn't change all that much really. It was a bit unsettling to see his cheek bones begin to move of their own accord. It was slight, but she was paying close attention. She noticed the sides of his face seemed to shift upwards a bit, as his upper jawbone seemed to lengthen. To accommodate his fangs, she assumed. He kept his mouth closed, but his face did look subtly different in shape.

Then, he opened his eyes. Felicity had to force herself not to flinch. His eyes...they were a golden yellow color, rich and bright, like marigolds. They each had a long black pupil, like a cat's. It was very disconcerting to see those golden orbs staring out from Cain's face, where his beautiful marine blue eyes used to be.

Felicity stared at him a moment, then hesitantly reached up to brush the hair from his eyes. She let her fingers trail down the side of his face and then gently part his lips, pulling the corner of his upper lip up to one side, to see his fangs. An incredibly sharp and thin gleaming point was there. She quickly pulled her hand away.

She stared into his eyes a moment and then said in disappointed little voice, "I wish your eyes were still blue."

She felt terrible when he looked down, almost ashamed. "What color are they?" he asked.

Now she looked at him with amazed wonder. "Don't you know?"

He gave a little shrug. "A vampire can't see its reflection. I haven't seen myself since I died."

"They're yellow."

He gave her a small nod. "Figured as much. Maribeth's are a very light golden orange, and most of my...offspring's are light as well, but some vampires have red. Guess it depends on your...lineage." He became increasingly uncomfortable, as she simply stared at him. "Are you done?"

Felicity couldn't help but become indignant. "No." She

looked at him for a moment and then slowly leaned forward, to give him a soft, hesitant kiss on the mouth; sweet, deliberate and unrushed. After an initial startled moment, he began to kiss her back and she even bravely let her tongue very briefly enter his mouth. She was vaguely aware of his fangs, but it wasn't distressing really. It was a kiss…from Cain. She then leaned back and looked into his eyes again. "Yes. I mean, whatever…it doesn't matter. It's still you."

Cain stared at her for a moment and then shifted back to his human face. His eyes began to well up with unshed tears as he looked at her in wonder. "Have I ever told you how incredibly in love with you I am?" She smiled.

"I think you may have mentioned it, yeah." They stared into each other's eyes for a moment longer. "Not that it matters, but *this* is definitely a better look for you."

Cain laughed. He was still looking at her in amazement. As though he couldn't quite believe she was still there, and not frightened away from him. Felicity gave him another shy little smile. "Well, we've got some experimenting to do, don't we?"

Cain became flustered, as though embarrassed to ask it of her at this point. "No, I don't need to…"

"You'd *better,*" she said playfully, trying to bring him around to being his normal self again. "Now who's being timid?" He still looked as if he didn't quite believe her. She knew that he really wanted to, but was afraid to give in to his desires, only to find that she would resent him for it. "I'd be safer if I were marked," she reminded him.

When he did not answer, she gently moved her hair to one side and tilted her head slightly, to expose her throat. He needed no further persuasion. Cain began to lean in towards her, when she hesitated and put a hand up to stop him for a moment. "Self-control, right? If it's okay with you, I would like to walk out of here with a heartbeat."

Now he smiled. "As you wish, my lady." He leaned in to her and she let him come first to her lips for a kiss, passionate and deep. After a time, once her head was nicely spinning with the venom of his kiss, his lips left her mouth to move down the side of her neck, until he reached almost the very spot where he had bitten her before.

Her heart began to pound, her pulse to race, as she anticipated the feel of his teeth at her throat. She tensed for the pain, but it was another kiss he bestowed upon her skin. He placed one kiss after another, until she was beginning to wonder if he would go through with it.

Then she felt the tips of his fangs pierce her flesh. He did it quickly and decisively in one swift bite, hugging her to him closely. So keen were the points of his teeth, that there was only a moment of pain...and then she felt *the venom.*

It was much more prominent to her senses, now that she recognized it for what it was. She could feel the warmth of it spreading from her throat, to move throughout her body. Her limbs felt heavy and the actual bite seemed almost numb.

Cain held her firmly as the dreamy, euphoric haze that often accompanied his kisses now grew into more and enveloped her mind until she felt almost as though she were floating. That's when he began to drink. At first, just a small and almost hesitant tug at her throat. She felt his lips seal over the spot in a gentle kiss, but then, he truly drank. He sucked strongly at her throat and as before, on the night of her first mark, as her blood filled his mouth, she heard him issue a low moan of pleasure. It was almost as though she could feel vibrations of it travel through her body, tugging at nerves that ran deep to secret places within her. His sucking felt like a tide of longing, washing over her, again and again. Waves of soothing comfort, pleasure and an ever-increasing desire for more.

She gave herself over to the rhythm of it, swooning in his arms and reveling in her surrender, but after only a few moments, she felt him withdraw. He covered the spot with little kisses and licks, and finally pulled back to look upon her face.

She felt dizzy and abandoned, left teetering on a precipice of passion. She tried to clear her mind and opened her eyes. It took a moment to truly focus upon his face. She wanted to ask why he had stopped, but some part of her mind chastised her for her foolishness. Would she have him drink her to death?

After gazing upon her for a moment with eyes once again blue, he leaned forward and she almost wished she could beg for him to return to her throat, but he only kissed the spot once more and then his lips moved to taste and tickle her ear. He kissed and nuzzled her cheek, and whispered, "I could have gone on far longer. I know how much you can safely give, but I thought it best I take things slowly, test the waters. Are you well?"

"Mm-hmm," was all she could manage to utter. She let herself lean against him, her head on his shoulder, but then he leaned her back so that his lips might meet hers. He tempted her with whispering little kisses at first, his tongue darting

23

about her lips with teasing little licks. Finally, she managed to pull herself from her haze sufficiently to wind her hand into the hair at the back of his head to hold him firm for a true kiss. The kiss was long and grew heated until she needed to lie back, longing to feel him over her.

She wanted to be covered and completely permeated with his presence, outside and in. She wanted him to...*own* her. Never a phrase she would have chosen before, but at this moment, it was a basic and carnal need, an apt description.

He left her lips to pull the pants from her legs and just as quickly discard his own. He then climbed back on the bed to straddle her with a leg on either side of her hips. She looked up at him through heavy lidded eyes. He seemed to tower over her, strong and masculine, dominating. And yet she had no fear of him, none. His words from the first time they had made love drifted back to her. 'Have trust, never fear' and she did have perfect trust.

He put his palms flat to her belly, cool and soft upon her skin, and slid them slowly upwards, to cover her breasts beneath the little tank top she wore. He cupped each breast for a gentle squeeze and then sought to find her nipples to lightly pinch and tease.

His hands left her breasts to support her back and sit her up, so that he might pull off the shirt over her head. Once he removed it, she lay back again and he ran his hands over her breasts once more, his fingers lightly rubbing back and forth and drawing little circles around her nipples.

Cain moved his body and parted her thighs, so that his knees could rest on the bed between them; and then moved down so that his lips might cover the nipple of her left breast.

He gently suckled her, and her body responded with warm and wet anticipation between her legs, but her breath caught in her throat when she unmistakably felt the tips of his fangs against the plump flesh of her breast. He did not bite her, but hovered there a minute as she held her breath.

He suckled her for a moment more, allowing her to breathe and then looked up to her pleadingly, with his now golden eyes. She was still unused to seeing him this way, but although it caused her heart to pound, she was not really startled or afraid. It was as though she were allowing herself to discover this new side of him now; not as something to fear, but something interesting and new. After a moment's hesitation, she gave him a quick little nod of her head. Let him do what he would, she was beyond worry over such things.

She lay her own head back to the pillow and could not resist but to move her hips against him and press her body to his, although it was only his smooth stomach that the downy hair between her legs rubbed against. He sucked upon and kissed her breast a moment more, before piercing it with his bite.

Felicity felt as though the room was spinning and needed to open her eyes to prove it wasn't so. The warmth and comfort of the venom was renewed within her and his suckling upon her breast to draw her blood, was an experience sensual and exquisite. He did not let it go on long though. As he left the bite, she felt the peculiar mixed sensations of the cold air against her skin and the warmth of the venom pulsing beneath.

This time, when he brought his lips to hers for a kiss, it was with a hunger that was passionate and demanding, as she had never felt from him before. It was tinged with the slightly metallic taste of her blood. She kissed him and wrapped her arms around his lower back, silently begging him to consummate their love once more.

The venom still caused her to feel as though she was floating upon a heavenly plane when the thrust she had awaited tried to bring her to earth. She only felt connected to her body through the hollow ache inside of it that he now filled with his own.

She wrapped her arms and legs around him, trying to anchor herself to the reality of their bodies intertwined. Desperate to be ever closer to him, she held him as though they could meld into one being. He rocked and moved within her slowly but with ever-increasing speed and intensity, until he began to gently impress his teeth to the tender place between her shoulder and throat. They felt flat and even, the teeth of his human self. Again and again, he gave her little play bites alternated with kisses, until she could hardly stand to feel the barrier of skin between them.

In breathless whispers, she begged him, the barest voice that only he could hear. "Please, do it Cain. Drink from me, **more**." The last was more a demand than a plea and it seemed to ignite his fervor. He began to build his movements to a degree that she had never experienced from him; strong, bold and desperate, where he had always been so gentle and patient before.

It drove her wild. She craned her head aside in a needy attempt to force him to drink from her before orgasm bore her away. He waited only a moment, and then once more sunk his fangs into her willing throat. With his first pull upon her vein, her body's climax caused her to grip and crush herself to him with all of her strength, though her muscles were surely nothing to his. He withdrew his fangs to let out a cry of his own pure pleasure. He held her firmly as she felt his body fill hers with the warmth and magic of his satisfaction and yet again, she was borne away to ecstasy.

When he loosened his hold upon her and caused his body to leave hers, he let his lips return to her neck. Not to bite, but only to gently kiss and suck upon the wound already there. Her muscles slowly untensed and she felt amazingly comforted by his tender attentions to her throat. Slight shivers and aftershocks of pleasure moved through her now and then from the venom within. Gentle sighs escaped her throat until finally he forced himself to leave her wound and find her lips instead. She felt herself in such a dream-state, that she found it hard at first to find the words she wanted to say. After a moment, she managed to tell him, in a whisper, "You don't have to stop."

He let out a low moan that ended in a little a laugh. "Yes...I do." He rolled onto his back and she quickly moved to keep contact with his body. Even to be only pressed against his side was so much better than to be separate. "The venom, it has a decoagulating agent in it."

As if that explained anything. She felt annoyed that he might expect her to actually *think* at a time like this. She had meant to tell him 'The venom's also got my head reeling at the moment. A deco- what?', but all that seemed to come out was a mumbled... "Huh?"

He laughed and sat up next to her. "It keeps the blood flowing freely so that it won't clot too soon. Not only have I taken just about as much as I should, but we have to make sure it stops bleeding. My licking and kissing you there, only makes things worse."

She could hardly keep her eyes open as she voiced her disappointment. "Mmmm, but it was so...*nice.*"

He laughed at her again as he softly caressed her cheek. "Yes, I think you've had quite enough." He used his finger to stroke the bite once more and then brought it to his mouth to taste. She watched him, dim and fuzzy, beneath her drooping eyelids. He seemed to inspect the wound at her breast without actually touching it, and then drew the sheets up over her body to her shoulders.

She was half-asleep and hadn't even felt him leave the bed until he returned with a tissue to gently dab her throat once more. She tried to smile at him as he leaned forward to place a kiss upon her forehead. The next she knew, the world was black.

~~~~~~~~~~~~~~~~~~~~~~~~~~~~~~

When next Felicity opened her eyes, it was to see Cain putting a paper bag down on the bar. He was dressed and wearing his leather jacket; he must have gone out. She hadn't even heard him leave. His return had awoken her, not from the noise, but from the feelings that his proximity produced. It was a bit startling, yet oddly familiar to recognize that her body was acutely attuned to his now, just as it had been when she was marked the first time, but now it was so much more. The connection was so meaningful now, and emotional as well. She found it very reassuring.

Cain's closeness gave her warm shivers and tingles of anticipation upon her skin; it made her long for his touch. It was his venom within her. She belonged to him now. She was marked for all vampires to see…as his. He noticed her awake and spoke as he took off his jacket. "Oh good, I was hoping you wouldn't awaken 'til I returned. I hadn't anything to leave you a note."

"Where'd you go?" Her voice sounded oddly thick and groggy to her ears. She cleared her throat and blinked her eyes to clear the haze of sleep, and tried to ignore the odd sensations that his nearness produced in her now.

Cain laid his jacket on the bar and smiled at her. "Well, I figured you might be hungry and I haven't got anything here; so, I thought I'd do some shopping."

Felicity suddenly realized that she was rather hungry. She rolled onto her side to see him better, without having to sit up. "What'd you get?"

"Now keep in mind I couldn't go far; I didn't want to leave you for long and it's nearly dawn. There's not much open around here at this hour." With that disclaimer, he began pulling items from the bag, naming them as he placed them on the bar. "Bag of pretzels, Chocolate chip cookies…"

"Ooh, Entenmann's?" she asked.

"Are they any good?" he inquired.

"Are you kidding?" she asked in disbelief. "What else?"

"Milk and orange juice. I didn't know which you'd want. That's it. Oh, and a beef jerky." He gave her an apologetic little shrug.

"Interesting assortment," she said with a laugh.

"I hope it'll do. The gas station doesn't exactly have a

large selection, besides, orange juice and cookies, isn't that what they give out at the hospital when you donate blood?" She giggled and he moved to sit next to her on the bed, gently moving the hair away from her face on the pillow.

He very slowly touched his fingertips lightly to her cheek, trailing them gently downward. As when marked before, she was amazed at the electric sensations that his touch caused on her skin. He leaned forward and gave her a tender kiss, which after a moment turned into lots of little kisses with which he smothered her face and neck, making her squirm and giggle. Each one was made into a magic little thrill by the mark upon her. He ended it by nuzzling the side of her throat and giving it a last very deliberate kiss over his bite there. He inspected the spot for a moment and then looked at her with almost bashful concern. "How are you feeling?"

Felicity smiled at him, instantly touched and amused. "Look at you, you're all concerned and worried about me. You're so cute!"

He stood from the bed. "Vampires are not *cute.*" He moved to behind the bar, crumpled up and threw away the bag.

"Well, *you* are. Relax, I'm fine…see!" To try and prove her point, she sat up far too quickly and suffered a major head rush. "Whoa." She slowly lay back down.

"Uh huh, think I'll bring the cookies to you. Milk or juice?"

"Milk, and I am fine. I just sat up too fast."

He poured her milk into a mug. "M-hmm."

Doubt tried to creep into her mind. "Why? You don't think I need a transfusion or something, do you?"

Cain laughed and then looked a little insulted as he opened the cookie box. "Of course not. I stopped well above what should be your tolerable level of loss. You just need some rest."

He brought her the milk and open cookie box. She smiled and sat up a little as he handed her a cookie. "You're going to serve me?"

"Always and forever if I could," he said with a very serious and genuine look of love, as he sat on the bed.

She held her cookie and snuggled close to him, as she nibbled it. "After last night, forever's soundin' pretty good. I wouldn't mind a forever filled with nights like *that*." She suddenly dropped the hand with the cookie back down to her lap, to look at Cain in seriousness. "Except for the zombies. I don't much care for zombies."

Cain laughed. "No zombies, got it." He gazed at her as she finished her cookie and took a swig of milk from her mug. He raised his hand to run his fingers through her hair and gave her a kiss on the cheek. She smiled, but then looked down at her lap in thought. "What is it?" he asked.

She shrugged. "Nothing."

He dipped his head to find her eyes with his own. "What are you thinking about, that's taken the smile from your lovely face?"

"I was just remembering...that night at Tommy's. Remember when Sindy called me a dog without a leash? She said I ought to have a license."

Cain shook his head in disgust. "Why do you think of such things now?"

"Well, I didn't really *get* it then of course, but she was

talking about me not being marked, right?" Cain acceded with a slight nod of his head. "Like I was your pet or something. I never really thought about what that could mean...until now, but a vampire could do that, couldn't they? Keep someone, like a pet. Someone to...play with, drink from."

"You're not my pet. I don't think of you that way and I'll thank you not to use the term. It's barbaric."

"I'm sorry. I know *you* don't do stuff like that, but others, vampires like Arif; they do, don't they?" He nodded. "*That,* with him, it just seems creepy. But being with you all the time, that doesn't sound bad at all. Call it whatever you want."

He became very uncomfortable and moved away from her a bit on the bed. "Don't talk like that. Is that what you want? To be shut up down here all the time, with nothing to look forward to but me?"

She smiled. "I'm sure you'd let me go out if I were good."

"Stop it. It's not funny. There are those, like Arif, who do that you know. And it's not always a *voluntary* thing."

That caused her to shudder. "Sorry, but that's not really what we're talking about here. Why couldn't I just stay with you? Not like a prisoner, but the way things are now. I think I could be very happy, spending all of my nights with you."

"There's one major obstacle there. You're not *like* me."

"So? That's okay. I can accept that now. In fact, right now, that's seeming like a pretty good thing. I may not have enough in me to feed you all the time, but my body is making more even as we speak." She smiled and spread her arms. "I'm a renewable resource."

Cain rolled his eyes and groaned. "Felicity, the fact that I'm a vampire in itself, is not entirely the problem, but think of what that means. You age, while I do not."

"So...what, you don't like old ladies?" she teased.

"Time is valuable for you, when it means almost nothing to me. Unless you were to decide, that a life like mine was what you really wanted... Well unless that were so, then time spent with me, for you...is time wasted, time from your finite and ever-advancing life. To spend all of your time with me, what kind of life is that? To not be accomplishing something, not to be actually doing anything of worth; to have no goals, no career, no family, no future; you deserve more than that."

"I could be with you and still have that stuff, a job or whatever."

"You have no idea how difficult it would be. You don't want to spend your life trying to hide me from your friends and family, or to lie and make excuses for me during every daytime event you attend. You shouldn't have to waste all of your energies on living a lie when you should be focused on your future in the real world."

"All that stuff seems so important to you. I guess it *should* be important to me too, but right now all that I can say really matters to me, is being happy. Being with you makes me happy. Doesn't it make you happy too?"

"Oh luv, what a question. You cause my heart to soar like none other before you. I would very happily keep you with me until the end of my time on earth, but it would be at the price of giving up many of your human ties. I don't know that it's not more than you should be willing to pay.

The life that I lead is certainly fulfilling and worthwhile in its own ways. At least I like to think so, even though it is very lonely much of the time. *If* you were to decide that truly, in your heart, you want to share in that with me...Well, I don't know that I *could* ever turn you away, but you are so young! Too young perhaps, to know what you want from life. You need to live, before you can die, or you will forever resent me for it."

"But why can't we just stay together the way that we are now? Things are good."

He smiled sadly. "Good for *me*."

"You don't think they're good for me too? I love spending my time with you."

"It all goes back to what I said before. It's time wasted. I can keep you selfishly to myself for a small period of time, but I could never justify more than a little while. Your life is going by. You can't be content just to let it."

He turned to face her more fully on the bed and took her hands into his own. He raised them to his lips, to kiss her fingertips, and then smiled as he gazed into her eyes as he spoke again. "Somewhere, out there in the world, is another man. A human man, and he's just waiting to fall head over heels in love with you; much as I am now."

"I'll never love anyone the way that I love you," she told him with a pouting voice.

He gave her a sad little smile. "I'd like to agree, but I have lived through love and heartache as you have not. I know it seems that nothing could be stronger than our love *now*. And I do hope that you will keep my love for you in a special place, always remembered in your heart, but you are a loving young lady, and your heart is big enough to love another as well as me. You'll see.

Someday you'll meet another and *his* love for you will

overshadow mine. I can't say I look forward to the prospect, but I know it must be true, as he will be able to give you all of the things which I cannot. I could care for your every need surely, but only he could take you for a walk in the sunlight. He can be a part of your life in the world, not I.

He will love you and protect you; treasure your precious heart and make you happy in all of the ways of which I can only dream. You'll have a place in the world, a career, a happy marriage and a family," he said with a broad smile. "Children, lots of them; you'll make a wonderful mother. You should have a real life." He held back unshed tears and tried to smile, as he continued.

"To stay with me might make you happy for a time. We could probably preserve restraint and safeguard your health through my tender drinks, albeit through great difficulty, but the years will pass and one day you'll look back to see that you've nothing. You'll have nothing in your life, but me; nothing accomplished, nothing achieved, nothing to show for your time spent on earth...with death looming ever nearer. You'll become bitter, vengeful and you will either leave me, to be old and alone for the last of your days...or you will then, beg me for the blood. Even if I were to give it to you, you'll be older then. And I will love you still, but how resentful might you be, to be trapped for eternity in a body no longer in the blush of youth? You will hate me for not giving it to you sooner, but if I did give it to you now, how will you ever know of the life you'll have missed?

No, to stay with me is the wrong decision for you to make in either case. No matter how badly I might long for you to make it. I try to tell myself that we could be happy together, always, but as you can see, upon closer inspection, all scenarios seem to fall apart. I can't do that to you. I will leave *because* I love you. I won't take your life away or make you waste it with me for my own selfish ends.

I've tried to be firm in the choice from the beginning, but loving you so, does cause me to waver now and again, but when the time comes, I *will* leave you. I'm not yet sure when that will be, but it will come sooner than later. And *you* will have to let me go."

He spoke gently and evenly, with a calm that she almost resented, but she knew that he was right. He was a good man trying desperately to do the right thing, though it break their hearts. Somehow, he remained composed, although she could feel the tears gently rolling down her cheeks.

She almost felt as though she wanted to beat upon his chest, to tell him that it was cruel and unfair, but anything she might say or do seemed only like a waste of their precious time. And so, she only crushed herself to him for an embrace and prayed that he would stay for as long as he could. After a time, he undressed and joined her under the covers. She held him tightly, as though afraid that he might leave her in the night, although she knew that was foolish. He held her as well, and eventually, they slept.

~~~~~~~~~~~~~~~~~~~~~~~~~~~~~~~~~~~

Felicity glanced at her watch, and then snuggled closer to Cain to give him a kiss on the cheek. He cracked open an eye to look upon her and then closed it again. "Morning!" she happily cooed in his ear. He gave her a weary smile. "Still tired?"

"I'm usually just heading to bed right about now."

"Oh yeah. Sorry."

He opened his eyes again as he smiled at her remorse. "It's alright. I wouldn't let you leave without properly seeing you off."

"I'm not leaving yet."

"Aren't you expected at work?"

"I was on from ten to four, but Mr. Penten said not to come in until twelve. Give them time to fix the windows, I guess. So that means I've got over two hours to kill before I have to get dressed." She snuggled closer to him and let her hands wander beneath the sheets.

He inched away from her a bit and laughed. "Aren't you tired?"

"Uh-uh," she replied with a smile, still seeking to fondle him under the covers.

He playfully pushed her hand away. "My dear girl, your appetites have become insatiable!"

"Aren't yours?" she asked.

He chuckled at her. "No, and you should be very thankful that they are not. Otherwise, we might have quite an unfortunate situation on our hands."

She smiled. "I didn't mean *that* kind of appetite."

"I haven't the strength for either, and neither should you. We've hardly slept and you haven't even had a proper meal since...when? Early dinner yesterday?"

"More like lunch, dinner was just junk from the café."

"See, you should get dressed and go to breakfast before work," he admonished.

"And don't forget, I also ate cookies," she reminded him.

He laughed at her. "You have to rebuild your strength." He gave her a kiss and whispered in her ear. "If you don't prove yourself of a responsible nature, I shall be afraid to repeat that magical experience we shared last night. Please don't take that away from me."

She climbed atop him and leaned down for another kiss. "I'm responsible. I'm going to make love with you and still leave myself a whole hour to eat something before work."

He shook his head with a grin. "Insatiable," he muttered.

"Oh *please,* you love it," she insisted playfully.

He did his best to sound very weary and put out. "I suppose I *might* let you have your way with me..." She raised her eyebrows at him and smiled in amusement at his phrasing. "On one condition. This is serious, really."

She made a great show of trying to look dead serious. "What is it?"

"You can't ask for me to drink from you." She smiled and was about to make a taunting remark when he stopped her. "No really, I mean it. You have no idea the effect that has on me. In the heat of things, to have you begging for me to taste your blood...well, I'm not infallible, you know. It's too soon. I shouldn't drink from you again, not now. So please, don't ask it. Promise?"

She smirked as though enjoying holding even an imaginary bit of power over him. "Okay, I promise, but can I do anything else I want?"

That startled him a bit. "I suppose," he replied with a smile. "What did you want to do?" She just grinned and disappeared beneath the covers.

~~~~~~~~~~~~~~~~~~~~~~~~~~~~~~~~~~~~

Felicity had left Cain with only a half an hour to get some breakfast, but he wasn't complaining. He had teased her though, in saying that she had better not return until nightfall, as he needed time to recuperate. 'Even a man of his hale and hearty constitution needed some rest,' he had told her.

She arrived at work to find gleaming new windows already in place, and the glass truck just leaving. Mr. Penten was just leaving as well. He told her again that he was glad for her safety, and thanked her for her dedication and level headedness the evening before. She felt like an idiot as she accepted his praise, remembering herself screaming and shoving the vial out in front of herself for safety.

Ashley was already inside, as well as Harold, working the café. The shards of glass had all been swept away and everything looked clean and perfect again. She still couldn't help but picture filthy walking corpses behind the counter though.

Ashley had rushed over to her, gushing with tales of Ben's supposed bravery. Ben had done a great deal to keep things under control, 'rescuing' Felicity and Alyson more than once, but to hear Ashley tell it, he'd fought off an entire gang of thugs, almost single-handedly. "I knew that girl was trouble," she'd told Felicity with a disapproving shake of her head. "Did you see how short her dress was? Even *I* have more couth than to wear something like *that.*"

About an hour before the end of Felicity's shift, Ashley

was off for the day. She stopped at the counter on her way out. "I'm outta here. When are you done?"

"I'm off at four."

"Cool. I have a manicure, and then I'll come back and pick you up to go check out Clarissa's."

? Oh yeah, the costume shop. "Oh, I don't think so."

"Come on. Even if you don't go to the dance, you're going to have to wear something on Halloween, right?" Felicity shrugged; she didn't quite follow that logic. She liked to dress up for Halloween, but without a party to go to, what would be the point? "Besides," Ashley continued, "I need someone to be there when I try on my costume, to make sure that it's perfect. Ben doesn't wanna come." Felicity just shrugged again. "I'll be back."

Sure enough, an hour later Ashley was out front ready to drag her to the costume shop. Felicity glanced at her own car and then back at Ashley's. It wouldn't be dark out for almost two hours yet, and it wasn't like she had anything better to do. She got in.

It was a bit longer of a drive than she had anticipated, but eventually, they arrived. It was also bigger than she'd expected. Felicity looked at the racks of clothes in wonder as they entered. "Wow, this place has a lot of stuff."

"Best costume shop in the county. Probably also the only costume shop in the county, but still...we're lucky they're so close."

"Yeah, only an hour away," Felicity said in sarcasm.

Ashley affected not to notice. "I think they mostly rent costumes for like, playhouses and stuff, but come Halloween they get pretty cleared out. I ordered my costumes months ago."

Felicity looked at the abundance of clothes in amused amazement, and then stopped to look questioningly at Ashley. "Wait a minute. You ordered both for you *and* Ben, right? How could you have ordered them so far ahead of time? You and Ben weren't even dating then."

"Oh, I know. I just ordered the uniform in a size to fit the kind of guys I always go with. I do prefer a certain build you know, tall and trim, broad shoulders. Ben's perfect, it'll fit." Felicity still had trouble believing half of the things that came out of this girl's mouth in genuine seriousness.

They had reached the counter, but no one was around. There was a large photo album filled with pictures of costumes. As Felicity began to flip through it, she noticed that many of the pages had pink 'post-its' on them, proclaiming to be sold out, or yellow ones saying 'on hold'. "Wow, yeah. Looks like most of the cheap ones are already taken, unless I want to be 'Harem Girl'."

Ashley came rushing over in distress. "You *cannot* be a harem girl! Then you and I would have the same pants and I do *not* do the twins thing."

Felicity grinned in amusement at Ashley's concern. "That's okay. I didn't really want to be a harem girl anyway."

Just then, a guy about their age in a purple pointed hat and sorcerer's robe came out to meet them. "Hello ladies. The Great Wizard Winterfarthing, at your service." He was pretty good-looking, under all the velvet. He noticed Ashley's flirtatious smile and gave her one of his own. "You can call me Brad."

Ashley batted her eyes at him for a moment. "Hi there, Brad. I'm a special order," she said, handing him her receipt.

"I'll bet you are." He glanced down to read it and then sized up Ashley some more. "Wow, yeah. You'll look great in that. Assuming you'll be wearing the Jeannie outfit, and not the military uniform." She giggled at him and looked at Felicity, who was thumbing through the photo book with an air of boredom. Brad took back Ashley's attention. "So, you got a 'Major Nelson' to wear that, or what?"

She smiled. "Well, the position's filled for tomorrow night, but it's not a permanent post."

He raised his eyebrows at her. "That a fact? Well, I'll just get this out, so you can model it for me, make sure it fits well in all the right places." Felicity rolled her eyes as Brad turned his attention to her. "How about you? You a special order too?"

She stared at him for a moment over the book. "No. I'm just here for moral support."

He laughed and then looked down at the book. It was open to a mermaid costume. "Wanna try that on?"

"No, that's okay," she quickly replied.

Ashley came up behind her. "Why not? What's the fun of coming, if you're not even going to try anything? At least try something on."

Brad smiled at her. "I'll get it for you. What size seashells you want?"

"Excuse me?" Felicity asked.

His grin broadened. "The top. Large?"

She blushed and looked back at the costume. It sported a

bikini top made of two large seashells. "Yeah, thanks." Brad disappeared into the back and Felicity turned to Ashley. "I am not going to wear that. And I can't believe the way you are flirting with him!"

"What? He's cute!" Ashley insisted defensively.

"So's Ben," Felicity reminded her harshly.

"Oh, big deal. A little harmless flirting never hurt anyone. What do you think Ben does when I'm not around? It's not like we agreed not to see other people or anything. What are you going to do, tell on me? Lighten up," Ashley demanded.

Brad returned with the costumes. "Here you are ladies. The dressing rooms are right over here."

When Felicity was reluctant to go, Ashley pushed her into the booth. "Come on. It'll be fun."

She took it all out and tried to make heads or tails of it...literally. She finally figured out how to put it on, but whoa, was it revealing. The scales for the fish tail didn't start until way low on her hips, far below her belly button. And the seashells were definitely made by someone who had a different interpretation of the word 'large' than she did. There was no mirror in the booth though. She'd have to go out to the big mirror to look at it.

"Felicity, are you done? I need help with this zipper." She heard Ashley call from next door.

It was Brad who answered before she could. "Want me to help you out with that?"

She heard Ashley open her door. "Yeah, thanks."

Felicity stayed huddled in the corner of her room, trying to decide if she should just take the thing back off. She heard Brad again from outside the door. "You look fantastic! Your wish is my command."

Ashley giggled. "That's *my* line silly." Felicity almost groaned aloud. "Felicity, come see. Aren't you done yet?"

"I don't think this is going to work for me," Felicity explained.

"Do you need help?" Ashley asked.

"No!" Felicity quickly replied.

"Then come out already!" Ashley insisted.

Felicity sighed, eased open the door and hesitantly stepped out. Brad let out a long low whistle that immediately made her consider going back in. Then she caught sight of herself in the mirror. Wow! She did look very sexy in it. She looked much better than she would have thought, but it was *too* sexy.

She noticed Ashley's expression in the mirror behind her. She looked a bit put off by Felicity's appearance. In fact, she got the distinct impression that Ashley was afraid that Felicity looked better than she did. That thought was confirmed by Ashley's negative words and attitude. "You look like a fish," she said sarcastically, taking hold of the end of Felicity's tail.

Brad gave Ashley a skeptical smile. "More like a fisherman's wet dream."

Felicity began to blush again, feeling very uncomfortable. "I don't think I can wear this."

Brad suddenly became the enthusiastic salesman. "Sure, you can! A few pearls in your hair, maybe a fishnet shawl. You look amazing!"

Ashley shook her head. "No, you're right. It's really not *you.*"

Felicity turned to look at her in amusement and noticed

44

Ashley's outfit. She really did look perfect. "Wow, Ashley you look great."

Ashley smiled, folded her arms and did the blink thing. "I'll have to do my hair of course." She quickly held her hair up, as if in a ponytail high on her head.

Brad smiled. "Better than Barbara Eden."

Felicity nodded. "You're going to look gorgeous. I have to go and take this off." She quickly stepped back into the dressing room.

"You want me to get you something else?" Brad called from outside.

"No, that's okay."

"I thought you looked super, but if you want something a little more...modest, well, we do have lots of other stuff. Maybe something more...elegant?"

That sounded interesting. Felicity peeked out of the dressing room. "Like what?"

Brad thought a moment and then broke into a big smile. "I've got just the thing! What are you, a size twelve?"

She tried not to grimace. "More like a fourteen."

Brad furrowed his brow a moment. "Well, I only have a ten or a twelve, but don't worry, the twelve'll fit. Don't move." He rushed off before Felicity could stop him and she was left standing there behind the door half dressed.

A minute later Brad came back with the most gorgeous gown she had ever seen. "How about the Medieval Princess?" he asked, holding it up proudly. The dress was the deepest royal blue with silver beads and sequins covering the bodice. It had deeply belled sleeves and the skirt was turned back and fastened with silver clips at a slit in the front, to reveal silver and white lace underskirts beneath. It was absolutely breathtaking.

"It's beautiful!" Felicity exclaimed.

Ashley came back out in her regular clothes, took one look at the dress and then looked accusingly at Brad. "That is the most expensive costume in the store."

Felicity's smile wavered. "How much?"

Brad looked hesitant to tell her, not a good sign. "Well, it's $349."

"Three hundred and forty-nine dollars!"

"It comes with a head piece." She had obviously lost any notions of buying it. "We do rent it, though. $50 for the whole Halloween weekend, due back on Tuesday morning."

Ashley scoffed at him. "Fifty bucks? Mine cost forty and I get to keep it."

Brad gave her a sly grin. "Yours uses considerably less material." Felicity couldn't keep her eyes off of the gown. Brad held it out to her. "Try it on."

"It'll never fit."

"One way to find out."

She tried it on. She did manage to get the zipper up without a problem, which was a relief, but even without the mirror, she felt as though she were bursting out the top. The bodice was cut to a low square shape in front. She knew from past experience, that the shape was usually a flattering neckline on her, but it was cut so *low*. She came out to look in the mirror. Brad bowed low before her, taking off his hat. "My noble lady."

Ashley was standing with her arms crossed. "I'll bet it weighs a ton."

Felicity looked in the mirror and smiled. "Cain calls me that, 'My lady'."

Ashley looked skeptical. "He *does?*"

Felicity smiled and nodded, admiring her reflection. "M-hmmm."

Ashley just rolled her eyes and pouted as Brad asked, "So I take it you've already got a 'Prince Charming' to go along with that?"

She smiled, thinking of Cain seeing her in the dress. "Yeah, I sure do."

Ashley eyed the dress some more. "Isn't it a little *tight?*"

Brad seemed to sense Felicity's self-doubt creeping in. "No, it's supposed to be like that. Haven't you ever seen a Shakespearean play?" He turned to Felicity reassuringly. "They all wear them like that, I swear. You look exquisite."

She knew he was just trying to sell her the dress, but he was right. It was perfect. "I'll take it."

"Excellent choice, you won't regret it!" Brad went back behind the counter to ring up Ashley's purchase while Felicity went back inside to change. She came back out and joined them at the register, just as Ashley was signing her credit card slip. "Great. Oh, and if you could put your phone number on there as well? For business purposes."

Ashley smiled. "Sure, and um, feel free to use it personally any time."

"Thanks, I sure will." He turned to Felicity. "Oh, I forgot to mention, there's a twenty-dollar deposit on that dress."

Felicity opened her mouth and slumped her shoulders in disbelief. "So, it's *seventy* dollars?!"

"Well, you get the twenty back. It's just in case you pop

some beads or sequins, you know? It's an expensive gown."

Felicity grumped at him. "I don't think I have enough."

Brad eyed Ashley, standing nearby. "Maybe you could…borrow it?"

They both looked at Ashley hopefully for a minute, until she caved in disgust. "Oh fine, put it on my charge." She dug out her card to give him back for the transaction, as Felicity gave Ashley her fifty.

"Thank you!" When all was said and done, they gathered up their purchases and receipts and bid the Great Wizard Winterfarthing/Brad farewell.

Chapter 2

And a large chocolate shake

Cain

Cain's house
7:15, Saturday night

Cain paced the upstairs of his home, waiting to feel
Felicity. He'd only been joking when he'd told her not to
come back until dark. Actually, he'd expected her to get some
dinner after work and then bring it to eat here with him. That
had been their usual routine for the past week or so, unless
they'd plans to go out. It had been full dark for almost an
hour and she still was not even within his range. Neither were
Chris or Marcus that he could tell, but that wasn't very
reassuring. At least if he could feel them nearby, he would
know that they were not near Felicity.

He wondered for the tenth time, if he should try and go
out to look for her, but he had no idea where she might have
gone. He was afraid that if he set out in the wrong direction,
he wouldn't feel her approach and they would miss each

other, so he continued to pace and worry.

Finally, he felt her presence begin to flicker into range in his mind. She was moving very fast. Good, she was probably in a car. She turned up the drive as he stood awaiting her in the doorway. She smiled, unconcerned as she walked up to meet him. She tried to give him a kiss hello, but he just gave her an admonishing look. "When I told you not to come back until dark, I didn't think you would actually *listen* to me."

She shrugged. "Sorry, I got caught up with Ashley."

"Do you have any idea the danger you've been in? It's been dark for an hour now. How can I protect you if you go putting yourself into harm's way without me?"

Her face fell downcast as she realized his concern. "Oh. Sorry, but I *am* marked now," she added by way of defense.

He stared at her levelly. "It's not nearly the safeguard you think it is. I haven't had the chance to assess just how seriously committed Chris is to all of this vengeance drama. He may not be able to *bite* you, but that's hardly the full extent of his resources. There are a lot of ways to kill someone. Marking is meant for territorial purposes, not true protection. You have to be more careful, really." The last of his words degenerated from scolding rebuke to anxious relief. He pulled her to him for a hug, gratefully soaking in the delicious feel of his mark upon her. He covered her neck with kisses and then held her back to look upon her face. "Don't worry me like that again," he gently scolded.

She smiled. "Sorry."

"Have you eaten?" he asked.

"No, and for somebody who doesn't need food, you sure worry a lot about it. You're always making me eat, I feel like you're fattening the Thanksgiving turkey," she teased. He looked rather alarmed and insulted at the reference, but she tickled him and made him smile. "Relax, it's a joke. In poor taste maybe, but...lighten up. Come on, let's go out to dinner," she insisted, heading back to the car.

He followed. "So, what were you doing with Ashley?"

"Oh, she wanted me to go with her to the costume shop, to pick up her outfit for the dance." They ducked to get in the car and she started it up while he watched her in silence. "I was thinking about it some more, the dance...I'd kind of like to go," she said in a quiet, hesitant voice. She looked up to see him staring at her.

He sighed. "Felicity, I've already told you, I really don't care to attend."

"Oh, I know. *You* don't have to go. If you'd really rather stay home, then I'll just go by myself. Ben and Ashley are going, and Karen and Jack will be there."

He still gazed at her levelly. "Because you had such a wonderful time at the last school function you attended?" She gave him an annoyed look. "By all means, don't stay home on my account. You can certainly do as you like. If it's that important to you, go."

She sat sulking at him. "I got a costume,"

He rolled his eyes and shook his head disapprovingly. "I've seen the costumes young ladies wear these days. What did you get? The 'sexy witch', the 'sexy nurse' or the 'sex kitten'?"

She became indignant. "None of the above."

"Don't tell me you got the little red leotard with the devil's horns and the tail on the back?"

"No! If you want to see my costume, you'll have to come to the Masquerade Ball."

He shook his head again. "A lady of your bearing should be above resorting to such coercions. I'm *not going*. Wear what you like." He nodded towards the gearshift. "We ought to get moving, it's getting late and I've got things to do tonight."

Rather than ask his plans, she sulked for a moment more. "It's a princess," she said quietly. She looked up to see his reaction. "My costume, it's a medieval princess."

He smiled at her tenderly. "Well, I rather *like* the sound of that. I'm still not going though. Perhaps you'll come by and show it to me after."

She still looked a bit sulky, but put the car in reverse and pulled out of the driveway. "Where should we go?"

"Better make it take out; I don't want you out here long." He suddenly remembered something with a start. Arif cloaked his lesser minions. He'd said it was simple. It probably was, Cain had just never tried it before. A marked human should be even easier to hide than another vampire. He concentrated on Felicity's mark as they headed for the McDonald's drive-thru. It was such a simple thing, that he didn't need more than one try. He felt a fool for never attempting it before. At least that was one less worry. They were both invisible to Chris now, as long as they were together. He probably couldn't hold it if she left him. They pulled up to the order speaker and Felicity studied the menu. "I'll have a chicken Caesar salad and a diet coke."

He caught her attention after she ordered. "Just a salad?"

"It's a *chicken* Caesar salad."

Cain leaned forward to address the speaker. "And a large

chocolate shake."

Felicity looked at him in annoyance. "I don't want a shake."

"That's all." Cain told the speaker. He turned to Felicity in amusement. "It's not for you." She smiled in surprise. Very rarely did she ever see him eat or drink anything other than his nightly coffee. "I treat myself now and then. I'm rather fond of them actually."

"Chocolate huh?"

Cain grinned. "Well, I don't think they come in 'Butter Rum Ripple'."

They got their food and headed home. Once they were unpacked and enjoying their purchase at the bar in Cain's room, Felicity asked, "So what are we doing tonight?"

"Not *we*, me. I probably should have mentioned it earlier, but I didn't want an argument. I'll be leaving you for the remainder of the evening." She began to protest but he held up a hand to stop her. "You can wait here if you'd like, but seeing as I haven't got a tele, you might rather spend the evening at the dorm. Have a girls' night and take your mind off things."

"Tele?" she questioned.

"T.V," he clarified with a laugh.

"Where are you going?" she asked.

He turned quietly sober. "I have to go and find Chris."

"But you can't. He hides himself; how would you find him?"

"Chris can hide but Marcus can't, and he's not exactly the 'self-sufficient' sort. If I can find Marcus, Chris will be nearby, I'm sure." No matter how well Arif had shown Chris how to cloak, Cain was betting Chris wasn't experienced or strong enough mentally to cover himself *and* another...he hoped.

"Cain, **no.** You can't take them both alone, they'll kill you!"

"Well, thanks for the vote of confidence, but I'm not planning to fight them, if it can be avoided."

"Then what are you going to do?" she asked in concern.

"Negotiate," he replied.

She stared at him for a moment. "Something tells me they aren't going to want to talk." She sounded as though she thought him very naive.

Cain smiled. "Not to worry. It's not as though I've never handled hostile negotiations before." He went to his bed to pull something out from underneath. "In fact, that's what this is for." It was a chain mail vest. Bundled in his hand, Felicity couldn't discern its true shape.

"What's that?"

He held it up for her to better see. "Insurance." He put the vest on over his tee shirt. "Can't say I've used it often in the past. I never much worried over the outcome of such confrontations. I've often wondered why I even keep the thing, but now...now I've got you, for no matter how short a time, and I can't say as I'm quite ready to leave this world yet." He then went to the laundry room to find something to put on over the vest.

"But a stake isn't the *only* thing that can kill you," she called to him in concern.

He came back out, wearing a thin blue cashmere sweater. He laughed a little at her. "My dear, if I can't manage to avoid being *beheaded* or *lit on fire,* then I probably deserve whatever happens to me." He modeled his sweater for her. "I don't look too lumpy, do I?" She laughed and came to give him a kiss.

She squeezed his biceps, and then brought her hands around and down to squeeze his buttocks as well. "Only in the right places."

He rolled his eyes at her. "Are you going back to the dorm?"

She quickly shook her head. "No. I want to wait for you here."

"It may take me awhile to find them. Chances are I won't be back 'til almost dawn. I think you're better off at the dorm."

"No. I want to be here when you get back. And you'd *better* come back."

"No worries." He gave her a kiss and stooped to reach under his bed and add another stake or two to the one he already carried in his boot. His sweater had tight cuffs at the end of the sleeves. Perfect to conceal a stake up his right arm, without having it slide out. He put another in his other boot and one in his back pocket. Felicity was watching him nervously. "Time to go."

She followed him to the door, where he turned to ask her one last time, "You sure you wouldn't rather the dorm?" She didn't even answer but gave him a look that told him not to ask again. "Well, I suppose you should be safe enough here. Read whatever you'd like, I've some books and things about. Stay downstairs; I don't want you near the windows. Chris and any he might bring aren't invited, so you should be all right."

He paused as an uncomfortable thought came to mind. Chris wasn't invited, but Sindy was. No one could issue an invitation but the one who resides in a dwelling, so it wasn't as though Sindy could come and then invite Chris in, but he didn't relish the thought of Sindy herself visiting Felicity, even if she weren't behaving dangerously. She probably wouldn't come...he hoped. Still..."I'm locking the door. If Sindy comes 'round, don't let her in."

"Why would *Sindy* come here?"

"She…bothers me now and again. Just send her away. Better yet, don't answer the door. You've no reason to answer it for anyone. I'll be back before dawn. Alright?"

She looked a little doubtful over the Sindy issue, but didn't argue. Maybe it was just his own guilty conscience. He gave her a kiss and locked the open door. "Don't worry; I've been doing this sort of thing since long before you were born. I'll be back."

He left Felicity, closing and checking the door behind him. He then thundered out into the night on his Harley Davidson Motorcycle. He hadn't really much of an idea where to start and just rode circles around town. Chris probably wouldn't stay within his range, unless he had a specific agenda, but Cain didn't want to chance going too far from Felicity, if Chris lay in wait.

After he felt that Chris was almost certainly not local, he headed out further. As he came upon the next town, he sensed a distraction from his objective. Sindy was nearby and quite obvious about it too. He followed her trace until he came to a motor lodge. She was in room #7.

When she didn't answer after the third knock, he briefly

revealed his trace. That brought her to the door after only a moment or two. She opened it fully, without fear. Her hair was dripping wet and she wore nothing but a towel. She was clearly happy to see him and he had a hard time keeping the stern face that he'd thought to use. She was so blatantly thrilled at his presence, although she tried to seem nonchalant as she uttered a throaty, 'Hi.'.

"I see the cloaking isn't coming along very well," he admonished.

She became indignant at his accusation. "I was in the *shower.*"

"So? That's the perfect opportunity. What else have you got to concentrate on in there?"

Now she flashed him a mischievous smile. "You might be surprised."

He resolved to remain business-like, refusing to let her bait him. "Can I come in?"

She kept the smile and moved to admit him. "Please do."

He entered the room and shut the door behind him. As he turned back around, her towel was just hitting the floor. He looked away from her body with a sigh. "Can't I shut a door without you losing your clothes?"

She laughed, drawing him to inadvertently look at her and nodded her head towards the bathroom. "Did you wanna join me?"

He shook his head no, doing his best to divert his gaze. She moved a bit closer to him. Finally, he looked up and did allow himself to run his eyes over her graceful form. His gaze rested upon her face and she gave him a sly smile. He kept his eyes focused on her own as he spoke. "If my heart could beat, it would surely be pounding out of my chest about now, to be in the presence of such a..." he ran his eyes over her lithe body once more, for her benefit more than his own, "desirable and tempting seductress." She was obviously pleased, but wary of the catch. She knew that he was flattering her before the fall. "But I must graciously decline."

She didn't take it to heart; she didn't give up so easily either. "Why? I won't tell. She'd never know."

"I would know."

"So? You said yourself that she was only good for *temporary* happiness. You gonna let that get in the way of something that could be *real?*"

"Sindy please, I said no. It won't happen again; not while I'm residing here."

"So, when are you movin'?"

He laughed, and tried not to stare at her pert breasts. "I don't know. Maybe not for quite some time and it's not as though I'm asking you to wait around for me. Perhaps we shall decide that we're not properly suited to each other anyway."

"So, why'd you give me money for this swell room?"

"For your safety. Did you plan to find yourself a cave in the woods?"

She shifted her weight and put her hands on her hips, drawing his eyes there. "Sure you can't be persuaded? Shame to waste a queen size bed."

He smiled and looked at the floor. "Quite sure."

She shrugged, an interesting movement, considering her lack of clothing. "So maybe you're in the mood for something a little more...liquid?"

He tried not to get annoyed, but looked up at her sternly. "Sindy, when are you going to stop throwing body and blood at me for long enough to show me the *person* you are?" She rolled her eyes and crossed her arms in a huff. "You are worth far more than only what you may *do* for someone." The words had only just left his lips when he quickly looked down, feeling repentant and ashamed. He forced himself to meet her eyes. "I suppose my actions the night we *were* together didn't do much to substantiate that claim, but it *is* true none the less. Do forgive me. My actions that night were deplorable."

She smirked at him. *"Forgive* you? I waited a long time to get you to give me that night."

Cain's shame was surely written upon his face. "All the more reason for you to be disappointed in me, as I am in myself. It shouldn't have been like *that.* I'm sorry."

"So, make it up to me. I'm sure you could do better if you tried," she taunted.

"Get dressed." She only stared at him, amused that he thought to give her orders. "I *am* going to make it up to you. After you cover your body, I will teach you to cover your trace." Now she did smile, genuinely. It seemed she would accept his lack of physical attentions, if he really would teach her to cloak. She had been trying so desperately and discouragingly to accomplish it without him, with such limited success. He smiled back at her. "And don't be all night about it, I have other things to do."

She smiled at him again and went to get dressed, before long she had donned one of her little black dresses and was sitting on the bed next to him. She didn't dry her hair, but brushed it out, to dry long and straight down her back. At first, she did attempt once or twice, to caress him and snuggle close, but he very seriously threatened to leave, and she gave up and lay back on the bed next to him, while he remained sitting.

He turned to face her. "Before we start, I have to ask, you haven't seen or spoken to Chris, I gather?" She just shook her head no. He sighed; he really should be out searching for Chris now, but Sindy was an intelligent girl. Once he showed her the way of things, this shouldn't take long.

"Alright. Cloaking. It's not hard to do, for one who's got decent mental control, but it does require great discipline and stamina. First, let's see what we're working with." She gave him an odd and almost insulted look. "What do you think your range is? How far away can you feel another?"

Sindy shrugged and thought for a moment. "Like...half a mile I guess."

"All right. I want you to sit up, and clear your mind." She looked annoyed that he should make her change position, but did as he asked. She sat facing him, with her legs folded underneath. "Now, take a deep breath and exhale it slowly."

"Why?" she asked.

"Because I said to."

"We don't even need to breathe, Cain; what's the point?"

"Would you stop being so difficult! It's to relax you and help you clear your head. I don't suppose you've any experience with yoga?" Cain inquired.

"You're kidding right?" she asked with a smirk.

"All right, come on, we're wasting time. Be quiet and clear your head. Now, I want you to stretch out your senses and describe to me, the first mark you see."

"The lady in the front office," she quickly answered.

"Don't use your superficial knowledge. Tell me what you can sense *only* from the mark. You only assume it's in the office, but you don't *know*. Use your mental image of the surroundings and not your memory. What do you *know?* Study the mark and tell me everything about it."

"Okay. Judging by the low life energy around the mark, I'd say it's someone alone in a building; hardly any plant or animal life immediately around. Based on direction, and the layout of this place, it's got to be the front office." She stopped to open her eyes and see if he would dispute her.

Cain just smiled patiently. "Go on."

Sindy closed her eyes again to continue. Cain knew that most young ones found it very hard to concentrate without closing their eyes to tune out their surroundings, but he was still impressed by Sindy's display of skill thus far. Marks were fairly easy for any vampire to see, but the surrounding life energies were of a different texture to the mind and usually went unnoticed. The fact that she could decipher them would make cloaking that much easier for her. She went on. "The mark is about a week old I'd say, not all that strong. This guy doesn't know how to use his venom. It's Paulie, he was one of my football guys, but even if I didn't know him, I'd say he's not all that powerful, and obviously real young."

"Very good. Read me another."

"Cain, reading marks is inherent, basic stuff. Let's move on."

There was only one more mark that would be within her range anyway. "Just read the other, please."

"Fine. It's kind of far away, but I can see it okay. It's

weak; the vampire's a real young one. Maybe one of the zombies, 'cause there was hardly any venom but the mark is real fresh, like from two or three nights ago. The mark itself is poorly lit, not a powerful vampire, gotta be a zombie. Happy?"

"Yes. Whether you know it or not, you read very well. What seems basic to you is difficult for some. Some can only tell the age of the vampire by its mark, and not whether they are well made, or the age of the mark itself. I also suspect that your range could be a bit further than you think. With practice and control, you might reach further. Now I want you to read me."

"I can't, you're cloaked."

"Then look at where I *ought* to be. What do you see?"

"Nothing." He watched with a smile as she sat with eyes closed, and realization came over her face. "*Nothing!* It's...too blank, like a black spot was put over the area. There is *no* energy there at *all*. That's like...impossible!

You son of bitch! All of this time you've got me thinkin' that I have to shut my light *off*, when I really just needed to cover it up?"

"I never led you to believe that, you came to your own conclusions. You cannot *shut off* your trace unless you cease to exist. No wonder you've been having such difficulty. That's why it's called *cloaking*. You're trying to hide your light, not put it out."

"Well, thanks for the tip. You could have told me that like three months ago."

"Three months ago, I couldn't be sure if you'd use the

knowledge to sneak up on me and put a stake through my heart."

She smiled. "And now you're sure I won't?"

"Now I am sufficiently sure that if you tried, I could take you out first."

"Thanks," she uttered sarcastically.

"Concentrate on creating a blanket. You want to create a blanket of blackness, with which to cover yourself."

"Wait a minute, I have a question. Now that I know the trick, why couldn't I just notice where the blackness is, and know that there's a vampire there?"

"You see it now because I'm sitting right in front of you. If you were any further than a few steps away, my black spot would melt into the scenery. It would be virtually impossible for you to find me mentally, without actually laying eyes upon me. To be honest, most other vampires don't notice other life energies anyway, or the lack thereof; they only notice marks; another testament to your mental prowess. Trust me, it works. Now see if you can do it."

It took her a few minutes to figure out how to begin, and then to cover her trace entirely, but she was fairly clever and with some proper guidance, she quickly got the way of it. In less than ten minutes, she had herself perfectly cloaked. She gave him a shove on the shoulder. "You jerk, this is so easy! You have no idea how I have been freaking over this."

He chuckled. "Creating the cloak is easy; it's holding it that's the trick. I must say, something tells me stamina won't be much of a problem for you." She grinned. "But have you got focused concentration?"

"What do you mean? I can hold it."

63

"You are doing well, even through a conversation, but what if you're startled or distracted? Holding it throughout the unexpected, that's the clever bit."

She raised her eyebrows. "Try me."

He laughed. "Well, it doesn't prove anything if you're expecting me to distract you, now does it? Let's just practice concentration. All right, let's see. What's twelve times twelve?"

She looked at him as though she were asked to speak Greek. "How the hell should I know?"

He laughed and tried to think of something else to ask of her. "I know, recite me 'Mary Had A Little Lamb'."

"You have got to be fucking kidding me. How about an Avril Lavigne song?"

Cain sighed up at the ceiling and then looked back to her face. "Forget it. Just answer me some questions, alright? What's your name?"

"Sindy," she answered, looking at him oddly that he should ask.

"Your *full human name.*" Now she looked annoyed. "Come on, what is it?"

"Cynthia Abigail Applebaum," she answered dutifully.

He raised an eyebrow. "Really?"

"Yes. Use it and you'll be missing teeth," she threatened.

He laughed. "Who was your first-grade teacher?"

"Ummmm, Mrs. Beltzer."

"Who was your first date?" Cain asked.

"Robert Melman," she answered, after some thought.

"Who was your first kiss?"

"Benjamin Everheart. This isn't a test, you're just being nosy."

"No, I'm not. I *should* be trying to fluster you to make you lose concentration."

She gave him an amused stare. "Cain, I have been living with six guys who have like nothing to look forward to in their nights but sex and blood play with me. It's gonna take a little more to fluster me than 'who was your first kiss'. In fact, it might be fun to hear you try, but don't even bother. You *can't* fluster me."

"You are holding your shield rather well, I must say." He briefly entertained the notion of actually trying. Although he always tried to conduct himself as a civil man, he surely *could* ruffle her if he tried. She had no idea, the true extent of his experiences. "Wait a minute, did you say Everheart?"

"Uh-huh, Ben," Sindy answered.

"The Ben that *I* know?" Cain asked incredulously.

"Yeah, so?"

"Nothing I just… I never knew his last name." Cain paused in contemplation before trying to resume the conversation undaunted. "He was your first kiss, huh?" Cain asked non-chalantly.

"Are we done?"

He smiled. It might be fun to shock her with recounted experiences; in the way she was always trying to fluster him, with the pretext of course, of testing her concentration, but no. He had been irresponsible enough in wasting time here. "Actually yes, I believe we are. You're very good at it," he said sincerely.

"Thanks." She actually became flushed with his

compliment. He got the impression that she was unused to true praise for anything other than her body.

"Keep it up, *all the time.*" He gave her a confidential little smile. "Even in the shower."

She laughed at him. "Yes sir." He got up from the bed. "You're not leavin' already, are ya?"

"Yes," he told her.

"You don't have to. Stay for awhile. I'll be good, if you *really* want me to be."

"You're wavering," Cain informed her.

"What?" she asked in distraction.

"Your shield. Sorry, I have to go. I've got some things to take care of."

She quickly hid her trace again. "Goin' to look for Chris, huh?"

He nodded. "You know where I might find him?"

She shook her head 'no'. "Sorry. You want back-up?"

He smiled at her. "No, but thank you. Stay out of trouble." He walked to the door and turned to see her gazing at him in actual concern. "By the way, the lack of 'soot' smeared about your eyes...it's very appealing." He probably shouldn't have said anything, but he couldn't help but let her know.

She stared at him for a moment, as though trying to decide how to take that. "Chris used to do it for me. Said it made me look like a model, from a big Paris fashion show or something." She took her eyes from his, a bit self-consciously.

Cain smiled sweetly at her. "Chris was a fool to cover up such natural beauty." She looked up in surprise, that he would give her such a genuine compliment. "Besides, Paris girls -

very snobby, far too thin and not at all appealing...to my eye anyway. Goodnight." He opened the door to leave.

"Be careful." She said it very 'off the cuff', as though she wouldn't really worry for him, but her eyes spoke differently.

"You too." With that, he left her and closed the door.

He spent the remainder of the night searching to no significant end. Now he had less than an hour left before he would need to head home for the dawn, and there had still been no sign of Chris. He felt a bit guilty for letting himself get side-tracked by Sindy, but the lesson in cloaking had been very valuable to her, and Cain was pleasantly surprised by her show of mental skill. The visit had also helped to ease the shame he had been carrying over the night that she had come to him and he had not turned her away. He was glad that he'd had the chance to apologize anyway.

Still, it was an hour lost, and he still had no idea where Chris might be, or what he could be planning. He had come across others later in the evening though. Two vampire males, younger than he, but hardly newborn. They were in the parking lot of a restaurant, talking to two human women. Cain didn't really know them, but was fairly sure they had been at Venus, the first night he had spied Arif. He got the distinct impression that they were Arif's men. They had a very slight aura of Arif's trace about their own. Part of his 'guard' Cain supposed. He couldn't see Arif anywhere about, but that meant nothing.

He thought of intervening, surely the ladies were in for more of an evening than they might expect, but he also did not wish to make enemies; he had enough problems at the moment. He sat watching them a moment more, from his bike across the lot. The men were totally unaware of his presence.

Cain decided that he just could not leave them in good conscience. He entered the restaurant. He carefully inspected the patrons, half-expecting to see Arif among them, but the man was not to be found. After a few minutes of indecision, Cain approached the payphone. He placed an anonymous 911 call to the police. He gave the address and explained that he had seen two women being attacked in the parking lot.

He quickly returned to his motorcycle, hoping he had remained inconspicuous. A casual glance in their direction showed that they were all still talking. It seemed as though one of the men was trying to convince the women to enter his car. He hoped they were wise enough not to be persuaded. He put on the helmet that he had purchased for Felicity; to help mask his identity, in case any glanced in his direction. Unfortunately, the Harley Davidson was not known for its 'subtlety'. He flinched as he started the incredibly loud engine and left, not wanting to be there when the police arrived.

He told himself he had done all that could be expected. He hoped it wasn't a foolish move on his part. He didn't want to distress the women, but he almost hoped that the vampires did attack them, so that when the police arrived, there would be no suspicion as to why they'd been called.

That event, and the time spent dawdling with Sindy was the extent of his accomplishments for the night. A bit anti-climactic maybe, but at least he had managed to help Sindy out, while successfully declining her propositions. To her, he probably had seemed as steadfast as always, easily turning down her advances. Of course, he did love Felicity. He had no desire to disrespect her, and no need to look elsewhere for attention, but he had to admit to himself, that Sindy had piqued his interest far more than he'd expected her to. All the way home, he tried to analyze why.

He loved Felicity, truly. It bothered him that Sindy should be able to turn his head, even though he had not submitted to his urges. It had always seemed a much simpler thing to turn Sindy away in the past. Of course, she'd usually been fully clothed, but he'd thought himself strong enough not to let that make a difference.

Finally, he was able to put his finger on it. In the past Sindy had been sure to have him see her in a certain way. She had always tried to appear confident, controlling and invincible. She still kept the habit of trying to project that persona most of the time, but he had seen her briefly, here and there, without artifice. It made a big difference in the way that he looked at her now. She had begun to let down her defenses for him now and then. As he had said to her this very evening, when she was not busy trying to ply him with her body or blood, he could see a bit of the *person* she was. When he wasn't busy fighting with her, or avoiding her advances, she could be rather appealing. In simple times like those, he could see a bit of the human girl left in her.

He pulled into his driveway as the sun was beginning to lighten the eastern horizon. The sky was just a lighter shade of dark in that direction, but he could see the coming dawn for what it was. He would have to continue his search for Chris tomorrow night.

The human girl, who bore his mark within, was still far more appealing to him than any other could be. Even as the thought came to his mind, he chided himself for being a fool. As he had told Felicity himself, their love seemed perfect and unequaled now, but he should know better. Someday soon, things would have to change, but for now, he would immerse himself in her affections.

Drinking from her had been everything that he had known it would be, and more. To add that dimension to their bed sport had excited and satisfied him better than he could have imagined. For a rare time in his life, he was very content. For this brief time, he felt that he did not have to struggle so hard to fight his vampire nature, and he needn't be lonely as a man either. The physical pleasures that he shared with her now were amazingly rewarding. He could very easily see how others could desire to keep humans this way.

Unfortunately, many of those vampires *used* the human they kept, unsympathetic to anything but their own greedy desires, and then cast them aside when they died of being poorly cared for, or the vampire simply grew weary of them. Cain would never do that to Felicity. He loved her dearly and would treat her with the respect due a queen if he could keep her with him, but no, he knew what the end results of such an arrangement would most likely be. For the hundredth time, he tried to convince himself; if things did not go just right...to take a chance with her life like that was unacceptable.

He had been sure to speak firmly and unwaveringly to her about his eventual departure, but truthfully, he could very easily be persuaded to spend all of his nights, loving and drinking from her. The fact that she had professed a desire for the same had startled him to realize that the burden really was on him to end it. Even through his disappointment, he had always felt somewhat comforted by the fact that she did not want him to turn her. Knowing that she refused to become his true mate was like a safety net for him. It was not his choice alone, to do the right thing. She would not allow otherwise.

The idea of keeping their relationship going on the way things were now had not really seemed an option to him before. He hadn't spoken to Felicity about his past experiences with others such as she, but it was a scenario that he had played out in the past...more than once. He hadn't seen the need to give her specific examples, but there were women that he had stayed with far longer than he should have, before they left him or asked to be turned into vampires themselves. It had never ended well, but somewhere in the back of his mind, he had begun to think that perhaps it could work this time, with Felicity. He was older now, more experienced. He was better able to discern safe limits for their play. If he filled himself mercilessly with animal blood, their relationship could continue safely for a time.

He'd even considered trying to model his relationship with Felicity, after that of Mattie and Alyson. They had kept things going well for *years,* but there were two major differences between his actions and Mattie's that he should be unwilling to change.

First of all, Mattie and Alyson only saw each other for a few days a month normally. Sometimes much more infrequently, even not counting this last long separation. In this way, Alyson was in less danger of losing too much blood, becoming anemic or too dependent on the venom. He couldn't be certain, but he had the feeling that it might be somewhat addictive. It certainly was psychologically addictive anyway. So, their time spent apart was probably wise, but he could never bring himself to be away from Felicity so often.

The other problem was one that he had spoken to Felicity about. Her life was going by. Obviously, Allie did date other men while Mattie was away, but Cain knew that none would satisfy her the way that her vampire lover did. Her heart belonged to Mattie and she would be unwilling to truly give it to another, if there were any prospect of his returning.

Cain could not do that to Felicity. It was terribly unfair. If he could not give her the life that she deserved, he should make way for someone who could. That reasoning is what kept him from trying to carry things on the way they were now. It was pleasurable sure, and he certainly was not going to end it before allowing himself to indulge with her in body and blood many more times to file away with his fondest memories, but his time with her was definitely limited.

It was with a heavy heart, thinking of such detestable truths that he entered his home. He felt Felicity's strong and comforting mark, glowing within. Downstairs, burning brightly; beckoning him, though she lay quiet and still. He went down to find her, asleep in his bed. Only his bedside lamp was on and she held a book in her hand, fallen aside as she slept. He moved closer to see what she'd been reading. It was the Bible of all things. That made him smile. Perhaps he should be reading it a bit more often himself these days. At least he could feel that his time with her had been *some* sort of good influence.

He gently took the book from her hand and put it aside as she opened her eyes. Yes, reflected there was the love that he'd been eager to see. He gave her a kiss and stood to undress and join her. He hushed her sleepy questions with more kisses as he joined her in the bed. The morning would come soon enough and explanations could wait for later. For now, he just wanted to lie with her safe, warm and loving in his arms.

~~~~~~~~~~~~~~~~~~~~~~~~~~~~~~

They eagerly enjoyed each other's attentions until the time came for Felicity to go back to her own room, to get ready for work. He had even allowed himself to drink from her again - although he was very careful not to take much. At first, he had thought to give her another day to recuperate, but she had actually *asked* it of him. Tentative and almost shyly she had asked if enough time had passed. Knowing that it could be safely done, he could hardly disappoint. She had obviously given herself over to admitting her enjoyment of it. It was an absolutely exquisite experience as before.

She asked him once again if he might reconsider attending the Masquerade Ball, but once more, he declined. She was disappointed but he explained that not only was he not interested in the event, but that he had much more important concerns. He needed to find Chris and extinguish any other thoughts of revenge that might be brewing. If Felicity was determined to attend the dance, then she had better be sure to stay in the company of her friends *at all times.* 'Even in the bathroom' he added, thinking of Ben's experience. She should be sure to have someone walk her to her car as well. He gave her a key to his house, so that she might enter and wait for him if he were not yet home when she returned. "I know that you're disappointed, but I really do feel that this is for the best. If you can't be persuaded to keep yourself home safe at the dorm, then I do hope that you'll end your evening here. Give me something to look forward to upon my return," he said, coaxing from her a smile.

She agreed to all of his precautions, still insisting that she would go. There was nothing for him to do but let her. It certainly was not his place to forbid it. Of course, he'd the feeling that if he did, she would obey him, but that was not the relationship that he wanted. She was an independent and intelligent young lady, only just learning to be confident in her own decisions. She'd been reminded of the dangers; he could only hope that she would use the utmost care. Hopefully, Chris would be busy elsewhere with Cain anyway.

She left him for the day and he tried to get some sleep before sunset approached. He'd an idea that he wanted to follow up with, and would need to leave just as soon as the sun would allow it. When the sun finally did dip below the horizon, Cain immediately set off on his motorcycle. He inspected the parking lot as he drove by the DownTime, both Felicity and Ben's cars were there. Of course, he could see their marks as well, letting him know that they were both within. He resisted the temptation to stop in and see her as the sensations from her mark grew strong at his approach. His body acknowledged the venom within her and sorely longed to taste her again. He did his best to ignore it and turned his attentions elsewhere.

He checked Tommy's lot as well when he rode by, but there were no familiar cars there. Good. He made his way through the streets until Alyson's house came into view. There was the car he'd been looking for; luck was with him, and she was at home. She looked very surprised to see him at the door. Especially when she looked up to see the brightly colored sunset still blazing in the sky. She stared at him oddly. "Hi. Did you *know* it's not dark yet?"

He laughed. "It's indirect light. The sun has actually set. No danger." She still just stood staring at him in puzzlement. He was a little surprised that she hadn't learned that from Mattie, but something told him that they spent most of their limited time together *inside* the house. "I wanted to speak with you. Would you like to come out?"

She smiled. "We don't have to stay *outside* to talk, Cain. You can come in."

He returned her smile as he entered her apartment. "Thank you." He hadn't wanted to put her in an awkward position, feeling forced to invite him. As he turned to face her, he noticed that she had plastic gloves on her hands. "Have I caught you at a bad time?"

She followed his gaze to the gloves and then took them off. "Oh, no. That's okay. I was just gonna do my hair. Hey, maybe you could help." She laughed at the look he gave her. "Don't worry, I wasn't gonna make you *do* anything. I just wanted your advice." Surely, he still looked rather doubtful. She continued, unconcerned. "See, I'd put lots of extra pink in, for the Homecoming dance, but it was too much pink. So now I added some green streaks, except it wasn't the color I thought it was gonna be...too dark. Anyway, I tried to get it out, but now it just looks like I had an unfortunate encounter with some pool chlorine. So, I have to cover it with something else, but if I do any more pink, I might as well just dye my whole head pink. Didn't really wanna do that."

He was staring at her hair throughout and studying the streaks of pink, purple and 'chlorine green' with bewilderment. "What was wrong with *blonde?*"

She chose to ignore him and kept on. "So, I've got this multi-color pack. I haven't got much left though, except a few I've never tried. What the heck is chartreuse? Do you know?"

He chuckled. "It's a yellow/green, like what you've got now."

"Oh. Then what's puce?"

"That's a purple color, if I'm not mistaken." He studied her hair again. "What happened to the blue?"

"Oh, I took it out. It didn't really go with what I wore to the dance, but it wouldn't come out all the way either. So, then I put pink over it, and that's how I got the purple that's in there now."

He laughed and shook his head. She put her hands on her hips and waited for him to meet her gaze again. He looked back up at her, pushing the hair back from his own face. "You should put back the blue. It'll bring out your eyes."

At first, she seemed to think that he was making fun of her, but he nodded reassuringly. She looked thoughtful for a moment and then smiled. "Thanks. I think I have some blue left." She was still looking at him thoughtfully, when she reached forward and swiped *his* hair out of his eyes again. "When's the last time *you* had a haircut?"

He shrugged. "I don't know, March? Actually April...yes, early April. You know, I had come here to talk to you about things other than hair."

"You should let me cut it for you," she offered.

He smiled, eyeing her wildly shorn locks. "Would I come away looking like you?"

She laughed, unoffended. "Even if you did, I guess you wouldn't know it, huh?" she teased. "No, I'm good with guys' styles, really. I do Ben's hair all the time and Mattie's too. I don't have my license or nothin', but I used to work in a hair salon, as an assistant, 'til I turned twenty-one." She shrugged. "Tommy's pays better."

"I can't. I really can't stay."

"You wanted to talk to me. You talk while I snip, it'll take ten minutes." She moved closer to run her hand across the side of his face. It startled him a little, as Felicity was often prone to such familiar gestures, but Alyson did it with a very business-like attitude. "You need a shave too. Unless you're really goin' for the 'gruff and rugged' look. I've got all the stuff in the bathroom. I shave Mattie. He says I've got a nice touch with it."

He shook his head again as she moved to the bathroom for supplies. "That's alright, really. I can shave later at home, but um...perhaps the haircut. If it really won't take long."

"Not at all." She came out with scissors, comb, and a smock, and headed for the kitchen. He followed and watched as she dumped her stuff on the table and pulled out a chair to the middle of the floor.

She eyed him appraisingly and then gestured to the sink. "It'll come out better if you let me wet it first."

He sighed. This was probably a stupid waste of time, but Chris and the others wouldn't even be awake yet. They always waited for well past full dark before venturing out. He let her put the apron over him and dutifully leaned over the sink. She spoke as she began to work her fingers through his hair. "You know, you might as well let me put some shampoo and conditioner in it, if we're going this far."

"Do as you like," he mumbled from under the water.

When she was finished, she toweled off his head and had him sit down so she could comb out his hair; otherwise, she'd never reach. He observed her as she moved around him. She was such a petite little thing. Not something he really noticed when dealing with her; she certainly had a large enough personality, but she could hardly be more than 5'2" and was just a thin little slip of a girl. He found himself marveling at how careful Mattie must be to take *any* blood from her. Surely, someone so slight hadn't all that much to spare.

She stood in front of him, brushing down and measuring out the bangs in front of his eyes. Now that they were wet, they hung down well past his nose, practically to his mouth. Allie laughed. "It's a wonder you could see! Why d'ya wait so long?"

He smiled. "I haven't got a proper hairdresser in these parts. Do well and I might give *you* the job."

Allie laughed again. "That's a deal. I've seen the way you tip Ben, and you don't even like him much."

"Just do me a favor, nothing fancy or striking. Just shorten it up. I usually take off as much as possible without getting a crew cut and then let it grow until it's in my eyes again."

"Well, that's a dumb system," she said with a smirk.

"It's convenient," he insisted.

"It's silly. You don't have to go half a year before your

next cut, just come back to me. Trust me, I'm gonna make you look good. Then if you let me give you a trim every six weeks or so, you won't need a major cut every time."

He became impatient. "Alright, whatever, let's just get started already." He gazed at her levelly for a moment as she came before him with the scissors. "I'm trusting you."

She smiled. "Can I go short in the back?"

"If you want. So, listen, about this Halloween Masquerade Ball." Allie began combing and cutting as he spoke. "Felicity seems absolutely set upon attending."

"And *you* still don't want to go."

"It's not that I don't want to go." She met his eyes with a smirk. "All right, I *don't* want to, but it's also true that *I can't*. I spent all of last night looking for Chris, with no sign of him anywhere. I can't assume that he's just given up and moved on. Especially when Sindy professes that he's a specific desire to harm Felicity. I need to confront him and convince him that to do so, would be seriously against his best interest. I will not rest until I have dealt with him personally."

"Goin' huntin' huh?" He slumped his shoulders. "Don't move!"

"Sorry. *I* don't do things that way. I just want us to have a chance to talk. I know Chris; he's not really a bad sort."

"Oh yeah? I find it hard to get to know someone when they're clubbing me over the head, or siccing animated corpses on me, so *I* wouldn't know."

"Well, perhaps he hasn't been all that friendly, but think of what *he's* been through; dying young, without properly being given a choice, having to take orders from Sindy and be treated as some sort of slave. And now with what happened to Luke...losing a close friend is a terrible thing, but he must be made to realize that what he does now cannot bring Luke back. Punishing Felicity or Sindy for past hurts can accomplish nothing. It will only make him enemies, and I am an enemy that he does not want, I can assure you.

He needs a sympathetic ear and to be helped to move past it. I know that he is capable of being far more of a man than Sindy ever gave him credit for. I want to help him to shake off the past, rise above it and begin anew. He needs to leave here and start a new life."

Alyson seemed doubtful of his confidence in Chris' ability to change. "To do what? Live like you? I don't think someone like him has it in them."

"And who are you and I to judge? I won't let him destroy those in his path, to be sure, but if he can manage to live in peace, let him be. He needs a chance to be the man that he never could while under Sindy's shadow. It is his choice what sort of man that will be. If he can find a life that will make him happy without hurting others, that will be a satisfaction far greater than killing these here now. That is what I must make him understand. And of course, I must warn him, that killing Felicity, or even Sindy for that matter, is not an option for him anyway. If he chooses to continue that fight, it will be against me. And he will not win. He should let it go, leave here and start a new life. One without such anger and hatred. I've shown him ways in which he might live without such strife. He must have paid *some* attention."

Alyson stood in front of him for a minute, looking at his face or his hair, he couldn't really tell. "You've got a big heart." He shrugged. "Don't let it get you killed."

"I'll try." He glanced down at the floor. "There's a bloody lot of hair down there."

"Relax. You're gonna look great. Just stay still, I'm not done. So, what does any of this have to do with me?"

"Well, I did have a bit of a favor to ask...since I really will be preoccupied, dealing with Chris and all, I can't attend the dance."

"So?" She seemed to know what was coming next.

"So, it still worries me to be so far from Felicity. Even if I've got Chris out of the way, so that he isn't a threat. Look at what happened last time. I can't chance such a disaster again. What if he's got allies, who might try to take her while I'm not there?"

"Cain, I don't wanna go, besides, what am I supposed to do?"

"I don't expect you to *do* anything. In fact, I would very much prefer that you stay *out* of trouble, but I would feel so much more at ease if I knew that you and Felicity were keeping an eye on each other. I worry for you both so."

"What are you worried about me for?"

"You're all alone. Do you think Mattie would ever forgive me if something happened to you right under my nose?"

"I can take care of myself," she informed him.

"Good, be a dear and take care of Felicity for me as well? Who else can I trust? I don't want you to try and fight anyone for me. Just keep aware of things and keep yourselves out of trouble. Please?"

"Well..." She backed away a bit and then moved to brush her fingers through his hair. "Look at you. How can I say 'no' to such hottie? Alright, I'll go. You're all done. Wow, you do look really hot"

He smirked at her. "That big a difference, eh?"

She laughed. "You looked good before, but now..." she played with his hair a bit more, "even better. I wish you could see yourself. I'm *good.*"

He laughed and ran his fingers through his hair. It fell down to just above his eyes. "It's still rather long in the front, isn't it?"

She put it back as it was and brushed his hand away. "No, it's perfect."

"It'll be in my face again before long," he complained.

"It's sexy, leave it alone. It was so long before, how can you even tell? Trust me, it looks good." She took the smock off of him and then got out a broom for the floor. As she began sweeping up, he took his wallet out, to see what he could give her. She saw his intent and held up a hand. "Na, first one's on me. You look great. Felicity is gonna flip, although...all that stubble kind of ruins the effect." She put her hand on his chest, as if to keep him in the chair. "Stay." She rushed into the bathroom and came back out with shaving supplies.

"That's really not necessary." He eyed the long straight razor she took out. "You sure you know how to use that thing?"

Alyson gave him a sly grin and struck a pose with her arm raised high in the air. "Are you kidding? At last, my arm is complete again," she quoted.

Cain rolled his eyes at the obvious reference. "I never much cared for Sweeney Todd."

"Relax. It's not like I'm gonna take your head off. You'll survive."

He laughed. "Thanks, very reassuring. You'll go to the dance with her for me?" He allowed her to lather him up with shaving lotion.

"Yeah, don't worry; I'll stick to her like glue. No problem. In fact, I'll tell her I need a ride. That way, she can't ditch me." He couldn't answer, as she had begun to carefully shave him and he didn't want to move. Actually, it kind of felt nice to be fussed over, and she did seem to know what she was doing. It didn't take long. "There you go. Not a knick. You look much better, trust me."

He flashed her another smile. "You have my gratitude. Perhaps I'll see you later. If she doesn't want to return here with you, feel free to join her at my house if you like; or the dorms. Not that you *have* to spend the whole night, but if you don't mind, I'd feel better if you stay together until I return."

Allie looked confused. "Shouldn't we pick a place to meet? How are you gonna catch up with us if you don't even know where we'll be?"

He dropped his eyes a moment, though why he should care what Alyson would think, he couldn't say. "I'll find her. She's marked."

"Oh." She stood silent for a moment, and then backed away for Cain to rise from the chair. "Well, it took a *little* longer than ten minutes, but if you could see yourself, you'd agree that it was well worth it." He met her eyes almost shyly, and nodded thanks. "While you're out looking for Chris...Well, you'll keep an eye out for Mattie, right?"

"Of course, but something tells me that when he does

come, it's straight *here* he'll be headed."

She looked at him accusingly. "And now I have to spend my night at this dumb dance. If he comes while I'm gone, I'm gonna be pissed."

"Odds are, he won't, but if I see him, I'll tell him to meet you there. I'd better get going. It's full dark by now." He paused once more by the door before leaving. "Thank you."

Allie shrugged. "What are friends for?"

Chapter 3 - Loyalties

Felicity

Alyson's house
9:00, Sunday night

Felicity sat in the driveway at Alyson's and beeped the horn for the third time. Finally, Allie emerged and turned to close and lock the door behind her. She looked as though she were dressed in a regular sweatshirt and jeans. As Allie entered the car, she seemed very impressed by Felicity's gown, but wasn't given time to say anything before Felicity verbally pounced on her. "Allie, where's your costume?"

"I'm wearin' it."

"No, you're not. Allie, you said you were dressing up!"

"I did...see." Allie had cut the collar off of her sweatshirt, to widen the neckline. Now she tilted her head to show off the two perfect red dots she had painted on her throat.

Felicity became annoyed. "That is not a costume."

"Sure, it is. Isn't it obvious? I'm a vampire victim. I was gonna go with a more gory/open wound sort of look, but I decided to be authentic instead."

"You should have been the cat. Why'd you change your

mind anyway? I thought you didn't wanna come."

"Yeah well, what else have I got to do? Besides, I thought it might be fun to hang out and make fun of everybody else's lame costumes. Speaking of costumes, what are you supposed to be, besides *beautiful?!*"

Felicity smiled at the compliment and adjusted her headpiece. It was a little crescent-shaped sort of velvet hat that was open to her hair at the top like a crown, with a veil hanging down the back. Felicity had been very pleased when she managed to use the hair comb Cain had given her, tucked into her hair at the base of the veil in the back. "I'm a medieval princess. Do I look good?"

"Let's put it this way, I know Cain hasn't seen you. 'Cause if he did, I don't think he could've pulled himself away! Girl, you are gorgeous!"

Felicity smiled, excited over speculation of Cain's reaction to her costume. "You think? I wish he had come. Why are guys so stubborn?" she asked in disappointment, as she pulled out of Allie's driveway.

"Come on, he's out there trying to take you off of Chris' most wanted list. Give the guy a break. He's only trying to make the world safe for human-kind. Don't be so hard on him."

"He didn't wanna come anyway. Wait a minute, how do you know what he's doing?"

Allie shrugged. "I just figured..."

"Uh-huh. And what was wrong with your car again?" Allie was just staring out the window. "Nothing, right? Cain told you to come with me, didn't he? I don't need a babysitter."

"I'm not a babysitter. We were just talking, and Cain

thought you could use some company. You're supposed to keep an eye on me too. We'll watch each other's backs. That's what friends do. You are like my only girlfriend you know."

"You've said that before. You know, you'd probably have more friends if you weren't so...abrasive all the time."

"I do that on purpose; I'm selective. If they can't survive the screening process, they're not worth my time. Who needs a bunch of fake friends anyway?"

Felicity shook her head at Allie's odd logic, but then her jaw dropped as she pulled into the parking lot in front of the school. The entire entrance to the building had been covered in a false facade, made to look like a haunted castle. It had painted 'crumbling' brickwork, complete with cracks. There were even false windows, lit from behind and sporting shadows of spooky figures within. It was amazing!

Felicity parked the car, and she and Alyson got out approaching the castle. Felicity turned to Allie with open-mouthed awe. "Wow."

Allie tried to act unimpressed. "Not bad." Felicity just smiled, and they made their way to the entrance. In front of the actual doors, a giant 'draw bridge' of plywood had been laid across the sidewalk, 'lowered' by chains attached to the building. The glow from the street lights revealed that day-glow colored chalk had been used to draw the 'moat' on both sides of the bridge over the sidewalk, in beautiful swirls of bright blue and aquamarine. A multi-colored and dangerous looking moat monster had even been drawn. They crossed the bridge into the entryway, which was flanked by two large and appropriately hideous stone gargoyles. Once inside, they paid their entrance fee to a robed and hooded ghoul, who motioned for them to drop it into a smoking cauldron.

The ballroom itself was decorated as well, with cobwebs, spiders and bats hung from every available surface. An eerie mist enveloped their feet, but rather than the spooky sounds one might expect to hear, it was dance music that accompanied them as they entered. After taking a few moments to check out the many costumed guests, Felicity spotted Karen and Jack. She sized up their costumes as she approached.

Karen looked very cute, dressed as a 'roaring 20's' flapper, complete with a feathered headband and mini dress covered in fringe. Jack wore a pinstriped suit, fedora hat, and toted a big plastic machine gun. Felicity and Alyson said their 'hellos' and complimented their outfits. Karen positively gushed over Felicity's gown. "You look so amazing! Are you here alone?" she asked in disbelief, looking around for evidence of Felicity's date.

Felicity and Allie shared a glance. "No. I'm here with Alyson."

"Oh, yeah, but I meant like, don't you have a date?"

"No, we're keeping each other company tonight. Our boyfriends couldn't make it." She had to smile at the word boyfriend. It sounded so strange and inadequate applied to Cain. What she and Cain shared was *so* intimate and indescribable. She was sure that Alyson felt the same about what she had with Mattie, *boyfriend* just didn't cut it.

Karen gave her a sympathetic smile. "You are so daring. I could never come to something like this *alone.*"

Felicity and Alyson shared another amused look as Alyson mumbled. "It's not *really* 1920, hon." Felicity considered reminding Karen that they were not alone, but had each other; and maybe even mentioning that she had planned to come alone in the first place. However, Karen wasn't even paying attention to her anymore.

When Karen finally did turn to her again, it was to point out another couple on the dance floor. Todd and Brenda were dancing nearby, gazing into each other's eyes and completely oblivious to their onlookers. They were dressed as Captain America and Wonder Woman, as promised, and they did look like a picture-perfect couple.

"Aren't they just adorable?" Karen asked. "Jack and I have been hanging out with them a lot since Homecoming, and they are just so cute together!"

Felicity hardly spared them another glance. That should be her and Cain dancing and sharing whispered secrets on the dance floor. How depressing. Why did she bother to come without him anyway? "Very cute. I'm going to get a drink." She turned to find Allie eager to follow.

They made it about halfway to the refreshment table when Allie stopped her to say, "Look, there's Ben."

Felicity followed her gaze to find 'Major Nelson' dancing with 'Jeannie' not too far away. Ben wasn't facing Felicity and Allie, and Ashley hadn't noticed them. Felicity could tell that Allie was eager to make her way over there. "Why don't you go say 'hi'? I'll get us drinks and be there in a minute."

"Great." Alyson left to meet Ben while Felicity continued to the refreshments. She ladled out cups of punch for her and Allie, from a cauldron of 'Witches Brew'. As she did, she eyed the odd assortment of snacks assembled there. Among the usual chips and pretzels, there were adorable little 'mummy' hot dogs, wrapped in strips of bread dough with little dotted mustard eyes peeking out, the baked potato ghosts, cut in half and painted white with sour cream even had little 'O' shaped chives for eyes and mouth. There were munchkin donuts with spider legs and cups of pudding and cookie crumb dirt, inhabited by gummy worms. A very eclectic but Halloween worthy assortment.

She took their drinks and joined Ben and Ashley, who had just begun talking to Allie. They still hadn't noticed Felicity. Allie seemed to speak louder for Felicity to hear, upon her approach. "I know, I wasn't gonna come, but then I got an invitation from someone I just couldn't refuse."

Ashley spoke up before Ben could respond. "So, where's your date?"

Allie smiled. "Getting me a drink."

Felicity had stopped just behind Ben, and could hear his voice begin to falter as he asked, "Who are you here with?"

"A friend of yours," Allie answered smugly.

That's when she realized what Allie was doing. Ben knew that Allie was eagerly awaiting Mattie's return. Alyson had not been seeing anyone else, in anticipation of his arrival. If she said she had a date, Ben would probably assume that it was his deceased friend. Considering the trepidation with which Ben thought of seeing Mattie again, Felicity decided it seemed rather cruel. She wouldn't let it go on any longer. Felicity leaned lightly over Ben's shoulder and whispered with a loud huff of air, "Boo!"

Ben jumped and spun around, almost making Felicity spill the drinks. She laughed and handed Allie her cup. Felicity then gave Ben a very tender and serious look as she said quietly, *"I'm* Allie's date for the evening."

Ben just stood there, staring at her and apparently trying to calm his racing heart. Felicity eyed him up and down, and then turned to Ashley. "You were right, Ashley. He *does* look dashing."

Ashley only smiled, but Ben seemed to find his voice. "So do you. I mean, you're not *dashing.* You're great. I mean, you look great."

"Thanks."

Ashley spoke up loudly. "I feel bad for you. It must be like a million degrees under all of those skirts. Aren't you roasting in there? Most of the people here are much more lightly dressed, so I know that the committee's keeping the heat up pretty high."

Allie took in Ashley's mostly transparent costume with an arched brow. "Well, maybe people wouldn't be cold if they were actually wearing clothes."

"And what are you supposed to be, 'white trash'?"

Allie smirked at her and pulled her shirt collar aside as she tilted her head to expose her 'bite'. "I'm a vampire victim. Or as Ben so quaintly puts it...a blood whore," she answered, aiming a sweet smile at Benjamin.

Ashley looked disgusted. "Come on Ben, let's go dance." Ben had blanched at Allie's statement, and looked more than happy to be led back onto the dance floor.

After watching them go, Felicity turned to Alyson. "You only dressed like that to bait him, didn't you? Why are you giving him a hard time? You know how unsettled he is about the whole 'Mattie' thing."

"If I don't keep shoving it in his face, he'll just try to

ignore it forever. Ben does that. Like if he doesn't acknowledge stuff, it'll just go away. If he's gonna stay in my life, he's gonna have to get a grip. I can't go back to hiding stuff anymore.

That's what he wants, you know. If I won't stop seeing Mattie, then Ben would like me to do it behind his back. That way he can go back to pretending that Mattie doesn't exist anymore. How can someone I love so dearly, be so dumb?"

"I think we all have stuff that we're dumb about. It's just hard to recognize the dumb stuff when it's your own. I mean, look at *us*. *We're* in love with *dead* guys. How dumb are we?"

Alyson just nodded her head towards Todd and Brenda. "If loving a dead guy's so dumb, then why aren't *you* over there dancing with Captain America?"

Felicity watched them dancing for a moment, and then scanned the crowd. There were plenty of good-looking young guys in the room, but not one of them could hold a candle to Cain in her eyes right now. She couldn't help but remember what she had said to her friend Deidre...Cain was going to leave some pretty big shoes to fill. She looked back to Allie, feeling a bit depressed. "I don't know. 'Cause I'm dumb. You wanna go find somewhere to sit? I don't feel much like dancing."

"Yeah, okay." Allie did not seem very happy to have made her point. They made their way to a table and sat down, not far from two guys dressed as The Mummy, and Frankenstein's monster. The guys looked them over and then asked them to dance. Felicity politely declined to her large green prospective partner. Alyson was a little more blatant about her refusal. She made an unfavorable visual appraisal of the guy dressed as

'The Mummy', and answered "No thanks. I don't like surprises." Felicity shot her a disapproving look as the guys walked away dejectedly. "Well, I'm sorry, but just *how ugly* do you have to be to want to cover your face in bandages for a social event?" Allie asked.

Felicity tried not to laugh as she looked back out into the crowd. Her eyes found Ben and Ashley dancing again. Funny, they were dancing together, but neither of them seemed to be paying any attention to the other. Ben was just sort of staring out into space. Meanwhile, Ashley looked to be putting on a show for everyone around her more than she noticed Ben, even though he did look very handsome in his uniform. It was so unlike the way that Todd and Brenda were dancing. Their actions reminded Felicity of how she had felt dancing with Cain at Tommy's on that first night that seemed so long ago. It had felt as though they were in their own private world. How hard was that to find with someone? Looking around the room, it seemed depressingly rare.

Felicity watched Ben and Ashley for a few more minutes before turning to speak to Alyson. "Does Ben really do that, ignore stuff? He usually seems like a pretty straight-forward and sensible guy."

Allie smiled. "He is, as long as it's not about him, or anybody he cares about."

"Well, I think all guys are like that to a certain extent."

"No, Ben is bad. I mean, it took forever for me to get him to believe in vampires," Alyson insisted.

"Allie, be fair. Until I'd seen them, I wouldn't have believed you either," Felicity admitted.

"But Ben is my best friend. He should have taken my

word for it. It took years," Allie explained.

"*Years?* How old were you when you first saw one?"

"Eleven. Never forget it. Fucked up my whole life," Allie said.

"Wow. What happened?" Felicity asked.

"I was going to the library with my mom," Allie began.

"You never talk about your family," Felicity observed.

"Yeah, there's a good reason for that. 'Cause they suck. My mom is a total bitch. My dad left us when I was nine, and I have a little brother, Henry, but he's a dick. That's why when they moved, I didn't. That was when I was eighteen; never regretted it.

So anyway, I think it was November. Yeah, it was after daylight savings, 'cause it was only dinner time and it was already dark out. So, it was just my mom and I; I think Henry was at Cub Scouts, and we were goin' to the library. You know, the little one over on Church Street."

"Oh, the one with the cobblestone and the slate roof? It's so cute."

"That's the one. It used to be a church you know. That's how they named the street. Somewhere along the way, it got turned into a library. Anyway, my mom used to work for a publishing company. She was like a fact checker or some shit. So, we're goin' to the library, and I'm helpin' my mom carry this shitload of books.

Now, not too long before, this new guy had shown up in town. A real slicker, always in a suit and drivin' a fancy car. He bought this real big house over on Wilshire. It's not there anymore, it burnt down, but you should have seen it; the thing was huge, like a fucking mansion. So, a guy like *that* in a town like *this* attracts some attention, you know?

So, this guy just happens to pull into the lot at the library same time as us. And as we're walkin' to the door, he comes rushing over to give my mom a hand. My mom's kinda hot, and after my dad left, she started dressin' like a real slut. I mean, there's snow on the ground, and she's wearin' a short coat with a mini skirt and freakin' 5-inch heels." Allie shook her head in disgust. "So, he's helpin' carry books and he goes to open the door for us, and I just happened to be looking at his face when the guy freaked. I mean he jerks his hand away from the door and drops all the books and his eyes...they turned red. I swear, the guy was looking right at me and I saw his eyes turn totally red."

Allie sounded almost desperate, as though she thought Felicity would question it. "I believe you."

"You're the only one," Alyson informed her.

"What happened?" Felicity asked.

"Well, my mom's all concerned for the guy, and I'm just standin' there in shock. I was totally convinced that I was standin' next to The Devil himself. That's when I dropped all *my* books. So, now my mom's all pissed, callin' me a klutz and wantin' to know what my problem is."

"What did you say?" Felicity prompted.

"I couldn't say anything, it's like I just froze. So, the guy tells my mom that he got stung by a bee. How lame is that? It's mid-November! And my ditz mom believes him and yells at me to start picking up books," Alyson told her.

"So, then what happened?"

"Nothin' really. We picked everything up and went inside. The guy didn't come in though. Said he was gonna go put somethin' on his hand, but as we were leavin', I stopped to check out the doorknobs. They're real old, original with the building. They're like brass with all these intricate designs worked all over them. Right in the middle of each one, is a cross. I swear. They're still there; you can go see them for yourself."

"Allie, I believe you," Felicity assured her.

"Later that night, my mom's on the phone with some friend of hers, goin' on about how great this guy is. So, I felt like I had to tell her. I mean, the last thing I needed was Satan for a step-dad. So, I told her."

Felicity prompted her again, "And?"

"And, she thought I was insane. I was all worked up about it, but she told me to shut-up tellin' her such lies. We didn't see him again and I don't know if I would've said anything else, but then the nightmares started.

Every night, I'd wake up screamin' that The Devil was comin' for me. Stupid nightmares. When my mom tried to tell me to forget them, I'd bring up that guy again. Never did know his name.

So finally, my mom takes me to see some jerk-off psychiatrist. I tell him the story, and he tells my mom that I'm having 'father replacement' issues. Unbelievable."

"That was it?" Felicity inquired.

"I wish. Couple of weeks later we're at the Christmas Parade over in Walton. My brother was on the Cub Scout float. So, the guy...he's there, standin' right on the side of the road, with all the regular people! I was already in so much trouble because of this jerk, and then he has the nerve to come over and start hitting on my mom, again! Can you believe it?! There was no way I was just gonna stand there and let that fly."

"What did you do?" Felicity asked uneasily.

"I stood right up to the guy, and I told him that I knew his secret. I told everyone loud and clear that this guy was a demon straight from Hell. I said he'd better stay away from me and my mom or I'd pray that God himself would strike him down with lightning."

"You said that?" Felicity asked in disbelief.

"Uh-huh. Maybe it wasn't the brightest thing to do, but I was only eleven. I wasn't really scared he'd *do* anything; we were in a crowd of people and it'd only prove me right. Still, I thought I was pretty brave. My mom, on the other hand, thought I was pretty psycho. That's when she sent me away to Hutchins School."

"What's that?"

"It's a school for troubled kids who need repeat psychiatric evaluations and treatment. Sounds fun, doesn't it? That's where *I* spent the second half of sixth grade."

"Oh Allie, that sucks."

"Tell me about it. When they let me come home for the summer, it was Ben who convinced me I should stop talkin' about it all. They all knew, Ben, Mattie, and David. Mattie and Davy said they believed me, but I know they didn't, not really. Ben didn't even try to pretend.

He told me that it didn't matter what I *thought* I saw, 'cause grown-ups just *didn't* believe kids about stuff like that. So, I should just keep quiet and try to forget it already, so they wouldn't send me away again.

He was right. Still, I didn't really care if everybody else

thought I was crazy, but the guys...knowing that my best friends thought that too, *that* hurt. Ben should have at least tried to believe me. I was closer to him than anybody else in my life, and I don't think the thought ever even crossed his mind, that I might be telling the truth. That hurt.

Sure enough, I shut-up and they didn't send me back. I still had nightmares sometimes, but my mom just told me that I'd better figure out how to deal with it. Nice, huh?

The guy had left town, something my mom never let me forget was my fault. 'A rich guy took an interest in her and I spooked him'. I probably saved her life, stupid bitch. At least he was gone, but kids never forget stuff like that. Especially since every kid in school thoughtfully reminded me each day by branding me 'Crazy Allie'."

Felicity felt an instant empathy. She also was no stranger to being teased in school. "Kids are cruel."

"*People* are cruel. Why do you think I don't bother with anyone? It's not worth it. I stopped worrying about what other people thought of me a long time ago. 'Cept when it comes to my guys, Ben, Mattie, Davy and I, we were like the Musketeers. We did everything together."

"Like hunting vampires?"

"I'm coming to that. The guy came back. It was on my seventeenth birthday. Some present huh? We were coming out of the movie theater and there he was. Smiled right at me. God, that guy gave me the creeps. Still looked exactly the same too; hadn't aged a bit. I guess he'd decided that things had calmed down enough to return. He didn't go near my mom though. Just went back to livin' in that big old house of his. We'd see him around now and again.

Davy started callin' him 'Drac', you know, like short for Dracula. He thought it was hysterical. I had done some research and the only creature I could find that couldn't touch a cross, was a vampire. I'd only ever seen the guy out at night. It made sense.

The boys had always poked fun at me a little about it. I mean, they're my good friends and I know they love me, so it wasn't hurtful, but they wouldn't quite let me forget it either. You know, like they'd point people out and say 'Gee Allie, that girl's lookin' awfully pale, think she's a vampire?' or 'How about that guy over there, couldn't you just picture him in a cape?'. I was so sick of being teased, that I told them I wanted to find a way to prove it. That's when Davy came up with 'The VanHelsing Club'."

"Are you serious?" Felicity asked with a laugh.

"Oh yeah. He said we should be vampire hunters. They all thought it was a splendid idea. You know, fifteen-year-old boys don't really need very much persuasion to get themselves into trouble."

"Wait, fifteen? I thought you said you were seventeen?"

"I was. I'm two years older than they are, well Mattie and Ben. Davy was sixteen at the time. Not that it ever mattered, by the time I was twelve they all towered over me, I'm so damn short."

"You're lucky to be so petite. You're like, automatically adorable," Felicity said with a twinge of jealousy.

"*Oh please!* Ben calls it my 'pixiness'. He used to beg me every Halloween to dress up like 'Tinkerbelle'. I'd like to sock him!" Allie exclaimed.

Felicity laughed. "It *would* look perfect on you."

"Shut up. Anyway, that's when we began sneaking out at night. We started out by snooping around Drac's house, but before we actually did anything, it burnt down. The paper said it was faulty wiring, but *I* think it was set by another vampire. Drac must've had bigger problems than us kids.

So then, we started looking for new vamps to uncover. We'd find a likely place, and wait. The back parking lot at the movie theater, the all-night gas station, out in the side lot at The Red Barrel. The guys'd sit and watch and I'd be the bait.

Can we just pause for a moment and pay tribute to the fact that I am still alive despite that incredible display of stupidity on my part? I'm a tiny little seventeen-year-old girl. 'Let me go stand out in a dark parking lot in the middle of the night and wait to be attacked.' God, I was stupid."

Felicity flinched, thinking of the night she had tried to avoid Cain coming to her in her room, by sitting outside by herself at night. "Everybody does something that they didn't really think through, once in awhile."

"Yeah well, the guys were supposed to be protecting me, but I don't think they were even watching half the time. They'd be sitting in the bushes with a six-pack of beer, comic books and a titty magazine, while Crazy Allie stood out there waiting to prove some kind of point. Even if there were *no* vampires, do you realize how lucky I am? I could have been kidnapped, raped, murdered by some human psycho, the possibilities are endless. And I expected protection from three half-drunk young teenage boys. Stupid."

"So, were you attacked by a vampire?"

"Three times," Allie informed her.

"Oh my God!"

Alyson nodded. "Yeah."

"Well, obviously you survived, and at least you proved you were telling the truth."

"You'd think. Here's what happened. I'm standin' out on the side of The Red Barrel mini-mart, and it's like midnight. So, the guys are sitting out behind a dumpster, with their usual entertainments...comics, porn, and beer. I'm actin' like I'm waitin' for somebody to pick me up. You know, lookin' around for cars, checkin' my watch and tryin' to look all scared and helpless.

So, this guy comes around the side of the building towards me. Looked like a real bum. Dressed in like three layers of dirty clothes, heavy beard, and I thought for sure he's comin' to hit me up for some money. So, I'm prepared to chase him outta here, before he scares away the vamps. The bum comes up to me, and freakin' lunges for my throat!

He's got me in a bear hug, tryin' to bite me and I'm screamin' and tryin to get him off me. Of course, the guys had all the weapons, another testament to my unbelievable stupidity. It seemed like it took them forever to come help. They were totally unprepared. I wish I could have seen them when they first heard me scream. I'll bet it would have been freakin' comical to see them scramblin' over each other and spillin' their beers to come to my aid.

Thing is, soon as they showed, the guy bolted. By the time they got to me, the guy was off in the woods. Davy went to chase him, but he was gone. Meanwhile, I'm tryin' to say I told you so, and they still didn't believe me! All they'd seen was a dirty old bum. Ben says he knows I'm mad 'cause they weren't really watchin', but I don't have to go pretendin' that the guy was a supernatural monster'. If Mattie hadn't held me back, I would've punched him right in the face."

"You didn't keep going out after that, did you?"

"Are you kidding? I couldn't wait to go out again. I was right! He was a real vampire! You have to realize; it was six years since I'd seen Drac get burned by that cross. I was almost starting to wonder if I *was* crazy, but now I had proof, even if only for myself. I wasn't just 'Crazy Allie' seeing things, it was real and now I was gonna show them, even if I had to get bit to do it. I was annoyed they hadn't seen it, but at least the incident did make us see how stupid it was, to leave me so vulnerable.

After that, Mattie always stayed with me while Davy and Ben promised to actually glance up at us once in awhile."

"Why always Mattie?" Felicity asked.

"Well, they didn't want to scare the vamps away, and Mattie seemed the most vulnerable of the three guys. Ben and Davy are much...taller." Allie's usual fast and easy cadence of speech seemed to falter as she caught herself. "I mean was...David *was* tall, like Ben." She stopped for a minute, staring vacantly at the dance floor. "David was a pretty big guy, even though he was only seventeen, when he died. They must have ganged up on him." She swallowed hard and continued before Felicity could say anything. "So, Mattie was the obvious choice. Not that he's 'little' or anything, but compared to them...I think he's like 5'9"."

Anyway, it took weeks before we saw anything else. We'd go out every Friday night. Mattie and I would hang out and talk while Ben and Davy 'kept watch' with their comics and whatever. As you can imagine, Mattie and I got pretty close.

He's so sweet, and I guess he felt like he could talk to me about stuff that he wouldn't ever bring up in front of the guys. One time, we were talking about something, I don't even remember what, but I put my hand on his leg. We were sitting facing each other on the ground, and I put my hand down like just above his knee. He was so cute; he got like hyper-conscious of it, and he was all nervous and red in the face. So, I'm askin' him what's the matter, and he's tryin' to shake it off like it's nothin', but I see him keep glancing down at my hand.

Mattie's always been kind of shy, and he was sixteen then, but I knew he'd never really had a girlfriend. I was almost eighteen. I'd been out with a few guys, all jerks, but I'd done my share of foolin' around. Mattie was so sweet and innocent, and absolutely adorable. I could tell by the way he was lookin' at me, that I wasn't just 'one of the guys' anymore. It was almost kind of funny, seein' him all flustered, *over me!*"

Felicity smiled. Alyson was practically glowing talking about Mattie. It was obvious how fond of him she was. Love was probably a very appropriate word. "So, what did you do?"

"I kissed him. Shocked the hell out of him, I'm sure. I know he was a little worried that Ben or Davy would see, but they weren't paying any attention to us. It was really sweet and soft. I mean, it's not like I attacked him or anything. After, he's just lookin' into my eyes with this shocked amazement, like he couldn't believe I did that, but *he's* the one who leaned over for another kiss. It was really nice. I was Mattie's first real kiss you know. I was Mattie's first *everything.*"

"Really?" Felicity smiled as Allie gave a little nod. "Was he *your* first?"

"No, but he's the only one that ever mattered." Allie's eyes had filled with unshed tears, and she stared out at the crowd of dancers again.

Felicity put a hand on her shoulder. "Don't worry. He'll come back."

"I know. He has to. We need each other. You know Ben and I are best friends, and he's like my reality check. He helps me deal with stuff, with life, but Mattie, being with him...he's like my *sanctuary* from the rest of the world, and I think I'm his. He understands me like nobody else does...not even Ben, and I get him too, you know? His life is different now and maybe there's stuff I don't know, but it's still Mattie. I don't know why I ever even bother with other guys. It's like I'm just killin' time. In fact, I'm startin' to think I'd rather just be alone when he's not around."

Felicity and Allie both looked up as Ben and Ashley walked by. Ben was being led by the hand; obviously, Ashley had a certain destination in mind. Ben smiled at them and might have stopped, but Ashley deliberately ignored them and kept walking. Rather than resist her, Ben just gave them a helpless and apologetic sort of grin and kept walking. Watching the two of them, Allie almost seemed nauseous. She turned to Felicity in disgust. "Being alone is definitely preferable to being led by the hand through life, by someone like that."

Felicity watched them for a moment more, and then went back to the prior conversation. "So, you said you got attacked *three times?*"

"Yeah. The next time was at the gas station. We were sitting off to the side and back a little, out of sight from the attendant. I was with Ben that night actually. He and Davy were sort of ticked off at each other over some girl. They weren't really fighting, but they didn't want to sit together. So stupid. So, Ben came with me, and Mattie stayed with Dave.

Ben and I are talking when all of a sudden, this guy comes from out of nowhere and punches Ben in the back of the head!"

"Oh my God!" Felicity exclaimed.

"I know! I must say, that David and Mattie did come pretty quickly that time, but I got him first."

"He was a vampire?" Felicity asked.

"For sure. After he punched Ben, he went 'vamp' and tried to bite him. The guy totally ignored *me*, like I wasn't even worth worrying about! I must say, I was highly insulted. He'll never underestimate me again!"

"What did you do?" Felicity asked uneasily.

"Well, after the last fiasco, it was decided that we should *all* have weapons, even me. And then there was *the pike*," she said with a laugh.

"What's a pike? I mean, besides a fish?" Felicity asked with a chuckle.

Allie chuckled. "It's a weapon. Sort of like a spear. Davy made it as kind of a joke. It was a long wooden push broom handle with the end sharpened into a wicked point. We decided it should stay with the bait. We'd just leave it on the ground nearby. Considering we were always in back lots near dumpsters and stuff, it just looked like another piece of junk on the ground.

So, this vampire had come around in front of Ben and was trying to bite him. Ben was doing a really good job of not getting bit, but he couldn't get away. So, I grabbed the pike and put it through the guy's back, to pierce his heart from behind. I hit it too!"

"Wow!" Felicity said in amazement.

"Yeah, but unfortunately I also kind of impaled Ben in the process," Allie admitted.

"What?!"

"I did, but it wasn't my fault! After it hit the guy's heart, he turned into dust and the resistance was gone. I couldn't help but come down harder than I meant to. It didn't go in deep," Allie said defensively.

"Oh my God, Allie, you could have killed him," Felicity said.

"I know, but I didn't. At least he believed me now, and I *did* save his life." Felicity was just looking at her in disbelief that she had come so close to mortally wounding her friend. "It left a scar; he was so pissed. Don't mention it; it's kind of a sore spot with him. It's barely noticeable, but he still makes sure I see it every time he takes off his shirt."

Felicity tried to remember when Ben had lifted his shirt to show her the bruises he'd received from Marcus. She couldn't recall seeing a scar, but it would have been hard to notice under all of the black and blues. "I never noticed the scar."

"Good, do me a favor and pretend you never do. Anyway, I would have been perfectly happy to stop goin' huntin' after that. Ben had seen the guys' fangs up close, and the others had seen him turn to dust. They believed me now, so...mission accomplished. I was never really out to save the world or nothin'.

Mattie wanted to stop because he was afraid one of us

was going to end up getting *really* hurt, besides, by that point he and I would rather have spent our Friday nights in private anyway. We had just started to get together alone sometimes during the week, and the guys didn't know. I don't know why we didn't tell them. It's not like we were ashamed or anything, but it might have made things weird for all of us together, you know? Messed up the group dynamic.

Davy on the other hand was psyched up and ready to go. He couldn't wait to stake a vamp. I don't know if Ben was quite as anxious, but that was when his mom got real sick. I think he just wanted to keep going out to get his mind off of things."

"His mom had cancer, right?" Felicity asked quietly.

"Yeah. She went through chemo. She was sick all through Thanksgiving and Christmas. It was real hard on her. At least it worked."

"Wait a minute, I thought she died?" Felicity asked in confusion.

"Well yeah, but not from that. It went into remission. Then she was fine." Felicity was a little confused, but Allie plowed on. "So, we said we weren't gonna do it anymore, but then Mattie and I found out that they were still goin' out hunting without us.

They hadn't seen any action. I guess two strapping young men don't make for very good bait. Mattie went off on them, for goin' without us. They didn't want to quit though. So, we all started goin' huntin' together again.

We had a few false alarms, but no more vamps. Until all of a sudden in June, we start seein' them. We didn't get any, and there was no proof really, but there were a lot of new suspicious characters around. We'd see them every night, but they always took off on us, before we could do anything. That's when Ben's mom died. They got her right in her own driveway."

Now Felicity sat back and eyed Allie with disbelief. "What? Allie, that can't be right. Ben said his mom died from cancer."

"Well, that's what they told *him,* and everybody else for that matter, but she'd been doin' real well, you wouldn't have even known she was ever sick. It was definitely a vampire."

"How do you know?"

"I saw it," Alyson replied.

"You saw her get attacked?" Felicity asked, with frightened awe.

"No. I saw the bite, on her body, at the funeral."

"Are you sure? Why didn't Ben see it?" Felicity asked skeptically.

"They had a lot of make-up on her and her hair was mostly over it, but it was there if you looked close," Allie confirmed.

"Didn't you tell him?" Felicity asked in astonishment.

"Yeah, but Felicity, we were at *his mom's funeral.* Think about that for a minute. He was only sixteen and his mom died. Now I have to try and show him that she was sucked dry by some monster? How fucked up is that? It wasn't until the last night of the wake that I got up the nerve to show him. He wanted to be with her alone for a minute, before they took her away. I made him let me stay, and I showed him."

"What did he say?" Felicity asked.

"He wouldn't believe it. He told me that it was a mark

from the hospital equipment or something. He just wouldn't
see it. At least, he wouldn't admit it to me, but I think he
knew, 'cause after that, he started hunting with a vengeance. I
think he was goin' out like every night, with or without us.
Vamps stayed away from him though. He was on such a
mission that he was probably just oozin' a danger vibe.
Vampires aren't entirely stupid, they all steered well clear.

There were a lot of them around still though. Somethin'
big must have been goin' on, and we couldn't stay lucky
forever. There was a night that they went without me. I had to
go to my stupid brother's graduation. I don't know exactly
what happened, but apparently, they ran into a big gang of
vampires who weren't scared of a couple of kids.

The guys took off running, and all of sudden, Mattie
wasn't with them anymore. Mattie never came back." Allie
was obviously still upset over it, even though Mattie had made
it through his ordeal. "They lost him! They said they looked,
but it was like he'd disappeared. I could have killed them!
They went without me and they let those vamps get Mattie!"

Allie paused for a deep breath. Felicity couldn't say
anything. She'd wanted to reassure her that Ben and Davy
hadn't meant for that to happen, but Allie already knew that.
It was just hard to live with. After a moment, Alyson
continued.

"I went lookin' for him. They didn't want me to, said it
was too dangerous, but I went anyway. Ben had told Mattie's
parents that they were attacked by a gang, so the police were
looking for him too, but nobody found anything. Then a few
nights later, *we* ran into four nasty lookin' vamps. I don't
know if they were the same guys who got Mattie or not, Ben

and Davy had said there were at least seven of them that night.

Anyway, I was the only one with a car at the time. I had this beat up old Suburban, so I used to drive us everywhere. I had it parked in a lot about a half-mile away. Seeing that there were more of them than us, I started running for the truck. For some stupid reason, the guys ran the other way. So, three of the vamps took off after them, and one followed me.

I made it to the truck in record time, closed and locked the doors. It was funny though, as soon as I was in, the guy gave up and took off back for the guys. You'd think he would've tried to break the window or something."

"He couldn't have gotten in," Felicity interjected.

"Why not?" Allie asked in puzzlement.

"A vampire needs an invitation for a car just like a house. It's your personal space," Felicity informed her.

"For real? I never knew that. That explains why he didn't bother. I always wondered about that, but Mattie's been in my car."

"You must have invited him without realizing," Felicity conjectured.

"I guess. So, the guy took off, and I didn't know what to do at that point. I wanted to go help the guys, but I was afraid to leave the truck. I couldn't drive to them because they were off in the woods, besides, if I moved the truck, they might not be able to find me if they came back. So, I sat and waited. It was awful, just sitting there.

Finally, Ben comes out of the trees, all out of breath and lookin' totally spooked. I'm talkin' white as a sheet and barely able to speak. He just got in the truck and asked 'Where's

Davy?'

Obviously, I didn't know. I asked him what happened and he just said they'd gotten separated. That was it, he wouldn't say anything else. So, we just sat there and waited. We waited all damn night 'til the sun came up and Davy never showed. We got out and searched and yelled for him, but we couldn't find him anywhere. So, Ben said he probably just went home. I don't think he believed that, but he was trying to keep me from freaking out. So, we go to his house and his mom checks his room, and he's not there.

Now, remember that this was right after Mattie had disappeared. None of us were supposed to be out at all, and his parents understandably freaked. They called the cops, and we showed them where we'd been. We told them we'd been out lookin' for Mattie. They thought we were involved in some kind of stupid gang war or something." Allie's voice became quiet and trembling as she tried to continue without getting too upset.

"They searched the woods, and they found Davy's body a little while later. When the vamps were done with him, they'd slit his throat, so you couldn't see the bite marks. I guess it looked weird that there was practically no blood, but the cops didn't make too big a fuss about it, not that *we* ever heard. Ben and I were kind of under 'house arrest' for a little, but they got a finger print off of a button on Davy's jacket. It belonged to some guy who was wanted for something a few towns over. Must have been one of the vamps.

That's all I knew." Allie stared at Felicity for a moment as a hard cold look came into her eyes. "You know Ben saw Mattie that night? He saw Mattie and *he never told me!* He knew how devastated I was. When we weren't out looking for him, I was crying for him like non-stop for three days. Then the night that Davy died, Ben saw him, and he just came back to the truck and he never told me!"

"Allie, you know Ben was only trying to protect you. If he had told you that Mattie was out there, you would have gone back out to try and find him. You would have gotten yourself killed."

"Felicity, look at me; Ben's like a hundred and eighty pounds and I'm lucky if I'm in triple digits. I think he could have stopped me if he tried. He should have told me."

"He didn't want to upset you," Felicity said in Ben's defense.

"He didn't want me to know, because he knew that I wouldn't turn away from Mattie the way that he did," Allie accused.

"How did you find out, about Mattie?" Felicity asked her.

"Next night, he came tappin' on my window. Oh God, Felicity. Talk about overwhelming joy and relief!" Allie's broad smile and tear-filled eyes made Felicity feel as though she were seeing the moment again through Allie's eyes. She could imagine the release it must have been, from the helpless devastation that Allie must have been going through. "I made him climb through my window so I could smother him with hugs and kisses. I couldn't believe he was there. It was like a miracle.

Then he told me. He told me that he'd changed, but you know what? It didn't matter. It was still Mattie. I *knew* him. He was just the same. I couldn't even see the change. He wouldn't show me, not that night. He put my hand to his chest though, under his shirt. We stood there, silent like that for a long time. At first, I didn't even know what he was doing, but then I realized. No heartbeat.

It didn't matter though. It still doesn't." Allie shrugged. "He's Mattie. You make this big deal about being in love with 'a dead guy', but I don't see it that way. Love is love. Every relationship has obstacles. Some are small, some are huge. You just have to decide if your love is worth overcoming them. Sure, being with Mattie makes it kind of hard to lead a normal life. I've been thinking about that a lot. You know what? I can't say I care. How's *my* life normal anyway? All I know for sure about my life, is that it really sucks when Mattie's not in it." Allie sniffled, and took a sip from her drink. She fought back the tears with a deep breath and went on.

"He wouldn't tell me what happened. Mattie's like that sometimes. He's so quiet and keeps stuff to himself. He'll only confide stuff to people he really cares about. And then some stuff, he just won't talk about at all. I asked, believe me, but he just wasn't talkin'. It must have been really awful; I had to let it go.

He did tell me about how he'd seen Ben though. He told me how spooked Ben was and that Ben just didn't understand that he wasn't some inhuman monster. I was enraged! I wanted to kill Ben for not telling me. I couldn't believe it! How could he have seen Mattie and not told me? How could he not see that Mattie was the same? How could he not understand? I told Mattie that we had to make him see. Especially now, after what happened to Davy. We had to make Ben see that Mattie was alright. How could he not be anything but relieved?

That's when I realized that Mattie didn't know what I was talking about. He didn't know...about Davy. I told him what happened and you could just see it hit him like a brick in the face. He didn't know. He was so desperately grief-stricken.

Then he realized that it must have happened while he was talking to Ben. That just made things seem worse. If Mattie hadn't told Ben straight off that he'd changed... If Ben hadn't been frightened of him, if only Ben had told him what happened. Mattie and Ben could have gone looking for Davy together and they might have found him in time.

Sometimes I think that Ben thinks that too. That's why he blames himself for Davy's death. We never talked about it though. Ben didn't even know that I knew about Mattie until now. Mattie told me not to say anything to him. Ben was just trying to keep me safe and I should try not to hold it against him. He knew it would just push Ben and me apart from each other. He said we needed each other more than ever now. We had to take care of each other. I think he felt bad that he couldn't be around for me.

I wanted Mattie to stay of course, but he said he couldn't, not yet. He couldn't let himself be seen; his folks were better off thinkin' him gone. Ben and I had stuff to do together that he couldn't be a part of. You know, with Davy's funeral and police questions and stuff. He told me that we should keep each other safe and be careful. Mattie promised me he'd come back when he could. He had his own stuff to do. He needed to learn how to live a new life."

Allie looked thoughtful for a moment. "You know, I always thought he was alone, but I guess I should have realized that he would have had a much harder time without help. I have a feeling that I owe *Cain* a really big 'thank you'. Sounds like maybe he took care of Mattie for me. What does he do, run a home for 'wayward vampires' or what?"

Felicity laughed. "I think it's more of a one at a time, case by case basis, but yeah. Something like that."

"He's a good guy," Alyson said admiringly.

Felicity nodded her head and tried to smile but she had a big lump in her throat. Alyson made it seem so straightforward. It made Felicity feel guilty, like the vampire issue shouldn't bother her. Was she really going to let such a wonderful man leave her life? She felt like she was stupid and cruel for not loving him enough to want to be with him…always.

Chapter 4 - Honesty

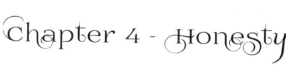

Cain

9:00, Sunday night

Cain rode his motorcycle through the dark streets of the town, much as he had the evening before. The chain mail that he wore beneath his sweater was a cold heavy weight upon his chest. He'd done a few sweeps of the area, and was confident that no other vampires were within the immediate vicinity at the moment.

He'd felt Felicity's brilliant and beckoning mark over in the direction of Alyson's house. He was grateful to Allie for following through with his wish that they be together. His body recognized the call of his venom within Felicity and urged him to move towards her, but he held his course and stayed clear. As tempted as he was to go and see her, he knew he must resist. She would only plead with him to stay and he really needed to get this business with Chris over with – alone. So, he stayed out of her physical range, hoping she would not feel him.

Luckily, his psychic range reached much further, so he could be sure that no other vampires were near – none that he could read. He dearly hoped that Chris was keeping Marcus with him. Chris had learned to hide his own trace, but had he realized that he could be traced through Marcus if they stayed together? It seemed a simple conclusion, but common sense was not usually a strength of Sindy's creations. With a silent prayer for Felicity and Alyson's safety, Cain moved on. He had one further stop to make before truly continuing his search. The closer Cain came to the motor lodge in Oxford, the more worried he became. He could not feel Sindy there. Not at all. Not even a slight telltale slip of her presence. Had she left? Where would she have gone?

He was unsure whether to worry that Chris had found and taken her, or that perhaps she had gone to him willingly. Sindy had told him that she was through playing games, but although he felt fairly certain that she would not seek to harm those Cain had chosen to protect, he had learned from past experiences that such assumptions could be dangerous. She had shown some amount of loyalty to him and he would like to trust her, but he was not a total fool.

He parked the bike out in front of room number seven, and went to the door. He was about to knock, wondering if he was wasting his time, when he heard slight sounds from within. He paused, and then purposefully rapped on the door. The one within was silent a moment, and then seemed to rush to the door, but it was not opened.

Cain stood outside, impatient but pleased. It had to be Sindy. She was so perfectly concealed that he had not seen her mark her at all during his entire approach, or even now. It was a wonderful display of psychic control and he could not help but feel almost inordinately proud of her. She still hadn't opened the door though. She had to know that it would be him. Was she pausing for effect, so as not to seem overly anxious, or was she only being cautious? As he had the night before, he briefly made his identity known, by momentarily dropping his shield. He heard her unlock the door immediately.

Sindy swung the door open wide and seemed to pose, with one arm stretched up to hold the doorframe, the other perched on her hip. Again, she wore the short black mini dress with the long flowing sleeves and a confident little smirk upon her face. No eye make-up. Probably impossible to attempt without a mirror anyway. She wore only lipstick and a hint of blush to accentuate her high cheekbones. She looked amused that he had come to her again, as if she thought that he could not bear to stay away.

He smiled and was still amazed that she held herself invisible to his mind so well and for so long. Even upon seeing him, she held it true. "Impressive."

She grinned and opened her arms wide as though to show off her sleek form. "Aren't I always?"

"Your cloaking," he clarified. "It's flawless."

"I know. Look at you all clean cut and handsome. You didn't get all dandied up for me did ya?" He raked his hand through his hair. Oh right, the haircut. He'd forgotten.

He smoothed his cashmere sweater over his chest, tugged the ends of his sleeves a bit, as though making sure his appearance was suitable, and then gave her a sly smile. "No."

She laughed. "Good, I hate it when guys try too hard. Come on in." She backed away from the door for him to enter.

As he followed her into the room, he refrained from turning to shut the door. "I think I'll let *you* close it," he said with a little smile, remembering the last two times he'd turned his back on her for such a task. She chuckled, closed and locked it he noticed. Perhaps behind her confident demeanor, there was a touch of worry after all. "Any news?"

She shook her head and held to her air of non-chalance tinged with boredom. She was rather good at that affectation he'd noticed. No matter what was happening around her, she always seemed to want him to think that she didn't care. "Nope, life is boring."

He smiled as she walked over and turned off the television program she'd been watching. "Boring also means safe. You're lucky."

She let herself collapse backwards onto the bed. "Yeah, lucky me. Nothin' but a big ol' empty bed and a boob-tube."

Always a bed reference. He wondered fleetingly whether she really did care so much for the physical pleasures of sex, as she liked to claim. Not that she shouldn't, but he'd the feeling that she considered it a priority, mostly because others seemed to. It was something that she considered herself good at, something to be valued for. It should be considered important because it was a commodity and a bargaining tool, more than for the rewards of the act itself.

She sat up and looked at him questioningly. "You don't even *have* a television, do you?"

"I read. I've found the few television programs that I've recently attempted to watch, to be banal and insipid."

Sindy gave him a blank stare for a moment before answering. "If that means they suck, then I agree." She sat up on the edge of the bed as he laughed, and then patted her hand on its coverlet, as though he should join her.

He shook his head to decline. "I'm not staying. I just wanted to check in...see if you needed anything."

She gave him a broad and mischievous smile. "Well, if you're asking..."

He quickly cut off any illicit request she might make. "Have you a refrigerator?"

She studied him a moment, annoyed that he would cut right to practical matters. Even when she knew he would decline, she always seemed to enjoy teasing him with her propositions. After a pause, she nodded towards the far corner of the room where a mini-fridge sat on the floor. "Already stocked. Thanks, anyway."

"Microwave?"

She made a face of disgust. "Just a hot plate."

"Whatever does the job. Right then, I'm off."

"Cain, I can't stay here."

He glanced around. The room seemed fairly clean and comfortable. "Why not?"

She slumped her shoulders and glared at him in exasperation. "Because it blows! What am I suppose to do, just sit here alone and watch TV all night?"

Cain sighed. "Well, your cloaking seems reliable enough. You can certainly go out if you'd like." Her face brightened as she smiled at him hopefully. "But you're *not* coming with me."

She slumped her shoulders again in a huff. "Why can't I?"

"You know I'm out looking for Chris," he reminded her.

"So? I got your back," she offered.

He let out a little chuckle. "Thank you, but no."

She seemed insulted by his response. "Don't you trust me?"

Now he looked back up at her with mild amusement. "*That* my dear, is another question entirely, but I'm not looking to fight Chris; I only want to speak with him. If I were to confront him with you, he would immediately become defensive and feel that we were ganging up on him. I need to do this alone."

"What for? You're wasting your time. After what he pulled, he doesn't deserve a chance to talk. You know letting him go is gonna come back to bite you in the ass one day. Just dust him."

He shook his head at her in disapproval. "I understand that you feel he's betrayed you, but if you pause for reflection, you might realize that the things you've done to him have been far worse." Sindy looked almost outraged at the idea. He put up a hand to forestall any argument she might have. "To be honest, your own personal quarrels do not concern me.

Now if you are looking for my *protection*, I suppose I might grant you that, but only in the knowledge that you are prepared to let grudges go and be done with it. Otherwise, if you'd both prefer to kill each other, go ahead. Just leave the rest of the world out of it, would you please?" She just rolled her eyes at him.

He pressed on. "Now I plan to go and offer Chris amnesty if he will take his newfound freedom and live peacefully elsewhere. Where do you stand?"

She thought about it for a minute, and then shrugged. "Well... I guess I don't really care what he does, as long as he stays out of my face," she replied grudgingly. "But I still think he's a lost cause. He's never gonna listen to you. You should just give up and stake him already, before he gets you first."

Cain gave her an insightful little smile. "I don't give up on people easily...lucky for *you*." She'd no answer for that, but only dropped her eyes to the floor. "Goodnight." Cain undid the lock and opened the door.

"Cain..." He paused, with his hand on the knob. "Can't you stay for a little?"

"No." He stood in the open doorway, looking out into the dark and nearly empty lot. When she didn't say anything else, he turned again to face her. She'd risen from the bed and stood before him. Her confident and superior attitude had disappeared. He stood firm. "I don't like not knowing where he is. I can't dally here."

She obviously still did not want him to go. She seemed almost embarrassed to have stopped him but was having trouble offering an explanation as to why. Finally, she looked up at him with large and honest eyes, although she did drop them to look at the floor now and again almost shyly as she spoke. "It's just... I've... I've never been alone before. I mean really alone. Like...disconnected, from *everybody*. Nobody owns me and I haven't got anybody either. I can't *see* you, or even Chris for that matter. Marcus' trace has Chris all over it now and he doesn't seem all that friendly towards me these days anyway. Only guy wearing my mark is *Ben*, and he'd be very happy to see me dead, so…that's not very reassuring. I've never been *alone* before. It's kind of…frightening."

Cain gazed at her in wonder for a moment. "Sindy, you have killed *dozens* of men. I have seen you be attacked by animated corpses and rip them limb from limb. And being *alone* is what frightens you?"

She became flustered and turned away. "You think I'm stupid."

He caught her arm to turn her back to face him. "No, I really don't. I think you're being *honest,* and I like that. Just making sure I've got it straight," he said with a sympathetic smile. "But you are an intelligent, independent and very strong young lady. You can stand on your own. Have faith."

She looked away, resentful and unsure. He took her by the shoulders to face him again. He looked into her eyes with a reassuring smile as he spoke. "You *can,* but you don't have to. You're *not* alone." He waited for her to smile back before he continued. "I'm still never sure whether to trust you entirely, but I really don't give up on people easily." She gave him another sly smile and laughed. "However, I can't take you with me, so you're going to have to let me leave now."

She didn't speak, but just bowed her head in acceptance. He knew she was embarrassed for him to have seen her as weak and afraid. As he looked at her now, he made himself realize that no matter how mature and worldly she often pretended to be, chronologically she was really only nineteen.

He let go of her shoulders and turned again to leave. Once more, she stopped him, but her voice sounded so quiet and hesitant that he couldn't be angry with her. "Cain...could you..."

He faced her again, but she wouldn't meet his eyes. After an interminable pause, he prompted her. "What?"

"Would you..." She finally lifted her eyes to his. He'd never seen her look so vulnerable. "Would you mark me?"

He stared at her for a long moment and then dropped his gaze to the floor, a bit uncomfortable with the prospect. She addressed his concern with the idea. "I know you're with Felicity now. That's your choice. Fine, whatever. This isn't about that. It's just... I'm not marked. I don't belong to nobody, it's like I don't even matter. I could die before dawn and no one would feel it, no one would even know...or care. I might as well not even exist. It's...scary.

If you marked me, at least I could feel like I'm a part of something, connected to the rest of the world again. It wouldn't have to be sexual. It's not like you'd be cheating on her or nothin'. It's just...a vampire thing. Honest."

He stood there, staring at her for what felt like a very long time. Just turning things over in his mind and unsure how to respond. After a moment or two, he could tell that she thought he'd decline. Finally, she turned to move away from him further into the room, her eyes carefully avoiding his own. "Forget it. It was stupid. Go find Chris or whatever, and be careful." He did not speak. She turned to look back at him, and found that he had moved into the room, and was shutting the door behind him.

He came to take her hands into his own and looked into her eyes. "You're not alone."

She looked away and tried to pretend indifference. "Yeah, I know. You'd better get goin'." She tried to move away, but he didn't let go of her hands. She looked back at him questioningly.

"I'll do it, if you want," he said quietly.

Her eyes widened just a touch and she stared at him for a long time, as though she didn't really believe him. He gave her a small smile and a slight nod. The relief was plain on her face. She seemed to ponder things a moment and then turned the inside of her wrist towards him and moved her arm slightly higher, in offering.

Cain felt as though he were seeing her in such a new light. He'd always suspected that there was a frightened little girl behind her fangs and false bravado, but now it was truly plain to see. How scared she must be, to actually admit it to him. She was so young, only sixteen when she'd died and become caught up in all of this. He knew that she was strong and could stand on her own, but being alone *was* frightening sometimes. He knew.

He dropped her hands from his own and opened his arms to her. "Come here."

Her eyes were bright and moist. She looked as if she would like nothing better than to collapse in his arms and cry in relief, but she didn't come to him immediately. Submission was not an easy thing for her, he was sure. She paused as though seeking a trap, or perhaps she was wondering if he would lose respect for her now. Little did she know that he held her display of true feelings in much higher regard than her usual air of fearlessness.

She finally surrendered to him. He enfolded her in his arms for a strong close hug. It took her a moment before she did truly give over to it. He held her for a time, a hug sincere and unrushed that she should feel connected to another; that she should know that he *did* care; and he then moved her back from him to look at her. He lifted a hand to sweep her long hair away from her throat on one side and let it drop down her back. He inched over the material of her dress, to leave her neck exposed and clear.

She seemed a little surprised; maybe she'd thought he would take back her wrist. Not that she seemed to mind. After gazing into his eyes for the space of a second, she closed her own and tilted her head subtly to the side. It was such a demure and supplicating gesture. It was very unlike her and he found it almost *too* appealing.

He gazed at her throat and let the change overcome him. As his vision shifted spectrums, he realized with mild surprise that her eyes remained closed. She wasn't watching him. He knew that to see him change usually excited her. To see him unleash the beast within seemed to give her a thrill. Patiently she awaited his bite. She really *was* trying to keep to her word. She didn't want him to feel that he was betraying his human lover by pleasing another. She held still and silent, her eyelids never lifted.

The last time he had drunk from her throat it was something savage and almost brutal. This would be different. It was not punishment, not foreplay, not even the purely practical act of marking. This was one creature clinging to another to keep them from feeling swept away by the lonely winds of the world.

He wrapped his arm around her waist and bent to her pale throat. She never even flinched as he pierced her skin decisively, with the utmost precision and care. Even as the first drops of blood began to envelope his fangs, he refrained from drinking. First, he would let the venom begin its task. He could feel his poison flowing into her body. She felt it too; she sagged against him a bit, as the first wave of dizziness came over her.

Sindy seemed hesitant to cling to him too strongly, as though he wouldn't want her arms around him. He used his own hold on her waist to crush her closely to him. She spoke, trying to keep her voice neutral and clear, though it wasn't much more than a whisper. "Drink. If you meet up with Chris and Marcus, you're gonna need it."

He couldn't wait any longer anyway. Did she really believe his will strong enough to keep him from such ecstasy? He held her tightly and sucked strongly upon her throat. She couldn't help but let out a low moan of pleasure, even as he fought to keep silent himself. Now she did bring her arms up around him. Surely, she would need his support just to keep herself standing through the waves of euphoria his drinking would bring. Her blood was like smooth liquid fire as it filled his mouth. It coated his tongue and burned its way down his throat as his body thrilled to the warm spice of its taste.

Again, he pulled upon her vein and it was almost as though the blood had a life of its own. His mind reeled with lightheaded fulfillment as it moved within him; finding its way through his body to fill not only his stomach, but also every hollow it could reach. It left a trail of warmth and shivers of pleasure in its wake, blood like this could never be confused with something human. It needed not a pumping living heart to propel it; it moved within him of its own accord. It was blood and yet mixed within it was truly something else, something alien and unknown. It was…vampire.

A disease? A separate entity of its own, seeking only a host? Cain did not know, nor did any he had ever met. Right now, it did not matter. It was life, blood, filling and completing him so that he might be a strong and powerful creature again. Her blood was an intoxicating pleasure that although he had not thought to sample again for some time, he had to admit was a very welcome and satisfying gift. His lips covered the wound as his fangs withdrew and he drank long and deep.

After a time, when Sindy seemed too inebriated with his venom to stand any longer, he used his arm to scoop her legs from under her as his other arm supported her waist and he carried her to the bed. He laid her down and forced himself to remove his lips from her throat, although the liquid ecstasy there was something difficult to disengage from. As he rose, she turned her face to try and meet his mouth for a kiss. His lips barely brushed hers as he lifted himself from her.

She looked up at him dreamily, obviously deep in a venomed haze. "Sorry, reflex."

He smiled and gave her a moment to recuperate. Her venom was surely fighting his own even now. He blinked his eyes and straightened, letting the vampire recede so that the man might resurface. He felt almost drunk with her unnatural blood.

Before long, she was sufficiently recovered to look upon him in clarity. He wondered if the fluids within her body saw his venom as an invading toxin or a kindred entity. It was a whole separate level of their existence that he suspected he would never understand. As long as the vampire within him was satisfied to let the man retain the lead, he was content not to delve further into the philosophy and true mechanics of it all.

He looked down at Sindy lovingly and stepped back from the bed. "I'll be leaving you now," he told her quietly. She only gazed at him with eyes rich and earthy brown like tilled soil. She still seemed loathe to let him go. He retrieved the television remote from the table and threw it to her on the bed. As he turned to leave, he heard it hit the floor as she threw it back at him with a laugh.

He came back to her. She pouted at him like a child. "TV sucks."

"So read a book," he told her.

"I haven't got any," she pouted.

He smiled. "Sure, you do." He reached forward to open the drawer of the nightstand next to the bed. Sure enough, there lay a Bible within.

Sindy chuckled. "You want me to read *that?*" Her speech was still a bit thick and slurred.

He shrugged. "If you want." He pushed up his sleeve to reveal his tattoo. He tapped the words 'Genesis 4:7' printed on the inside of his forearm for emphasis. "Look it up. It's a good passage." She smiled and shook her head slightly in amusement at him. Without saying anything further, he let himself out. He was only just closing the door as he heard her whisper "Thanks".

Part 2

Stakes and Sunshine

Chapter 5

Top of the food chain

Felicity

Masquerade Ball
11:00, Sunday night

Felicity stared out onto the dance floor to try and get rid of that nagging guilty feeling she had over the uncertain future of her relationship with Cain. Allie seemed to think the fact that he was a vampire shouldn't have any bearing on her feelings towards him. Was she just being narrow-minded? But Alyson had been involved with Mattie *before* he'd been changed. That made a difference in how she saw things...didn't it? Why did everything have to be so confusing? She and Allie sat quiet for a little, watching the party goers in their various costumes go by.

There was a couple dressed in matching pirate outfits of black, white and red, the guy in pants, the girl in a mini skirt. Another girl was dressed in a red devil leotard much like the one Cain had described when trying to guess Felicity's costume. Felicity was definitely the most elegantly dressed girl there. She felt stupid. What did she get this dumb gown for anyway? Cain wouldn't even see it. Somehow, she'd thought he would surprise her and come.

As she looked over the crowd, she kept glancing to the door, as though Cain would appear, like she lived in the last scene of some dumb romantic movie. While watching the door, she saw a girl come through. At first, she thought the girl was dressed as 'Morticia', from 'The Addams' Family'. Then she caught an awful chill as she realized...it was Sindy. She spoke to Allie as she kept her eyes towards the door. "What's *she* doing here?"

As Allie followed her gaze, her expression instantly became hostile. "Let's go find out." Sindy knew they were there. In fact, she stood with her hands on her hips and waited for them to approach. Felicity realized that Sindy had seen her mark. Alyson stalked right up to her. "Sorry honey, Ben's dance card's full tonight. Although I have to admit, I almost don't despise you quite as much as I do his current girlfriend. *Almost.*"

Sindy smiled and gazed up to unerringly find Ben dancing with Ashley across the large ballroom some distance away. She found him so easily; she must still see his mark in her mind. They were far enough away though, that Ben hadn't noticed them. Perhaps the physical aspect of his mark was beginning to fade a bit. Sindy smiled at Allie. "I'm not here for Ben. Unless you think he'd like me to be."

Felicity spoke before Allie had a chance to say anything else. "Why *are* you here?"

Sindy gave a little shrug and a smile. "I thought maybe

Cain could use some help."

Allie was quick to respond. "He doesn't need any help from *you.*"

"How would you know what Cain *needs*…from me?" She licked her lips and smiled.

Felicity said quietly, "Cain's not here."

Now Sindy turned her attention to appraising Felicity's ornate gown. Felicity knew she looked beautiful, but somehow, in front of Sindy, she found herself just feeling silly and over-done. Sindy smirked at her. "And look at you, all dressed up with no one to show. Poor baby. Still, *I* thought Cain'd be here too," she added, glancing around.

"Why? Did you see him tonight? Did he tell you he was coming?" Felicity said, regretting the *too* hopeful anticipation in her voice, as soon as the words came out of her mouth.

Sindy smiled at her maliciously. "Yeah, I saw him, but no, he didn't mention your silly little dance. Sorry. He was looking for Chris."

Alyson spoke up again. "Then why are you *here?*"

"I was following Marcus."

"Marcus is here?" Both Felicity and Alyson asked in alarm.

Sindy slowly finished their thought. "And Cain isn't…"

Allie spoke hopefully as they each glanced around the room. "Well, maybe Cain *is* here, and we just haven't seen him yet."

Both Sindy and Felicity answered her identically, until Felicity faltered upon hearing Sindy echo her. "Cain's not here, I would have…felt him." Felicity eyed Sindy in alarmed confusion. Sindy just grinned at her distress.

"Where's Marcus?" Alyson asked Sindy, trying to cut through any new discussion before it started.

Sindy seemed unconcerned as she glanced from one girl to the other. She gestured vaguely off to the left. "He's over that way, and he's not alone, but they're still pretty far off. They're not in the building yet or anything, but they do seem to be on their way here."

Alyson spoke, as Felicity was still uncomfortably staring at Sindy. "Then Cain is probably on his way too. If *you* managed to find and follow Marcus, Cain's probably doing the same thing."

"I don't think so." Sindy smiled thoughtfully. "When I saw Cain earlier, he was nowhere near here. He might have gone in totally the other direction."

"Where were you?" Allie asked.

"Oxford." She turned another smile on Felicity. "In my hotel room." Felicity didn't say anything, but dropped her eyes to the floor.

Alyson rolled her eyes and let out an exasperated sigh. She turned to Felicity. "Don't listen to anything that comes out of her mouth. I don't even know why we're wasting our time."

Sindy laughed. "Believe what you want but if I were you, I'd get anybody you didn't want sucked dry and split, 'cause Marcus is heading this way, and subtle is really not his style." Allie just stared at her for a moment, trying to assess whether she was telling the truth. Sindy glanced over at Ben again, who still hadn't noticed her. "It's time to go. Do you wanna get Ben, or shall I?"

"I'm not going anywhere with *you*. Why should we believe you anyway?" Allie asked suspiciously.

Sindy shook her head and laughed again. "You're right; you caught me. I was just putting you on. Marcus isn't coming here."

Felicity found herself sounding foolishly hopefully again before she could help it. "He's not?"

"Why don't you stay and find out? You guys are so stupid! I'm trying to do you a favor here. I know what's up and whether you'd like to admit it or not, I'm the only person in this room worth listenin' to. So if I say it's time to go, you'd best listen."

Alyson became very annoyed. "Just because you can see things that we can't, doesn't mean you get to order us around. Who the hell put you in charge anyway? I don't even know whose side you're on!"

Sindy stood a little straighter and took on an air of confident superiority. "I'm on *Cain's* side. Unfortunately, that seems to align me with *you,* but I can do whatever the hell I please. Let me let you in on a little secret. *I'm the top of the food chain here.* Vampires are far superior to humans, in every way. I'm the *lioness* in this room, and you guys are just a bunch of little jumpin' gazelles. Get over it, 'cause it ain't never gonna change." She looked up in Marcus' supposed direction. "Now it's time to leave. Let's go."

Alyson glared at her for a moment as Felicity shifted her weight uneasily, watching the door and trying desperately to feel Cain. He was still nowhere near. After an interminable moment, Alyson spoke. "I really don't like you."

Sindy shrugged with a breath of a laugh. "Like I care."

"Stay here. I'll go tell Ben." She turned to Felicity. "Don't go anywhere. I'll be right back."

Felicity watched uneasily as Allie rushed off to get Ben. After a moment, she nerved herself to look at Sindy again. She knew she was better off not saying anything. Sindy would only try to upset her, but she couldn't help but ask. "What makes you think *you* could feel if Cain was here?"

Sindy laughed. "Wouldn't you like to know?" She gave her a level gaze for a moment. "It's a vampire thing. The kind of stuff you'll never understand. When are you gonna realize, you're just not the kind of woman he needs? Cain is a vampire, a pretty powerful one. He needs another vampire by his side, not some whiny little vamp bait like you. Having to protect you all the time's only gonna get him killed. You really ought to step up or step out."

Felicity would like to tell herself that Sindy was only seeking to fluster her, but disturbingly enough, she knew Sindy to be right. Still, she felt compelled to try and stand up for herself somehow. "How do you know I won't...step up?"

Sindy looked her over in amazement. "*You?* You would try to let him make you into a vampire? Ha! You wouldn't last one night!"

"Why not?"

Sindy's voice became falsely sweet and condescending. "Sorry sweetie but you just haven't got what it takes. A pathetic little milksop like you couldn't handle it. Trust me. You really ought to go back home where it's safe and leave real life to the big girls." Before Felicity could reply, they looked up to see Alyson and Ben bearing down on them with Ashley following behind.

Ben was obviously pissed off by Sindy's presence. It was

also obvious that he was trying to get Ashley to go elsewhere, and was very annoyed when she wouldn't listen. He moved to speak to Sindy, but as soon as Ashley laid eyes on her, she spoke first. "You again! What are *you* doing here? You'd better not have your gang buddies showin' up after you again. The decorating committee laid out a lot of money to rent some of this stuff, and if it gets trashed there won't be enough left in the budget to decorate properly for the Christmas Gala!"

All eyes were on Ashley in bewilderment. Sindy asked Ben, "Is she for real?"

"'Fraid so. What the hell are you doing here? I'm really getting tired of paying to come to these things only to have you show up and ruin them."

"Well, believe me, unless you leave now, you're gonna think the last one was much more fun." She eyed Ashley again. "Of course, you might think that anyway." She licked her lips and mouthed him a little kiss.

Ashley became offended. "Hey, you know I'm his date and I'm standing right here!"

Sindy glanced at her again but spoke to Ben without bothering to address her. "You should leave her. I'll bet she'd make a nice distraction for Marcus. She looks delicious."

A commotion at the far entrance drew their attention. Frankenstein and the Mummy were standing in the doorway when they yelled in annoyance against someone who simply shoved them aside to move through. As though summoned by his name, Marcus appeared.

"Told you it was time to go," Sindy said with impressive nonchalance. No sooner had Marcus entered, than three other evil-looking men came up behind him. They were unmistakably together, and it took only a moment for their gazes to find Felicity across the room.

Ben spoke quickly. "Let's go, something tells me they're not afraid of making a scene. We're not safe here."

As they all moved towards the exit, Sindy spoke in annoyance. "Oh sure, everybody listens to *him*."

Chapter 6 - Connections

Cain

A Motor Lodge in Oxford
10:30, Sunday night

Cain clicked Sindy's motel room door shut behind him with a smile. He then looked up to his motorcycle to find it flanked by four fairly large men and backed by a long black car. They were vampires, and they were undoubtedly Arif's by the look of their garb and demeanor. Wonderful.

They stood patiently awaiting him. They didn't seem to expect him to run. He would be stupid to try. It would only seem foolish and cowardly. If Arif wanted something, Cain couldn't avoid him for long. If they indeed were Arif's men, better to see what they wanted and get it over with. He briefly considered summoning Sindy as an ally, but quickly dismissed the notion. Not only was she weakened from his drinking, but involving her would probably only make things worse anyway. Surely, Sindy had no idea they were there, as he had not. They were cloaked. He wondered if one of them was projecting it or if Arif was nearby.

The largest among them spoke. He was a tall, muscular, bald black man with a commanding demeanor. He wore black dress pants with a silk shirt, as did the rest of them. Not one of them wore a jacket, although it was surely below forty degrees. "Arif will see you this evening," the man said in a steady clear voice.

Cain smiled in amusement at his presumptive attitude. "Oh, he *will?*"

"*I* say he will. Do you dispute it?" was the man's reply.

Cain surveyed the four men and then looked back to their 'leader'. "I suppose I've time for chat." Not one of them cracked a smile. Cain glanced at his Harley. "Lead the way."

At this, another of them spoke. He was the shortest of the four, though still stocky and muscular as they all were. The expression on his face told Cain that he was most likely to be the troublemaker of the bunch. The man stared at Cain haughtily. "Leave the bike," he said, and then indicated with a nod of his head, that he expected Cain to get into their car.

Cain gave a snort of amusement. "I don't think so."

"Well, *I* do." Now the man smiled and gave the bike a nice shove.

It fell over with a loud crash and Cain had to fight to hold himself still and unresponsive. He prayed that Sindy would not hear it and come out to investigate. Again, he surveyed the men. He locked his eyes upon their leader once more. "Before this goes any further, perhaps you'd like to take a moment to reflect upon just what it is your *master* wants from me." As he said the word 'master', he turned his gaze upon the one who'd pushed his bike. Men like him always hated to be reminded of their superiors. "If Arif desires an exchange of information, perhaps he would also desire that I arrive in an amicable mood. If that is the case, you may lead me to him, or provide the address and time for a future meeting.

But should you expect to force me into your vehicle and bear me away against my will, I can assure you that not one of us will arrive in a condition conducive to conversation. If Arif *does* wish only to talk, I would think that he would be less than pleased."

The leader seemed to be weighing his argument, and coming to think that he was right. Of course, the little one was having none of it. He sneered at Cain in contempt. The black man who seemed to be in charge of the group spoke. "Tony, pick up the man's bike."

Tony seemed outraged. "What for? Let him get in the car. Elric, you let him ride and he's just gonna skip out on us first chance he gets."

A different man spoke quietly from behind Tony. "Tony, this ain't some little chicken shit. Don't you know who this guy is? He's even older than the master."

"So what? He doesn't even keep a court. No guard, no harem, no scouts, nothing. He a rogue."

The black man, Elric, seemed embarrassed that they should squabble before him. "Tony, do it. *Now.*" He turned to Cain, as Tony and the man who hadn't spoken yet, righted his motorcycle. "Follow," Elric said simply, and got into the front passenger seat of the car. The one who had seemed awed by Cain's presence got into the driver's seat, leaving the other two to finish standing his bike. Tony and his friend glared at him haughtily.

Finally, Tony got into the back, leaving the door open for the other. The last man spoke to him with a nasty tone. "You'd better keep up. 'Cause if you try to get lost, we'll find you... and dust you."

Cain smiled in amusement as the man got in the car and closed the door. He mounted his Harley and fired it up. It reverberated loud and echoing in the parking lot. The long black sedan before him pulled out onto the road, and he followed. He never even considered leaving them. Not that he was frightened of any juvenile threat, but he might as well see what Arif wanted, better than to leave it hanging over his head.

He still worried for Felicity though. He felt no sign of Chris or Marcus, but if they were near Felicity, they would be beyond his range at this point. Knowing that Alyson was with her did ease his mind a little, but he hoped he could take care of this nonsense with Arif quickly and be on his way.

They wound their way through mountain and forest until they turned onto a private road. Deep into the thickly wooded property, they came upon a very large log cabin type dwelling. It was almost big enough to be considered a lodge. It fit in very well with its wilderness surroundings, but was hardly the type of structure he would picture Arif to live in. Actually, Cain rather liked it.

Separate from the main building was a four-car garage. One of the doors opened as they approached. The car stopped in front of the main house to let out its occupants before the driver took it to be parked. There were other vampires psychically visible inside, although Arif's own trace remained hidden.

Cain parked his motorcycle outside the garage, just to the side. As he dismounted, the driver of the car exited and approached him. He stopped to wait for Cain; it was the man who had been impressed by Cain's age. He was about the same height and build as Cain, with short straight brown hair and an honest face. He looked to have been in his early thirties, though Cain couldn't tell his true age. He couldn't gage much about any of them while they remained psychically concealed.

As though prompted by Cain's thoughts, the marked presence of the four men suddenly became visible to his mind. Cain looked to Elric, the leader. He was most likely the one to have been cloaking them. Undoubtedly, he had dropped the shield to announce their presence to those within.

He was rather old that one, compared to most Cain had met anyway. By his trace, Cain would guess that he'd existed as a vampire for nearly a century. His trace was strong and powerful, he was well made. The vampiric age of the driver was perhaps fifty, while the other two hovered around the twenty-year mark. Although their strengths were fair, none was as clearly potent as their leader.

The man who had driven the car was still standing next to Cain. After a moment's consideration, Cain decided to reveal his own trace as well. It seemed only polite. He could plainly read them. Let them read whom they were dealing with as well. Cain knew that Maribeth had made him well. His mark was clear and bright. His powerful trace would show him to be not only old, but a competent, capable vampire as well; his intelligence and memories unmarred by his death. The vampire within him was strong and he dropped his shield to let it show.

The man next to him stepped back a pace as Cain's mark was revealed. He was obviously quite impressed and practically bowed his head in reverence as he moved his arm to show that Cain should pass him and approach the house.

Cain kept his eyes on the leader as he came near the porch where the men waited. He could swear that a smile was playing about Elric's lips as Cain climbed the few steps. Yes, this man was impressed by him as well. The other two looked only sullen and annoyed. Elric moved to open the door for him, another sure sign of respect.

The house did look to have been a hunting lodge in times past. Warm and inviting, its furniture was rustic and the front room was decorated with many trophies. The heads of large antlered bucks adorned the walls and there were many stuffed and mounted small game animals about. A huge fireplace dominated the far wall, and there were many chairs and ottomans scattered before it. It looked the perfect place for comfortable camaraderie, but the room was unoccupied at the moment, except for Cain and his escorts.

Elric turned to the man who had driven the car. "Byron, go before us to the master. Tell him that all is well, and we seek audience."

Byron left without question or hesitation. Elric looked back to Cain. "I will bring you before Arif shortly, but first, I must ask if you carry any weapons."

Cain smiled. "Of course, I do."

Elric returned his smile and then gestured to the man who had helped Tony to lift Cain's bike earlier. "Joseph." He came forward carrying an empty box retrieved from a niche in the wall near the doorway. Elric spoke again to Cain. "No personal weapons are permitted in the presence of the master. You may retrieve them upon departure."

Cain had to smile at the reverent and awesome attitude that Arif had instilled in his minions. Cain knew that some vampire elders kept an elaborate social structure around themselves, but he had very rarely encountered it personally. He had certainly never had opportunity to observe it to this degree. It seemed such a silly game to him. To keep oneself surrounded by guardsmen and courtiers, so that you might be constantly reminded of the imaginary status you've decreed upon yourself.

He concluded that he was best off playing along. He had already allowed himself into their presence. If things took an unsavory turn, it was not as though a stake or two would make the difference in helping him to fight his way out. At this point, concealing weapons would only make them mad. If things went wrong later, he would just have to improvise. He could probably cow them with age and attitude anyway. They were obviously well taught to respect their elders, even beyond the degree that their instinct urged them to. It was plain that none of them had ever seen a vampire as old as he before.

Cain withdrew the three stakes that he held on his person. He never let on that he was wearing the chain mail vest though. Surely, they never suspected it and he wasn't about to take it off. It was not a weapon and so he needn't reveal it. He was rather glad that he had it on though. He placed his stakes into the box and watched Joseph put the box back into its place by the door.

Elric nodded his approval, and seemed very glad that Cain had not resisted. Cain wondered what they might have done if he had. The men just stood there; arms folded. Apparently, they awaited approval before venturing further into the house.

Cain once again surveyed their surroundings. Everything seemed well maintained and dusted. He wondered how Arif had obtained such a dwelling. Surely it was inhabited by humans until fairly recently and Cain knew that hunting season for big game would begin shortly, in November. The place should be preparing to be filled with guests.

A large stuffed bobcat guarded the door through which Byron had disappeared. Now he returned, and stopped just inside the doorway. He faced Elric and nodded his head in acceptance. Arif would see them now.

Cain followed Elric and Byron through the doorway, while Joseph and Tony trailed behind him. They made their way through the house, passing many closed doors along the way. A few rooms held the traces of lesser vampires within, but none that Cain knew. He could feel seven marked humans in another room ahead that they approached to pass. Even before they neared the door, he could hear dulcet voices and squeals of feminine laughter from within. Elric stopped at the door, gave a sharp rap upon it, and then opened it about halfway.

From the slice of the room visible to Cain, he could see that it was a lushly decorated bedchamber. Two of the girls within were visible to Cain through the opening. One of them had been among the beauties that Arif had brought to the bar the night that Cain had seen him.

The room became immediately silent and the girls lowered their eyes to the floor. Elric said nothing. He only stared at them for a moment, and then closed the door. Apparently, they were meant to conduct themselves in a more demure manner when company was in the house.

Cain and his escorts continued on to the back of the house until they reached a stairway to the basement. They descended into a lower level that was surely as large as the rest of the house, although it was divided into separate rooms, rather than be mostly open as Cain's basement was.

The room that the stairs let out into was decorated with rich wood paneling and made to be a sort of game room. It sported a large pool table with a rack for accessories, two dartboards and a small bar in the corner. They crossed through to a doorway in the back. Elric paused and then knocked respectfully upon the door.

"Enter." Arif's voice came from within.

Elric looked to Byron who then opened and held the door for them. Elric entered the room and Cain followed. When Joseph and Tony had been admitted as well, Byron moved further inside the room and closed the door.

It was an office, albeit a very lavishly appointed one. This room had its own small fireplace also. Arif was not behind the desk that had been pushed into the corner, but reclined in a large armchair before the fire. He gestured for Cain to take the smaller chair next to him. The rest of the men stood awaiting orders.

Arif smiled to Cain. "And so, we meet again. Please, be seated. Byron, bring the man a drink. Rum and Coke, isn't it?" he asked. Cain gave a light nod as he sat.

Arif turned to Elric. "Thank you, Elric, you never disappoint. You may await summons in the parlor."

"Thank you, my Lord," Elric responded with a nod. He then ordered Joseph and Tony to leave the room before him. As soon as they left, Byron returned to give Cain his drink. They were then left alone.

"Glad you could come," Arif said with a smug smile.

"Well, a less urgent invitation with some notice might have been nice."

"Yes, I understand that you are a busy man of late, but I consider *my* business with you this evening more pressing than your dispute with young Chris."

Cain couldn't help but give Arif a resentful look, that he should assume his desire to speak with Cain to be more important than the well being of Felicity. What the hell did he want anyway? "Might I inquire as to just what is so important?"

Arif smiled and turned towards another door at the far end of the room. "Come," he called to those within. "I would like to introduce you to two of my most trusted men." As the vampires Arif spoke of entered the room, Cain had to stifle a groan.

They were the men from the parking lot of the restaurant, the ones that he had reported to the police the night before. He had practically forgotten the incident, as other things had seemed more pressing.

Arif noted the look upon Cain's face as they came to stand at Arif's side. "Am I to assume that you have already met?"

Cain avoided the men's angry stares as he answered. "We haven't been formally introduced."

Arif remained reclining casually in his chair as he gestured towards the men. "Let me do the honors. This is Tomas and Richard, two very highly valued members of my household. In fact, I have been particularly pleased with them of late. To reward this, I had granted them an evening of leave.

They had my blessing to entertain themselves as they would among the local populace, using appropriate discretion of course. Unfortunately, their evening was spoiled by a misunderstanding with local authorities. A misunderstanding that they seem to believe was caused *by you*."

Cain did his best to keep his face neutral and unincriminating. "Is that right?"

To their credit, the men said nothing, although Cain was certain that they would love to have leave to speak their minds. They stood silent and let their master speak for them. "In my house disputes are handled swiftly and fairly. I will not have unrest and dissension unsettling my men. So, I am certain that you will appreciate the importance of your presence here, so that we might settle the matter expediently. My men should be assured that I consider their requests as matters of importance worth investigating."

Cain only lowered his eyes a bit and ventured a small smile as he pondered just what to say. Although it was doubtful that his involvement could be proved, Cain decided it would be best not to try and deny his part in the issue.

Not only did he always try to maintain scrupulous integrity, but also if the men already suspected him, he must have been seen. He had no idea by whom or how accurately he'd been identified. It may even have been by Arif himself. Cain took pride in the fact that he considered his word to be unquestionable. He wouldn't let these men think any less of him by trying to dance around this issue. He looked to the two men. "My apologies for any inconvenience you may have endured."

The men only stared at him coldly as Arif spoke. "Then you do admit to playing a part in their misfortune?"

"I do. However, I must submit that any actions taken on my part were motivated not by any political or manipulative desire for vengeance. I act only as my conscience tells me that I must. It's nothing personal against you or yours, but only my own personal obligation to uphold certain standards of conduct. I cannot hold myself blind to that which I perceive as improper. I regret if I misjudged the situation harshly."

Arif sat up a bit straighter and gazed at him in seeming admiration for a moment. He must have expected denial. Arif then looked back to his men. "Tomas, what say you to this?"

The man's icy glare towards Cain never wavered. "I say that a man's conscience is meant to dictate his *own* conduct and not to judge that of others. If he disapproves of my actions, let him address me of it openly, and not act through humans, like a coward."

Cain could not help but feel ashamed by the man's words. He was well spoken and had valid argument. Cain said nothing.

"Richard?" Arif inquired.

"I agree. Jiminy Cricket should be taught to mind his own damn business. I'd be happy to do the teaching, if you would permit."

Cain could not help but smile, although he was certainly not in the best of positions. How did he manage to get himself into such predicaments? He really never sought such troubles.

Arif waited a moment to see if Cain would respond, but Cain thought it better to remain silent for now. What else could he say? Arif smiled upon him and then turned back to his men. "I do agree that your point is valid and you've every right to anger." His gaze found Cain once more. "Such a trespass upon my men cannot be ignored."

Cain smiled and shrugged. "You know what they say, 'no good deed goes unpunished'."

Arif returned his smile. "To follow conscience can be a challenging and often foolhardy venture, as far as personal welfare is concerned, but it is commendable to some extent all the same."

Tomas and Richard lost their satisfied expressions as they realized that Arif seemed to be looking upon Cain with admiration and acceptance. Arif spoke to them with an air of finality. "I must also conclude that although this act has been inconvenient and unfortunate to be sure, no true harm was done. I have righted the situation with regard to the police, and it will be forgotten to the world.

I must also inform you, that while I may have been inclined to seek retribution for this deed, I have chosen instead to view it as repayment for past actions already taken. In the past, I did grant Sindy aid, albeit in an indirect fashion, against those in the care of this man; and so, he has reciprocated with indirect action against mine. It is done, and no further debt is owed. There is no need for hostilities. Do you accept this verdict?"

The men stared coldly at Cain for a moment but then bowed their heads towards Arif in acceptance, albeit grudgingly. "Good. Let no further action be taken against him. You are dismissed." Richard and Tomas left the room through the door they had entered by, leaving Cain and Arif alone again. Arif turned to him now with an air of casual camaraderie. "I hope you will understand the need for such displays. I do seek to keep satisfaction among my ranks. Have you ever kept underlings of your own?"

Cain sipped his drink, glad for the distraction. He did not want his relief over the incident to be too apparent. "No. I've never had the desire to explore such an arrangement. You've quite a large family."

Arif smiled. "Yes. I think that soon it shall be time to grant a certain number of them leave to part from me. I am thinking that Elric shows great promise as a Lord, though I will miss him. He is loyal and levelheaded. I do not think that I should worry for any problems from those under *his* control, should I allow him freedom."

"He does seem a man of good character. However, I'm not prone to speculation over such political issues. I prefer solitude, or the company of only a select few."

"Yes of course. You need freedom and mobility to carry out your quest." Cain had trouble deciphering if the remark was meant as a sarcastic jibe, or was simply said in earnest.

"If we are finished here, I do have other matters to attend to."

Arif grinned. "Yes, I know, but while I have you here, there is something else which I have longed to bring to your attention." Cain looked at him in confusion, wondering what else Arif might have in mind, when the door he had entered by was opened, startling him. It was Elric. Cain was at first very surprised that the man would enter unbidden to interrupt them, but then he realized that Arif seemed unsurprised at his presence. Most likely Arif had summoned the man mentally.

Arif nodded approval at the man's entrance and then turned back to Cain. "Before I explain, I must ask you something. How did you find my men when they approached you?" Cain only looked at him in slight confusion. "Was their invitation polite?"

Cain could see that Elric was a bit apprehensive over his answer. It was obvious at this point, that Arif thought Cain a man due some respect. When first Elric and his men had encountered Cain, perhaps they had not been well informed as to Arif's true feelings about him. After Cain had revealed his trace however, Elric had seemed respectful as well. "It served its purpose," Cain answered.

Arif pressed on. "Were there any among my men who treated you less than cordially?"

Cain only smiled and shrugged. Arif smiled as well. "Noble of you not to say, but I know my men. Elric, I would like you to fetch Tony, Joseph and Kieran, bring them to us in the Armory."

Elric seemed a little surprised at the last name, as was Cain; he had never heard of the man. Still, Elric left to his task without question or comment. Arif rose from his chair and gestured Cain towards the other door that had been used by Tomas and Richard. "Come, I'd like to show you something."

They exited the room into a hallway. A few doors were passed along the way to a final pair of large double doors at the end of the short hall. Arif produced a key to open these doors and reveal a large room that had indeed been turned into quite an impressive armory. It held a few glass cases displaying shotguns and rifles that had no doubt been left by the previous owners of the house, but the rest of the walls had been covered with an amazing array of weapons.

Racks and shelves of all types held swords, axes, crosses and stakes of every description. They ranged in age from modern crossbows to such items as the medieval mace and chain. Cain looked about in wonder and appreciation. There was even a large freestanding covered urn to one side, with an ornate cross depicted on its' cover. Cain assumed there was holy water within.

Arif looked pleased by Cain's open admiration of his possessions. "You approve of my collection? I must admit that it is a bit cumbersome to travel with, but many of the pieces within hold special personal value. I do admire a good weapon, don't you?"

Cain smiled. "Indeed. I had an extensive collection of my own back at my estate in the U.K. Unfortunately, it's mostly been sold to museums and such. You've some intriguing specimens here. Still, I don't see what this might have to do with me. Not to be rude, but I do worry for the humans in my care. I should be going."

Arif seemed unconcerned. "Fear not. I do have those of my own whom I use as scouts. They have been keeping track of the one whom you seek. They will alert us if any troublesome activity ensues. I like to know what goes on around me.

As a matter of fact, that concerns what I would like to show you. You see, I make it my business to know the happenings not only where I reside, but in neighboring provinces as well. As much as practicality permits anyway." Arif's attention was distracted for a moment. Cain could sense Elric approaching with the others.

Arif addressed the door. "Enter." Elric opened it, as bidden and Tony, Joseph and the one who must be Kieran entered the room. Arif spoke to Elric. "Thank you. You may stay. You might find this of some interest."

Arif continued his conversation with Cain. "As I was saying, I like to be well informed. Kieran is one of my runners. I use him to send messages to others and to scout ahead areas that I plan to visit."

Cain studied the boy. He was very young in appearance, perhaps fourteen when he died. His trace revealed him to have lived 'undead' for about thirty-five years beyond that. He was a slight young man with long wispy blonde hair and large bright green eyes.

Arif smiled at him. "You should know that I trust him implicitly. That which Kieran reports may be considered unquestionable. He has good insight and judgment of character and he is always invaluable in guiding me, but as I have mentioned in the past, in matters of great consequence I believe only that which I observe. A wise man reserves final judgment of a situation until he has seen it from all sides.

Kieran has informed me of some very interesting developments he observed, prior to my arrival. He is of course very skilled in the art of cloaking his presence, a necessity for my use of him as a scout. No doubt, you were unaware that Kieran surveyed this very area before I did arrive here myself. That which he reported back to me was very odd and interesting indeed. It seems there was some altercation between minions of Sindy's making and yourself with two of your human companions, in the cemetery a while back. Do you know the instance of which I speak?"

Cain thought back. Ah, yes with Ben and Felicity. He'd no idea that they had been watched. He nodded to Arif of his remembrance. The incident had happened shortly before Arif and his brood had arrived. In fact, later that same evening Cain had observed Arif himself for the first time, at Venus with Sindy.

"Kieran tells me that you and your humans fought well, easily defeating her minions. This in itself was not particularly of interest to me. It was that which occurred *after* that I wish to question." Cain furrowed his brow in thought. He'd no idea to what Arif might be referring. Was he seen spying upon them at Venus perhaps? Why should that be of interest to Arif anyway? "I am told that you engaged in a small demonstration for your humans in the cemetery afterwards. Kieran has reported that you were seen *holding* a cross."

Cain laughed. "Oh... yes. I held a cross, that's true enough, but the act was not without repercussions I can assure you. I did only that which any of us might, with sufficient bravery and strength of will."

"Is that so? Would you mind then, demonstrating such an act here for us now?"

Cain could not help but look at them all a bit oddly. What was the point? Surely, they had experienced such things before; they shouldn't need him to demonstrate. Were Arif's children so unversed in the consequences of such an act? Arif could plainly read his speculative thoughts. "Please, humor me. You needn't keep it for long. Tony, bring the man a cross." Tony seemed more than eager to oblige. He went to the wall, donned a thick glove from a lower shelf, and then brought down a particularly large and ornate cross from the rack. He came to stand before Cain with it.

Cain eyed Arif for a moment, who gave him a little nod of reassurance. Fine, he would humor them. He accepted the cross with his left hand. As Tony stepped back to give him room for display, Cain held it out before him. All eyes were trained closely on Cain's hand, awaiting the inevitable reaction. His skin did slowly begin to heat and then burn as he kept contact with the holy object. Cain was sure to keep his face blank and his arm steady. After a minute or so, wisps of smoke began to curl from his skin. Once the smoke was clearly apparent, he looked to Arif. "Satisfied?" Arif smiled and nodded. He seemed incredibly amused, although Cain could not imagine why.

"Thank you." Arif's men seemed rather amazed. "Tony, I'd like to see you do the same." Tony seemed a little startled at the request, but then looked back to the cross in Cain's hand. Cain still held it out before him, as it steadily emitted a thin trail of smoke, and tried not to let on that he very much hoped to be relieved of it soon.

After a moment's consideration, Tony seemed to decide that he would not let Cain show him up. Arif spoke as the man stepped forward for the cross. "Do keep it until I should take it from you," he said. Arif held out his hand to Tony, who gave him the glove. At his words, Tony seemed much less anxious to take the cross, but he would not back down now.

After a moment, he held out his hand to Cain. Cain gave over the cross with some relief. Tony flinched as he took it, but closed his hand about it. He held his arm out before him as Cain had. Within seconds, smoke began to rise. Still Tony held on to the cross, desperate to prove Cain was no better than he. Cain's eyes widened as an actual tendril of flame arose from the man's hand. Tony stifled a whimper and looked desperately to Arif, who had him hold it for a few seconds more, before relieving Tony of the object. Just as Arif took the cross into his glove, Tony's hand seemed to burst into true ignition with a great whoosh of heat, air and fire.

Tony let out a cry and pulled his hand from the object to smother the flames in the material of his shirt. He brought the hand close in to his chest and managed to put it out. When he held it out again to inspect the damage, his hand proved to be darkly blackened and raw with burns.

Cain stared in amazement and then looked down to his own hand. He brought it higher before his eyes as he observed the small pink and bubbled blisters there. It was damaged certainly, but he had not sustained nearly the injury that Tony had. Yet Tony had held the cross for barely a minute while Cain had held it for at least five.

Cain looked back to Arif in bewilderment. Arif simply nodded with a knowing smile. Cain shook his head in confusion. "I don't understand."

Arif held up a hand for silence from Cain. The other men were already quiet with nearly reverent awe. Tony nursed his hand while glaring at Cain. Arif spoke. "Wait. There is one more experiment I would like for us to undertake, if you will accede." Cain slightly nodded his head in confused uncertainty.

"The Holy Water, if you will. Just a slight touch will do." Cain eyed the urn and then shrugged. He approached it and slid back the lid. Its mechanism allowed for it to be opened without actual removal. Sure enough, clear water was held within. It looked harmless enough, but Cain knew that a priests' blessing could turn it into a painfully acidic fluid to a vampire.

He looked at those gathered around him and then pushed up his sleeves. Using his left hand again, he closed his fist, and then exposed only his pointer finger. He slowly dipped his finger into the water. It felt very warm to the touch. After only a moment, he felt its heat begin to grow. He kept his finger submerged until the water felt as though it should be boiling, although of course it remained calm and clear. Cain could see his finger becoming scalded beneath the surface of the water. He pulled it back out to show the redness of it to the others. It was raw and tender, and he greatly wished there was some plain water that he might immerse it in.

He stepped back from the urn and looked to Arif who wore a broad smile. "Joseph."

The man in question seemed to jump guiltily and was rather hesitant to step forward. He did though, and silently approached the urn. He looked to Arif, who nodded for him to repeat the act that Cain had just completed. Cain found that he was more than a little curious as to what would happen next. He stared intently at Joseph's finger as it dipped below the surface of the water.

Joseph bravely tried to keep it submerged, but could not last long. The second his finger was enveloped in the Holy Water, he seemed to stifle a cry as it immediately became as red and scalded as Cain's was. After less than a minute Joseph jerked it back from the water and cried out in pain. Cain watched in disbelief, as layers of skin from Joseph's finger seemed to slough off into the water and disintegrate. He held his finger in the air and tried in vain to blow on it and end the agony it must have been causing him. It was a truly gruesome sight. Any longer in the water and it would very probably have been stripped to the bone.

Cain stood speechless as Arif addressed his men. "I should think that in the future you would do well to be polite and respectful of your elders, whatever the circumstance. You are all dismissed."

The men filed out and Cain was left staring at his hand in disbelief. He looked to Arif when the door was shut once again. "What does it mean?" Cain asked.

"I had hoped that *you* could tell me. Have you not heard the rumors that circulate about you? Obviously not or you would not be looking so thoroughly perplexed. I had heard stories of your crusade to tame all vampires, to be civil and harmless creatures. With this news, I once heard that you were immune to such Godly weapons as cross and Holy water. I disregarded it of course.

When Sindy told me of your presence here and Kieran reported to me his observation of your doings, I was greatly intrigued. I must admit however that I still had trouble accepting such a thing until witnessed personally. The story I had heard at the first *was* exaggerated, but Kieran's description was as usual infallible."

"I don't understand. Are you telling me that there are none who might do as I have done?"

"None that I have seen," Arif admitted.

"My age perhaps. Am I the oldest that you have encountered? I know that the venom does grow more potent with years, perhaps defense grows as well. I am certainly not fully immune as you can see." Cain held up his slightly injured hand for Arif to see again.

Arif smiled. "I had suspected that theory would hold true…but I was mistaken. You see, *I* am this year 268 years of age. My damage would be identical to that of my men, I have tried it.

I also chanced upon another not very long ago. One almost as old as you. Gwenyfara was her name. 312 she claimed to be, with a strong, old and even mark to convince me it was so. I had not the opportunity to know her well. Apparently, she had some distaste for my lifestyle." Cain had to smile at that, and to refrain from asking Arif where he might find such a lady.

"I did have the fortune however, to observe the effects of a cross upon her fair skin. With only a touch she was quite badly burned. I do not believe age to be a factor."

"What then?" Cain asked.

Arif gazed at him evenly for a moment. "What else is there that would set you apart from other vampires?"

Cain dared not speak as he pondered the implication in his mind. Arif continued. "Might I ask, the name 'Cain', I assume that you chose it for its significance in the Christian Bible, did you not?" Cain nodded slightly. "I wonder if you realize just how well you have chosen.

I like to travel, and I do come across other vampires from time to time. Research into various claims of the powers and origins of our kind interests me. In a life so long, we all need something to peak our interests, no?" Cain smiled. "And so, as I do visit different regions, I like to hear the folklore and myths of each area and the boasts and claims of other vampires. Comparison of such tales often proves quite intriguing, but this is grist for the mill of discussion for another time.

I find your choice of name intriguing also. You must know well the story of Cain and Abel."

Cain gave a bitter smile. "A little too well."

"Indeed. I find it interesting that in punishment Cain is made to be a wanderer of the earth, a vagabond unable to work the ground for its crops. Our kind *are* wanderers by nature, and it is true that crops no longer serve us."

"Yes," Cain agreed.

"As you surely know, God did also place a mark upon Cain, that as he walked the earth none should kill him. An interesting idea when applied to a man like yourself – truly marked in his own way, and immortal.

Did you know that there is another version of this tale? In Turkey we have a story of the 40 morns and eves, are you familiar with it?" Arif asked him.

"No, I can't say I've heard it," Cain admitted.

Arif smiled. "It too includes the story of Cain and Abel. In *this* tale, it is not for slighted praise over crops that Cain kills his brother; it is so that he might take the woman promised to be Abel's wife. It seems Cain did find her fairer than his own."

Cain stared at Arif steadily, trying not to betray the fact that he was a bit shaken by the accuracy of the tale. His face had surely gone a bit pale, but his voice did not falter as he spoke. "No. I had not heard the story." Just how much did Arif know about him? Could he have had his spies listening as he told Felicity of his history? The thought made him feel a little ill that their privacy should have been so intruded upon without his knowledge.

"There is a more interesting version even than that. The Italians also have their own story in which Cain kills his brother Abel. Abel has more money than he and when Cain begs a share, he is refused. He kills his brother and then passes himself off as he to escape reprimand."

Again, Cain felt the odd shock of unforeseen recognition in the story. Hadn't he allowed himself to be mistaken for Charles by authorities to escape punishment of his own? He did not interrupt, but let Arif go on with the tale. "God's punishment of Cain in that instance is what truly stirs my curiosity. I believe the exact phrase is 'Thou shalt be imprisoned in the moon, and from that place shalt behold the good and evil of all mankind.' Do you feel yourself imprisoned in the moon? I know that I surely do, every morn when the moon slips away and I also must flee the coming rays of the sun.

I cannot say though, whether I find myself in a position to behold the good and evil of mankind in better perspective. I do hold myself rather aloof from such things. *You* however, seem very interested in acts of conscience. Mayhap you perceive yourself to be in clearer understanding since your... fall from grace."

Cain tried to gauge Arif's seriousness. He felt almost as though the man was mocking him; daring him to draw a connection between such strange coincidences. The cross, the Holy Water, his own personal 'crusade'; could there be a connection? "I do consider myself enlightened, in comparison to my past, that much is true. I cannot draw conclusion however as to what tonight's events may insinuate."

"Perhaps if I better understood the specifics of your existence, I could help you to speculate on the occurrences we have witnessed. It was 1692, the year of your transformation?"

Cain looked at him with odd amusement, that Arif should be so bold as to admit to such thorough research into his background. "Yes."

"And when was it that you chose to no longer take human life? Surely you drank fully at the start."

Cain eyed him for a moment. "There is a detail in my life of which you've not been previously informed? I was coming under the impression that anything I might divulge had already been reported."

Arif smiled, unperturbed. "I like to know whom I deal with, be not insulted but see it as a compliment. Most aren't worth the effort of such thorough research."

Cain gave the man a brief smirk. "1734. After that year I no longer drank deeply or for thirst. Not that I haven't my transgressions mind you, but it was 271 years ago that certain insights changed the way I view the world and the relationship between the vampires and humans within it."

"Do you truly believe that you can persuade every vampire in existence to lead their life by your model?"

"Some are very accepting of my ways, and grateful for the knowledge." Cain replied with a shrug. "Some need a little longer to digest the idea."

Arif leaned closer with a confidential smile. "I can tell you, there are many who will take a long while indeed."

Cain grinned. "I've got time." Cain tore his eyes from Arif to look to the door as they were both distracted by the quickly approaching mark of Kieran. "My Lord!" he called from the hall.

Arif must have acknowledged him with a mental urging, for the boy quickly opened the door. "I've just received word, the one you watch… Chris, he and his brood are on the move. Their purpose seems to be confronting the girl that Cain owns."

Cain became immediately distressed. Arif calmly questioned the boy further. "How long before they reach her?"

"The call came from Peter's post. He says they walk. At least twenty minutes I would think." Kieran dared to glance at Cain. "You can meet them if you hurry."

Arif nodded to the scout. "I thank you for the news." Kieran nodded and left them. Arif turned back to Cain. "It seems you must be going."

Cain thought to ask for a few men to back him up, but realized that it really was not Arif's responsibility to offer such assistance. *He* had no quarrel with Chris. In fact, he was most likely the one who had taught Chris to cloak. Cain was grateful enough that Arif would report Chris' whereabouts to him. "If I might inquire, how many does he lead?"

"Sindy's mindless behemoth Marcus follows him now. Added to that he has created three others. I must admit that the boy has begun to learn the way of it. He has corrected past mistakes and is creating much more useful allies of late."

Great. Cain eyed his hand once more, hoping it would not impede him. Arif noticed his concern. "Do accept my apologies for your injury. Let me offer compensation." Cain hoped he would send Elric or some other to help, but Arif had something else in mind. He gestured to the wall. "Why don't you choose yourself a gift? Something to keep peace between us."

Aid might have been more welcome, but this was better than nothing. Cain studied the weapons for a moment; very aware that time was of the essence. He was about to just grab anything when an odd-looking sword caught his eye.

The hilt and shape of the weapon were average enough, but what caught his eye was its sheen. It did not gleam under the lights as the other silver metallic weapons did. Upon closer inspection, he saw why. It was not made from metal. There was a thin keen edge of metal blade running along each side, but the very point of the sword and its main body, from tip to hilt was made from wood. Like a giant stake with a handle and a sword's cutting edge. Against a vampire, it would be a perfect weapon. Cain reached to retrieve it from its place up high on the wall.

Arif shifted weight and sighed; the first unnecessary gesture Cain had ever observed from the man. Cain inspected the weapon in delight. "You have chosen a very unique piece. That is 'Ash bringer' and she is one of very few weapons designed against our kind. I am attached to her, but in respect for you, I will part with her." Arif bowed his head as Cain smiled broadly and experimentally sliced through the air. "Guard her well and make me not regret my gift."

Cain looked up to him. "Perhaps I should take a lesser weapon. This obviously holds personal value."

"No. It is yours; you must accept it or you will insult. Some night you will return that I might tell you of her history." Arif went to the wall and brought down the sheath, that Cain should not carry the blade naked. Cain hooked it to his belt, and housed the weapon within. "Besides, recent events urge me to think that you are a man I would rather not have quarrel with. I wouldn't want to raise hand against you only to be struck by lightning and heavenly wrath!" He laughed and nudged Cain jokingly. Cain could not help but wonder whether Arif might believe the statement to hold a grain of truth. Tonight's events had been odd indeed. "Now go, I have kept you overly long."

Quite right. No time for such philosophic considerations and theology. "My sincerest thanks. For the weapon… and the demonstration."

Arif smiled. "Another time will perhaps permit for further speculation and discussion. Goodnight, Elric shall show you out."

Sure enough, Elric was just approaching as Cain left the room. The man eyed the weapon with some surprise. All humor aside, Cain had the feeling that it had been meant as a sort of 'peace offering'. Age did have its advantages. Before long, he was speeding towards the college. He desperately hoped that he would arrive in time to confront Chris, before Felicity became directly involved.

Chapter 7

Fears, tears, and fire alarms

Felicity

Halloween Masquerade Ball
11:30, Sunday night

Felicity, Allie, Sindy and Ben headed to the exit on their side of the ballroom, with Ashley trailing behind them. As they were leaving the room, Felicity turned to observe the actions of Marcus and his new friends. Two faculty members were trying to have words with them as Marcus' eyes were eerily trained on Felicity across the room.

Just as she was turning to follow the others, she saw one of the guys Marcus was with end his heated argument with the faculty by shoving a man roughly to the ground. Felicity turned to grab Ben's arm before he disappeared. "Wait, shouldn't we do something? I mean, what if they hurt someone?"

Ben glanced at her in disbelief and then looked back up to what was very close to escalating into a brawl in the front of the ballroom. "What are *we* supposed to do?"

Sindy gave an amused little chuckle. "In case you hadn't noticed honey, they're here for *you*. You gonna go jump into their waiting arms?"

"Aren't they looking for you too?" Felicity asked.

Sindy laughed. "Sorry sweetie, you're the prime directive. I'm just a bonus at this point. Besides, they can't even see me. You're the one shining like a beacon. They're following you."

Ben stopped to give Felicity a disgruntled look. "You're *marked*?" She looked at him ruefully and gave a little nod. She didn't think 'Seemed like a good idea at the time' would be a well-received answer. He looked disgusted and disappointed in her, but he didn't say anything else about it. He began walking again, pulling Felicity with him. She used one hand to try to gather and hold her voluminous skirts out of the way so she wouldn't trip over them, as Ben didn't seem in a very forgiving mood. After a moment, he spoke to her again over his shoulder as they walked. "If they are following *you,* then if we get the hell out of here, they'll probably just pass through without bothering anyone else. They wouldn't want to lose you."

Ashley caught up and grabbed Ben to stop and look at her. "Wait a minute. We *want* those guys to follow us? What exactly is going on here anyway?" She was trying to look very stern, but it was kind of difficult to take her seriously while she wore a bright pink sheer harem outfit trimmed in gold sequins.

Ben tried to dismiss her and keep walking, but she wouldn't let go of his arm. As they moved out into the hall, he gave an exasperated sigh. "Ashley, you don't want to get involved in this. You should stay here. Go stay with the crowd and no one will bother you. Someone's probably calling the cops as we speak."

"What are you going to do?" she asked.

Ben glanced at the other three girls. "I don't know. I figure if we lead them on a wild goose chase across campus, maybe then we can circle back here in time for the cops to arrive before they catch up to us. Make sure someone calls the police, okay?"

"Wait a minute. You're ditching me? I don't think so. You're *my* date and I'm not leaving you to run off with *her*," she said with a pointed look at Sindy, who smiled and mouthed her a little kiss.

Ben looked at Ashley in incredulity. "What??"

Allie threw up her hands in annoyance. "We don't have time for this crap!"

Ben looked back to see Marcus and one of his friends slipping through the crowd, as the other two were left fighting and arguing with the man who'd been shoved and those who'd come to his aid. He took Felicity's hand again. "She's right, come on." Ben led them away from the ballroom and down the hall. They were about to make the left turn that Felicity knew led down a corridor to the exit, when Ben stopped dead in his tracks. "Shit." Felicity peered past him to see a metal security gate stretched and locked across the hall, barring their way.

Sindy came up behind them to see the problem. "Nice going fearless leader."

Felicity turned to her, trying to defend Ben's choice of exits. "He didn't know. I guess they want everyone to use the main entrance. How did *you* get in without a ticket?"

Sindy smiled and licked her lips, a favorite gesture of hers it seemed. "Guess the doorman thought I had a pretty face."

Alyson eyed her for a moment and then muttered, "Freakin' succubus." She gave Felicity a little push on the shoulder. "Keep movin'."

Felicity resisted. "If all the doors are locked, we should go back."

Allie turned to look behind her, past Ashley and through the ballroom doors. Marcus and his friend were almost through all the people on the dance floor. They were headed for the doors and gaining fast. "I don't think so." Allie turned to Ben. "What's down that way?" she asked, gesturing further down the way they had been going.

"That's the gym," he answered, although his expression showed that he thought it an unpromising direction.

"Does it have a separate entrance?"

"Yeah, but *it's* probably gated too," Ben said as he reluctantly began to follow Allie, who had started down the hall.

Allie started picking up speed and the others rushed to keep up. "Well, there has to be a fire exit or something right?" No one had a chance to answer before they heard a yell from the ballroom behind them. Someone had tried to stop Marcus, and Felicity and the others turned just in time to see the man get thrown through the doorway into the hall.

Without further word, they started running. They could hear a commotion coming from the ballroom, but it was doubtful that the vampires within could be delayed for long. They may be hesitant to bear their fangs, but they were hardly worried about following rules or civilized social restraints.

They passed another short hall to an outside exit on their left, but it was gated like the first. "See," Ben said in a huff as Allie passed him to the double doors ahead. Alyson reached the gymnasium and quickly pushed open one of the doors to usher Felicity through.

Ben and Ashley followed and then Sindy entered last, closing the door behind her. "I don't think it has a lock," she said, studying the door.

Felicity turned to face the room and couldn't help but remember the last time she had been in the gym… with Cain. Now she sorely wished she had continued having him teach her self-defense, rather than take her for picnics and dancing. The main gym was a large area of hard floor, half of which was covered by the mat that she and Cain had worked on. Locker rooms were on the left side of the gym and the equipment cage and sign in desk were on the right next to the door. The near left and far right corners of the room each had a staircase that led up to the second floor, which made a sort of balcony that completely circled and overlooked the main gym.

Alyson began looking around near the ceiling of the first floor for an exit sign. "Where the hell is the back door to this place?" The back wall of the room was lined with bleachers, which were mostly folded against the wall at the moment. Allie spotted the red exit light in the far-left corner next to the bleachers and rushed over to try the door. Felicity had never spent much time upstairs, but she knew that the weight equipment, stair-climbers and treadmills were up there, and that further back the track circled the room along the walls.

Sindy grabbed hold of a large display rack of health and nutrition pamphlets near the sign in desk. "Ben," she called for his attention to help her drag it in front of the door. Ben pulled his arm away from Ashley to help push the heavy wooden rack of shelves.

Allie stormed back to them in a huff. "It's locked." After a moment, she ran off into the ladies' locker room to look for another door. Felicity went over to the sign in desk and picked up the telephone receiver. She had thought to try and call the police, but despite dialing '9', she couldn't seem to get an outside line.

Just as Ben and Sindy were finished moving the display rack, Sindy quickly backed away. A second later, a loud thump was heard from outside the door. It rocked the rack and some of the pamphlets spilled out onto the floor. The door did not open however. Ashley, who had backed into the left corner near the staircase, screamed and ran up the first few stairs. Felicity dropped the phone and went back out in front of the desk to stand by Ben. He glanced at her and she wasn't very reassured to see that he looked just as worried as she felt.

Allie pushed open the door to the ladies' locker room with a loud bang that made them all jump again. She didn't say anything; she just strode over to the men's locker room and disappeared inside. Apparently, she hadn't any luck finding another exit.

Ben eyed the display rack, and then went to lean up against it, to help it hold the door closed. Sindy watched with a condescending sneer. "This is stupid; we never should have come in here. It's not like we can *hide,*" she added with a pointed glance at Felicity.

Felicity flinched at her words. Did Sindy have to keep reminding Ben that she was marked? Not that she was ashamed of it really, but she knew that Ben disapproved. The door was pushed against strongly again from the other side, forcing Ben to push back in order to keep his feet. He glanced up at Felicity who was standing a few feet away, staring at the entrance in fright. "There's got to be a back way out. Anyway, I thought we could cut through and outrun them, but we're never going to get far enough ahead; they can see your every move." She just looked at him with apologetic worry as he turned back to Sindy. "Isn't there some way to shut off that damn mark? Cain says they can't see him. Can't *you* do that too?" Ben braced himself against the shelf with his back as Marcus pounded against the door again.

Sindy stared at him for a moment. "I've been doing it for me. They probably don't even know that I'm here, but I don't know if I can do it for her too. If we're trapped in this damn gym, it won't make much of a difference anyway. They already know where she is."

Ben looked at her seriously for a minute. "I'm working on that. Please... would you try?"

Sindy almost looked as though she'd like to comment on Ben asking a favor of her, but after a moment's consideration and a sidelong glance at Felicity, she gave him a small smile and nodded. "Sure."

Allie came bursting out of the locker room with a scowl on her face. "Nothing!" No one answered her, so after a moment she stalked back to the far exit again. Felicity started after her as the pounding on the front door became worse. As she rounded the bleachers, she saw that big white letters across the red back door proclaimed it to be a fire exit. 'Do not open – alarm will sound'.

Allie began pounding on the push bar, to no avail. After a few minutes of banging and cursing Alyson turned to Felicity. "It's fucking locked! Can you believe that? I'm gonna sue this damn school. How do you lock a fire exit?" They started back towards the others to try to devise some sort of plan.

Just then there was an incredibly loud crash as the door was pounded against again from the hallway. Ben was taken by surprise and thrown to the floor. The door only opened a crack, but the shelf was knocked over onto Ben and the rest of the pamphlets scattered over the floor. Felicity stifled a yelp of surprise that came to her throat. Sindy tried to help Ben out from under the display rack, but he jerked his hand back from her as though her touch was painful. His mark, it wasn't entirely gone yet. Sindy backed off under his warning glare. As he worked his way out from under the shelf, he seemed more annoyed than hurt and really didn't want her assistance. Felicity went to join Ashley on the stairs. "What do we do?"

Ashley looked at her accusingly. "What do those guys want with you anyway? Why won't anyone tell me what's going on? Ben?!"

Ashley was ignored as Allie stalked over to the foot of the stairs and looked up to Felicity. "Still no sign of Cain?"

Felicity just shook her head. The pounding against the door continued.

Ben and Sindy were busy trying to right the display rack again, to keep the door from opening. Ben glanced back at Allie. "You *can't* lock a fire exit from the inside only the outside locks. It must be stuck. Try again."

"I tried!" Allie glanced around the room and then back to Felicity. "Maybe we can get out a window?" she asked hopefully. Felicity looked up behind her to see the windows that Allie was talking about. She and Ashley quickly ran up the stairs to inspect them as Alyson went to try the back door again.

As they reached the top of the stairs, Ashley ran off across the track to check the windows on the far-left wall that was closest to them. Felicity quickly glanced around to see that the only other windows were at the back of the room over the spot where the bleachers were downstairs. The others were all interior walls. She made her way out onto the track and jogged towards the back wall, but even before she cut through the maze of treadmills, she could see it would be no use. The windows were far too high to ever reach.

After a moment, Felicity heard the front door get slammed against so forcefully, that it knocked over the bookshelf again. She looked down to see that Ben and Sindy had scrambled out of the way to avoid it landing on them. Allie's cursing and banging on the back door below Felicity started again. Ben ran to try and help her.

Felicity looked across the space that was open to downstairs, to see Ashley dejectedly making her way back through the weight equipment. "I can't reach them, unless you want to help me pull a weight bench over."

Felicity glanced up at the windows again. She couldn't even tell how you would open them anyway. She ran and leaned over the railing of the balcony so she could see Alyson and Ben at the back door. "I don't think we can get out from up here. Any luck?"

Ben told Allie to back away as he raised his leg and kicked strongly at the push bar of the door. As he did, Sindy came running towards him. "No, don't open that door!"

Too late. The door bar unstuck and pushed in with a loud click, followed by the wailing of an alarm. Ben was backed up a few steps from the force of his kick pushing off of the door. The door only opened a crack, but was caught and opened from the outside by the two vampires that they had left in the ballroom. Having been thrown out of the dance, they must have decided to follow Felicity's mark around the building to this door.

Sindy came up to join Allie and Ben by the door, giving Ben a scolding glance. She must have seen them coming by their marks, before anything could even be said, the other door came crashing open. As Ben, Allie and Sindy turned to see Marcus bash through the front door, the other two vampires moved into the room just enough to shut the back door and silence the alarm.

Marcus kicked the front door open further and heaved the display shelf aside. The other vampire he was with came around him into the room and surveyed its occupants.

Surprisingly, none of them seemed to look upstairs at Felicity on the balcony. She glanced back to Sindy and saw that she seemed deep in concentration. She must be doing it; she was hiding Felicity's mark! Felicity never felt so grateful, although it couldn't help for long. She silently prayed that Cain was on his way, and tried to inconspicuously move back a little from the railing to escape notice.

Unfortunately, Ashley had just been coming out from behind the treadmills at the other end of the balcony, when Marcus and his friend had come in. As Marcus was throwing the display rack aside, Ashley screamed, drawing his attention. Marcus looked confused. He was probably unsure what to do, being unable to see Felicity's mark. Upon seeing Ashley flee back from the railing again, he decided to start up the stairs. 'Thanks a lot Ashley', Felicity thought with a frightened shudder. She ducked down behind a stair-master and tried to crawl to where she could still see everyone below, but would hopefully remain hidden. She couldn't see where Ashley had gone and hoped that she was hiding well.

The two vampires by the back door moved forward, preparing to try and push their way further into the room. They only reached the front edge of the bleachers before being blocked by Allie, Sindy and Ben. The other vampire, by the front entrance, looked them over. He seemed to decide that the vamps by the back door needed no help and moved to wait for Marcus at the bottom of the stairs. He didn't seem to realize that there was another staircase in the corner by Felicity. She thought about using it, but once downstairs she could never cross the room to the front door without being seen. She didn't want to leave her friends anyway. She was probably best-off staying put for now. She desperately hoped that Cain would come looking for her soon.

Marcus was picking his way through the equipment across the way, to where Felicity couldn't see him well. A second later, he must have spotted Ashley again, because she screamed. So much for remaining hidden. She couldn't just leave Ashley to try and fend off Marcus alone. Felicity crept in and out of exercise machines trying to make her way over to the other side of the balcony unnoticed. As she neared the railing, she saw Ben below. He didn't see her, but neither did the vampires in front of him, so that was a good thing. Ashley screamed again from the other side. "Ben!"

As the vampires by the bleachers moved to come further into the gym, Alyson spoke to Ben. "Go help her, we're alright," she said with a glance at Sindy.

Sindy smiled and stepped up closer to Allie, looking over the two guys and crossing her arms in front of her. "Yeah, we got it."

The vampires looked at the girls in amusement. Ben seemed just as bemused by the girls' confidence as their foes were, when Ashley screamed again. Allie turned to him in aggravation that he was still standing there doubting their competence. "Go, we got it!"

Felicity saw Ashley dart out from behind the weight bench she'd been trying to keep between her and Marcus. She tried to run, but he moved to block her into the back left corner where there was only a small glass front refrigerator, no staircase. She opened the refrigerator and began throwing water bottles at Marcus, who seemed unfazed and was steadily advancing on her. "Hey!" Felicity yelled for his attention, standing up from behind the treadmill where she'd been crouching. "Weren't you looking for me?"

Marcus turned to face her. Slowly recognition crept across his face. Felicity wondered whether he actually recognized her or if Sindy had stopped hiding her mark, being forced to concentrate on other things. Felicity started backing away and Marcus began to follow her.

As she came closer to the rail of the balcony, she could hear Sindy and Alyson talking to the vampires below. Sindy was all 'attitude and confidence' as she asked, "Who the hell are you guys anyway? What do you want with us?"

"We owe Chris a favor. He wants the girl," one answered.

Sindy laughed. "Well, you may want to go back and tell him that his favor isn't worth your life. 'Cause if you want Felicity, you're gonna have to get through *us* first," she said with a smug grin and a glance at Allie.

The guys laughed at her. Felicity knew that Sindy could be a dangerous and formidable opponent, but her skills hardly looked to lie in the physical combat arena. Of course, Alyson's petite little form was deceiving as well. "No problem." One of the vampire's replied with another chuckle.

Felicity couldn't pay attention to the girl's reply, as Marcus was almost upon her. She'd managed to draw his attention from Ashley, but now what was she supposed to do? Where the hell was Ben? She heard fighting coming from the front left stairs. Ben must still be trying to get past the other vampire that had come in with Marcus. Ben should have used the back right stairs. Maybe he didn't know they were there. Anyway, Ashley's scream had come from towards the front.

She couldn't afford to worry about Ben at the moment, she had her own problems. Marcus stalked up to her with a nasty grin. Even through her frantic thoughts of escape possibilities, Felicity couldn't help but absently wonder whether Marcus had been told to kill her or bring her back to Chris. Would he even know the difference? He didn't look like someone who could handle complex instructions.

Felicity was trying to decide if she would break her legs, should she try to jump over the railing (unfortunately she was not above the mat at this point) when there was a terrible thud and Marcus collapsed to the floor. She looked up in disbelief to see Ashley standing behind him with a dumbbell in her hands. She had whacked him in the back of the head with it.

Ashley smiled and shrugged as Felicity glanced back down at Marcus in bemused relief. Ashley looked to have cracked his head open. His hair was a damp bloody mess. Felicity knew that he'd probably live through it, but he didn't look to be getting up any time soon. "Wow, thanks."

Ashley smiled. "*You* distracted him." She dropped the weight onto the floor with a loud thump and gave Marcus a little kick. "Big dumb oaf. What's his problem anyway?" Ashley backed up a step and looked up to Felicity in sudden worry. "You don't think I... killed him do ya'?"

"No. Definitely not. Don't worry about it. You did great."

Just then, they heard Allie yell "Kiyaa!" followed by what sounded like a man's surprised yell of pain.

Felicity ran to the rail to see Allie beating the heck out of her opponent. She went after him with a flurry of strikes and kicks, and he hardly seemed to know how to respond. He was trying to grab her but she kept slipping away.

His friend had originally seemed to think it was kind of funny that a little girl was beating up a big vampire, but he was suddenly distracted by Sindy who must have changed, because she went straight for his throat. She pierced his skin before he even had a chance to react. It certainly wasn't what he was expecting. "Holy shit, she's a vamp!" he screamed as she pounced on him. Sindy must still have been cloaking herself.

"It's her! It's the other one that Chris wanted." Yelled the guy who was trying to fend off Alyson.

"Well get her off me!" Sindy had wrapped herself around the guy and was surely drinking deeply. He couldn't seem to extricate himself from her and soon fell to his knees. His eyes turned orange and Felicity could see a flash of fangs in his mouth, proving that he had shifted as well. He couldn't seem to summon the strength or leverage to bite Sindy back though. She'd gotten too much of a lead on him. Her venom had probably started to affect his reflexes.

Felicity realized that the muscle relaxant in the venom paired with whatever else he might be feeling from her bite, would probably keep him from fighting back very hard anytime soon. After a few moments, she dropped him to the floor and wiped her mouth as she shifted back to her human state. "Mmm. I needed that," she muttered with a smile.

Felicity's attention was drawn from Sindy to see Alyson jump up onto the bottom bench of the bleachers in front of the guy she was fighting. She delivered a kick to his chest and then jumped down on top of him as he stumbled backwards and doubled over. Allie's elbow came down to hit him in the shoulder from above and he dropped to his knees. Allie never even gave him a chance to try and use his fangs. She ended the fight by giving him a swift kick to the head. He hit the floor and she pulled out a stake to finish him. He exploded into a big cloud of dust.

Felicity was startled by Ashley strongly grabbing her shoulder. "Oh my God! What did she do to that guy?! Where'd he go?! Did you see that?!"

"Yeah. I think they've got things under control down there. We should see if Ben needs help."

"But... I don't get it. Did you see what happened to that guy? What did she do to him? Why won't anybody tell me what's going on?!"

Felicity just started pushing Ashley towards the front stairs. "Ben'll tell you later." As they reached the staircase, they practically collided with Ben running up them, his arms covered in ash.

"Are you girls okay?"

Ashley started rambling in hysterics as she flew into his arms. "Ben, oh my God! Did you see what Allie just did to that guy? And that girl you know, she grabbed the other guy, and I think she *bit* him! It was so bizarre!

That giant dufus was chasing me and then Felicity distracted him and I clonked him on the head with a dumbbell and knocked him out cold! *I* did! Can you believe it? I hope I didn't kill him!"

Ben glanced up with a smile to see that Felicity was okay, and then put an arm around Ashley to start walking her down the stairs. Felicity was about to follow when she realized that she was beginning to feel Cain's presence, coming from somewhere behind her.

Finally! She stepped towards the rail and leaned over to see Sindy opening the fire door in anticipation of his arrival. He must be outside, coming towards the back door... and Sindy *could* feel him, just as she'd said. Cain was always cloaked, why would *Sindy* be able to feel him?

The door alarm began to wail and Felicity shook off troubled thoughts. At least he was here. She adjusted her headpiece and fluffed her dress in excitement to go down and see him. She headed towards the far-right stairs, as they would put her closer to the back door.

She was holding up her skirts as she cut in through the treadmills towards the corner. She had just crossed the track and stopped at the stairwell when suddenly a hand slipped over her mouth. She felt herself grabbed from behind and dragged backwards. She tried to scream but barely let out a thin shriek before her mouth was covered. Surely no one heard her over the alarm. She shook her hands free of her gowns' sleeves to claw at the arm around her and thought briefly that she should try to flip its owner, but she caught her heel in the lace at the hem of her skirt and could hardly even keep her feet. She was pulled back behind a rack of free weights and then pushed to the ground. The hand was only taken from her mouth for a rag to be shoved into it.

She struggled and looked up in dismay to see Chris leering down at her. He knelt down atop her in the same way that Luke had the night she'd killed him. Unfortunately, Chris seemed much more in control than Luke ever had. He had wasted no time in getting a firm hold of her long flowing sleeves, making her unable to use her hands trapped within. He used the ends of her sleeves to pin her arms to the ground over her head and showed no sign of giving her a chance to twist free. She tried to kick and wriggle from under him, but her legs only became hopelessly entangled in her skirts and it was no use. After a few moments of struggle, she became almost frozen in fear.

Fleeing from the others and taunting Marcus had been different. She had been pumped with adrenaline and surrounded by her friends. She had been scared, but somehow, she hadn't really thought anything truly bad could have happened, however naïve that might have been. This was different, back here alone with Chris behind the exercise equipment. Her friends were still nearby, but no one could hear her, no one would see, no one would even know... until it was too late.

But Cain was here, she'd felt him! She didn't think he was in the building yet, but he was certainly close. The alarm was still going off; they must be holding the door open for him. She couldn't even hope for them to hear something with that racket going on, but could Chris possibly hurt her in the few minutes it might take for Cain to get here, even against her mark? What was taking Cain so long?

With a sudden flare of frightened insight, she realized... Sindy was hiding her mark. There was no way for Felicity to know if she'd stopped, but until she did, Cain couldn't see her. He couldn't tell where she was. He would feel the physical awareness of her presence, but without her mark to guide him, it would be vague and hard to follow. She was... alone.

Chris glared at her in hatred and leaned down close to speak into her ear. "You thought you'd kill my best friend and get away with it?" he asked her with a rough shake, knocking her head against the floor. "You thought the 'almighty Cain' could protect you, but you thought wrong." He bared his fangs at her with an evil hiss. She scrunched her eyes shut and turned her head this way and that, trying to keep him from her throat.

As he held the ends of both sleeves pinned down with one hand, he used the other to rip the hat and veil off of her. He grabbed a handful of hair on the right side of her head, pinning the side of her face to the floor and leaving the left side of her throat exposed.

Felicity's scalp hurt and her neck ached, her muscles taught from hopelessly pulling away from him to no avail. Chris dipped down to the tender place where her shoulder met her neck but as his fangs touched her skin, he pulled back with an angry snarl. He eyed her in annoyance. "Went and got marked again did ya? Too bad. I was really looking forward to drinking from Cain's private stock." He untangled his fingers from her hair, and then shifted his weight so that he could pull something from his pocket.

He held a shiny silver switchblade up for her to see with an evil smile. "Guess I'll just have to lick it off the floor." She struggled with renewed intensity as he brought the blade to her throat. The blare of the alarm seemed to fill the world as it screamed in her ears and her heart tried to pound its way out of her chest. This could not happen! This was how it would end? She would have her throat slit by this creep while her friends and her love were not twenty feet away?

Felicity tried harder to pull away, but there was no room left to move, she was pinned. Her hands were trapped down in the long sleeves of her dress so that she couldn't use them to get free. Chris sat atop her, a heavy weight upon her stomach and chest so that she could hardly breathe. She scrunched her eyes shut tight as tears began to roll down her face.

Chris put the blade to her throat up high under her ear and she was forced to turn her face aside and strain her head up to keep it from stabbing her. She tried again to scream around the rag in her mouth, as he jerked the knife upwards and the point of the blade poked into her flesh. The cold steel made a puncture sharp and painful, so unlike her lover's bite. It stung as she felt it cut through her skin. He pushed it in deep before beginning to move it across and under her chin.

Felicity opened her eyes to see Chris looking down at her with a cold and sinister grin as he began to slit her throat. Then he jerked forward a bit, his eyes wide and his mouth opened in protest. Before she could wonder why, he seemed to explode. There was nothing left but dust to collapse upon her. The blade in her throat was jerked painfully further upward for a second and then fell dead upon her neck. It snagged there with its point beneath her skin for a painful instant and then dropped onto her chest as the hand holding it was transformed into ash.

She simply lay staring up at the ceiling tiles, through the swirl of dust that still hung in the air above her where Chris had been. Then another face came into view, Ben. He was holding a stake in one hand and holding the other out to help her up. She hardly believed that he was there. He must have come up the stairs while Chris was distracted with her.

Everything in the world seemed reduced to the sting of the cut at her throat and the blaring siren in her ears. Ben was smiling down at her when his face suddenly seemed to collapse upon itself in shock and distress. Her throat. She was bleeding she knew. He must not have seen the knife when Chris was in the way.

"Felicity!" He knelt down over her and pulled the rag from her mouth in an instant. She tried to speak, to tell him that she was alright. It was just a cut, it couldn't be that bad, but when first she opened her mouth, no sound would come.

His eyes seemed wide with fear and he grabbed and threw away the blade that had lain upon her chest. She ventured a small smile and he leaned down close to move the hair from her face. He took the rag that Chris had used to gag her, and pressed it against her throat.

The stupid alarm was still going off. It seemed deafening and she found it hard to even think. She closed her eyes, and then there was suddenly silence. She was frightened for a moment that perhaps she had passed out, but when she opened her eyes, Ben was still there and it was the alarm that was gone. They must have finally closed the damn door.

She found herself staring at the shiny buttons on Ben's NASA uniform for a moment before looking back up to his eyes. "Looks like you got to be a superhero after all," she whispered with a smile.

It took him a moment to realize she was referring to his Halloween costume. She was a little surprised to see a tear of relief slide down his cheek. It fell onto her face as he let out a little laugh. She knew that her face was already wet with tears of fear from a moment ago. She blinked as Ben leaned forward and gave her a small kiss on the cheek near the corner of her eye and took her last tear away.

He leaned back and moved the rag to inspect her throat. "I think you'll be okay." Ben tried to wipe most of the dust pile that had been Chris off of her stomach and then helped her gently to her feet, as she moved her own hand to continue holding the rag to her cut. She stood and Ben held onto her strong and sure for a moment as she gained her balance. She looked up at him again, thinking to thank him. He smiled at her with such touching and sincere relief that she was alright, and she forgot what she'd meant to say.

"Felicity?!" It was Cain, down below. He sounded terribly worried. The others must have filled him in on the evening's events. They had to know of Chris' presence now, for Sindy must have felt him die.

"Oh sorry." Sindy's voice. She must still have been cloaking Felicity, and Cain could not see her. He had to feel that she was near, but that only gave a general sense of direction. Felicity was afraid to yell and hurt her throat.

Ben yelled for her as they moved slowly towards the stairs. "Up here." Cain must have already been on his way up because he was upon them before Ben was hardly done speaking, before she knew it Ben had stepped away and Cain was holding her in his arms.

"Careful, she's hurt. Her throat," Ben admonished.

Cain leaned her back to look upon her in concern. He seemed confused. "But... how? He couldn't have..."

Felicity tried not to wince as she swallowed and it caused her throat to burn again. "Switchblade," she whispered. Cain looked devastated that she had been hurt without his protection and made her move the rag for him to see.

"I thought you weren't coming," she said lightly, trying to tease him as he fussed over her wound. He looked into her eyes again as she whispered, "and you're late."

He gave her a lopsided grin. "Yeah, I know." He looked on her with loving concern for a moment, and then seemed to remember something. "But look, I wore a costume." Felicity held the weight rack to keep steady as he let go of her hands for a moment to pull his sweater off over his head, revealing the chain mail vest that he wore underneath. She ran her eyes over him to see that he had added to it a large sword at his belt. He took her hands back into his own and made a little bow. "Your 'knight in shining armor', my lady." He seemed almost choked with remorse as he spoke. "Sorry I didn't get to slay the dragon for you." He glanced over at Ben. "Thanks." Ben just shrugged and looked away.

Felicity gazed at Cain for a moment. She still felt a bit disoriented and the side of her throat was a burning nagging sting that would hardly let her think, but something was tugging at her mind that she couldn't quite place at first. "You look different." Suddenly she placed it. "Your hair! You cut your hair!"

Cain smiled sheepishly and ran his hand through it. "Actually, Alyson cut it for me. Does it look alright?"

At the mention of Allie, Felicity noticed that Ben looked back at Cain in surprise and then became annoyed. He turned from them and went to lean on the rail a few paces away. Felicity surveyed Cain's' newly shorn hair. Allie had done a wonderful job. He looked so sexy! It was very short at the back and sides, but the front was just long enough to still fall forward a bit and look 'casually messy'. It was still 'him', just neatened up and a little more polished. She smiled. "You look really good."

Cain smiled at her adoringly for a moment. "You look lovely as well." She let out a small breath of a laugh, knowing she was probably a terrible mess. He took her gently by the elbows and helped her to the stairs. "Come on princess, let's get you cleaned up."

Felicity looked down at her dress as they began to descend the stairs. It was covered in ash and blood, and was trailing a long-ripped swath of lace from the bottom in the back. She looked back up at Cain. "Can I borrow $329?" He gave her a confused laugh and a nod.

Sindy met them at the bottom of the stairs, seeming a bit shaken. She looked up to the balcony, where Ben stood watching them, and then back at Cain. Her eyes seemed to fall on the sword. "Can I borrow that?"

Cain had no time to question her before she pulled it from the sheath at his side. She began to climb the stairs with it as Cain turned to rebuke her. "That's not to play with!"

She called back to him over her shoulder as she topped the stairs. "Don't worry; I'm not planning to enjoy this." Ben eyed her warily as she approached him. "Duck," she said as she closed on him.

"What?" Ben asked suspiciously.

"Duck!" He did, revealing Marcus just coming up behind him. Sindy swung the sword up over her shoulder like a baseball bat and then sharply brought it to swing around over Ben's hunched form. Felicity heard Ashley scream as Marcus' head came flying at them from over the balcony accompanied by a splattering spray of blood. His face was twisted into a frightening grimace of surprised anger. It turned to dust before it hit the floor. Felicity cringed in surprise and disgust as a few droplets of blood struck her arm, but was even more surprised when they disintegrated into ash as well.

Felicity looked up just in time to see Marcus' body transform into dust and then collapse upon itself in a sort of silent explosion, showering Ben with his ashes. Sindy dropped the sword and fell to the floor clasping her throat.

Alyson had been climbing the stairs to follow Sindy, unsure what she'd had in mind for Ben. Now she ran the rest of the way to reach them. Ben was just sitting up to see what had happened.

Cain had tightened his grip on Felicity's shoulders in surprise. He must have been so worried for her, that he hadn't noticed Marcus moving again. Now he looked down and caught her wincing in pain as she tried to swallow. "You alright?"

Felicity weakly smiled and nodded. She told Cain she just wanted to sit on one of the lower benches of the bleachers for a minute to recuperate. He helped her to sit and after watching her for a moment, presumably to assess whether she really was okay, he turned to examine the vampire that Sindy had left on the floor next to them. Felicity watched as Allie reached Ben on the balcony. Alyson squatted between him and Sindy, with a hand on Ben's shoulder. "You okay?"

"Yeah, what happened?" Ben asked.

"Marcus, behind you." Allie looked over to see Sindy beginning to stir. "She... beheaded him."

Ben stood up with a dazed expression on his face and tried to clear himself of Marcus' ashes. Ashley went running up the stairs to him. "Ben!" She practically tripped over Sindy and threw herself into Ben's arms. "Are you okay? What is wrong with these people? They keep exploding! I thought she was going to kill you! Come downstairs, let's get out of here!"

Sindy opened her eyes to look up at Ben. He met her gaze for a brief moment. "Thank you," he uttered. He looked almost surprised that Sindy would have done that for him. He opened his mouth as though to better express his gratitude, but wasn't given the chance. Ashley pulled at his arm insistently and Ben suffered himself to be led downstairs without another word. He hadn't the chance to say anything else as Ashley fussed over him and dragged him away.

Allie watched them until they disappeared from view and then turned to see Sindy sit up. She looked ill as her eyes met Allie's. "I am seriously starting to reconsider the whole 'be fruitful and multiply' thing. Turns out that pain is a pretty good incentive to keep your blood to yourself," Sindy muttered.

"What the hell are you talking about? No one even touched you!" Allie exclaimed.

Sindy tried to smile, but then shuddered as she looked down at Marcus' ash all around her. "Transferred pain. I made Marcus, so I get my own special sharing experience when he dies."

Allie gazed at her in shock. "You mean you... *felt* it, just like him?"

Sindy nodded. "Uh-huh."

Allie grimaced and looked from the ash back to Sindy. "That sucks."

"Tell me about it," Sindy agreed. Sindy's eyes were trained on Ben downstairs, who was trying to talk to Cain while Ashley alternately smothered him with kisses and pulled at him to leave.

Allie followed her gaze through the railing. "That was cool, that you did that for Ben."

"He doesn't seem too impressed."

"No, I wouldn't think that *you* should expect showers of gratitude from him." Alyson watched him for a minute. He and Cain seemed to be trying to bring around the last vampire on the floor that Sindy had drained. What were they going to do with him? She looked back to Sindy who was still staring at Ben. "But *I* think it was cool. Did it hurt a lot?"

Sindy shrugged. "You had some pretty cool moves down there yourself. Where did you learn to fight like that?"

"I used to take Jui Jitsu. I'm a brown belt. Haven't trained for a while though. Sucks I never got my black. I ran out of cash. My Dojo let's me train for free sometimes, but you know... it's a big commitment. I kind of got side tracked."

"No wonder you always manage to kick my ass."

Allie smiled up at her, amazed that she'd admit it. "I do, don't I? I've seen you pull some interesting tricks though."

Sindy grinned. "Oh yeah, being a vamp does have its advantages if you know how to use them."

Allie gave her a little grin, intrigued. "Like what?"

A sly smile stole over Sindy's face as she surveyed the people below them. "Keep your eye on Ben."

Alyson looked a bit nervous. "Why?"

"Just watch." Sindy stared at him intently for a moment. Felicity trained her eyes on him as well, wondering what Sindy could possibly have in mind. After a moment, he began to fidget and then gave a violent shudder and stumbled a step in Sindy's direction. He turned to look up at Sindy with an angry glare. He didn't seem hurt at all, just extremely annoyed.

Sindy chuckled as she and Allie moved back from the edge out of Ben's immediate view. Alyson gave Sindy a little shove on the shoulder. "What did you do?"

"Relax, he'll get over it." Sindy peeked over at Ben again, who no longer paid the girls any attention. "He hasn't got much of my venom left in him. I could do much more with the guy on the floor." She nodded towards the vampire who seemed to have come around and was being quietly questioned by Cain and Ben.

"But I don't get it," Allie persisted. "What did you do?"

"My venom is in him. When I'm close enough to him, it recognizes the blood and venom in me. It *wants* to be with me. Just a little urging makes it try to get his body to come to me. It wants us to be together," Sindy explained with a smug little smile.

Allie looked as uncomfortably confused as Felicity felt. "*It* wants? I thought it was just like... a poison."

"I don't really know what it is, but it sure can make things interesting. Since there's hardly any left in him, I haven't got the power for something long sustained and subtle, but if I focus it just right, it's good for a quick burst or two. Not very useful, but still... fun."

Alyson shook her head and stood up. Her expression was a strange mixture of disgust and amusement. "Leave him alone," she said mildly as she started down the stairs. Sindy retrieved Cain's sword from the floor where she'd dropped it, and followed. Sindy stopped next to the bleachers by Felicity.

Cain came over to meet them, as Allie went to talk to Ben and Ashley. Sindy handed Cain back the sword. "Where'd you get that thing?"

Cain smiled as he sheathed it at his side. "It was a gift."

"It's *wood*," Sindy said with an odd look.

"Yes, that's kind of the idea." He laughed as he made a motion in the air as though staking a vampire.

Sindy's eyes went wide with comprehension. "Neat."

Cain laughed again and then had Felicity tip her head up and remove the rag so he could see. He shook his head disapprovingly. "It's still bleeding a bit. It looks deep. I think you need stitches. Feeling alright?"

She slowly stood and answered in a low and rasping voice. "I'm a little woozy. It hurts, but I'm okay."

"Yes, I think an ER visit is definitely in order."

Felicity looked up at him in alarm. "I don't wanna go to the hospital." She raised her voice a bit in her distress but the pain immediately made her return to the level of a stage whisper. "What if my folks find out? They'll make me go home."

Cain studied her for a moment. "You *are* going to the hospital. I'll pay cash if you like so you don't have to use your parents' insurance, but you have to see a doctor… now."

Felicity pouted sullenly at the floor but allowed Cain to hold her arm to help her down off of the bleacher bench. Sindy caught his attention. "What are you gonna do with him?" she asked, nodding to the vampire that she had bitten. He was still sitting on the floor.

Cain shrugged. "I shouldn't think he'll be bothering us again. Let him be."

Sindy eyed him appraisingly. He was in his mid twenties, kind of good looking actually. Sindy gave Cain a pleading little smile. "Could *I* have him? Like to play with a little? I won't hurt him or try and get him to attack you or nothin'. Promise."

Cain rolled his eyes and shook his head, looking a bit disgusted. "He's certainly not yours or mine to command." Sindy's smile showed that she thought otherwise. After witnessing Sindy's use of venom and psychic control, Felicity was leaning towards agreeing with Sindy. She probably could control him very well if she'd a mind to. Personally, Felicity would be very content to give Sindy someone else to focus her attentions on for a change. Cain just waved her away. "Do as you like, just stay out of trouble."

Sindy grinned, looking at her new catch. "No problem. I can play nice, when I have to." The guy in question got shakily to his feet as she sauntered over to him. At first, he eyed her apprehensively, but relaxed when she stopped a few paces from him. She looked him up and down and then smiled. "Told you that you wouldn't get past me."

He smiled a little and shook his head. "I didn't know you were one of *us*."

Sindy glanced at the spot where a few ashes of the guys' partner could still be seen on the floor. "Was he a friend of yours?"

The guy shook his head with a bit of a shudder. "No, not really."

Sindy gazed into his eyes a moment. He seemed mesmerized. "Wanna make a new friend?"

After taking a second to clear his head, he gave her an odd look and then smiled. He jerked his head towards the fire exit. "Let's get out of here, before the cops show up."

Cain turned to the man as he and Sindy prepared to leave. "Has someone called the police?"

"They threatened us they were gonna, but I don't know if they really did."

Cain groaned. "Wonderful. Ben, do me a favor and fetch down the knife that Chris used on Felicity. It must still be up there, right?"

Ben and Ashley had been about to leave by the main entrance. Now Ben stopped and looked annoyed. Felicity couldn't help but think that Cain's use of the word 'fetch' was probably a poor choice. "What for?"

Cain stared at him for a moment as the alarm briefly sounded while Sindy and her new friend left the building. After it was silenced, Cain spoke. "I do spend a decent amount of effort trying to keep things like this out of the papers. We'll have to clean up this mess. Secondly... *you* reached Felicity first." He looked almost pained to acknowledge that fact.

"So?" Ben asked.

"So, did you touch the knife? If you did, it's got *your* fingerprints on it. A detail you may want to take care of *before* police get a hold of it."

Bens' mouth became a hard line. He made Ashley let him go so he could climb the left front stairs and go find the knife. As he reached the top, Cain yelled up to him. "You might want to try to scatter the ashes up there a bit as well, make them less noticeable." Ben grumbled something that it was probably fortunate they couldn't quite make out.

Allie went over to try and stand up the display rack by the door. As soon as Cain saw what she was doing, he went to help. Once they had it standing, Alyson began replacing the pamphlets. "You should go," she told Cain. "Get her to the hospital. I'll fix this."

He smiled at her in appreciation. "Don't stay too long. You don't want to be the only one here if police do arrive. And Alyson... thanks." She smiled and waved him off to leave.

As Cain turned to leave, he noticed Ashley standing by the front doorway with her arms crossed. Cain watched her a moment and then gave her a smile. "Would you mind?" he asked gesturing towards the flyers and booklets surrounding Ashley's feet.

She glanced down, looking astonished that he would expect her to help. Cain just stood there smiling at her hopefully. Finally, she gave in and started helping Allie with the pamphlets. "There'd better be a good explanation for all of this. You guys ruined my dance." She eyed Allie a bit apprehensively. "And you... you'd better stay away from me. I saw what you did to that guy. That was... spooky." Allie just laughed.

Cain returned to Felicity and they made their way to the back exit. Felicity noticed that he tried to kick and scatter the little pile of ash from Allie's kill as they passed. Just before they came to the exit, Ben leaned over the railing above them. "Isn't this your hat?" he asked. He threw Felicity's headpiece down to them, with its veil fluttering behind.

Cain caught it and turned it over in his hands. "It's not a hat, it's a coronet."

Ben left the rail with a 'whatever.' Felicity called up to him. "Thanks." She looked back to Cain curiously. "What's it called?"

"A coronet. Sort of like a tiara made of velvet. High fashion among noble ladies of my day."

Felicity gave him an odd little laugh. Her hand shot up to her head as she realized that she'd been wearing the comb he'd given her as well. It was still there, although hopelessly tangled in her hair. She breathed a sigh of relief. Cain handed her the headpiece and she felt very silly putting something so lovely atop her unruly mop of waves and tangles. She pouted at Cain. "I really did look lovely, honest."

He laughed and gave her a kiss. "You always do. Now stop stalling. If there's one thing I know about, it's blood loss. We've wasted enough time as it is. You've a date with a doctor." As they exited the gymnasium by the back door, Felicity couldn't help but think that she would be very happy never to hear another fire exit alarm again.

Chapter 8

Fresh air and sunshine

Cain

Arriving at Cain's house
5:45, Monday morning

Cain was very relieved to pull Felicity's car into his driveway and shut the engine. She was sitting silent and still in the passenger seat, probably sleeping. It was becoming uncomfortably close to dawn. He'd thought they would never be done in the emergency room. As it was, they were cutting things rather close. He had less than a half an hour to get inside before the sun would peek over the horizon. More than enough time really, but still, nerve racking after an evening of stressful events.

He looked to Felicity, to tell her that they were home, and was a bit surprised to find that she was awake after all. She sat staring out the window, seemingly deep in thought. She hadn't said much since leaving the gymnasium. He'd been terribly worried and guilt ridden over the fact that he hadn't gotten to her in time. Once in the hospital, by her side, holding her hand as they injected her with antibiotics and sewed stitches through her tender flesh had been almost unbearable. He was unused to witnessing such things. In his world, either you healed quickly on your own, or you were dust. Such drawn out and painful intercessions were unnecessary. To see her go through that after her already trying experiences, feeling that he could have prevented it all, was maddening.

Felicity had told the medical staff an unlikely story of pumpkin carving and playing around foolishly with a kitchen knife. She'd said her friends were teasing and chasing her. She'd been running with the knife and then fallen, stabbing herself. It sounded ridiculously irresponsible and unbelievable to Cain, but the nurses barely blinked an eye. It seemed they had dealt with far worse on Halloween's eve.

He turned to her now and wondered if the evening's events had damaged her more emotionally than the physical damage the knife at her precious throat had done. As the evening had worn on, through the hospital ordeal and then the ride home, she had become more and more withdrawn. "Felicity?" he gently prodded. "We're here." She barely acknowledged him, but then took off her seatbelt. He'd thought she would rather go back to the dorm. She had nothing of her own to change into at Cain's, but she had quietly insisted that she wanted to go to Cain's house. He'd driven her with the car to the hospital of course. Even now, he wouldn't let her drive home. He'd have to return for his motorcycle tomorrow evening, after things had settled.

He left the car and went around to help her from her seat, giving her the car keys to put into her purse. They went up to the house and after he let them in, she passed him and headed straight for the stairs. He worried that she would trip over the welter of skirts her gown sported, but she managed to navigate the stair without event. Once reaching the bottom, Felicity dropped her purse and headpiece. She stood waiting for him to cross the room and turn on a light. He lit the lamp by his bed and turned to face her. She stood quiet and contemplative as he ran his eyes over her once gorgeous gown. Her hair had been pinned up at the sides with only a few curls meant to hang down. Of course, now it was a bedraggled mess, but he was certain that at the start of the evening she had looked every inch a royal princess.

Lovely and demure, she had dressed so beautifully for him. Why hadn't he just gone to the stupid dance? She had been so full of innocent excitement when first she'd brought it up, but he hadn't wanted to go. Later he had reasoned that he couldn't go. He'd thought it would be wiser to finish things with Chris before they escalated to a more dangerous level. It seemed almost foolish in retrospect. Why did things never work out the way that he planned?

He found her gazing at him in thoughtful seriousness. He tried to coax a smile from her with one of his own, but after a moment, she only yawned and looked at the floor. He went to her. "Here, let's take that gown off and let you have some rest." He took her hands into his own, to spread her arms and look at her one last time. "You look like true nobility. A vision of beauty… under the ash, blood and bandage that is." She did not meet his eyes or smile as he'd hoped. Instead, she only sighed as she dropped his hands and turned around for him to help her remove the dress. He opened the button at the top and pulled down the zipper. "I don't believe it's entirely ruined. Perhaps I can have it cleaned for you." She only shrugged and turned back around, holding the dress up to her chest. He met her eyes and brought a hand up to gently caress her cheek. She didn't really smile, but did close her eyes and seemed to enjoy his touch. The tingle of her mark *did* make each touch its own special experience.

Cain gently placed his hands upon her shoulders and then slid down the sleeves of her gown. She dropped her arms to her sides, letting him guide it down to reveal her breasts, and then down over her hips to the floor. He was rather surprised as he knelt on the floor and helped her step out of it, to find that she wore a garter belt made with black lace and midnight blue ribbon. It held her thigh high black stockings in place. He wanted to smile at her for it, but could only feel overcome yet again with guilt and remorse. She'd gone through such trouble to please him and it had all been ruined. Surely, she had planned to end the evening here in his bedroom, to be carefully undressed by him as she was now, but this was not the romantic and exciting experience she had surely anticipated. Instead, she was wounded and weary... and he had failed her. He forced upon himself a smile and looked up to meet her eyes after she daintily stepped from the dress with a hand on his shoulder to steady herself. "This is new," he said, running his finger gently over a strap of the garter belt.

She looked down for a moment as though she had forgotten she was even wearing it. She gave him a thin smile. "I went shopping."

"So I see," he said with a playful grin, fingering the lace.

She did not seem in the mood to play however. He could hardly blame her. He removed the gown from the floor at her feet and laid it across the bar. He then came back to her and eyed her hosiery with a smile. She sighed and asked, "Do you know how to take them off?"

Cain couldn't help but let out a little breath of a laugh and give her a sly grin. "Yes." He knelt before her again and slipped the shoes from her feet. Then he undid the clasps that attached the belt to her stockings in the front. She turned around for him to undo the ones in the back and he looked up with a bit of a start to give her a little tap on her bare bottom. "You *do* realize that there's quite a shortage of material back here?" he asked with a chuckle.

When she turned to look down at him over her shoulder, he saw that she'd a slight blush to her cheeks. That made his smile broader. It seemed a long time since he'd made her blush. He always found it so delightful. "It's a thong," she answered with a tinge of bashfulness.

"I see. Can't say I've much experience with one. Perhaps you'll wear it for me again sometime?" She just gave him a weary smile and turned back around.

He completed the task, removing stockings and belt. He left her thong panty for her to remove herself if she'd like. He couldn't help but feel her presumed disappointment weighing on him. By the time he'd brought her hosiery to the bar to leave with the dress, he knew that something must be said. She'd mentioned nothing of the evening's events to him. He'd been filled in a bit by Ben, but he had no idea of what she'd really gone through. He wouldn't ask her to relay it all to him;

she would tell him when she was ready. Just the same, she had no knowledge of his doings either.

The things that he had experienced at Arif's were too puzzling and detailed for him to go into now... if at all. He was almost frightened to speculate on their meanings himself. One thing he did know from experience and the reading he had done, was that The Lord *did* work in mysterious ways. Seldom if ever in history was one given concrete evidence of heavenly approval of one's doings. Those who thought to interpret odd phenomenon to such ends were almost always deluded and found themselves following their own praise down a path to destruction.

No, he would not dare to presume that he could understand the meanings behind his partial protection from the heavenly weapons of holy water and cross. He would simply carry on, satisfied in the knowledge that he was living in a manner that he found morally sound. That would have to be enough to sustain him. He did however want to tell Felicity of his troubles in finding her. She shouldn't think that he'd simply dallied overlong in other pursuits and not reached her in time. The fact that he had arrived *after* the fact seemed inexcusable. It was a thorn in his side that he felt he needed to justify. He wanted her to understand and not be resentful of it. She'd never said a word to that end of course, but he couldn't help but feel that way. Her quiet demeanor towards him did nothing to help.

He came back to her where she stood unmoving and took her hands into his own once more. After gazing into her eyes for a moment wondering where to begin, he simply poured out what was on his mind. "Felicity, I am so sorry that things turned out this way. I should have done as you asked. I should have gone with you. I had thought that I could prevent such things. I had thought that it was better to find him on my own and reason things out, without putting you into danger. That he could be made to change if given the chance. I worried so much for helping others that I almost lost the one I hold dearest of all. I've failed you terribly, haven't I?"

She said nothing. She didn't really seem disappointed in him, only lost in thought. He pressed on. "I didn't think he would go so far. I thought him to hide behind his creations as he did before, afraid to try for you himself. You're marked; safe from his bite or any lesser vampires that he might have made. I hadn't thought things would get so dire in so short a time. I came as soon as I knew his minions to be moving towards you. I thought to reach you before they ever could.

I sped towards you at a breakneck pace but then… you disappeared! Your mark, it was gone! I was beside myself knowing not what to think. I hadn't known that Sindy could hide you or ever thought that she *would*. I didn't even know that she was there. A mark can only be truly extinguished by death. Gave me quite a start I can tell you! But they hadn't reached you yet, I could see them still. They hadn't been quite upon you when your precious light went out. No one had seemed to touch you, unless Chris himself was cloaked and had gone before them, but that just didn't seem to fit.

I reached the dance hall but they wouldn't allow me entrance. I don't know what I would have done, but then I *felt* you. Your mark was still disguised but I could feel your physical presence within. Not in the very ballroom, but somewhere beyond. You've no idea the relief that brought! Of course, I don't know if the physical aspect of your mark would remain after death. Never had the unfortunate circumstance to discover that myself, but I had to believe that you were all right, alive and well. Still, it was a difficult task to locate you from the outside. In fact, if it weren't for that bloody fire alarm wailing through the night, I don't know how I ever would have found the door. It was a ghastly racket but I was powerfully grateful for it. That was right clever sounding that alarm. You felt me too, didn't you? That's why you had them open the door."

Felicity had been silently staring at him throughout. She gazed at him a moment more before answering quietly. "That was Sindy actually."

Cain continued on. "That's another thing! I reached the door only to find Alyson, Ashley and Sindy there. I asked for you and Allie said that you were fine, but then Sindy stumbled as though struck and fell to the floor. It took her a bit before she could mumble that it was Chris. It suddenly hit me that if Chris was in difficulty, it was most likely over you. That's when I called out for you. Thank God you're alright." She just stared at him strangely. He leaned forward to give her a kiss on the cheek. "Shall I help you to bed?"

She raised her fingers to lightly touch the plastic bandage taped in a rectangle to the side of her throat. "They said I could shower."

"Oh, of course." He gave an awkward glance towards his distressingly small bathroom. "I've only a stall shower though. It's not big enough for two. I'd thought to help you. What if you get dizzy?"

"I'm okay."

"I'll bet there's a tub upstairs. Yes, there's sure to be. We should go up; I'll carry you if you'd like. You can take a bath."

She eyed him for a moment and then left him for the downstairs bathroom. "I can do it." Before he could respond, she'd shut the door. He stood there for a moment, not knowing what to do. He heard her start the water. After listening to it run for a minute or two, he went to the laundry room.

He came back with a couple of towels and tapped on the door. She couldn't hear him over the water. He hesitantly opened the door a crack. "Felicity, everything alright? I've brought you towels."

"Thanks."

He entered the steam-filled room and put the linens down on the edge of the sink. He was careful to close the door and not let the warmth escape. He noticed that she had left her thong and the hair comb he'd given her on the edge of the sink as well. He touched the comb lightly with a smile. "You want a wash cloth?" She only held her hand out from the curtain for it. He gave it to her and stood there a moment more. "Do you need anything else?"

"No, I'm fine," she replied shortly.

"Careful not to get the bandage too wet." She mumbled an 'uh-huh' through the water. He left her alone. He went to the bar, thinking to brush off the dress a bit for her. After closer inspection, he realized that it really was in need of professional assistance. Most likely, it was ruined. Not knowing what else to do he went to turn down the bed. He took off his boots and then went back to the laundry room.

He found a t-shirt and a pair of his pajama pants for her, and then undressed to don a pair of sleep pants for himself.

The water was turned off and he sat down on the bed, awaiting her. After a few minutes, she emerged from the bathroom, wrapped in towels. She had one around her body and had her hair wrapped up in another on her head. She came to the edge of the bed looking flushed and exhausted. He watched her look at the pajamas and then at him. She picked up the shirt, and went back into the bathroom, leaving the pants behind. She didn't entirely shut the door, but he waited for her on the bed. He couldn't help but feel a little hurt and confused that she didn't want to change in front of him. Then he realized that she'd gone back for her panties.

She returned without the towels, wearing the shirt. It only came down to the very top of her thighs. She was trying to brush through her wet hair with her fingers. She went around the bed to the side that she usually used and sat, slipping her legs beneath the covers. He turned to face her, looking at her long, wet hair. "You don't want to go to bed with it wet, do you?" She remained sitting and shrugged.

Cain quickly went to the bathroom cabinet and came back with his brush and hair dryer. He plugged it in, put it down on the bed with the brush and then moved to sit behind her on the pillows. "Can I do it for you?"

She shrugged again. "If you want."

He carefully moved the brush through her hair a few times and then turned the blow dryer on. He took his time, just drying and brushing out her hair. She jumped once when he went over a sore spot near the top on the side. She quietly explained that Chris had held her down by the hair. He felt almost enraged to hear it, but sat quiet and still. She offered no further recount of her experience. He refrained from asking for more detail and went back to her hair, being cautious to try and avoid the spot again. She would talk to him when she was ready, he wouldn't push her.

He didn't really try to style her hair, he'd no clue how he should even try. He just brushed it out long and straight from underneath and down her back. In the dim light he watched as it turned from a dark wet chestnut brown, to the beautiful auburn color he so loved, with just a bit of crimson glow where the light touched it. She sat silent throughout. Even when it was fully dry, he spent a few more minutes just brushing and running his fingers through it. Finally, she turned to look at him. "Thanks." She seemed troubled.

"How's your throat?" he asked in concern.

She sighed and raised her fingers to the bandage again. "It hurts a little. I think the stuff they gave me wore off."

He looked at her in concern. "Something I can do?" She just gazed at him thoughtfully. "How about a nice cup of tea?"

"You have tea?" She looked surprised.

He pretended to take offense. "I'm an Englishman; of course I've got tea!"

Now she laughed a little. He was glad to see it. "But you always drink coffee."

He smiled and wrinkled his nose at her. "Yes, but sometimes you just need a good cup of tea."

She lightly shook her head. "Maybe later."

"Are you sure? I've got Earl Grey," he said to tempt her.

"No thanks," she told him.

She lay back on the bed beneath the covers and he got in to join her. He reached to shut the light and then turned to give her a kiss. "Sleep well." She lay still on her own side of the bed and he felt obligated to do the same, although he wanted nothing more than to hold her. Finally, she turned towards him and snuggled into his arms, her face buried in his chest. He felt so relieved to have her there. Her attitude had been so oddly cold and he sorely just wanted to wrap his arms around her and feel her melt into him as she did now. He knew she'd been through a lot and didn't want to judge her actions harshly, but he'd been a bit put off that she didn't seem to want him to comfort her at all.

After snuggling with him a bit she wriggled herself up to place a few kisses upon his throat. He wondered if she knew how strongly that always affected him, even if for no good reason. Her lips found his chin, his cheek, and then his own lips, but they didn't stay there for long. After a few light kisses she moved to have him kiss *her* neck, on the side away from her injury. He gave her the kisses there that she seemed to desire and then once again took back her lips, but she would not give him the deep kiss that he sought. She kept turning away to offer him her throat until it was undeniable that his kiss was not what she really desired. He only kissed her there once more and then leaned back from her, though she seemed desperate to press her flesh to his lips. "Felicity, stop."

She seemed confused and hurt as she looked up to his face. "What? I just thought…"

"You're hurt. You need rest, not further trauma." He tried to say it teasingly, hoping he wouldn't sound too stern.

She lay back and seemed to pout. "I can't sleep."

He eyed her for a moment warily, wondering her true thoughts. She enfolded herself back into his arms. He held her close, trying to understand how she must feel. Once again, she brought her lips to his throat. This time not only to kiss, but also to gently suck upon his skin. Yes, she had to know that it thrilled him to feel her there. Yet he knew that she was only trying to coax him again to her own throat. Sure enough, before long she thrust her skin to his lips. He pushed her back firmly. "No. You'll not be drowning your worries in venom this night." He couldn't help the slightly harsh tone in his voice. He was annoyed that she wanted his bite more than his other attentions. She seemed very hurt by his words, but to be bitten had obviously been her intent. He spoke to her in a milder tone. "You've lost enough blood for one evening."

She lost her look of aggravation and turned to him hopefully. "You wouldn't have to actually *drink* any."

He stared at her in flustered disbelief. "That's asking a bit *much*, don't you think?"

She glared at him coldly and then rolled over, turning away from him. "I wouldn't think you'd be thirsty for *my* blood anyway. Haven't you had your fill elsewhere?" she asked acidly.

He froze for a moment, staring at the back of her head. "What?"

She waited a moment before elaborating, but didn't turn to face him again. "You drink from Sindy, don't you?" She spoke again before he could think what to say. "I know you have. She can *feel* you... just like I can."

He closed his eyes and felt his heart sink. No wonder she'd been cold towards him. "I did... drink from her, but there were reasons…" She turned to give him a look that dared him to try and justify it. "…that I'm sure you don't care to hear. I drank from her this evening, but it was only to mark her. It was only blood… nothing more."

She sat up in anger. "Only blood? *Only blood!?* How can you even say that to me? It's never *only* blood. You told me that yourself, remember? *'It's much… much more'* were your exact words, I believe." She gave him no chance to try and defend it. How could he anyway? He'd only meant that he had not indulged in Sindy's body as well, but he couldn't honestly say that her blood hadn't pleased him, even if he hadn't been trying to be untrue to Felicity.

"Is that how you did it?" she asked. He had no idea what she could mean. "Is that what you did, back before I let you drink from me? You told me that it was difficult, but that you could keep things under control. Is *that* your control? To quench your thirst for *my* blood by filling yourself with *her?*"

"No! It's not like that at all! I drank from her yes, but it's not like it's been a regular thing." She didn't look like she believed him. "Once. Once I've drunk from her, since you returned to me."

"Returned to you? When did I leave you?"

"It was technically *I* who left. The weekend that you went home, for your birthday. I told you that I wouldn't see you again. I didn't want you to be hurt. I didn't want to ruin your life. I didn't think for a moment that you would return to me. Not after *that.* And it was only after that, when you returned to me that I truly allowed myself to believe that we could be together."

"How many times? You drank from her once *since* my birthday. How many times before that?"

She sat looking at him directly, trying to read his eyes. He would never use false words to lie to her anyway. "You came to me, asking that I protect Ben from her, do you remember? I drank from her then. I found her and I asked that she leave Ben alone. She wouldn't listen. We argued and then... I drank from her. I drained her. Drank until she lost consciousness, and left her there, in a field. That's why she wouldn't touch Ben again. It was a warning. I did it for you, to keep your friends safe."

She looked confused, as though trying to place something. "You came to see me that night, at my window."

"To tell you that your friends were safe," he told her.

"You were all... giddy and romantic." She looked ill.

"I was relieved that you wouldn't have to worry," he said.

"You were *drunk*... on *her* blood!" He opened his mouth in protest, but again she wouldn't let him speak. She looked disgusted and appalled. "She's got venom too, right? Like you. Drinking from her must give you venom and blood. That must be better than drinking from *me* ever could be," she conjectured.

"No, it's really not. Vampire blood *is* different but... it's not like that," he insisted.

"When else?" He began to shake his head. Did she really expect him to recount every instance? "Tell me!"

He gave her a level gaze. "Twice more." She only answered with expectant silence. "There was a night; I was coming to meet you at work. She was there."

"The night of our picnic, right? I knew. Ben felt her. You were out there for a long time and I kept waiting for you to come in, but you didn't. You stayed out there with *her*."

"We were only talking for most of the time… really. Then she offered me her wrist, for my thirst. 'Twas only her wrist and I never asked for it… but I did drink, some. I never meant to hurt or betray you."

"You sure as hell didn't *tell* me!" she exclaimed in disgust. He sat silent, awaiting the inevitable. He couldn't bring himself to offer the information, but he wouldn't withhold it from her. She asked. "When was the last? You said twice more, when was the other time?"

He felt almost ill in remembering. "When I sent you away. You went home for your birthday and I told you not to come back, so that I wouldn't hurt you. She came to me then, and I didn't turn her away. I drank from her that night as well."

Felicity stared at him long and hard. Surely, the guilt and loathing he felt for his actions that night were written upon his face. "And was that… *only* blood?" Her eyes were welling with tears. She knew that there was more. "You slept with her, didn't you?"

"Once." Her face seemed to crumple. "I thought I had lost you! Look at you. You are so beautiful and innocent; perfectly pure with such a loving heart. I don't deserve someone like you! All *I* could ever do is ruin your life. I tried to tell you, that's why I sent you away. She came to me that night and I let her. I told myself that I deserved nothing more. I was miserable to be without you and I tried to drown my sorrows in her, I did.

Do you think she's what I want? Do you think that I could be happy with someone like her? It's *you* that I love, but I can't *have* you. Not really. Not forever. I thought to resign myself to the truth. To face the fact that I am not human no matter how I may long to be, and that another monster like myself is all that *I* could ever hope to deserve. It was *not* what you might think it was... believe me, but then... then you came back. Despite the warnings, despite how I tried to turn you away for your own good, you came back to me. You were like a breath of fresh air being offered when I was drowning in sorrow. How could I not breathe you in? How could I send you away to seal my fate?

I tried. I wanted to do the right thing for you, but you wouldn't let me. And God help me but I've never wanted anything more in my life than to show you my love. You came back and you let me, being with you has been happiness I never thought to know. Since that day, *never* have I touched another with impure intent. It's not as though I haven't opportunity, but it's you that I want. Don't you know that?"

There were tears streaming down her face, but as much as she looked as though she would like to come back to his arms, she held herself still and apart from him as she spoke. "Tonight. Instead of coming to the dance, you went to see her... in her hotel room. Why would you do that without telling me? And now I'm supposed to feel grateful that it was *only* blood!? Have you been spending time with her all along?"

"You're with me always! I was looking for Chris; I've checked with her, thinking that she may have seen him. I've seen her now and again but not for any indecent purpose. I taught her how to cloak, to defend herself. And now, tonight... I marked her. She asked for my protection and I granted it. I spurned her advances but I'm not going to throw her to the wolves."

Felicity turned away from him to look down at her lap. After a moment, she took her legs from the covers. She reached to the end of the bed, where the pajama pants he had left for her lay folded. She picked them up and put them on without saying a word. He kept on. "You must understand. I've only been trying to do right by everyone. I never meant to hurt you. I love you so dearly. I suppose I should have told you, but I've known all along in my heart the strength and loyalty of my love; so, I never thought it need be questioned. Felicity?"

She had stood from the bed, taken a glance about and then headed for the stairs. Now, as he called her, she stopped to look at him. Her face was streaked with tears, but she didn't seem to be crying any longer. Instead, she had a most disturbing look of confusion and almost panic upon her face. When she spoke it almost seemed that she was talking to herself, as she didn't meet his eyes. "I can't believe this. I can't believe that I should have to question you. I trust you. I trust you with my *life*." Now she did look up at him, her eyes pleading for him to make his admissions untrue, her breaths coming quick and unmeasured. "You're supposed to make me feel safe. You're my protector. My true love, my everything. I have given you *everything*. My body, my blood, I'm yours... *only* yours. And *you* are only supposed to be for *me*. Isn't that how it works?"

She took a deep gasp for breath and suddenly turned again for the stairs as if unsure what else to do. He tried to go to her, to hold her, but she wouldn't let him. She grabbed her purse from the floor by the door and began to climb the stairs as he followed. "I *am* yours. I love you, but I haven't been unfaithful; it's not the same.

I am a vampire. I can't always profess to like it much but it remains a fact. I live in a different world, with different aspects to be considered. The things I've done were for reasons that you may not be able to comprehend. You're human. I love you so, but you have to accept that a vampire must sometimes live by rules that you cannot understand."

They reached the front door and he held her arm to stop her from opening it. Before he could say anything else she asked, "Has she... ever drunk from you?"

He closed his eyes for a moment in relief that he could answer something for her without guilt. "No. Never. My blood remains my own... for a long time now. I won't share it lightly, but I *would* share it... with you," he told her truly.

He couldn't tell what she thought of that. She only stared at him blankly, although she surely understood the offer. It had always been there, but never so directly voiced. She said nothing. "Felicity please don't go. I love you. I need you."

She gazed at him quietly and he could see the love still in her eyes amidst the tears. He wouldn't lose her, not like this. She wouldn't leave him, she couldn't. She lightly pulled her arm away. She took a very deep breath and exhaled with a shudder. "I love you too, but right now, I think I need some sunshine."

She opened the door and he was forced to back away as the bright early morning sunlight filled the entryway. He barely had the chance to realize that she was actually going to leave, before she moved outside and closed the door.

Chapter 9

An offer I can't refuse

Felicity

Monday morning
Cain's house

Felicity stepped out into the cold morning air and squinted in the bright sun. She headed straight for her car, never looking back although she heard Cain reopen the door. He didn't call out after her and she hurried to the car, hoping that he wouldn't. She felt as though she were walking on ice as she padded over the cement in bare feet. It was autumn still, but winter was waiting in the wings, and up here in the mountains, it wouldn't wait for long. The warmer seasons often seemed fleeting, and winter was always quick to make its presence known and over-stay its welcome. The cold breeze blowing against her tear-wet face made the 35-degree morning feel more like 20.

Short sleeves and no coat, she didn't care. The air felt frigid in her throat as her breaths came out in little gasps of fog before her face. She jumped into her car and slammed the door, trying to cut herself off from the rest of the world. She didn't dare glance back at the house. She dug through her purse for her keys to start the engine, finally found them and started the car. She turned up the heat only to be rewarded with a blast of cold air in the face, forcing her to turn it down until the car had warmed up. The seat felt freezing on her legs through the thin pajamas.

She couldn't wait. She put the car into gear and took off for the dorm. She just wanted to get into bed, pull the covers over her head, and cry herself to sleep. She didn't want to think, to reason or try to sort out her feelings. She just wanted to sob and cry unobserved and then sleep all day, but she couldn't be lucky enough to escape turning it all over in her mind on the ride home. His words replayed over and over in her head.

Cain. She kept trying to stare at the road and not hear his voice in her ears. He made his love for her sound so grand and unfailing like something from an epic romance. He made everything he ever did sound so reasonable and understandable, as though she shouldn't be able to help but feel sympathetic and forgiving.

His eyes brimming with tears and his voice trembling to melt her heart; everything he said always made her feel as though he were the wise and mature one and she was unreasonable and cruel not to understand. Like he endured such torture in his daily life that she should feel instant leniency towards anything that would be viewed as a transgression if committed by someone else. As though *she* should be comforting *him* with an arm over his shoulder saying 'of course, perfectly understandable, who could blame you?'.

She'd known that she had to leave. She needed some time alone, to get some perspective. If she had stayed, she only would have forgiven him; how could she not? He was so gentle, loving, charming and persuasive. She would have stayed in his bed and wept in his arms until she'd fallen asleep. After that, things would go on as if no wrong had been done. He obviously felt justified in his actions, even if he wasn't entirely proud of them.

Not to say that she wouldn't *ever* forgive him. The thought of losing him was bad enough, but to give him up before she had to, seemed unbearable, but she had a right to be angry, didn't she? She knew she did, and she wasn't going to let things be smoothed over so easily.

He hadn't told her! To know that he had been with Sindy was just sickening. He'd had sex with her only a day or so before Felicity herself had come to him! To know that that haughty, condescending whore had put her hands on Cain's body... That after all of the nights that he and Felicity had spent together dancing and talking and kissing goodnight, building anticipation for the precious moment of their union, he'd gone and fulfilled his desires first by fornicating with that witch!

Felicity understood that he hadn't really thought to see her again. The explanations he gave of his rationale about his misery over losing her and trying to see himself as deserving only another vampire were heartbreaking and believable, but it didn't make it any easier to accept. Just because she could almost understand why he'd done it, didn't mean that she thought he *should* have done it.

Even putting the fact that they'd had sex aside, (albeit with great difficulty), he had drunk Sindy's blood... four times, and he had never told her! She knew about the experience of *drinking* blood, only from what he himself had told her, but judging by the feelings she experienced when being drunk from, she could imagine what it might be like for him. He had called drinking 'the ultimate experience'.

Vampire blood had to be different from human blood. He had even admitted that it was. No matter what kind of rational, logical and unincriminating reasons he might have for drinking from Sindy, he had to have *enjoyed* it. She knew that he must have. To do that without telling her just seemed wrong.

Could things even go back to the way that they were? The thought of him with Sindy made Felicity positively ill. To picture Sindy clinging to him as he penetrated her throat with his fangs and made her feel things that Felicity tried to imagine were only for herself, was crushing. To know that he'd had sex with her as well... how could drinking from her *not* have brought back that memory for him? Just because he didn't repeat the act, should she feel vindicated that he was hers? He had still done things behind her back. Even if sex and blood sharing weren't the same, they *felt* the same to her. It was unacceptable. She'd always thought that Sindy'd had some nerve to act so damn possessive over him, when she shouldn't have any grounds for such an attitude. Now she knew why.

Felicity parked the car in the dorm lot and got out to race across the dew-wet lawn. A few girls were emerging for breakfast before classes. They gave her wide clearance and odd looks as they turned to snicker and whisper to each other as she passed. Crying, barefoot, dressed only in men's pajamas and clutching a dark blue velvet purse; Felicity knew that she must have been quite the odd sight. 'Who cares; what the hell do they know about real life anyway?'

Felicity took the stairs two at a time and practically flew into her room, closing the door behind her. She collapsed onto her bed gasping as though she'd run the whole distance home. She wanted to cry, but her tears seemed to have deserted her now and all she could feel was a growing, burning ball of anger in the pit of her stomach.

He'd lied to her! Not with words but with actions. He knew that she believed herself to be the only one to take physical liberties with him. He may try to explain his deeds as innocent, unhurtful and as having practical purpose, but the plain truth was that he had deceived her. She didn't have to be a vampire to know that he must have enjoyed drinking from Sindy. That's why he hadn't told her.

If he was that hell bent on protecting Sindy with his mark, he could have found another way. He could have explained it to Felicity. She wasn't totally heartless. Maybe she could have accepted it if he'd drunk from Sindy's wrist, in Felicity's presence, briefly and only for marking. That would be a truly platonic and wholesome act, but no, he had kissed Felicity goodbye and then snuck off to Sindy's hotel room so that he could enjoy her blood in private.

Cain. She could smell him. It was the pajamas. They smelled faintly of his aftershave. Roughly, she raised herself from the bed and tore the t-shirt off over her head. She didn't want him here, not even in some abstract representation. Not now.

She caught the scent of him again as the shirt came off over her head. With an almost frightening force, she felt a sudden surge of longing for him. It was like a physical need. Like being hungry. Her body *wanted* him. She quickly threw the shirt into the corner, as though it were something disgusting. "Go away Cain, I don't want you here!" She yelled, feeling creepily shaken.

She stared at it for a moment, in shock. It was only a shirt, but the smell reminded her of him and the venom in her body must recognize that somehow. Sindy had said it could be like that, hadn't she? Creepy, but apparently true. Her body was infiltrated with his venom. It was all throughout her. She'd never really thought of it as its own entity before. The idea that she was host to something that might try to control her actions was very disturbing. She'd never had cause for concern over it before. She'd never even noticed it as anything more than an interesting and pleasurable addition to her experiences with Cain.

She felt stupid for freaking out, but also leery. She stood for a minute, waiting for further evidence of unwanted urges. Nothing. He wouldn't try to *call* her would he, the way that Sindy called Ben? She shuddered remembering how upsetting it had been to be marked the first time, when she didn't understand. To feel compelled to go to him, without realizing why; the panic and anxiety, the hot flashes and chills it had caused her.

But this was different. The first time had been a big adjustment, but she'd gotten used to it and it didn't seem nearly as severe once it was understood. She'd been marked for a while now. She was accustomed to it. Her body was used to feeling him near. Usually, it was a comforting thing. Now if she felt it, she would recognize his calling. She felt confident that there was no way that she would be drawn to him against her will. He had to know that trying to summon her would only make her furious. No, he wouldn't dare.

It wasn't as though she was frightened of *him*. It wasn't even like she hated him or anything. She was just angry and she wanted the right to be angry. Let him sit there in that dark barren basement alone. She ripped the pants from her legs and after a moment's thought, she took off the stupid thong as well.

She donned new panties from her drawer and found her sheep pajamas in a pile on the floor. Good enough. She just wanted to hide under the covers, forget everything and go to sleep.

At least she probably wouldn't have to worry over having nightmares of Chris and Marcus. They were gone, and now she had what seemed to be much more disturbing fare to darken her dreams.

~~~~~~~~~~~~~~~~~~~~~~~~~~~~~~~~~~~~~

Felicity awoke to a knock at the door. For a second, while half asleep, her heart leapt with joy that it might be Cain.

Then she realized that not only was that stupid remembered happiness and not really what she wanted right now, but that there was sunlight streaming in the window. It wouldn't be him. Even if by some heroic act he had made his way here through the sunshine, she would have *felt* him. It wasn't him.

"Felicity, you in there?" It was Ben.

"Yeah, come on in." She rolled onto her back to stare up at the ceiling.

He let himself in and closed the door behind him. Dropping his stuff on the floor, he turned to face her. "Finally! I have been calling your cell phone all day."

She sat up in bed, offering him a look of apology. "Sorry. I think I turned it off."

He eyed her sheep pajamas with a smile, but didn't mention them. She suddenly realized that the thong she had worn was on the floor right next to the bed, in plain view. She desperately hoped that he wouldn't notice it. "I would've come by sooner, but I had classes. To be honest, I wasn't even sure you'd be here."

Felicity gave him a dejected sigh and lowered her eyes. "Here I am."

Ben stared at her for a moment. She knew he was wondering why she wasn't at Cain's, but she certainly wasn't going to tell him. He gestured towards the bandage on her throat. "How are you feeling?"

She almost automatically said 'fine', but then she stopped herself to give him an almost impish smile. "One," she said quietly with a little smirk.

It only took him a moment to get the reference, and then he laughed. "I can't be the only person to have asked you."

She shrugged. "Do dead people count?"

He avoided answering and sat down on the bed next to her to check out her bandage. "Was it bad?"

"Eleven stitches," she informed him.

"Ouch," he said, wincing in sympathy.

"Yeah," she agreed.

"I hope you don't mind, but I didn't think that you were going to feel like going in to work tonight, so I asked Lucy to cover your shift."

Felicity sat up a little straighter, slightly alarmed. "Am I on tonight?"

"3 to 9," he told her.

"What time is it now?" she asked worriedly.

"Almost 4:00," he admitted with a smile.

"Oh. Oops."

Ben laughed. "Don't worry about it."

"Thanks." She suddenly realized that if it was 4:00, Ben should be there now too. He always worked on Mondays. "Aren't *you* closing tonight?"

"Na, I never work on Halloween," he explained.

"Oh yeah, I forgot that was today," she said.

Ben stood up quickly and went to the door as though remembering something. He grabbed an orange plastic shopping bag from the floor. It had a picture of a ghost on it and read 'trick or treat' across the top. He brought it to her on the bed and sat back down next to her. "I brought you some candy."

She opened the bag to look at the varied assortment of loose, bite-size candy bars. She looked back up at him with an arched eyebrow. "You went trick-or-treating?"

Ben laughed, shaking his head. "No, I *bought* it. You know, to give to kids. Somebody's got to give the little rug rats their sugar rush. My dad's been out of town, besides, kids are cute. I like to see their costumes."

Felicity smiled. "Yeah, me too."

"I didn't know what you like, so I gave you a few of everything."

She glanced in the bag again. "That's an awful lot of candy."

"Yeah," he said with a little laugh. "There's a slight possibility that I may have gone overboard."

"Thanks," she said with a chuckle.

"I'm just glad you're okay."

"Thanks to *you*. And to think that all this time I've only known your 'mild mannered alter ego'," she added with a grin.

Ben shrugged. "Too bad I wasn't a few minutes sooner," he said quietly.

"Good thing you weren't a few minutes later." She gazed at him in all seriousness. "Thank you," she said sincerely. He just shrugged and smiled at her. After a few minutes, she broke eye contact to pull out a candy bar from the bag. She came out with a Butterfinger. "Want one?"

"No thanks," he said.

"So, what did Ashley think of everything?" she asked, unwrapping her candy bar and taking a bite.

Ben sighed, shaking his head. "I had to *tell* her."

"Well, yeah," she agreed.

"She…didn't really believe me."

"What?! How could she not? She saw at least two of them dusted like right in front of her!"

"Yeah well, she's kind of holding to the theory that it's more something that was done *to* them, than the possibility that they were actually vampires," he explained.

Felicity's mouth opened in disbelief. "What could you possibly do to someone to make them explode into ashes? That is like the stupidest thing that I have ever heard! Then again, look at who we're dealing with." Just after she said it, she realized that she was insulting Ben's *girlfriend*. She looked up at him in embarrassment. "Sorry." Ben just lowered his eyes and slightly shook his head. She could have sworn there was a hint of a smile playing about his lips. "But you tried to convince her, right? So, if Ashley doesn't believe you, then what does she think... that you're crazy?"

"No! I mean, well... I don't think so. She still wants to see me tonight," he admitted.

Felicity looked back down at the bed. She felt bad to have said anything derogatory about Ashley, and couldn't help but wonder just how serious Ben really could feel about her. "Where are you going?" she asked quietly.

"Well, my annual tradition is to hang out at Tommy's and make jokes about Allie's tail, but... Ashley doesn't want to go. In fact, I think she's kind of scared of Allie now... which is really pretty funny when you think about it," he said with a laugh. "I'll probably just take her over to Venus. They've got a Halloween thing going on. She wants to wear her costume again."

Felicity dropped her eyes with a little smile. "She did look really great."

Ben gave back an almost embarrassed grin. "Yeah, she did." There was an awkward silence for a moment. Felicity dug into the candy bag again for another bar. She pulled out a Snickers and looked up to find Ben gazing at her intently. "So did you," he said quietly. She tried not to be too obviously flattered and began eating her candy bar. "That dress was beautiful. Did it get ruined?"

She took a bite and shrugged. "It was just a dress."

Ben smiled. "Yeah." They just sat there for a moment as she finished her candy bar. Then Ben took a deep breath and sighed. "Well, I'd better get home before dark or I'm going to have about five pounds of candy left." He stood from the bed with a laugh. "Don't forget to call Mr. Penten and let him know when you'll be back to work."

She nodded. "I will. Thanks for the candy."

He picked up the rest of his stuff and turned back to her from the door. "See ya."

"Bye. Thanks again… for *everything*," she said earnestly.

"Don't mention it," he replied.

~~~~~~~~~~~~~~~~~~~~~~~~~~~~~~~~

Lying on her back in bed, Felicity turned her head to observe the clocks' glowing red display of the time: 12:00 p.m. It was noon on Tuesday… wasn't that part of a song? Oh yeah, Sheryl Crow. 'All I wanna do is have some fun'; not a concept that Felicity felt all that familiar with these days. Fun seemed something long forgotten. It hadn't really been very long since she'd been blissfully happy, spending her nights with Cain; unaware of danger from Chris or deceit from her lover, but it felt like forever.

Halloween night had come and gone without event. Not long after Ben had left, she'd pulled on jeans and a sweatshirt and wandered down to the cafeteria in search of some dinner. Students were running around campus in costume, preparing for parties, acting foolish and generally having fun. She'd gotten some cold chicken and taken it back to her room.

She was up half the night. After sleeping all day, it was difficult to rest all night as well. She was used to staying awake late these days anyway. In fact, if it weren't for forced daytime attendance of her classes, she probably would have adopted a completely nocturnal schedule by now.

She'd sat up half the night trying to catch up on her homework and searching for 'feelings' of Cain. She had thought that she could almost sense him once, but it was fleeting, and slight enough to make her doubt herself. She wasn't really expecting him, and she certainly wasn't hoping for him to try to use psychic influence over her, but she was still a little disappointed not to feel any trace of him at all. As mad as she was, and even unsure whether she'd *like* to see him; shouldn't he at least *try*?

Now it was noon on Tuesday. She was skipping classes again. She had a doctor's note until Wednesday, might as well use it. She sat up in bed. What was she going to do all day though, sit here and feel sorry for herself? One of her first instincts last night had been to call Deidre. They had always been in charge of 'damage control' for each other's love lives in the past, but things were so different now. Deidre could never understand. It would be more frustrating than helpful, but who else could she talk to?

Felicity was startled by an authoritative knock on the door. Curious, she got up to answer it. She opened the door a crack, and then swung it wide upon seeing who it was. "Allie, hi," she said with some surprise.

"Get dressed. I'm taking you to lunch." Felicity just stood looking at her for a moment in slight confusion. "You *can* eat right?" Allie asked, looking at the bandage on Felicity's throat.

Felicity gave her a bemused little smile. "Yeah, I'm allowed to eat. I just thought you might be kind of busy today."

Alyson glared at her until Felicity backed up a bit to allow her into the room. Alyson stalked inside seeming in a considerably less than cheerful mood. "Yeah well, so did I; and yet here it is, another stupid bright and sunny day and I have absolutely nothing else to do. So, I'm taking you to lunch."

"Well, there's an offer I can't refuse," Felicity mumbled.

Allie gave her a look of annoyance. "Get dressed."

They ended up at the diner picking at tuna salad sandwiches, cole slaw and pickles. Felicity's original thoughts of relief that she might have an understanding ear to confide in were displaced by the fact that Alyson would barely talk to her since leaving the room.

Obviously, Allie was having her own problems, but she wasn't in the mood to share. Mattie must not have showed. Felicity felt bad for her, knowing how long she'd been waiting, but every attempt at conversation was met with a brash comment and then sulking silence. Felicity was trying not to become annoyed, but she felt in just as sour a mood as Allie, and was having a hard time being very understanding.

She took another bite of her sandwich as she watched Allie absently dismantle and destroy hers with a fork. "Allie, why did you even order that?" Alyson just shrugged. Felicity decided to try one more time to get Allie to talk. "Still no word from Mattie, huh?" she asked gently.

Allie glared up at her. "What do you think?"

"You don't have any idea where he is? He didn't tell you?"

"If I knew where he was, do you think I'd be wasting my time here?" she asked harshly. After a moment, she looked up in apology. "Sorry, but this sucks."

"Halloween was only yesterday. I'm sure he just got delayed." As she said it, Allie looked up in alarm over what kind of 'delay' Felicity might mean. She quickly corrected herself. "I mean like a regular delay. You know, like maybe his car broke down." Allie shook her head lightly and took a big gulp of soda. "Don't worry; I'm sure he'll be here soon. It's got to be difficult, only being able to travel at night and you don't know how far away he's been. He'll be here."

"Yeah well, he'd better be. I already put in for vacation. Took two whole weeks off work, starting tonight." A secret sort of little smile stole over Allie's face for a moment. "There's this place...a little bed and breakfast in the Poconos. We go there sometimes, like for long weekends. It's real quiet and secluded. He loves it there. We haven't been in over a year." After a moment, she returned to looking petulant and disappointed. "He'd better get his ass back here soon, because I made reservations."

She looked up at Felicity again while viciously stabbing her fork into the coleslaw before continuing. "I told Cain that Arif and his goons better stay the fuck away from him too.

He'd better give them the message, because if I find out they've kept him away from me, I swear I'll stake 'em all."

Felicity watched as the anger drained from Allie's face after a moment and she seemed to shake it off. She took a deep breath and looked back to Felicity with new concern. "Speaking of Cain, enough about my shit and on to *your* problem." Felicity took another sip of her diet Coke, hiding her face momentarily behind the glass. Allie just stared at her until she put it down again. "I saw Cain last night."

Felicity stared into her glass. "Yeah?" she asked sullenly.

"What did you do to that guy?!" Allie asked.

"*I* didn't do anything!" Felicity blurted in a huff.

"Well, somethin's goin' on, because he just holed up at a table in the back right after sunset and drank all night. He didn't even go for coffee first."

"Big deal," Felicity muttered.

"Seven bottles Felicity. When I brought him the first drink, he tells me to hold the sugar water and just bring the rum. He drank seven bottles straight. Well four bottles of rum, then we ran out and I had to switch him to scotch for the last three.

He wouldn't talk to me hardly at all. I told him to keep Arif away from Mattie and he just handed me a pile of money and said he'd do anything I wanted tomorrow, but tonight he just wanted to be left alone with the rum. What happened? It can't be over *that*," she said, pointing at Felicity's bandaged throat.

"No." Felicity took a deep breath and looked Allie in the eye. "He's been drinking."

"Well duh, I just told you," Allie replied.

"*Blood* Allie," Felicity clarified.

"Oh. Well, no kidding. He's a vampire, that's what they do."

"From *Sindy*," Felicity added.

"...Oh... So, I guess she wasn't just blowin' smoke, huh?"

"Apparently not," Felicity agreed.

They sat in silence for a moment as Felicity tried to take another bite of her sandwich. She put it back down and pushed it away instead. It just didn't seem very appetizing anymore. Allie seemed to be having trouble deciding what to say. Finally, she asked, "Are you sure? 'Cause that just really doesn't seem like something he would do."

"Yes. I'm sure," she said with insulted annoyance. "He drank from her the night of the dance, Allie. That very night! I'm sitting at the dance wishing he was there, and he's off sucking on that whore!"

Allie looked surprised and almost amused at Felicity's choice of words, which only pissed her off more. She glared at Alyson who quickly dropped her small smile. "Take it easy. He actually told you that?"

"Not in those *exact* words, but yes," Felicity told her.

It was plain to read on Alyson's face that she thought Cain must be a fool to have told her. "What else did he say? I mean, he must have given you some kind of an explanation."

"Of course he did. He was only marking her, you know, for protection from the others. So even though it was in her hotel room, behind my back, that makes it okay right?" Allie actually seemed to be thinking it over. "It's such a load of crap! It's not like that was even the first time!"

"How many times did he do it?" Alyson asked her.

Felicity glared at her in annoyance that she should even have to ask. "More than once, *does it matter?*"

Allie leaned forward a little to put her hand on Felicity's arm. "I'm just trying to understand. It's hard to picture *Cain* doing something like that. I'm sure he never meant to hurt you."

"Sure, take his side. Hey, you saw him before the dance too, didn't you?" Felicity asked.

"Well yeah, but *I* only gave him a haircut, I swear. And I told you about it, so it's not like I'm hiding anything. Well, I told you I talked to him, but I didn't tell you about the haircut, but only 'cause I thought it'd be a cool surprise."

Felicity rolled her eyes. "I'm not accusing you of anything, but did he say anything to you?"

"What, you mean like 'Bye, I'm gonna go suck Sindy's blood now'? No sorry, he didn't mention it. He was after Chris, that's all I know," Allie insisted.

"Yeah, until he just happened to bump into Sindy at her hotel room all the way in Oxford? He went there on purpose," Felicity said accusingly.

"Chris was after her too. Maybe he thought Chris'd be there. You know that he couldn't have been there long, 'cause then Sindy showed up at the dance with us," Allie pointed out.

"Yeah, all haughty and full of herself knowin' that Cain had just drunk from her." Felicity stared at the table with a scowl on her face, thinking of the attitude and possessiveness over Cain that Sindy had displayed while talking to she and Allie at the dance. At least Cain hadn't really paid her much attention once he actually got there.

Well, except for the fact that while Felicity was being rescued by Ben from having her throat slit, Cain was busy attending to Sindy who must have collapsed from feeling Chris' death. Good, she hoped it hurt…a lot.

"He's a vampire Felicity. Maybe he had a good reason for needing her blood. You don't know what kind of stuff goes on for them. Mattie's always been pretty solitary, but I think the ones that live in groups have all kinds of social rules and stuff. I think it's kind of like being part of a wolf pack. The Alpha male needs to prove dominance to keep control and stuff," Allie explained.

Felicity had met her gaze as Allie spoke and was staring at her with ever increasing disbelief and disgust. "I can't believe that you are sitting here trying to defend him! *You* know what it's like to get bit. How would you feel if you found out *Mattie* was drinking from some other girl?"

Alyson gave her a steady look before answering. "He prob'ly does Felicity. I don't *ask* him about it or nothin', but I wouldn't be surprised. I mean let's face it, he's a vampire. I'd like to think that he'd rather always take from me, but I'm not going to delude myself into thinking that he's never even tried it from someone else."

Felicity ran her hands through her hair in aggravated frustration. "It's not the same anyway. It's not like you're together all the time, besides, I haven't even told you the worst part. He slept with her! Try to tell me how *that* was for practical purposes!"

"That night?!" Allie asked in disbelief.

"No, not that night." Felicity admitted, "It was a while ago, but still…"

"Was it after you guys were together?" Allie asked.

"Yes." She said it forcefully, but her conscience wouldn't let her leave the statement stand. "Well, we had kind of broken up, but it was only for the weekend, and I never really believed him that we wouldn't see each other again.

I guess technically he did break up with me first, but it's a stupid technicality! He still had sex with her... like right after I left!" At first, Allie did seem to sympathize, but after a moment, a little smile crept over her face. "What the hell are you smiling at?" Felicity demanded.

"I'm sorry, but... did you ever watch 'Friends'?" Felicity stared at her in uncomprehending annoyance. "Ross and Rachel? 'We were on a break!' I'm sorry, never mind. Not really all that funny."

"Allie, you are supposed to be 'the supportive friend' here. You're not helping! You're supposed to sympathize and tell me that Cain is a jerk. Get mad and offer to stake him or something."

Allie tried not to smile as she raised an eyebrow. "You want me to *stake* him?" she asked in amusement.

Felicity crossed her arms and sat back in a huff. "No, but it's the thought that counts," she mumbled.

"Look, I'm sorry. I guess I'm just kind of jaded 'cause I've been out with *lots* of guys and they're *all* jerks. Do you realize how very few decent people there are in this world? It's really depressing.

But Cain *is* a good guy. It sucks that he slept with her, and I can't tell you to forgive him for that. It was a shitty thing to do... but everybody fucks up once in awhile.

241

As far as drinking from her goes, I can't really tell you what to think about that either. I don't really see it like you do… but that doesn't matter, 'cause it's not me.

I guess what you really have to decide is where you want things to go from here. I mean honestly. Are you in it for the long haul, or are you just having a good time? 'Cause if it's not a long-term thing… then you're gonna have to let him look elsewhere eventually. What do you expect?"

Felicity tried not to feel betrayed, but Allie's words reminded her unkindly of the things Sindy herself had said that night at the dance. Alyson was a bit kinder about it, but the concept was the same; 'step up or step out'. What *did* she expect from him? Total devotion, when she wasn't prepared to offer it in return?

No. It's not the same. Just because she wasn't willing to give him eternity shouldn't mean that he couldn't at least give her total devotion for the time that they *were* together. What he had done was wrong. She knew it and she wouldn't let herself be talked into believing that her own narrow mindedness was to blame.

She sat quietly for a moment, trying not to let her eyes fill with tears. "I expected him to be honest with me…entirely. He had to have known how I would feel. Even if we can't last forever, shouldn't he be only with *me* when he's with me? It's *after* he leaves that life goes on. It shouldn't be going on behind my back."

Allie let that soak in a moment. Then she looked sorry and severely chastened for trying to defend him. "You're right." Allie took a deep breath and sighed. "He's a jerk. You want me to stake him?" she asked quietly.

Felicity rolled her eyes. "No."

"I could you know. I'm tougher than I look," Allie assured her.

"What do I do now?" Felicity asked dejectedly.

"What do you want?" Felicity kind of shrugged, deep in thought. "Do you want to go back to him?" Allie asked.

She looked up at Allie in angry determination. "No." Allie seemed very surprised. "I want *him* to come back to me, begging, on his hands and knees."

Allie smiled. "*Then* do you want to go back to him?"

"No. Then I turn him away because he should suffer more first." Alyson laughed as Felicity described what *should* happen. "But he can't live without me. He begs for my forgiveness like every night. And he *doesn't* give up. And he *doesn't* go back to *her*. Oh my God Allie! What if he's with her right now?"

"Relax, he's not," Allie assured her.

"How do you know?" Felicity asked.

"Because it's broad daylight," Allie pointed out.

"So? That doesn't mean anything. She could have been waiting for him when he got home this morning."

"Felicity, let's not get crazy here. He's sitting home alone and depressed just like he should be…with a hangover."

"Vampires don't even get hangovers. How's that for injustice?" Felicity grumped.

"Oh yeah." After a minute, Allie looked back up at her thoughtfully. "So, the ball's in his court?"

"I guess. It's not like I never want to see him again, but he's got to know that what he did was *not* okay. I want him to come back; it just shouldn't be so easy. I can't believe he didn't even *try* to come and talk to me last night."

"He probably just figured that you needed some space. At least you know that he wasn't out havin' a 'happy time'."

"None of us seems very happy these days."

"I don't know about that. Ben seems to be getting along okay. He didn't show up at Tommy's last night. He *never* misses Halloween. I figure he must have been over at 'Jeannie's' getting wishes granted or somethin'."

Felicity laughed. "They went to Venus."

Alyson looked up in surprise. "You talked to him?"

"Yeah, he stopped by yesterday," Felicity told her.

"That's just great," Allie muttered sarcastically.

"Why, what's the matter?" Felicity asked.

"That means it's only *me*. He's totally avoiding me, Felicity. I thought that if I tried to make him face the fact that I'm not gonna give up on Mattie, eventually he'd just accept it, but instead he's being stupid and stubborn and he's hardly even talking to me anymore. I'm kinda runnin' out of time here you know? Once Mattie shows up, I can't be playin' these stupid games. Ben's just gonna have to deal, like it or not. Why won't he understand?

He's my best friend. Does he really think he can make me choose…'Mattie or him', like a friendship ultimatum? I can't do that, it's just not fair! I think that stupid bimbo girlfriend of his must be brainwashing him against me."

Felicity couldn't help but laugh. "I don't think so. He's just being stupid all on his own. He wouldn't let Ashley push him that far. In fact, and this ought to give you a laugh, Ashley's kind of scared of you now."

"What?"

"Yeah, 'cause she saw you dust that vamp. In fact, she's so stupid that she won't even believe Ben that they were really vampires. She just thinks you put some kind of whammy on the guy. Even Ben thinks it's pretty funny."

"She is such a moron. How can he stand her?"

"I don't know, but you'd better try and talk to him again before Mattie gets here. In fact, he's the one you should be having lunch with, not me. Go find him. You know his schedule; wait outside his class or something. He'll come around; he has to. I know he cares about you enough not to let this stay between you. He's just stubborn."

"Yeah. Stubborn he is, but I didn't think he'd hold out this long. You're right; I should go talk to him. Ashley can't have turned his brain entirely to mush. He'll come to his senses, right?"

"I hope so. Go ahead. I got this," Felicity said, waving her hand over the table to include her half-eaten sandwich and Allie's mutilated mess. Allie thanked her, dropped some money on the table, and rushed off to find Ben.

Felicity sat back and sighed, wishing that her problem could be so easily solved. She could go and talk to Cain, but what would she even say? What did she want? She had no idea. She wanted to know that he desired no one but her. She wanted him to love her like he would never love another… and then what did she want him to do? Leave?

He wanted her to stay with him. He'd even offered it, his blood. What he had done behind her back had hurt her, of that there was no doubt, but he *did* love her. She knew that he did. He wished that they could be together, just the two of them, forever. If she went to him… If she asked him to be true to her… If she asked that he pledge unflinching faithfulness and loyalty to her, he would. She knew that he would. He loved her.

He was sorry to have hurt her and she knew that she would forgive him. She had just needed some space, but how much space did she want? Not enough to make him think that she had decided to go on without him. She couldn't lose him like this, it was all wrong. To be angry and wounded and not fix it was unthinkable. She wouldn't leave him like this, she couldn't. Could she even leave him at all?

She had told herself all along that she would, when the time came, but that had always seemed to be something in the far distant future, not a prospect to face now, but why should he stay? He had come to deal with other vampires. Chris and Luke were gone, Marcus was gone. Obviously, he and Sindy had come to some sort of understanding, so he really had no reason to stay from that perspective.

Sindy. What would *she* do when Cain left? Go back to her old ways and start causing havoc again? Doubtful; she valued Cain's opinion of her too highly. Felicity knew just what she would do, she would follow Cain. Why not? With Felicity out of the way there was nothing to stop her from seducing Cain for herself. She'd done it once, why shouldn't she try for him again?

Cain would have no further reason to reject her advances. Felicity would be some distant memory of a 'human' that he had dallied with for a short while. Hardly anyone of great note in his amazing life. And Felicity herself would be here, left to carry on her mundane existence. To concentrate on school, spend her free time at work and go home for weekends with her family.

Unless…

What would it be like, to be with him… forever? What kind of life would that be? She tried to imagine.

Cain. Handsome, strong, confident, kind, gentle, and adoring. Spending all of his time with her, loving and laughing. They could make each other so happy.

Hardly ever seeing her family, if at all. No sunlight. No career. No children of her own…

No school. No job. No responsibilities. Never worrying for money. They could go anywhere, do anything; travel and explore the world together.

No heartbeat. No reflection. Hiding her true self from the world.

No aging. No disease.

No food, only… blood.

Felicity thought back to the times she had let him drink from her, in his bed. She never would have admitted it to herself before, but now she could almost understand how he could get so caught up in that, how someone could *desire* blood. It was still an imperfect understanding, but somehow it just didn't seem as repulsive as it once had.

He loved her. She loved him. Allie had made it all seem so simple that night at the dance. *Was* it that simple? Aside from the whole prospect of immortality and freedom, they could finally just be happy, together. The decision was in her hands to walk away, or to be with someone she loved, forever. To be together always, what more did she want?

Felicity was startled from her thoughts by the waitress. She approached the table with some trepidation, eyeing the scattered remains of their lunch. She gave Felicity an odd look. "Do you want something else?"

"No, I don't."

Chapter 10

Until we meet again

Cain

Tommy's Place
Midnight, Tuesday

Cain sat staring out into the gloomy bar and tried to drown out the thoughts in his head with another swig of rum. How had things turned out this way? Perhaps he should have been more honest with Felicity from the start, although he'd never really sought to deceive her. He'd never meant to hurt her or be untrue. Once he'd realized that she needed to know about his encounters with Sindy, he had tried to speak the truth in as gentle a manner as possible. He wouldn't try to hide anything from Felicity, but it had hurt her. He knew how she felt about him. He felt the same about her, but he was the first person that she had so completely given her heart to. The fact that he had shared an intimate experience with another was something she could not accept.

Knowing that he had had sex with Sindy was surely a devastating blow to Felicity. In truth, he probably felt almost as bad about it as she did, but he *had* sent Felicity away never to return before it happened. He had tried to convey to Felicity that it truly was an act of self-depreciation more than any sort of illicit reward. He hoped that somehow, she could understand and forgive him that, but as much as the sex did disturb her, that did not even seem her main concern. It was the intimacies of blood sharing that seemed to turn her ire most. Something that Cain knew she could not understand, but he himself did not even really see as a trespass.

If he were to be completely honest with himself, then yes, he had known that she would probably not approve, but he had spoken truly when he had told her that *he* knew all along in his heart that his love for Felicity was strong enough not to be swayed by such things. The blood was an entirely separate matter.

He tried to see things from her perspective, to find an analogy that would help him to understand how she must feel, but the truth was, there was nothing that he could think of that would be the same. She could not drink from another, she was human. Even if she could, he wouldn't be hurt by it. It was not the same as infidelity in a relationship, although she seemed to think that it was.

Cain had never lived as a part of a large group of vampires the way that Sindy and Arif did, but he had lived with a select few at different times in his life. When he had shared relationships with other vampires in the past, sharing blood was a natural thing; with ones' lover, and with other vampires one was close with as well. It was not done lightly, or with someone that you did not care for, but it was not the exclusive act that Felicity seemed to think it should be. It was a tie to another, meaning that you were allies, friends, family. A blood tie was a serious thing but not an exclusive endeavor by any means.

Felicity could not understand all of the implications and meanings assigned to drinking from someone. Cain wasn't even sure if he did, but it was undoubtedly more than just the physical taking of blood, especially between two vampires. He had drunk from Sindy not only to mark her, but as a connection for her. Instinct played more of a role in the existences of some than others. Whether it was vampire instinct or human loneliness that drove Sindy to crave his mark, he did believe that she felt incomplete in being alone. It was a basic inherent need to feel a part of a group or family for some. That was most likely the reason that lesser vampires subjected themselves to occupying a lower rank in a social structure such as the type that Arif enforced. They could not stand to exist alone. They would rather give up their freedom to obey an elder, than be without family, purpose and security.

The intricacies of blood sharing were complex and almost unexplainable. It was not something that he felt Felicity would even try to understand, so he hadn't tried to defend himself with explanations. Perhaps he really had been in the wrong not to tell her anyway, but he did believe for himself that he'd had no impure motives. He really did love Felicity enough not to want to endanger her fragile heart, but some things were driven by his vampire nature and that was a command difficult to ignore. Even apart from instinct, his human nature softened his heart to Sindy at times as well. Was that wrong, to feel for another if it was not sexual in nature? Should he have left Sindy to deal with her own insecurities, knowing that Felicity would not understand?

It was beyond debate, it was done. She'd felt betrayed, and had left him. This was not the way that he had wanted things to end. Such an abrupt and unpleasant parting, but that was not the worst part. The awful truth of it was that although she probably wanted him to, he really should *not* go looking to smooth things over. As unforeseen and painful as the other morning had been, it was a catalyst for something that he really should have been working up the nerve to do all along. He should leave her. She showed no signs of desiring a life like his and he really had no place in hers. Staying for much longer would only make things that much harder. He should leave now, while she was angry with him. It would probably be easier on her that way.

She really was a creature different than he. He could not fit entirely into her human world without great obstacles to overcome, and she obviously could not handle being with him if he were going to continue to deal with other vampires. Each of their worlds had social complexities that the other could not fully adapt to. Such convoluted thoughts were too much for him now. His attempt to get drunk enough to become blissfully unaware of the situation was only being rewarded with a slight dizziness and the onset of a pounding headache.

He looked up again to survey the crowd around him. Young adults drinking, laughing and appraising each other's value as potential mates. Why does everyone have to assign such meaning to everything? Why can't things just be bloody simple for a change? Why can't one just do what *feels* right without worry for what *is* right by social and moral standards? He knew it was the vampire within him speaking now. Whispering in his ear to be the beast and not the man. Such a strange breed vampires were. Not man, not animal, but something with attributes of each. The instincts and desires of an animal with the mind and nagging conscience of a man. Could something so at war with itself, really have been *meant* to be? Enough philosophy. More rum.

As he drank, his eyes inadvertently tried to focus on a form moving towards him, although his mind was trying to ignore all else in the bar but the glass in his hand. The figure stopped before him and would not be ignored. He put down the glass to make himself look up and acknowledge the face. Alyson. He watched silently as she stood there appraising his state and the table before him. Three bottles of rum, two empty, one still half-full. You'd think it would be taking better effect by now. She smirked at him with her arms crossed before her. "I see you've got another full evening planned."

He gave her a weary smile. "They told me you weren't working."

She sighed. "I'm not, but I couldn't stand to sit home anymore. I left a note on the door." She eyed him for another moment and then gestured to the bottles on the table. "So, what's with the stockpile?"

He spoke with a measured, depressive air, as though it were exhaustive to have to explain himself. "No table service tonight. They said you weren't working and that I would have to go to the bar. I don't like having to get up and go to the bar. It inhibits my rate of consumption and interferes with the pathetic attempt I am making to get sodden drunk." Allie laughed at him. He found the very slight fog that had been hovering over his mind was clearing already. Very annoying. "It's not funny. This stupid body of mine nullifies the alcohol so fast that a good stupor is damn near impossible to achieve."

"Well, you're gonna need more than that," she said with another gesture towards his bottles.

"That's all they'd let me buy, said I had to leave some for everyone else. Your boss is very annoying. He said if I wanted more, I should visit a liquor store."

Allie pulled a chair over from the table opposite and sat down on it backwards with a laugh. "Man, you're even worse off tonight than I am."

He eyed her quizzically. "What's *your* problem?" Allie gave him a pointed look, as though he shouldn't be so rude as to make her say it. Of course, he should have realized... Mattie. "Oh. Well at least yours is easily remedied."

She shrugged, with grudging acceptance. "So's yours. She wants you to go to her."

He let out a resigned sigh and answered her quietly. "I know."

"So why are you sitting here?"

He took another large gulp of rum from his glass. "I am trying to drink up the nerve to leave."

She looked at him curiously. "The bar?"

"Town," he clarified.

She didn't seem to take to that well. Neither did he really, hence the rum. "Why do you want to leave?"

"I don't *want* to leave, I have to. It's no good, my being here."

She looked annoyed, although he couldn't imagine why. "Not good enough for who?"

Who did she think, him? "Her."

Alyson leaned down to drag his gaze from the glass before him and make him meet her eyes. "Do you love her?"

"Of course, I do," Cain insisted.

"Enough to make it only her?" Allie asked.

He drained his glass. Why was she even asking? It was beside the point. "Yes."

"You sure about that?" she asked with an arched brow.

He gave her an exasperated look and refilled his glass from the bottle. "Devotion is not the problem, believe me."

She nodded and smiled in acceptance. "So… You want her, she wants you… What's the problem?"

He drank almost the entire glass before answering her. Finally, he looked back up to her and put it simply. "She wants *me*, not *it*."

She looked as though she thought he was making a big deal over nothing. "*That's* the problem?"

He became annoyed. "No, that is not the problem. The problem is that I would like for that to be the problem."

She stared at him for a moment, trying to decipher what he meant. "Are you sure you're not drunk?"

He took the last swig of his drink and clunked the empty glass down onto the table. "The real problem is that I should not even offer *it*."

"Why not?" Alyson asked.

"Because, she deserves her life! She doesn't really want *this*." He raised his arms to signify his annoyingly inhuman body. "It's not fair for me to use the love she has for me to sway her towards something that she does not want. Not that I could even sway her if I wanted to. She's no desire to live in darkness and I can't say I blame her. She's a whole future ahead of her and it's not right for me to take that away."

"It's not taking something away, its giving something new, but I don't even know if that's what she wants. I don't think *she* even knows what she wants, but you can't just leave, not like this."

He buried his face in his hands for a moment. "You're right, I can't. I'm not allowed to leave without telling her first, I promised."

"Good, don't." Allie told him.

Why did she have to go and make him promise? She knew how important it was to him to keep his word. That was why. It was going to be hard enough to leave, but to have to face her first… "Does a note count?"

Allie glared at him in disapproval. "No!"

Cain picked up the bottle and poured the last splash of rum into his glass. He put the empty bottle down and was about to raise the glass to his lips, but his hand froze halfway there as he broke into a broad smile. "Speaking of notes…looks like someone got yours."

Alyson's eyes went wide as she interpreted his words. She spun and stood nearly knocking over her chair to see what Cain saw. It was Mattie, at last. Their friend stood at the entrance trying to reason with the doorman, who was apparently telling him that he was not old enough to come inside. Cain smiled as he could practically feel Allie's relief. She didn't even waste another glance on Cain but began pushing patrons out of the way, as she ran to the door.

Mattie did look awfully young. No matter how long he lived, Cain had a difficult time getting used to the fact that vampires did not outwardly age. He had very few long-standing associations with others. Most he dealt with, he knew less than a year. Mattie was different, they always kept in touch. He'd known Mattie since days after his death a little over three years ago. Not a very long time, but in the life of a young living man the difference between seventeen and twenty would certainly be apparent. Cain hadn't seen Mattie in almost a year, yet of course, he had not aged outwardly at all. He'd let his light reddish blonde hair get a bit shaggier than usual. As his skin had begun to pale from lack of sun, it caused the smattering of freckles across his nose and cheeks to become a bit more apparent; but he still looked to be the same young man that Cain had come across newly turned and alone.

The doorman was just stepping away, having decided to allow him in. Mattie smiled, thanking the man, and was just turning to face the room when Allie caught him by surprise. She barreled into him, throwing her arms over his shoulders and challenging him to keep his feet. It took not a moment for Mattie to wrap his arms around her as well. He caught and held her by the waist, letting the force of her rush to him spin them around as he lightly lifted her off the floor. He then let her back down to her feet, but still held her crushingly close. He bent with his face buried in the crook between her neck and shoulder; not to bite, but only to feel her close against him and to breathe in her familiar scent. They seemed to stand there forever, just holding each other.

Not a person in the bar who had noted their embrace could help but smile. The love and relief of reunion after long separation was clearly apparent and would tug at anyone's heart. Cain smiled as well as he watched them from across the room. He too was happy and relieved that his friend had arrived safely. Not that Cain had really worried for him. Other than the misfortune that he had met on the night of his death, Mattie usually had a knack for keeping out of trouble. Mattie was the sort to get along well with people wherever he might go. He usually kept to himself, but he was respectful and polite with such a friendly, easy-going smile, that he always seemed to fit right in.

Although a bit young, Mattie did look to blend rather well with the usual crowd of college students in the bar tonight. He wore the pullover tunic that Cain had bought for him in Mexico two years ago. It was striped with blue, green and black and brought some color out of Mattie's very pale blue eyes. Cain smiled remembering Mattie's insistence that they cross the border for a weekend after they finished business Cain'd had in Arizona.

Since they'd met, Cain had watched Mattie grow from a quiet and shy youth to a young man filled with confidence and inner strength. The first year had been hard as he mourned the loss of his natural life, but once he'd accepted his death to the mortal world, he'd begun to feel liberated; freed from responsibility and unafraid to explore and enjoy the world around him. He was still cautious to be sure, but was eager for new experiences.

Cain had indulged him with plane tickets and spending money, although rarely accompanying Mattie in his travels unless it coincided with business of his own, but of the weekend in Mexico, Mattie had insisted. Cain was glad he'd gone; it was a fond memory. Now Mattie had paired the tunic with a very faded pair of blue jeans that had a hole in one knee bordered by frayed strings, and a pair of brown leather boat shoes with no socks.

Cain was probably the only other besides Mattie himself, who could hear Alyson's mumbled words in Mattie's ear. "I was so worried about you." Mattie held Alyson back by the shoulders so that he could look at her. He ran his eyes over her face and seemed to note the new colors in her hair with a smile. She was grinning from ear to ear, although there was a telltale sparkle of tears in her eyes.

She glanced downward almost shyly for a moment as Mattie looked at her hair again and ran his fingers lightly through it. Then she met his eyes again with a bold reproach. "Don't you ever stay away from me that long again. Not ever!"

"That's a promise." He gave her a watery smile as he held back tears of his own. "God Allie, I've missed you," he whispered as he pulled her close for a kiss. It began as a crushing, desperate reunion but after a moment, Alyson threw her arms back around his neck and their kiss turned passionate, unrushed and deep, it went on and on.

Cain turned back to his glass, reminded of his own love soon to be lost. There was only a swallow of rum left. Damn. He downed it and looked up to see Mattie release Allie from their embrace. She smiled up at him adoringly, but then gave him a rough shove on the shoulder. "You said Halloween," she reprimanded, although she couldn't drop the smile for long enough to really appear disappointed in him.

"I know. I'm sorry. It took a little longer to get back than I thought," he explained.

"Where were you?" she asked.

Mattie gave her an impish little grin. "Colorado."

"Colorado! What the hell were you doing way out there?"

Mattie smiled and laughed. "Oh, it's beautiful Allie, you should see it. I got great pictures. I've been lookin' around a bit, for a good place to settle down, get a house."

Allie took a step back and gave him a very curious look. "You bought a *house*, in *Colorado*?"

Mattie grinned and shook his head. "No. Colorado's pretty, but so are a lot of places. I bought something else... a surprise." Allie just tilted her head as though trying to figure out what he could be up to. "Come on, it's outside."

Mattie was clearly excited to show her, and took her arm to lead her out, but she stopped him, remembering something. "Wait, before we go... there's a friend I should say goodbye to."

Mattie gave Allie a steady stare for a moment and then began to scan the bar, seeming a bit out of sorts. Cain could guess who he might be looking for. Cain himself was sitting down in the back and was mostly blocked from view by other people. Mattie didn't see him. "An old friend or a new friend?" he asked warily.

Allie gave him a thoughtful smile. "New friend of mine... old friend of yours."

Mattie looked around again seeming very perplexed. "Who?"

Allie took him by the hand with a smile. "You'll see. Come on."

Cain put down his glass and sat up a bit straighter at their approach. Even when Mattie's eyes first fell upon him, it took a moment for recognition. Cain was probably the last person Mattie expected for Alyson to know, and surely, he looked a bit different with the new haircut. It was almost odd to finally see the two of them together. These two friends that he had known separately and grown so fond of. They would make an interesting balance of personality, and they were obviously very much in love. Cain definitely approved. As they stopped before Cain's table, Mattie's eyes went wide with shocked surprise. "Cain?" He turned from Cain to Alyson and back a time or two as though completely bewildered.

Cain stood with a grin and took one of Mattie's hands into both of his own. "Welcome back. Always good to see you safe and sound."

Mattie finally gave him a broad smile, but still looked very confused. "What are you doing here? Were you looking for me? Is something wrong?"

"No, no." Cain laughed as he sat back down and Alyson and Mattie took seats at the table. "I'm here on my own business. I arrived back in June and spent the last five months being served drinks almost nightly by this feisty young lady here," he said with a nod and smile at Allie. She had her arm wrapped around Mattie's as though afraid to let go of him. "Wasn't 'till last month that I put her together with you though. Gave me quite the shock, I can tell you."

Mattie looked from Cain to Alyson. He still couldn't seem to believe the two were acquainted. "You really *know* him?" he asked Allie hesitantly.

She laughed. "You mean that he's a vamp? Yeah, I figured that out back in July."

Mattie was suddenly worried as he turned to Cain. "She didn't try to stake you, did she?" Cain laughed and shook his head no. "She does that sometimes. Could have been very embarrassing."

Allie gave him a little shove as Cain answered. "Not at all. She's been a very good friend," he said with a tender look at Allie. He then realized that Mattie, although smiling, might be wondering just *how* good of friends Cain and Allie had been. Cain continued very sincerely to Mattie. "You are a very lucky man, to have such a loyal and devoted young lady eagerly awaiting your return."

Mattie gave Allie an adoring smile. "I know."

"And you should not have kept her waiting," Cain added sternly.

Mattie looked properly abashed. "I know, but I'm only one night late. Pretty good considering... I had a good reason." Both Cain and Allie looked to him expectantly. Rather than answer, Mattie stood from his chair and motioned for them to do the same. "It's outside. Come see."

Cain and Alyson shared a curious glance and then followed Mattie from the bar. As Mattie held the door for her, Alyson walked out first into the moderately full parking lot. "What exactly am I supposed to be lookin' at?" she turned to ask Mattie.

He smiled and pointed over to the far side of the lot. "That." It was a very large and obviously brand-new, first-class motor home.

Alyson looked back at him in surprise. "That's yours?" Mattie just smiled and nodded. "You bought a *motor home?*"

"It's an Alpine Luxury Motor *Coach*. And technically... Cain bought it for me." He gave Cain an apologetic and hopeful look. "You know that bank account that was supposed to be for emergencies?"

Cain gave a little laugh, lightly shaking his head. "What are you going to do with that thing?"

"I'm going to live in it. It's a house on wheels, so I can live anywhere... everywhere. Isn't it great?" He looked back at Allie hopefully. "Please tell me you think it's great."

Allie smiled at his enthusiasm. "Yeah. It's great."

Mattie shook his head impatiently. "Nah... You can't tell anything from out here, wait until you see the *in*side." He took Alyson eagerly by the hand and crossed the lot to the object of his excitement. Cain followed with a little laugh at Mattie's joyful glee over the thing.

Cain followed them inside to a surprisingly spacious living area. It was appointed with rich cherry wood paneling and warm, inviting shades of green, purple and burgundy. It had a couch and recliner facing a large flat television screen. The driver's seat looked like a cozy armchair and was swiveled completely around to face the room, as was the passenger seat, which even had a fold out footrest. There was a little dinette area with a booth type table and benches, and what looked to be a full-service kitchen. Cain looked around in amazed wonder as Allie's mouth dropped open. She was obviously quite impressed. "Mattie this place rocks!"

"You like it?" he asked with a broad grin.

"It's awesome!" She walked around running her fingers over the stone kitchen countertop and testing the plushness of the cushions on the couch.

"That folds out into a bed," Mattie informed her.

"No shit? That's the bed?" Alyson asked in surprise.

Mattie smiled. "No, that's *a* bed. *The* bed is back there," he said, gesturing towards the little entryway to the back room.

Allie got up and ran past the bathroom into the bedroom, and by the sound of it, jumped onto the bed with a little scream of joy. "Oh my God, this bed is huge!"

Mattie laughed as Cain turned to face him. "There's nothing left in that bank account is there?" he asked with a resigned little smirk.

Mattie dropped his smile to look at Cain with a little anxiety. "No, not really, but I'll pay you back, I swear. At least I won't have to spend money on hotel rooms anymore."

Allie came back out to them wearing a big smile. "Wow. I totally approve, but you can hardly see out the windows."

Mattie and Cain shared a glance as Mattie answered. "Extra dark mirror tinted thermal windows. It's kind of a safety feature for someone like me."

Allie gave them both an awkward smile. "Oh yeah."

"There's really heavy curtains too. And look," Mattie moved to show them a recessed panel door that slid out and across the room behind the driver's seat. "During the day I can close off the drivers cab and make this a separate room.

That way I can hang out in here without getting sun through the windshield. Someone else could even drive if they wanted," he said with a smile at Allie.

"Very cool," she answered.

Mattie turned back to Cain, almost fearfully awaiting some sort of response. "Isn't that cool?"

Cain was staring at it in wonder. "Ingenious."

Mattie still seemed apprehensive over Cain's reaction. "It's okay right, that I bought it? You know I'll pay you back."

As if money were an issue. Cain eyed Mattie's hopeful face for a moment. "Consider it a gift," he said with a smile.

Mattie looked very relieved that he wasn't mad. How could he even think that Cain might be? Mattie never asked for much and often worked odd jobs for his own money. Cain had never denied him a request. Mattie smiled in appreciation. "Thanks. I was kinda hopin' you would say that. What do you think of it? Really?"

Cain looked around again in disbelief. He'd never been inside such a thing. He'd no idea how luxurious it could be. He'd thought a motor home to be little more than a glorified bus. "I have never seen the like. And you can actually drive this thing? Live where you please?"

Mattie nodded and smiled at Cain's wonder. "That's the idea. You like it?"

It was so endearing, the way Mattie always looked to him for approval. He often felt like a father figure to the boy. Their relationship actually reminded him a bit of the bond that he and Charles had shared when Cain was a young human of Mattie's age back in England; Cain now in the role of the older and wiser brother, guiding and sheltering him from harm. Of course, Mattie was much better behaved and far more agreeable than Cain had ever been at that age. 'Let's hope we have a happier ending as well', Cain thought to himself sadly of the relationship. He smiled to Mattie in endorsement of the purchase. "I think that it's a fine investment. Enjoy your new home. I'll still see you at the house though, right?" he asked.

"Yeah, of course."

Alyson looked at them both questioningly. "What house?"

Cain answered. "I've got a house up near Buffalo. Tenants are moving out, end of the month. I'll be staying there for a little. Mattie was originally supposed to meet me there, after his visit here of course," he added with a smile. "Well, you two don't want me hanging about all night. So, I'm going to take my leave," he said, turning for the door.

Allie grabbed his arm and stopped him in a commanding tone. "You can't *leave*." She looked at him sternly and he knew just what she meant.

Cain turned back to face her, but it was Mattie who looked at her with raised brows and asked, "Why not?"

Allie realized his confusion. "Oh, he can leave the *trailer*." She turned back to Cain and added in a stage whisper. "I *want* you to leave the trailer."

Cain smiled at her knowingly as Mattie corrected her. "It's not a *trailer*. It's a luxury motor coach."

"Whatever. Cain you *cannot* leave town, not without talking to her first."

"I know. I won't."

"And none of this 'quickie goodbye' crap either. You'd better stick around and really talk things out. I mean it." Cain averted his eyes as she pointed her finger at him accusingly. "Because if I come back to find her a sobbing broken mess, I'm gonna hunt you down and stake your ass! Even if I have to go all the way to Buffalo to do it!"

Cain smiled at her phrasing and then sighed and met her eyes again for a long and serious moment. "I will talk to her, but I can't tell you what'll come of it, and one way or another, I *will* be leaving." He just stared at her silently for a moment, trying not to become emotional about it all. "All I can tell you is that I *do* love her. Whatever you find her emotional state to be when next you see her, most likely mine will be the same. Good or bad and where that will be I honestly don't know. We'll just have to wait and see what unfolds."

Mattie was respectfully quiet, although he would surely question Allie later. Alyson looked as though she might cry, but seemed to accept his answer. She gave him a little smile. "So, then I guess…this is goodbye."

Cain leaned to give her a fond little kiss on the cheek and then looked into her eyes with a pause for serious reflection. "Until we meet again," he said with a loving little smile. He then looked to Mattie with sincere precaution. "Take care," he said meaningfully. Mattie gave him a solemn nod. With that, Cain did take his leave of them. Out into the cold dark lot and away into the night. At least for Alyson and Mattie, Cain felt reassured that he knew all would be well. They were lucky to have each other. If only Cain knew what his own future would hold.

Part 3

Evolution of Love

Chapter 11

You just don't understand

Felicity

Felicity's dorm room
11:30, Friday night

Felicity hadn't worked tonight. Mr. Penten had seen the bandage on her throat yesterday and told her that she should take some more time to recuperate. She really *was* fine, but she wasn't going to argue.

It had been five whole days since she had left Cain standing in the doorway to his house. Five! This was the fifth night and it was already getting late. Wasn't he even going to *try* to come and see her? After her talk with Allie, Felicity had decided that although she wouldn't rush to seek Cain out, she would certainly be receptive to him when he came to speak to her. Why hadn't he come?

By midnight, she began to worry terribly that he wasn't ever planning to come to her at all. In fact, she suddenly had the terrible fear that perhaps he had packed up and left. She

269

quickly threw on some clothes and went out to her car. Not that she really wanted to go to him. She was still feeling stubbornly angry enough that he should have to come to her, but she just *had* to drive by his house, just to be sure he hadn't disappeared on her. He'd promised he wouldn't, but still...

At first, she was very relieved to see that his motorcycle was still there, at the top of the driveway. He would have taken it if he was going to leave town, but as she slowed in front of the house, she still could not *feel* him at all. Her mark could not be gone already, and she knew from experience that if he were in the house, he would still be in her perceptive range from the street. He wasn't there.

He must have walked somewhere. Where would he go? Only one place came to mind. Tommy's. In fact, now that she thought about it, she *had* felt a flickering tug of his presence when she'd passed the bar on the way to his house, but she'd been so intent upon reaching his house that she'd been going rather fast, and she hadn't paid the feeling proper attention. He must be at the bar. Was he planning to sit at the bar every night until she went to him? Stupid plan. She wasn't coming. He was the one who had messed everything up, he should come to her. Didn't he realize that?

She drove back, thinking that she would pass Tommy's Place and see if she could indeed again feel him there. Then she had an annoying thought. He could see her mark. Long before she felt him, he would know that she was there. In fact, it was probably already too late to hide the fact that she'd been out looking for him. His psychic range reached pretty far. She wasn't sure of its exact distance, but chances were that from the bar, he had seen her leave the dorm and head off in the direction of his house.

That made her feel kind of dumb. It rather defeated the purpose of the whole 'aloof' image she was trying to achieve. Oh well, too late now. Might as well satisfy her curiosity and see if he was even there.

Allie's. She would drive to Allie's. That way she could pass Tommy's but maybe still try to maintain the illusion that she had concerns other than Cain. What she would pretend to be doing visiting Allie in the middle of the night she didn't know, but that shouldn't matter. She'd just stop at Allie's for a few minutes and then leave. Cain probably couldn't tell if she actually went *in* anyway.

As she neared Tommy's, she slowed the car. Not too much, she didn't want to be obvious, but she couldn't just fly by. Yes, he was definitely there. Her body recognized the feel of his presence with a desirous sort of ache. 'Creepy venom' she thought with disgust. Not that she didn't desire him anyway, but it would be nice to acknowledge it on her own and not feel like some other influence was pushing her at him.

When she had first been marked and understood about the venom, it had felt rather nice. Like she always had a part of Cain with her. Such an intimate and personal connection with each other. She still wanted to see it that way, but ever since overhearing Sindy and Alyson's conversation about it, she couldn't help but feel a little creeped out.

Sindy spoke of the venom as if it were its own separate identity. Like the venom itself had its own motives and desires. That was very unsettling, but it was still something that had come from Cain, and Felicity tried her hardest to see it that way. It was venom, a drug, an inanimate substance. It's not as though anyone was consciously controlling the way she felt. Cain didn't use the kind of powers that Sindy seemed to enjoy playing with. He had never tried to summon or control her. She just felt him when he was near. It was like an addiction, a craving that her body had for more venom, like people had for something like a cigarette. Right?

She kept on to Allie's, wondering if Cain had noticed her closeness. He must have. Even if he had managed to get himself drunk, sensations like those her proximity to him caused could not possibly be ignored. She wished she could see his mark the way that he could see her, to know whether he left the bar to follow her, or what else he might be doing. She sincerely hoped he was alone.

Allie's car was parked out in the street in front of her apartment. Felicity pulled up next to it and sat there for a minute. No lights were on inside. It was after midnight. She could be sleeping, but Felicity doubted it. She knew that Allie was used to working the night shift. Most likely she just wasn't home.

Maybe Mattie *had* come, and they were out with his car. She hoped so, for Allie's sake. Nothing left to do but go back to the dorm. At least she knew that Cain was still around. Of course, the fact that he was sitting at the bar instead of coming to see her was aggravating, but it could be worse. She went back to her room, quickly passing Tommy's and feeling Cain's fleeting presence once more, and then went to sleep.

The weekend came and went. Her mom had called, but being unsure how much to say about her throat and visit to the hospital, she ended up saying nothing. The pumpkin-carving story might have gone over alright at the hospital, but her parents were certain to be a bit more discerning. She was afraid that any attempt to give a false account of things would lead her into tripping up her story and making her mom suspicious. It was easier to just pretend nothing out of the ordinary had happened. She'd said that she had to work and had a lot of studying to do, and wouldn't be home this weekend. She hoped when the time did come to go home, her injury wouldn't be too noticeable.

Monday would mean back to work, back to classes, back to routine, but still no word from Cain. How could she possibly just fall back into daily life without him? He *was* her life these days. She felt as though all of her time was spent missing him and keeping herself from going to him.

What was he waiting for? He was the one who had kept things from her and made her feel betrayed. She was emotionally hurt *and* physically injured. Wasn't he even going to try and see her, to see that she was okay? Could he possibly think that she wouldn't want him to come? She spent her evenings catching up on schoolwork and sitting around the dorm wondering what she should do.

Monday morning she had to miss algebra (not *too* disappointing) to go back to the hospital for a follow up visit, and then she returned to school for lunch. Felicity was just paying for her chef salad in the cafeteria line when she noticed Ben waving at her from a table. He was already eating, alone. Felicity had not seen Alyson since their lunch at the diner on Tuesday and this would be the first time she'd spoken to Ben since then. She wondered how things had gone, and whether Allie might join them for lunch; if Allie was even around.

As the days passed without word from her, it seemed more and more likely to Felicity that Mattie had returned and they were off spending time alone together. How romantic it seemed. Where was *her* romance? Why was Cain being so stubborn? After spending decades alone, was he *that* out of practice in being with a woman that he couldn't figure out that he should come and apologize to her? She almost wished she could send Allie to go and talk to him. Maybe Ben had seen her. She waved back to him and went to join him at his lunch table.

He greeted her as she put her tray down and got settled. "Hey, no more bandage!"

"Yeah. I got my stitches out." She tried not to be self-conscious about it. She had noticed that she'd picked up the habit of raising her hand to her throat as though to cover the spot. She purposely kept her hand on the table. "How's it look? Is it very noticeable?" she asked Ben hesitantly.

"Na. You can hardly see it. Go like that." He tilted his head back to demonstrate exposing the side of his neck. Reluctantly, she did the same. He examined her throat and then shrugged. "It's there, but it's not obvious unless you're lookin' up at the ceiling."

She tilted her head back down and kept her eyes on her lunch. She knew that it was an ugly scar. It was a few inches long, and still a bit puckered and red. The doctor had assured her that it would fade quite a bit as it healed and at least it was mostly under her chin. Hopefully no one would notice it under regular circumstances.

Ben seemed to realize that she was still uneasy about it. "Hey, I have a vampire hunting scar. Well, technically it's not from a vampire though. Allie staked me…" Felicity couldn't help but smile, recalling Allie's account of what had happened. "You're smiling? It's true, really. She did."

Felicity chuckled. "I know, she told me."

Ben gave a little nod and chuckle. "I was holding off this vamp and Allie came at him from behind, you know like to stake his heart through the back. She got him, but then she got me. Another inch or two and I could have had a real problem on my hands."

"She said you'll never let her forget it."

"It hurt!"

Felicity smiled. "So, let's see it."

Ben looked around, taken aback. *"Here?* In the middle of the cafeteria?"

Felicity smirked at his affected modesty. "I showed you mine."

Ben laughed with an arched brow and then pulled up his shirt. She leaned forward to examine his chest. Now that she was looking for it, it was obvious. Right in the center of his chest was a slightly raised and shiny stripe of scar tissue.

After a moment, Felicity leaned back and looked up at him, unimpressed. "Mine's bigger."

Ben started to laugh as he dropped his shirt. "First time I ever lost *that* contest."

"What? The thing's barely an inch long; you can hardly even see it!"

Ben began laughing hysterically as Felicity gazed at him in confusion. Finally, he tried to fill her in. "That was supposed to be a joke."

"I don't get it," Felicity replied.

Ben finished laughing and stared at her for a minute, as though trying to decide whether she really knew what he meant. "I wasn't necessarily referring to the *scar*."

Felicity went over the exchange again in her head and began to blush fiercely with comprehension as Ben smirked at her. She averted her eyes as three guys approached their table. They were clearly friends of Ben's and stopped to say hi. They had lunch trays in their hands, but the table was too small to accommodate them. They only paused on their way to sit elsewhere.

After their initial 'hey's and what's up's', one of them turned his attention to Felicity. "Who's your red friend?" he asked Ben with a smile.

Felicity had obviously failed at her attempt not to be embarrassed by Ben's comment, but finally looked up with a smile as he introduced her. "This is Felicity. 'Liss, this is Pete, Jeff and Tim."

She gave the guys a timid 'hi'. They were all older than her, probably juniors and seniors. They turned their attention back to Ben.

"Shouldn't you be in 'research mode'? Don't be slackin' on us," Pete scolded.

"Relax, I've got it," Ben answered.

"I hear Benson's tough," Jeff added.

"I got it. He's toast," Ben assured them, unconcerned. They laughed and headed off to sit at another table a bit away.

Felicity turned back to Ben quizzically. "Got what?"

"Oh, I'm heading a debate later," he said, taking a bite of his sandwich.

Felicity looked back over at the guys, who had settled at their table with much joking and laughter. Felicity looked back again at Ben, quietly eating his lunch. "How come you don't sit with them?"

Ben glanced back at the guys briefly and then went back to eating his lunch. "I see those clowns all day. Lunchtime is always reserved for... Allie."

They sat in awkward silence. Felicity refused to say anything, she only watched him expectantly. Ben was going to have to talk to her about Allie on his own. She was getting tired of trying to play the mediator and pull information out of them.

Finally, he spoke. "Have you seen her?"

"Not since Tuesday. Didn't she come see you?" she asked.

"Yeah, she cornered me outside my physics class," he said.

"And?" she prompted.

Ben looked as though he'd rather not answer. Finally, he replied grudgingly. "And, the first sentence out of her mouth had the name 'Mattie' in it. So, I told her I didn't want to hear anymore and I walked away."

"Ben! You didn't even let her talk?! She wanted to talk to you before she went away!"

Ben appeared very distressed by that statement. "Where is she going?"

"She said she was taking some time off work, to go to the Pocono's."

Ben nodded, with a relieved little laugh, as though he should have expected as much. "She does that sort of thing a lot, takes long weekends and stuff. I always used to think it was with *different* guys though. I can't believe she spent the last three years letting me think that she was so... undiscriminating."

Felicity just stared at him for a second in disbelief. As though he were in any position to judge. "Funny, you seemed to accept *that* better than you reacted to the truth."

For a moment, Ben looked as though he would become angry and argue with her. He never took his eyes off of her face, but finally he sighed and spoke quietly instead of yelling. "You just don't understand."

"You're right... I don't," she told him.

"You know, if it was just some vampire... I would still find it sickening." Felicity gave him a pointed look as he continued. "But the fact that it's *him*. I just can't stomach that."

Felicity tried to put aside the reference to a vampire relationship being 'sickening' and focus on Ben's problem with Mattie. "Can I ask you a question? How would you have felt if you had known they were seeing each other *before* what happened to Mattie?"

"That's another thing! Why didn't they just tell me? They had to hide it? What did they think I would do?" he asked.

"I don't know. I guess they just figured it would make things kind of difficult between you," she tried to explain.

"Right. And this has been so much better," he answered sarcastically.

"Ben." She gave him a look to let him know that she was in no mood for sarcasm.

"I would have been happy for them. Why would I have objected to two of my best friends being together?"

"Why *do* you?" she asked.

"Felicity, you just don't get it. He's not Mattie anymore; he's a vampire *pretending* to be Mattie. That's what they do. Vampires are the 'Great Pretenders'," he said.

Felicity sat very still. "Who told you that?"

"It's what they're made for 'Liss. That's how they survive. They pretend to be human but they're not. Mattie is dead. I went to his funeral! Just because some demon made its way into his blood and reanimated his body doesn't mean I'm going to welcome it with open arms!"

"But it's not like that! Just because he's been changed physically doesn't mean he's not still the same inside."

"How would you know?" Ben asked.

"Allie says he's the same," Felicity told him.

"Allie's being a fool!" he replied.

"Ben, this isn't 'Invasion of the Body Snatchers'! It's like a disease," she insisted.

"No, it's not! It's more like an... unexcorcisable possession." Ben just sat there for a minute as she glared over the table at him. "Felicity, *it takes over* a person. It changes them. They may have the same memories, the same mannerisms, but they develop the instincts and priorities of the new creature that they become. They *become* a vampire. Their human life is *over*. It may be more subtle in some than in others, but I refuse to be fooled. They're not the same. They're just *not*. You think you know, but you don't. You don't know any from *before*. I've seen before and after.

279

Look at Sindy. She has tortured and killed so many guys. You've seen what she's done to them... what she'd like to do to me! She is a manipulative and conniving, heartless bitch; an inhuman, unfeeling predator. Do you really believe that I would have dated someone like that?"

Felicity held his gaze sternly. "I have no great love for Sindy, *believe me*, but isn't that an awfully harsh description of someone who saved your life? If she were just some 'unfeeling predator', why would she do that? Shouldn't she have just let Marcus kill you and had a good laugh over it?"

Ben glared at her for a moment. No doubt, he was unhappy to be reminded of the incident. "Sindy marked me. I'm *hers*. She was just defending her own right to the kill."

Felicity rolled her eyes and dropped her face into her hands for a moment in exasperation. "Oh God Ben, give me a break." It was almost pointless to argue with him. He could find an answer for anything. "Anyway, the point is, the fact that *you* dated her once or twice is hardly proof of character. You had some nerve calling Allie undiscriminating, like *you've* got such high standards. You're dating *Ashley*."

Ben opened his mouth in outrage. "That is so unjustified. Ashley may not exactly be... long-term material, but she is a decent person, and at least she's *human*."

Felicity just sat there glaring at him and daring him to say something about her and Cain. He didn't. He went on. "Mattie's not. Not anymore. When those things took my friend, *he* became *it*, a vampire. It uses the knowledge of its past life to behave like a human so that it can hunt them. It's a predator... and we are the *prey*."

Ben sat there staring at her over the table, his eyes pleading for her to understand and believe. It was a very convincing argument, except for one thing. Cain. She *knew* him, better than Ben knew any vampire, she'd wager. She didn't know if Cain was any different than before he died, and he was definitely host to something other than himself in his body, but it hadn't entirely *taken him over*. He was a good man. No matter what he had done to hurt her feelings and make her angry, she just could not think of him as some ruthless animal devoid of emotion. It just wasn't true. He may be a vampire, but he was *also* a man. "Where did you learn that?" she asked Ben quietly.

He shrugged. "I'm observant... *and* I've overheard some conversations that made an awful lot of sense."

"Ben, just because something sounds good, doesn't make it true. Or haven't you learned *that* from the debate team? We are not talking about senseless animals here; we are talking about people. People suffering from... an affliction."

"An affliction that makes them kill other people. I'd say that makes them animals in my eyes."

"Don't be stupid Ben. Stop putting aside your common sense just so you can win an argument. We are not talking about those mindless vampire-zombie things here. You know that Cain isn't like that, and neither is Mattie.

They're not entirely ruled by instinct. They have free will. They have self-control. They don't even live off of *human* blood! Did you know that?"

Ben squinted his eyes at her and answered sarcastically. "Yeah, I can tell by the holes in your neck. Or is that just for special occasions?"

Felicity felt the sudden rush of tears welling up in her eyes. She felt overwhelmed and misunderstood. "That's not fair. I can't be expected to sit here and try to defend a whole race of creatures that I don't even fully understand."

"Then don't!"

"But it's *not* the way that you think it is! Cain is a good person, and so is Mattie."

Ben sat forward in alarm. "You've *met* him?"

"No, but I know how Allie feels about him and I trust her judgment of people. Why can't you just let her be happy?"

Ben held her gaze in silence for a long moment before answering. "Because I love her.

My whole life Allie has been a sister to me. You have no idea what that's been like. It sounds very touching I'm sure, but I have spent the past eighteen years watching her make bad decisions. Look at her life! You don't think I've had higher aspirations for her than 'local bar maid'? She's smart and strong and she could do so much more, but she gets so passionate about things that she loses all perspective. Trying to talk her out of something only makes it worse. She is so damn stubborn that she would fuck up her whole life just to prove a point!"

"Gee, doesn't *that* sound familiar?"

Ben ignored her. "All these years I have tried to make her recognize a bad choice *before* she makes it and she just won't see. I can't watch her ruin her life 'Liss. It hurts too much. **I** can't do it anymore."

"Well, you know what? It's not about **you!** It is *her* life. You want to give her advice; you want to let her know that you don't approve? Fine! Have your say, but then she will do what she wants, and if you love her, then you will just have to deal with it.

You know, someone once told me that when your heart truly chooses to love someone, you can see past their faults to the person inside. You may disagree with their decisions and they might do things that you disapprove of, but you don't stop loving them. If you love her then you can tell her how you feel, but then you have to let her make her own choices. And if things turn out badly…you'll be there to hold her when she cries, but that's all you can do.

This - what you're doing now is only making things worse. If you do love her, then she needs to know that. She needs to know that you're still her friend – no matter what."

Ben spent a long time staring at the table before them. The cafeteria around them seemed like nothing more than undefined white noise. Finally, he looked up to her eyes. "You're right."

Felicity was so relieved that he would actually admit it. She gave him a little smile. "I know." She reached across the table to take his hands into her own. "You're going to be a great lawyer someday… but make sure you're arguing for the right side."

He gave a little breath of a laugh and took his hands back. "This doesn't change how I feel about them." Felicity knew that he meant not only Alyson and Mattie, but all vampires in general. She looked down at the table again, wishing she had the right words to make him understand. "But I will talk to her. As soon as she gets back. I will."

"Good."

~~~~~~~~~~~~~~~~~~~~~~~~~~~~~~~~~~

It was Thursday night; this would be eleven nights without hearing from Cain. *Eleven.* She'd non-chalantly checked his whereabouts now and again. He was invariably at Tommy's. She had even thought she might have felt him approaching her now and again, but he always seemed to change his mind and leave before she actually laid eyes on him. It was maddeningly frustrating. She felt heartsick and driven almost to distraction without him. It had been well over a week, almost two! There was no way that she could spend another night just waiting for him. No way, but if she went back to him, would that be sending the message that she'd decided what he had done was okay?

One more night. She would tough out one more night alone and then tomorrow night she would go to him. Go to him and give him hell for not pursuing her that way that he should have. Was she *that* easy to ignore?

She had dinner alone and then wandered back to the dorms wondering what she could do to keep herself distracted for the evening. She went up to her room and was rather surprised to find that she was actually all caught up on her homework and had none left to do. She stared at her notebooks in disbelief for a moment. That never happened to her. She always left her assignments until the last minute. It was a bad habit but she didn't expect it to change anytime soon, no matter how good her intentions might be. The combination of having days off from class and work, and not seeing Cain had given her the time to catch up. She thought about trying to study extra... maybe even read ahead.

No. She just couldn't force herself to do it. In fact, she so despised the idea that she cleaned her room instead. That done, she sat on the edge of the bed. She still felt nothing from Cain. It was after eight o'clock already, and daylight savings time had moved sunset to an early 5:30. He certainly could have come to her by now if he'd wanted to, but there were still a lot of hours left in the night.

She found herself knocking on Karen's door.

Karen answered quickly but seemed to be in a distracted rush, and was very nicely dressed. She probably had plans to go out with Jack for the evening.

"Oh, hi Felicity. What can I do for you?" Karen asked.

"I thought I'd see if you felt like hanging out tonight. I guess you've already got plans huh?" Felicity conjectured.

Karen grabbed earrings off the dresser by the door and began to put them on as she spoke. "Actually, I do. Sorry. Jack and I are going out with Terry and Paul. Do you know them?" Felicity just shook her head and shrugged. "I'd invite you, but it's kind of a 'couples' thing."

"Yeah. That's okay, I understand," Felicity assured her.

"I don't really have time to talk. Jack's going to be here any minute, but you know, if you're looking for something to do, I think some of the girls have a T.V. movie planned," Karen said.

Felicity thanked her and Karen smiled, giving a little wave as she closed the door. Felicity looked back down the hall towards the living room. There were a bunch of girls gathered on the couch and love seats. Felicity didn't really know any of them very well though.

In fact, she had been spending so much of her time at work and with Cain, that she hadn't made many friends at all. She hadn't cared before, but she was beginning to regret it now. Oh well, at least she knew some of their names.

Hesitantly she left the hall to enter the living room. Not sure whether she should just sit down and join them, or say something first, she stood awkwardly eyeing the girls for a moment. The conversation came to a stop as they noticed her.

There were five girls in the room and all were wearing their pajamas. She knew Regina and Bridgette, who were sitting on the big couch. Both had dark hair, Regina's in a short pageboy cut, Bridgette's long and flowing in beautiful waves over her shoulders. Regina wore a pair of plaid pink and orange sleep pants with a large pink t-shirt, Bridgette had on a long pale green t-shirt style nightgown. They were both Freshmen like herself and had always been friendly to Felicity.

Penny was another freshman Felicity knew by sight but had never really spoken much to. She wore her strawberry blonde curls in childishly cute pigtails and had on red shorts, a white t-shirt with little red hearts all over it and big fuzzy pink slippers. She sat on the love seat with two girls that Felicity didn't know.

The girls she didn't know looked older, sophomores or maybe even juniors. The one perched on the arm of the sofa was a black girl with dozens of long, thin, finely done braids. She wore camouflage patterned pajama pants with an olive-green tank top. Felicity remembered seeing her once or twice before.

The other girl sitting with Penny however was much more familiar. Felicity didn't really know her either, but she knew that she was very popular. She certainly had the presence of a 'Queen Bee'. She was tall and thin with shoulder length hair that was originally dark, but was now perfectly highlighted with even streaks of blonde and a warm caramel color. She had it loosely tied back from her face with a headband made from a piece of ribbon. She wore dark blue satin pajamas with matching ballet type slippers. She'd been the one speaking when she noticed Felicity standing there.

Felicity searched for something to say. She focused on the couch with Regina and Bridgette on it. At least she knew that they knew who she was. "Hi, I heard you guys were going to watch a movie?" she began hesitantly, Bridgette smiled but it was the black girl on the other sofa who answered her.

"It's 3-P Thursday," she said, as though Felicity should know what that meant when she obviously didn't.

"3-P?" Felicity asked.

"Pizza, Popcorn, and P.J.'s. How can you have lived here since September and not know that?" the girl inquired haughtily.

Felicity gave an awkward little shrug. "I guess I've been kind of wrapped up in my own stuff."

Regina spoke up. "Anyone who doesn't have plans hangs out down here on Thursday nights. Maggie's got her bridge club, so she's never home until late. She's rents and leaves a bunch of movies for us. I guess it's her way of trying to keep us out of trouble while she's out. The pizza's all gone, but you can join us if you want."

Felicity gave her back a grateful smile as Bridgette added, "There's still time for you to go put on your p.j.'s before the second movie starts."

"Thanks." Felicity headed back upstairs to change into her sheep pajamas. It was better than sitting in her room by herself worrying about her problems with Cain. She was going to have to get some new p.j.'s though. Her sheep were getting worn just as fast as she could wash them. All of her other nightgowns were over-sized t-shirts that were far too short for her to wear downstairs. She didn't really like to have her legs covered in bed but she was too self-conscious to wear her short nightgowns in front of anyone. Oh well, the 'sheep' would have to do.

She came back down to the other girls who were now sharing two bowls of popcorn as they talked, Bridgette motioned for Felicity to come sit on the big couch. She was glad, because she had been trying to decide if she should do that or sit alone on the other empty love seat.

As she crossed the room, she couldn't help but feel as though everyone was staring at and judging her. Penny smiled and spoke as Felicity sat down. "Those pajamas are cute."

Before she could reply, the girl in blue satin added, "Yeah, *big* improvement over the ones you had on outside last Monday."

It only took a second for Felicity to make the connection. The girl in blue and the one with the braids had been among those out on the lawn when Felicity had come home from Cain's crying, the morning after the Masquerade Ball. Wonderful. Penny asked, "Oh, were you the girl outside in her pajamas on Halloween?"

Felicity felt her cheeks grow flushed and began to fiercely wish she had stayed upstairs and read her textbooks. The girl with the braids answered Penny. Felicity noticed that she wore a necklace with her name written in little diamonds. It read 'April'. "They weren't *her* pajamas; they were *men's* pajamas."

Felicity stared at the floor for a minute and then decided that it was better to answer than not, since she wasn't likely to be swallowed into a black hole the way she'd like to be. She looked up at Penny and answered. "Yep, that was me."

It was the girl in blue satin who replied. "So… rough morning, or really lame Halloween costume?"

Felicity averted her eyes and sighed. "Rough morning."

"Don't sweat it," Regina interjected, giving the girl in blue an annoyed glance. "We've all been there. Guys suck."

The girl in blue gave Regina an irritated stare. "Speak for yourself."

Bridgette interjected. "Well of course *you* wouldn't know what it's like Deborah. You've been hooked up with Bobby Gavin since like *forever*. You are so lucky."

Penny quickly turned to Deborah with an excited smile. "Oh my God Debbie, he is so hot!"

Regina answered, looking disgusted at Debbie's smug smile. "Yeah, yeah, we're all very jealous. Maybe you could get him to spring for a room once in a while, so the rest of us can get some sleep?" The girls all seemed very amazed that Regina would actually say that. Felicity was just happy to have the focus off of herself. Regina smiled at them all. "Oh, come on, somebody had to say it." She fixed Deborah with a steady look and a little grin. "You guys are shameless."

April, the girl in camo spoke up. "So what? We've all of us had a guy in our room at one time or another."

"Speak for yourself," Regina replied, mocking the tone that Deborah had used earlier. "I have a little more class than that."

April made a face at her. "Or a little less opportunity. Don't act like it's so unheard of, because if you haven't snuck a guy in, you're the only one."

Penny laughed. "*I* haven't. I'll bet Felicity hasn't either."

"Yes, she has!" Regina said gleefully. All eyes turned to Felicity as she looked over at Regina in surprise. "Ben Everheart," Regina told them with a grin.

"Oh wow, you're dating *Ben*?" Penny asked.

"No," Felicity quickly replied.

Regina continued. "Maybe not *anymore*. It was almost two months ago."

"He came over to visit but we're just friends, really," Felicity assured them.

"Too bad. Kim Davies used to date him, and boy did she have some stories to tell," Regina said with a smirk.

Felicity wasn't usually one to gossip, but couldn't help but turn to the girl and ask. "Good stories or bad stories?"

Regina grinned. "Good. A little *too* good. They couldn't be true."

Bridgette gave her a light shove on the shoulder. "Shut up." She looked over to Felicity reassuringly. "I know Ben. He's a nice guy. It's just that when it comes to dating, he's kind of known for having a short attention span."

Regina started to chuckle. "It's not the length of his attention span that Kim was telling stories about."

Bridgette stared at her in disbelief. "You are so lewd!"

April tossed a throw pillow that hit Regina in the side of the head — not all that lightly. Regina glared but it was Deborah who spoke. "Ladies please. You're being rude to our new friend. So, Felicity, if you're not dating Ben, who's pajamas *were* you wearing?"

Felicity glanced down uncomfortably at the floor. "Oh… he's not a student."

Debbie's eyes seemed to pierce through her for a moment. Then she asked, "Are you sleeping with Professor Eldrige?"

"No! No, you just don't know the guy. My… boyfriend. He's not really from around here."

Bridgette put a hand on her shoulder sympathetically as Debbie asked, "Did you break up?"

"Well…" After a second, she shrugged. The last thing she wanted was to divulge details and run the risk of getting at all emotional in front of these girls. Crying out on the lawn was more than enough of a display. "We had a fight. I don't really want to talk about it."

"That's okay," Bridgette said, and then glanced over to Debbie. "Leave her alone."

Debbie smiled and April held her hand up for a moment as though to stop things. "Wait, wait. I just *have* to ask. What happened to your throat?"

Felicity mentally assured herself that her scar wasn't really noticeable. The girl had seen her with the bandage on Halloween. "I cut myself. On accident," she quickly added. "It was a whole… unfortunate… pumpkin carving thing."

April looked at her skeptically with a raised eyebrow, as though she wanted to laugh. "You were carving pumpkins… and you accidentally stabbed yourself in the neck?"

Regina shifted in annoyance and picked up the remote for the T.V. "I'm starting the movie." Felicity gratefully broke eye contact with April and sat back on the couch. She hadn't even asked what they were watching. Truthfully, she couldn't care less.

It turned out to be a romantic comedy. As long as it wasn't a vampire film, Felicity was happy. About halfway through the movie, they ran out of popcorn. Felicity volunteered to go and make more. She was having a hard time concentrating on the story anyway. She grabbed the bowls and went into the kitchen. The box of microwave popcorn was already out. She put in the first bag and leaned back on the counter as she listened for it to be done.

Was she being stupid… not going to see Cain? Why was *he* being so stupid and not coming to see her? Fears that he was with Sindy popped into her head as they had when she had spoken to Allie at the diner. No. He wouldn't be with Sindy again. Not now. After the argument they'd had, Cain wouldn't see Sindy unless he had truly decided never to see Felicity again. No, he was just giving her space, spending his time alone. She had to believe that.

The time between pops began to slow down and after a second more Felicity took out the popcorn so that it wouldn't be burned. She put the second bag into the microwave, and then dumped the contents of the first bag into a bowl.

As she was crumpling up the bag for the garbage, a very odd feeling came over her. Like a wave of dizziness. She put her hand out for the counter and paused on her way to the garbage pail. Cain. It *was* Cain, wasn't it? After a moment, she felt it again. A slight shiver shook her and she felt a dizzy little wave of longing for Cain wash over her. Yes. It was definitely him, but this was much stronger than the fleeting flashes she'd felt from him now and again in the past week. She threw away the empty popcorn bag and examined the feeling. Where was he?

He didn't feel very close yet, but he was coming closer. Was he coming *here*? It was hard to tell. She was almost too distracted to fully analyze it because her body suddenly seemed absolutely desperate for him. She stood herself fully upright and mentally commanded herself to take control of things. She might miss him, but she wouldn't let her feelings be guided by some superficial addiction.

It was getting stronger. So strong in fact, that for a second she wondered in surprised annoyance if he was actually trying to *summon* her. Would he go so far as to do that? Is that why he hadn't come to her, because he wanted to *make* her come to him?

No. He just wouldn't do that. It must feel so strong only because she'd been away from him and sorely missed him. The microwave beeped and she was startled from her thoughts. As she opened the door, she realized that the smell of burned popcorn was filling the kitchen. Great. She quickly poured it into the other bowl and hoped it wouldn't taste too bad.

The strength of Cain's presence had seemed to stabilize and she decided to hand off the popcorn to go up to her room and change. For all she knew, he would be waiting at her window. She headed back out to the girls in the living room. "Here's the popcorn. Sorry it got a little... burned."

Cain. He was standing just inside the front entrance. Apparently, Penny had let him in. She was standing there next to Cain by the door and smiling at Felicity. She seemed very impressed. In fact, all of the girls did, and everyone was staring at Felicity, including Cain. He was standing there looking smolderingly handsome, but in an unintentional, casual sort of way. He wore his usual black jeans, boots and his black leather jacket with a light blue t-shirt underneath. He looked so sexy and yet his expression was very humble and disarming. He was giving her just the slightest smile with large and hopeful eyes. "Hi."

The room was so quiet that you could have heard a pin drop. They must have paused the movie when Penny got up to answer the door. Felicity found her voice, though it was little more than a whisper. "Hi." After a second Felicity glanced down and realized that she still held the two bowls of popcorn. She quickly handed them off to the person sitting closest to where she stood. It turned out to be Deborah, who looked none too pleased to have Felicity shoving popcorn bowls at her. She did take them though. Felicity couldn't care less what she thought; what any of them thought. She wiped her buttery hands off on the legs of her pajamas.

Cain took a step forward and she noticed that he held a single long stemmed red rose in his hand. "I brought this back to you," he said as he lifted it towards her, back? Oh. The stem of the rose was threaded through the tines of the antique hair comb that Cain had given her. She had left it on the edge of the sink in his bathroom. "Be a shame for you to lose it. I really *want* for it to be yours."

She took a few steps towards him and accepted the rose with a 'thank you' that even he might have had trouble hearing. She took it from up high on the stem, near the bloom, without touching Cain's fingers. He seemed very aware that she had purposely avoided his touch, but she didn't want their first electric physical reunion to be in front of a room full of onlookers.

He turned those soulful and heartbreaking eyes of his on her and she thought she would melt. 'He was keeping things from you! Sneaking around behind your back!' she tried desperately to remind herself. It didn't seem to matter. As much as she might like the idea of trying to make him unsure of her acceptance of him, she knew that she couldn't deny him for long. She just stood there staring at him, not trusting herself to speak. "Do you think that perhaps we could talk?" he asked her quietly.

She breathed a quiet sigh of relief. Yes, talk. He wouldn't just assume that all was automatically forgiven because he'd brought her a rose, but it did seem terribly romantic and she really just wished she could fly into his arms. She kept herself still where she stood and gave him a shy little smile and a nod of her head. "Yes. I'd like that."

She was startled by the sound of the movie 'un-pausing' itself after its five-minute grace period, and was reminded that they had an audience. She glanced at the girls who were all shamelessly staring at them, and then looked back to Cain. "Maybe we could talk... *up*stairs?"

"As you wish," Cain said with a little grin. He took a step back to let her by as she headed towards the staircase. Cain surveyed the room with a charming smile. "Ladies," he said with a nod of his head, by way of departure. He then turned and followed her up.

She held onto the rose and climbed the stairs, trying not to glance at the girls and very glad that in walking behind her, Cain couldn't see the grin that she could not keep from her face. The other girls in the room were silently smiling as well and Felicity knew that Cain had made quite an impact on them. Of course, the last thing she should worry over at this point was what they would think, but she had to admit, it felt good.

They reached the top of the stairs, out of view of the others and crossed the hall to Felicity's room. She opened the door and entered, Cain following behind her.

Suddenly she heard him let out a quiet but sharp exclamation of pain. "Ah!"

Felicity spun around to find him standing in the hallway. His shoulders were hunched forward and his hands were clenched to his chest in obvious pain. "Cain! Are you okay? What is it?" He looked as though he were having a heart attack.

He took his hands away and shook his head a little as though trying to shake it off. "I'm alright." It was difficult to believe him, as he seemed very disturbed.

Felicity couldn't help but be a little frightened for him. When he finally did look back up at her though, he didn't seem worried or truly hurt anymore, only a bit embarrassed. "What happened?" she asked.

"Apparently I'm… *un*invited," he answered quietly.

Felicity's eyes went wide. "*I* did that? Oh Cain, I'm sorry. I didn't mean to. You can come in. Of course, you can come in. Please… I invite you. You're *re*invited. Come in." She backed away from the door with her hand held up to the base of her throat feeling absolutely stricken. He tentatively followed her into the room. It seemed to work. The invisible guise was lifted and he had no further problem entering. He still looked kind of hurt though, emotionally. "I am so sorry. I never meant to keep you out really. I was angry. I was mad at you and… I guess I said some stuff. It wasn't on purpose."

He gave her a little smile as he moved deeper into the room and she passed behind him to close the door. "*Very* angry you must have been, to have been yelling at me aloud when I wasn't even here." He said in an amused but hurt sort of tone.

"I wasn't really yelling at *you*," she said uncertainly. "It was more at your… shirt." He eyed her dubiously, but she felt awkward to try and explain. In any event, her recent distaste for the whole 'venom thing' was beside the point. The evidence of his dis-invitation from the room had brought back the memory of how she had felt that morning. Alone in her room, feeling violated by his venom and betrayed by his actions; feeling completely deceived and distraught because of this man who was supposed to be her 'protector', the man that she loved and had always made her feel so safe. "Anyway, I think I had a *right* to be angry."

He looked down to the floor with a little smile. "From your point of view, I suppose you did."

She squinted at him in disbelief. "You *suppose?*"

297

He ventured another smile. "I suppose that was also an unfortunate choice of words."

She stood staring at him with one hand on her hip, the other holding the forgotten rose by her side. "Ya think?" So often, she felt that his age and experience gave him better perspective than she had, and gave him an advantage over her in most situations; as though she should automatically defer to him, but this time she refused to be so easily swayed. She would forgive him, but he'd been wrong and he should admit it.

At the same time, his physical closeness to her was distracting almost to the point of over-whelming her. She tried to use the feeling to fuel her stubborn free will and to steel herself not to be too easily persuaded, but... she couldn't remember ever feeling such strong desire.

How could he just be standing there, seeming so unaffected and strong? He was so close to her! How could he stand to be so close to her without kissing her? Didn't his body feel it the way that hers did? Her body was practically screaming for him! All she wanted to do was to forget arguments and past hurts; to hold him and kiss him and feel herself pressed up against him and... Uggghhh!!!

In an effort to hold herself still, she unconsciously tightened her grip on the rose and stabbed herself with a thorn. She flinched and broke eye contact with him to pull her thumb loose from the point. Yep, she'd been stabbed pretty good. Nice going Felicity. She brought it to her mouth to suck on the small stinging hole there. As soon as the metallic taste of blood filled her mouth, she was reminded of the first night that she had allowed Cain to drink from her. He had kissed her after and had tasted just the same.

She quickly pulled her thumb from her mouth and looked up to find him staring at her. Immediately uneasy and aware of their awkward tableau, she dropped her eyes again and walked over to the dresser to put down the rose.

When she turned back to face him, she noticed that he was standing before her other dresser, just opposite the mirror… in which he had no reflection of course. She found herself just staring into the mirror at the reflection of the 'empty' room as she tried to think what to say.

After a few expectant moments, he looked at the mirror and seemed to become annoyed. "I'm over here," he quipped sarcastically.

She just gave him an irate glance and sat down on her bed. He didn't move at all towards her, but stood his position and crossed his arms over his chest. After a pause, he spoke, sounding must less amicable. "Look, I understand that I've upset you, but I honestly don't think that I've anything to be ashamed of."

She looked up at him in disbelief. That's how he was going to start? He continued. "Just because you cannot empathize with my position does not change what I am. I am a vampire and I should act accordingly. You're not, and you shouldn't be expected to understand. In fact, if you search your feelings, I'm sure you'll come to agree that this is all for the best. Our relationship was bound to come to an eventual end. T'was inevitable really. Our misunderstanding the other morning was a bit more brash and abrupt an end than I might

MELANIE NOWAK   EVOLVING ECSTASY - PART 3 - EVOLUTION OF LOVE   CHAPTER 11

have liked, but the fact that it should force the issue is actually a bit of a relief."

She just sat there watching his mouth move and trying to figure out what the hell he was trying to say. It sounded almost like rehearsed gibberish. Partly because she didn't want to hear it, but mostly because for every statement that came out of his mouth, his facial expression and body language seemed to be screaming the exact opposite. The desire and pull that she felt towards him with each passing moment was so strong that she was absolutely certain that it had to be more than some passive side effect. He *was* summoning her. Perhaps it was just an unconscious spill over of his true emotions, but it was undeniable.

She stared at him for a moment in disbelief, and finally just blurted out, *"What?"*

He looked at her as though they were acting a play and she'd said the wrong line. "It's time I moved on. I don't want to see you anymore. I'm leaving."

His words came out strongly but his face was so forlorn that she couldn't believe him for an instant. She kept staring at him, waiting for him to take it back. He held firm. Meanwhile, his intangible calling to her grew stronger than she'd thought possible. It was a good thing she was already sitting on the bed. It would have been difficult to keep her feet through the waves of desperate need that seemed to be pouring out of him. She was hardly able to believe that she hadn't thrown herself into his arms already.

Finally, she smiled. He seemed to find that disturbing. Apparently, he'd expected a different reaction. She spoke. "I know that I've told you before what a terrible liar you are, but this is just pathetic. I wish that you could see your face," she said, with a gesture at the mirror. "You look like you're about to fall apart."

She had started with a smile, but as she spoke, emotion began to well up from within her. "You're telling me that you want to leave, and yet even as you say the words... *you're calling me.* Did you know that?

I feel like I'm being smothered in feelings for you. Like I'm hopelessly tangled up in you and you're telling me to go away even as you pull me in. Do you even realize that you're doing that?"

He obviously *hadn't* realized. He seemed almost shocked, and then he did begin to fall apart as she predicted. He said nothing, but was having a terribly hard time keeping tears from his eyes. She knew that her own were already welling with them. She asked him sincerely. "What are you trying to do?"

After a minute, he seemed to give up trying for the 'cold and distant' look that he wasn't achieving anyway. He sat down next to her on the bed and put his head into his hands. "I don't know. I haven't got the words. You've gone and messed it all up and made me forget what I was supposed to say."

She almost would have laughed if she weren't already crying. His nearness to her was overwhelming. She was breathing deeply and trying so hard just to sit still and not move to touch him. God, but his venom must be so strong! She felt as though she wanted nothing more than to drape herself across his lap and bare to him her throat. He looked up with moist eyes and must have seen something in her face that alarmed him. "Are you alright?" he asked in concern.

She closed her eyes for a moment and then whispered to him. "Cain please. The summons. You have to stop. I can't think."

He seemed terribly disturbed and looked closer at her as though perhaps she was teasing him. He sat up straighter and appeared to concentrate. She felt the almost oppressive desire she had for him begin to lift. It receded until she felt that she could talk to him again, but it was only lessened. It never actually left her.

She had raised her eyes to his face as he tried to rein it in. When he looked up at her, he seemed very apologetic. "Sorry. I haven't much practice with that. It's hard to control something that you never use. Looks like it kind of ruined my plan." She raised her eyebrows inquiringly. He explained. "You were supposed to believe that I wanted to go. You were supposed to be mad at me."

"You *wanted* me to be mad at you?" He was staring vacantly into his lap as he nodded yes. "Then why did you bring me the rose?"

He looked almost sheepish and more confused than she was when his eyes found the rose and comb on her dresser, as though he hadn't thought it through. "Well, I wanted you to have the comb back. If I wasn't going to tell you that I was sorry, then it seemed only right that I offer some token of apology. I guess it was a bit contradictory. And when I saw you, I must admit that I almost lost all resolve right then and there. You *are* a sight for sore eyes. I really am bad at this aren't I?"

She looked at him with a confused little grin. Had he really been so socially isolated all these years that he was having such a hard time dealing with his feelings over this? "But why did you want me to be mad?"

She dropped her smile when she realized how exasperated he was with himself. He seemed so hopelessly distraught. As he spoke, his voice wavered with emotional turmoil. "You just don't understand. I spent these past nights trying to find the best way. I drank and I thought and then I drank some more. When that didn't work, I went home and I prayed. I prayed desperately over you but every solution that came to me was unbearable to accept. I couldn't carry it through. I knew that I wasn't strong enough. I just knew it.

So, I decided that you should be mad. That's why I stayed away, let you be angry with me, because you see, if you were angry then you could be strong. It would empower you against me and make you fight for yourself, for your life. I need you to be strong... because one of us should be. I am old and powerful as a vampire, physically robust as a man, but my heart... My heart is feeble and weak and it cannot let you go."

A tear slid down his cheek and she found her fingers lifting to it before she'd even thought the act through. As her fingertip touched his face to wipe away the tear, the tingle of his mark upon her was like a warm enveloping current. It shivered through her fingers and traveled down her arm, seeming to land in her heart. She took a long shuddering gasp of breath. After it passed, she exhaled and whispered, "Then don't."

She caressed his cheek again and after a brief moment, he took her face into his hands and came to her lips for a kiss. This time the electricity of his touch ran deeper and further within her. She let herself melt into his arms and give herself over to him as his psychic call had tried to demand and had made her so vividly imagine, but venom or not, she knew that at this moment there was not a thing on earth that she needed more than his touch.

He kissed her with the passion of a love he'd thought lost. She thought that he would lay her back on the bed, but after the initial heat of reunion subsided enough for her to breathe, he leaned back from her with his face turned aside. He seemed to be concentrating on something.

"What is it?"

He gave her a slight smile and glanced at the door. "I believe we have an audience," he whispered. Felicity pulled herself from the haze she was in and looked at the door. She couldn't see any shadow to block the light shining through the space beneath. When she looked back at Cain, he nodded. "They smell like popcorn."

Felicity giggled and sniffed, wiping the tears from her face. "That's probably me."

He fixed her with a very steady gaze and a slight smile. "Yes, you smell delicious… as always," he breathed. She had to drop her eyes, lest she melt back into his arms. "But she…" he nodded once again towards the door. "has the scent of popcorn mingled with cherry lip-gloss and… pepperoni pizza. It's the one who answered the door, with the pig-tails," he whispered so quietly that Felicity could barely hear him.

Felicity looked again at the door and then back at Cain in disbelief. "You can really smell her?"

Cain looked almost ashamed of the ability. He shrugged. "Some talent, eh? Anyway, perhaps we could finish this… conversation back at my place?"

Felicity smiled and dropped her eyes. They still did have talking to do. She planned to chastise him severely for ever keeping anything from her, but she still felt desperate for his touch. She kissed him again. It was softer and sweeter but still just as deep and no less satisfying.

He eyed her for a moment and then stood from the bed. He spoke in a tone that she knew was meant for anyone outside the door as well as for her. "I'll wait downstairs, so you can change in private." He didn't let her speak; he just smiled at her and then went for the door.

He paused a moment more, presumably to be sure the way was clear, and then opened it to step out into the hall. He closed the door behind him.

Chapter 12 - Almost human

Cain

Felicity's dorm
11:00, Thursday night

Cain left Felicity's room, almost grateful to leave her presence for a moment to regain his composure. He'd been rather flustered by how powerfully she affected him. He had stayed away for as long as he could stand in trying to find the courage to end things as he should. He'd told Felicity as much.

What he had not told her was that he'd also hoped for the venom she had received from him to have weakened a bit. Unfortunately, that hadn't worked out nearly as well as he'd hoped. He'd last bitten her almost two full weeks ago. Her mark would still last for another week or two, but the venom itself should have reached its half-life and be on its decline by now, lessening her awareness of its effects. Apparently, he hadn't taken into account just how strong his venom had become. He knew that he really should have waited longer, but he just couldn't stay away. He'd thought that its effect would have at least been weakened by now.

Not only was it disappointing to know that she was still feeling so strongly drawn to him, but he had fiercely underestimated his own need for her. Of course, he missed her and wanted to be with her and hold her, but this was so much more than that. It was thirst. The vampire within him had not been fed human blood for almost two weeks now. It was dissatisfied with the purchased blood that he endeavored to quiet it with and was thirsting for more gratifying sustenance.

It recognized Felicity and it wanted her, *badly*. It was distracting to say the least. Once he found himself alone in the room with her, it was impossible to ignore. He'd focused intently on simply blurting out the things that were necessary to be said, in order to take himself from her presence and end his torment. He had not even realized that he had been sending her a psychic summons throughout. He longed for her in so many ways that he must have broadcast it unconsciously.

The realization shook him and made him realize that he could not do things the way that he'd planned. Not that they were working out very well anyway. No, the vampire in him wanted her just as badly as the man and was loathe to leave her, thirst unsatisfied. Her mark was fading, however slowly and he needed to claim her once more. If he did not, the vampire within would never allow him to let her go.

He would give in to desire, yet once more. For a short time. He would make amends with her, love her, and fulfill his needs. Then, when the beast within him was silent and satisfied he would tell her that he had to go. He would make a swift departure before his inner vampire could rebel against it.

It seemed almost cruel to tease her so, seeking her affections, knowing that he would leave, but it really was the only way. It sat better with him than trying to pick a fight with her anyway. She was a smart and perceptive girl. She saw right through his poor attempt at indifference to her, but she had also known all along that eventually he would have to leave.

Besides, he couldn't honestly say that he didn't relish the idea of having a bit longer with her. He loved her so much and it was going to be heart wrenching to have to leave. To spend a few more days with her would build fond memories and ease their hurt somewhat. They would spend the next few days bathed in lover's bliss, and then, depressing as it may be, he would have to inform her that it was time for it to end.

As Cain descended the stairs to the entryway, he could see that all five of Felicity's dorm mates who had originally greeted him were obediently sitting on couches in the living room watching their movie. Even the one with the pigtails, although Cain could tell that she was a bit out of breath. He smiled to himself and stood to wait by the front door. After a moment, he noticed them looking at him expectantly. "I'm just waiting for Felicity. We'll be going out for a bit."

He was met with knowing smiles from the girls. The one in the blue satin pajamas spoke. "Why don't you come and sit? Make yourself at home while you wait," she said, tapping the couch cushion next to her as an invitation to him.

He gave them a small grin and nodded his acceptance. Things were so different these days. Not one of these girls was dressed in any more than her nightclothes, and yet they seemed totally unconcerned. Not that they were really wearing anything very revealing, but it was a far cry from standards of propriety in his day. It still seemed a bit inappropriate to his old-fashioned sensibilities.

As he sat amongst them, they seemed very interested and observant of him; as though they were excitedly expectant to see what he might do. He realized that they were using him as a judge of Felicity's status among them. Young girls were such a strange breed. It was like they had their own little society that he would never aspire to understand. He hoped that his presence had somehow gained Felicity a bit of respect among them. He was conscious to keep his British accent apparent. He'd noticed that ladies always seemed to admire it.

The girl in blue spoke to him again. She seemed to think of herself as the 'leader' of the group. "So, Felicity tells us that you're not from around here."

"No, I tend to travel quite a bit," he answered.

"For business?" she asked.

"Mostly."

"So, what do you do?" she pressed further.

Her tone was a bit flirtatious but her main agenda seemed to be information, fodder for future discussion and speculation over him. He hoped that his vague answers would still put him in a positive light. "I guess you could say that I'm sort of a 'Guidance Counselor'. A 'Life Coach', if you will." He was met with a blank stare. "I give advice."

She cocked an eyebrow at him. "To young girls?"

He grinned. "Not usually. No, I have a rather elite clientele, but they're usually very fond of their privacy, so I'm sure you'll understand if I can't get into specifics or name names."

The girl in green with the long dark hair seemed suitably impressed. "A Life Coach. I've heard of that. The big stars use them, like to help them make decisions and stuff. I bet they'd pay anything if you could help them keep up a good image for the tabloids."

Cain just smiled and lowered his eyes as the girls exchanged impressed glances with one another. Only the young lady of color in the camouflage pajamas seemed skeptical. Her necklace proclaimed her name to be 'April'. "Aren't you a little young to be giving people 'life advice'?"

He met her eyes and gave her a charming little smile that seemed to disarm her almost immediately. "I'm a bit older than I look, and I dare say that I've led a rather educational life." He leaned forward to her confidentially. "I can assure you that my disciples are always well satisfied with my credentials." He hadn't really meant for his tone to sound particularly alluring, but was rewarded in seeing that he'd actually brought a bit of blush to her perfect mocha complexion.

He really was uninterested in any other here save Felicity, but he had to admit that it was rather fun seeing these young ladies become impressed with him. The girl 'April' seemed of a very strong and confident attitude, uneasy to win over. She was lovely as well. All of them were in their own ways. Silly as it was, he was glad that he seemed to meet their approval.

Unfortunately, although he himself was uninterested in these girls for more than passing conversation, the vampire within him was beginning to recognize them as very appetizing fare. After being awakened by his closeness to Felicity and yet denied, it was eager for a hunt. He would never touch these girls of course, but little things were starting to distract his attention. For one thing, they all smelled very appealing. His keen sense of smell could not help but dwell on the pleasing and varied bouquet of scents that they carried. The way that they giggled and gathered so closely around him, seeming to hang on his every word, was very tempting to the predator within him. The girl in blue sat so close to him that his heightened senses were clearly aware of her heartbeat.

The girl with the pigtails worked up the courage to ask, "How old are you?"

He smiled at her tentativeness and tried to keep his mind on making small talk rather than acknowledge his thirst. "Twenty-seven."

The girl in blue reasserted her dominance over the conversation. "You must think we're terribly rude. We haven't even introduced ourselves," she said, leaning forward to rest her hand lightly on his knee in a gesture that seemed just a bit *too* familiar. "I'm Deborah." She batted her eyes and gave him a sly little smile. She was definitely flirting now. He must meet her approval. Perhaps she thought it would be fun to see if she might turn his eye from Felicity. Not a chance.

Their attention was drawn to the staircase as they heard the true subject of his desires emerge from her bedroom. Rather than continue his conversation, Cain sat silent with his eyes trained on the stairs in anticipation of her. She descended, dressed in jeans and a peasant blouse of a pleasing paisley pattern done in shades of blue, green and purple. Her beautiful auburn hair was left loose to flow down her back, its lovely waves bouncing as she came down the steps. Cain noticed that she had a winter coat draped over her arm. Good, she'd need it. He'd brought the bike.

He stood from the couch as she entered and surveyed the room. She didn't seem overtly jealous of the girls flocked around him, but he was certain that she was curious as to their conversation. He couldn't resist a parting display for Felicity's sake. He turned back to his hosts. "If you'll excuse me girls, you've been charming company, but my lady awaits," he said with what he hoped was not too much dramatic flair.

He noticed that Felicity had dropped her eyes to the floor and was trying to hide her grin. Hopefully he had made an impression that would please her. He went to meet her with a tender kiss on the cheek. It surely appeared chaste enough, but the bond that they shared through Felicity's mark made even such a simple gesture hold an almost indecent little thrill.

She closed her eyes and breathed deeply as her heartbeat was momentarily quickened. Then Cain took the coat from her arm and helped her on with it. "Shall I drive? I've brought the Harley." She just nodded with a smile. He opened the door for her and gave the ladies in the living room a smile and parting nod goodbye.

~~~~~~~~~~~~~~~~~~~~~~~~~~~~~~

The ride home was a nice respite from having to try and fight his urges and strive for normalcy. Felicity sat behind him on the bike with her arms wrapped around his waist. Funny how his cravings for her seemed satisfied to let him be for now. His vampire nature still wanted her blood… desperately, but knowing that she was with him seemed to stay it for now.

Knowing that he was whisking her away to a place where they could be private… that he had 'landed his prey' seemed sufficient to ease his thirst for the moment. He hoped that things would go well between them so that he might silence his inner vampire quickly and simply enjoy being with her as a man.

They reached his house and she dismounted the motorcycle and followed him to the door without saying a word, before long they found themselves in his bedroom. She still said nothing, but went to sit on his bed as he turned on the light. He wished that they could forgo all of the preliminary mediations and just get under the covers to lose their problems in love and laughter.

He thought perhaps she felt that way too. Unfortunately, neither one of them was likely to admit to preferring such physical desires over the discussion of their less tangible obstacles. He had to at least attempt to ease her concerns over the past. She seemed to have the same thing in mind as she spoke. "You kept things from me. No matter what you say you did or didn't do with Sindy, you still hid it from me. That is just… unacceptable. You can't do that; you can't hide things from me. We're supposed to be honest with each other; always, no matter what."

He sat down next to her on the bed, and looked upon her sweet face. Trying not to notice her alluring scent and the gentle throb of the pulse beneath the skin of her throat, he accepted her accusation. "You're right. Just because I felt justified in my actions does not mean that I should not have shared them. I suppose I knew that you would look upon it unkindly, but my heart has always belonged only to you. And since you came to me to declare your love, I've given no other leave to touch me in any intimate way... no matter what I might have done for them. I hope you'll not judge me too harshly."

She sighed, searching his face for a moment before giving him a little half-hearted smile of acceptance. She wasn't happy about it, but she seemed to have lost the will to fight with him much more. She would forgive him. Thank God, because his desire for her blood was becoming once again difficult to ignore. For probably the hundredth time since his death, he cursed his unnatural body for keeping him from being able to relate to someone without such illicit thoughts and urges.

He made a mental check of himself, to be sure that he hadn't resumed 'calling' to her again. "I am sorry about the whole 'summons' thing. I really never meant to coerce you. I wasn't even aware that I was sending it. I guess I just wanted you so desperately... no matter what I might have said."

She gave him another little smile. "I figured it was something like that."

She didn't seem at all upset over it. If anything, he thought perhaps she was flattered. Didn't she realize the extent of her effect on him? "It's not troubling you now, is it?"

"No, not really. It's still there, but you seem to have gotten things under control," she answered.

With an impish grin, he realized that she actually seemed to like the idea that he found her irresistible. He *had* usually displayed better restraint in the past. Perhaps she didn't fathom the extent of her attractiveness to him. He leaned a bit closer to her and whispered, "It's not easy I can assure you. You bring out longings in me, almost impossible to harness."

She grinned and turned away with flushed embarrassment. Yes, she was pleased, and his closeness was strongly affecting her as well, but she wasn't quite ready to give in to him yet. "Flattery will get you nowhere. I'm still mad at you."

He gently touched her face to turn her back to him. "Are you sure about that? Isn't there some way that I might regain your favor? Because I have to be honest, as much as I would never seek to steal affections from you unsolicited... I don't know how much longer I can keep myself from you."

She looked up at him in startled realization. She definitely felt her own urges from his mark upon her as well as any natural feelings she might have. Now she seemed to study him and try to assess the full extent of his desires for her. How could she not be able to tell that he barely restrained himself? If she hadn't seen it before, she noticed it now. Rather than be disgusted as he had been afraid that she might be, it appeared to arouse and excite her.

He implored her with a soft but urgent whisper. "Please, forgive me. I do love you... and I *need* you."

She looked almost shocked to see that she held such power over him. Although the power she held was only by his decree. He could certainly have taken her at any time that he liked. He waited for her assent by his own resolution. He had made a promise to her once. He would never touch her again without express consent. He silently begged her for that consent now.

Rather than answer, she kissed him so vehemently that he felt as though floodgates had been opened to finally unleash all that had been restrained. He kissed her deeply and passionately, but it was not only her kiss that he required. She knew it too. She didn't seem at all disappointed when he ended it. She tilted her head to offer her throat to him without word or hesitation.

He felt a bit guilty to put such desires before all else, but all he could think was to bless her for her generosity. His lips moved eagerly to kiss the skin that covered her willing vein. He paused only a moment, and then let the change overcome him. His eyes had barely finished changing the spectrum of his vision when he pierced her skin with his newly unsheathed fangs. As the first drops of her precious blood touched his tongue, he felt a great wave wash over him of longing and relief rolled into one.

He hadn't the patience to wait for his venom to work its way throughout her system. He knew that she would feel its effects eventually as he fed and it wasn't as though he need worry that she would panic or try to flee from him. She knew the euphoria that would be forthcoming.

Felicity let out a small gasp at his first real pull upon her. He hoped he hadn't hurt her at all. He hugged her closer, forcing himself to be gentle as he drank. Her blood was a thick and rich reward for his wait. Sweet and fulfilling as nothing else could be. This beautiful girl with such an open and giving heart, her blood was like love liquefied. He loved her more than he had ever dared to think that he could. Not only for her giving nature but for the fun and simple joys that she brought to him. How was he going to give her up? He knew that he should, but *could* he?

Her blood was a welcome physical reward. A much-needed respite from the desperate thirst that he had faced. Of course, the affections that she displayed for him with her body were pleasurable as well. Yes, their lovemaking was an indulgence that he had denied himself for so many years. He did fully enjoy her attentions, but what he treasured most from her were the plain and simple times that they spent together.

While Felicity had come to appreciate the physical rewards of his vampire nature, she did not love him because he was a vampire; she loved him in spite of it. She had never treated him as anything less than a man. She was truly concerned for his feelings and well-being. She was always there for him. She had listened to his confessions with a sympathetic ear and a consoling manner. She shared her own joys and concerns with him and looked to him for comfort and camaraderie. Just being with her was gratifying in its own right. Time spent with her could be so blessedly normal. Just a man and a woman, enjoying each other's company. An indulgence that his life of recent past had been so sorely lacking.

He loved watching her make new discoveries and gain confidence within herself. He loved being a part of that. He loved just sitting with her... anywhere. The café, the park, his own secluded bedroom, it didn't matter. Quiet conversations and fond glances. He loved to make her smile. The way that she would blush and giggle at things that he said, or even at her own newly uncovered boldness at times. Those things were so precious to him.

This… this purely selfish act of drinking her blood was sinful ecstasy. It was such exquisite gratification, but her love meant so much more. He needed to pull back from this wicked feast. To keep his senses and be sure that he would please her as well as himself. As soon as he had lessened his thirst enough to regain full control, he made himself disengage from her.

He studied her face, hoping that she hadn't been too startled or disappointed by the abruptness with which he had bitten her. Hopefully his venom was strong enough that it would affect her even without a deliberately full dose. She had been without it for a while, so it shouldn't take much to subdue her pain and bring her the lightheaded contentment that she had grown accustomed to.

As he gazed upon her now, he could see that she did display signs of becoming intoxicated. His venom usually worked rather well on her. That was something for which he was grateful. At least he could feel that his guilt over wanting her blood could be eased by the fact that she was gaining some pleasure in the exchange as well. He let her eyes focus upon his own before he spoke. "I'm sorry, I couldn't wait. I didn't hurt you, did I?"

She shook her head no and took back his lips to resume their kiss. She kissed him with fervent ardor and passion that he would have been surprised to receive from her back in early days of their relationship. Now these expressions of the secret fire within her were a delight that he eagerly looked forward to each time they made love. After fully conveying her desires to him through her kisses, she left the bed to remove her clothing. He watched her try to steady herself with a hand upon the bed as she impatiently stripped the material from her body. He undressed himself as well.

Cain had to smile, thinking of the first time that she had disrobed for him. It really was not all that long ago, but what a different girl she had been from the confident woman she was now! She had stood across the room and slowly, shyly removed her dress. She'd been so hesitant and worried over his impressions of her. Now she could hardly wait to bare herself before him.

She removed all save her panties. He wondered at that for a moment, but then he saw why. She had worn the thong for him. The one that he had shown an interest in when he'd removed her gown after the Halloween Ball. She gave him a seductive little smile as she climbed back upon the bed to kneel before him where he sat. He gave her an approving little grin of his own as he raised himself to his knees and sought to embrace her for kisses once more. She stopped him with a hand upon his chest and looked up to his eyes. "From now on you have to tell me everything. I mean it."

He couldn't help but smile. Her words were slightly slurred and she looked as though she was having trouble keeping focus on his eyes, but she would not let it go. She continued. "I'm not hiding anything from you."

He moved her hand away from his chest so that he might take her into his arms. He let his hands leave her lower back to explore the edges of the scanty garment she wore. "Well, that's obvious," he replied with a teasing grin. She rolled her eyes at him as he cupped and squeezed her fully fleshed and bared derriere. He waited for her attention to come back to his face so that he might make her see that he was serious as he spoke, although he did not remove his hands. "Full disclosure, from now on. You've my solemn word."

She seemed pleased but did not answer. She only closed her eyes and took a very deep breath and sighed, after which she leaned her head against his shoulder. As she did, her head was tilted to the side once again baring her throat, although whether it was an invitation or simple chance he could not tell. He graced her bared throat with a small kiss, during which she never flinched. Of one thing he was sure, she was fading fast. His venom must be affecting her very strongly after their hiatus.

"Felicity." He gave her a little squeeze. She looked up at him once again with a dreamy smile. "The night is young and we've other pleasures still to explore. You mustn't leave me yet," he teased. He moved his hands to her waist for some tickling to rouse her.

That brought her around. She giggled and squirmed from him to lay down on the bed. "I'm all right, just give me a minute."

He looked down at her with a smirk and then dropped himself to lie over her legs. He slowly made his way up her body as he spoke, bestowing kisses along the way. "You're going to lie here on my bed, baring this beautiful body of yours before me, smelling of blood and wanton desire, and you expect me to have the discipline to wait?" He reached her lips and took them for a kiss. "I *would* wait until the end of time if you asked it of me, but surely you'll not be so heartless as to torture me so." He teased her with a thrust of his hips as he spoke, though the thin silk of her panties was still between them.

She seemed to be lifting herself from the fog she'd been in. Now she laughed with a playful sparkle in her eye. Yes, he liked that much better. He knew the venom was pleasurable for her, but he'd never been at ease with the notion of bedding a woman drugged into submission. He much preferred her to be lively and spirited in their sport. Once Felicity had overcome her initial inhibitions, she'd learned to tease and pursue him with almost the same enthusiasm with which he sought to please and seduce her. He wouldn't allow her to simply lie in wait for him.

After taking a moment to gather her strength, she pushed against him. He allowed her to roll him onto his back so that she might lie atop him. He knew that while she did like for him to take the lead much of the time, she had also been tentatively discovering her own fondness for assertiveness with him. He did his best to encourage her to have confidence and to be unafraid to make known her desires.

She lay over him now, 'pinning' him to the bed, although of course he could escape her easily if he tried. She lifted herself from him just a bit and pouted at him, trying to hide her slight smile. "I should make you wait... torture you. It'd be fitting punishment."

He sighed in exasperation. Would she never let this go? Sindy must be more of a thorn in her side than he'd realized... He stopped his frivolous discontentment with the issue mid-thought. How would he have felt? Maybe sharing blood was a poor example because he did not see that as she did, but what if, unbeknownst to him, she had been spending time with another, someone who irked him already? Perhaps someone like... Benjamin? He suddenly felt much more sympathetic.

She tormented him with little wriggles against his body and teasing thrusts of her hips now and then as she lay atop him. He closed his eyes a moment and drew breath to subdue his passions. "Felicity, I know that you want us to forget it and enjoy each other, believe me, so do I." She gave him a knowing smile. "But I don't want you to forgive me only because we seek pleasure of the moment. I want this to be right with you. I really do. I'll never keep anything from you. Never again. I promise."

She'd been focused on him intently throughout. She appeared to have cleared herself of her intoxication a bit. He really hadn't drunk from her for long; it was just that the initial dose of it had been a shock to her system. He continued, "Felicity... my love, no one could ever hold a candle to you in my eyes; *no one*. I would have to be mad to seek affections from another. I only didn't tell you of time spent with Sindy because I did not see it as private or intimate time really. It was *vampire* time. Time spent pursuing the goal I have set for myself to educate and civilize other vampires. I treated her as a student and comrade, not a lover. *You* are my only love.

I try to keep those details of my vampire life separate from you not to hide them, but because when I'm with you, I can forget... almost. Time spent with you is like... Do you know what it's like in Spring, when you lie out on the grass at mid-day with your eyes closed and the sun shining down full upon your face? The amazing warmth and comfort that it can bring? I do. I *remember* what that's like. It's like being with you. *You're* my sunshine.

I don't want to think of blood and restraint... tactics and lessons in psychic control when I'm with you. When I'm with you the dark parts of my life seem to fall away, and I can be... almost human."

She looked as though she would cry. He felt that himself. Then she became very thoughtful, and worried almost as she asked, "Aren't there... good things? About being a vampire, aren't there *perks?*" They both had to give a little laugh at the way she said it.

She sounded so hopeful, that his life should contain something good and rewarding. "Yes, I suppose there are, but every power I hold, every benefit I enjoy has one horrible drawback... they're all part of something that keeps me from *you.*"

She grinned and gave him a small kiss, seeming to be actually happy with his response, although it seemed an agonizing unfairness to him. She looked into his eyes with a glint of promise that he could not understand. "Let's not worry about that for now."

He wished he could be as optimistic. He felt so cheated and forlorn inside, in knowing that this may very well be their last intimate time together. "I love you."

"Oh Cain, I love you too." She kissed him fervently and then lay back down, holding him close and tight. This was a moment that he wanted fixed in his memory. Something to take out again and remember during long and lonely nights. He held her that way for a very long time, hoping she wouldn't notice the tears in his eyes.

After he let the grief of their pending separation leave him, he decided that they should enjoy the time left. He had always known it, but it seemed from now on every moment would be that much more precious. He began to let his hands caress her lower back, and then once again explore the border of the thong that she wore. She leaned up again to look at his face with a smile as he spoke. "So, do you think that you might remove this for me?" he asked with a playful tug on the strap of her thong.

She grinned and adopted an air of surprised innocence. "I thought you liked it?"

"I think I'd like it better on the floor."

She laughed and began to lift herself from him, smiling and edging herself away from him on the bed. "Is that right? Well, if you want it off…you're going to have to catch me and remove it yourself."

He did.

Chapter 13

Take a break and have a life

Felicity

Cain's house
Friday morning

Felicity awoke from her sleep with a comfortable and contented smile. She rolled over to snuggle against Cain… but he wasn't there. Opening her eyes with a start, she searched the empty bed; then heard a noise and looked up to the bar.

It was the clink of him putting his mug into the sink. He was wearing his pajama pants again and had been behind the bar, drinking apparently. He looked up at her now as he came back to the bed. She sat up a little and asked him sleepily, "What time is it?"

He shrugged. "The sun's been up for about an hour. I was just coming back to bed actually."

Felicity lay back down, rolling onto her side in irritation. "I don't want to get up."

Cain got into the bed next to her under the covers. "Then don't."

She frowned as she lay on her side facing away from him. "I have early classes."

He moved himself up against her back and wrapped his arm around her, leaning forward to whisper into her ear. "Would you be terribly disappointed if I asked you to miss them for me?"

She smiled and looked up at him in surprise. He was usually so adamant about her attendance at school. "Special occasion?" she asked.

He squeezed her close and kissed the back of her neck, just under her ear. "Something like that." He rolled her towards him and tried to kiss her lips but she turned her face away.

"Hold that thought," she said, wriggling out of his embrace. "Got any toothpaste?"

He laughed. "In the bathroom."

"Thanks." She jumped up off of the bed and ran to the bathroom to brush her teeth with her finger. Cain spoke to her from the bed as she did.

"Are you working tonight?" he asked.

"Yeah, 6 to 10," she answered with disdain.

"That's not so bad," he assured her.

"Yes, it is. I'm closing with Harold," she explained.

Cain laughed. "I'll come and sit with you. How about tomorrow?"

Felicity finished up and came back out to him. "6 to 10 again, with Ben. Mr. Penten's been keeping my hours pretty light since my... accident." She made a quick little gesture to her throat. "Like he thinks I'm in a delicate condition or something. Not that I'm complaining." She sat on the bed close to him and smiled. "*Now* you can kiss me."

He met her lips with his own. After the kiss, he leaned back and inspected the healing wound at her throat. "How is it?" he asked tentatively.

She shrugged. "It still hurts a little, but as long as I don't poke at it, it's all right." He hadn't asked her about the injury she'd received from Chris until now. She wondered if that was because he knew that she would be self conscious about it.

"I'm so sorry that you got hurt." He seemed to still feel guilty over it. That's when she realized; he hadn't asked about it not for her self-consciousness but for his. He still sounded worried over it. "How long does something like that take to heal?"

She looked at him a little oddly. It sounded like such a strange… alien question. She had to remind herself that he hadn't dealt with such human concerns in over 300 years. His injuries began to heal almost immediately upon his receiving them. Must be nice. "The redness and soreness is supposed to be almost gone. Then it should fade a little every day after that, so it will look better. It'll always be a scar though." She shrugged and tried to pretend that it didn't bother her. "At least it kind of follows the shadow of my jaw line, so you don't really see it. And… I wear my hair down a lot."

He turned his eyes down to the bed for a moment. There seemed an awkward silence until she leaned forward and kissed him again. "Don't worry about it, I'm fine."

He met her eyes with heartfelt sympathy. "I'm sorry."

"It wasn't your fault. It was just… one those things."

"Right. Just *one of those things*. Every young girl gets her throat slit now and then."

"Cain, it really *wasn't* your fault."

"If you look at the big picture, in the larger scope of things, then yes it really was." She sat looking at his face. He stared right back, unwilling to give up the blame.

"If you want to look at the big picture, then you really should look back at the night we met. If you hadn't been there, Sindy would've drained me dry. Then she would have had her boys hold down Ben so that she could do the same to him. Of course, *he* probably would've gotten a cool new immortal bod in exchange for *his* life, but somehow, he doesn't seem the type to appreciate the advantages of something like that. I'm thinkin' over all, it's a pretty good thing that you were there. So – big picture, I'd have to say that *you* have been a pretty *good* influence on my life." She leaned forward for another kiss, and then looked back at him with a smile. "Yes, I've enjoyed your influences *a lot*."

The slightest smile came to his face, and just as quickly, his eyes seemed to glaze with unshed tears. He reached a hand up to lovingly caress the side of her face. "That's why I've got to leave now, before I go and spoil it."

Cold fear struck her heart and she dared to hope that she'd misunderstood. "What?"

Cain took a very deep breath and expelled it slowly, eyes closed. When he looked again upon her, he seemed very calm, sad and resigned. "I'll have to leave soon. Please don't make me go into all of the responsible rationalizations and arguments over it. 'Cause I just haven't got the heart for that right now. I know that you understand the reasons, however cruel and unjust they may seem."

She dropped her eyes to look down at the bed. Now? Already? It seemed like she'd only just regained him! "It's too soon."

He moved his hand against her cheek to make her look at him again. "I'd like to agree, but it isn't only the intangible arguments that chase me to leave. Morals and ethics aside, I would dearly treasure unlimited time with you, but we've more immediate physical concerns as well." He dropped his hand from her face and sighed. "The vampire within me has been very carefully kept dormant these past decades. Scrupulously maintained on the very barest amounts of animal blood.

Now I've awakened it, with you. I would say that I wish that I could have waited; held out longer, refrained from drinking your precious blood." He eyed her throat for a moment and she could see the longing in his eyes. "But I don't really think that'd be true. In any case, awakened it is."

He gazed at her with staid gravity, that she might know the severity of his struggle. "The more I drink, the more it wants. It's not very satisfied with animal blood any longer, though I've practically been drowning myself with it. I'm making the local butcher's quite rich, and I've been buying the stuff almost faster than they can get it.

It doesn't seem to help much though. Perhaps it's only in my head, but the stuff just doesn't seem to do the trick the way it used to. It's getting very difficult."

She tried to pout at him and reject his seriousness. "I'll wear turtle necks."

That did make him smile. "It's not even just *you* anymore. It's becoming hard to be around *anyone*."

"Okay, so then stay away from everyone else." She changed tactics and smiled at him playfully. "I'll feed you. Every day, every drop that I can."

He gave a little laugh. "Right, and quickly become weakened and anemic. And that'd be the least of your problems." He leaned forward and gave her a little kiss. "No.

I haven't told you every bit of my past. There've been others. Few, and none that've touched my heart as deeply as you, but still..." He lightly shook his head with a distasteful frown. "I've tried such arrangements. It never ends well. I can't do that to you. I won't. I have to leave... now, before I start to lose control."

Felicity just sat there staring at the crumpled sheets before her. Her bottom lip began to tremble and she tried so hard not to break down and sob as she'd like. Her vision blurred and turned watery with tears.

After an interminable moment of trying to hold back her grief, she felt it recede as a new calm came upon her. She looked up to his face. He gazed at her with such love, devastated surely, but hopeful that she would not fight him.

She loved him, truly, deeply. What was it worth, not to have to let him go? She just sat there for a moment more, watching him. He looked so human. Was he really all *that* different inside? She knew that he was, and yet how bad could it be?

She put the thought aside. They had to have *some* time. A few more days at least. He waited patiently for her to speak.

"Could we just pretend like you don't have to leave? Just for the weekend?"

He gave her a watery sort of grin. "That was sort of what I had in mind."

"Then let's not talk about it anymore. 'Kay?"

He nodded his head lightly and reached up to brush her cheek once more. He seemed to be studying her face, memorizing every detail in anticipation of lonely nights ahead. "I love you," he whispered.

"I love you too," she replied.

After the tears began to clear from her eyes, he let his hand wander down to trace her jaw. He seemed to be studying the line of her injury on her throat beneath. "I could do something about that maybe... your scar."

She just furrowed her brow at him, unsure as to what he could mean. He clarified, "There's an old vampire trick that Maribeth and I learned back in days of the hunt. Wouldn't do to have a bunch of bodies left behind full of holes. People talk you know.

A few drops of vampire blood would usually do the trick. Vampire blood is quite the odd substance. I do believe it's got a life of its own. Right good at fixing things, it is. Keeps my body working long past what it's any right to.

See the blood, it regenerates tissue. That's how those awful zombies manage to up and walk around; constantly being repaired, they are. In fact, if they can manage to survive long enough and get themselves fresh blood, they can eventually be restored to a life-like appearance... like me. They'd still be brain-dead creatures of instinct though. There are limits as to what can be done.

Anyway, Maribeth and I would put a few drops on a victim's bite and the blood would go to work. We would 'heal' them, as it were." He was quick to banish Felicity's hopeful thought. "They'd still die, blood loss, you know? But the visible injury would be banished. The blood grows the tissue back together and covers the holes. Doesn't always work perfectly, but it helps."

He seemed to guess her next question before she even asked. "I couldn't have done it to help you, the night it happened. I suppose I might have tried if your life truly depended on it, but really the wound was a bit large for that. It would have taken more than a drop or two. And... it was open. It's really better if your blood and my blood never meet, trust me.

But now, it's begun to heal on its own. It's closed and on its way to recovery. I can't guarantee the results, but a few drops of my blood might help to speed it along. Perhaps it could smooth and fade the mark on your skin, lessen the inevitable scar. I could try... if you'd like."

She looked at him thoughtfully for a moment, and then smiled. "Okay." He smiled back and she knew that he was grateful that she would let him try to help. He did take on guilt so easily. She hoped it would make him feel better. She couldn't imagine that it would actually work, but it *would* be nice to look in the mirror and not be reminded of Chris lying over her with a knife at her throat. "What should I do?"

"Lie back." She lay back down on the bed with her head on the pillow. Cain closed his eyes and sat very still. She wondered what he would do. Shouldn't he get a knife to cut himself?

He opened his eyes to reveal that they were now a bright golden yellow. Oh. He brought his hand up before his face and used his fangs to puncture the length of his finger.

Felicity just lay there, watching him. It was so strange. It felt like the *first* time that he had changed for her to see. It seemed so long ago. Since then, other times that he had transformed himself before her had been rather surreal. She had always been swooning with passion and the venom of his kisses. She hadn't really looked upon him and studied his change with such a clear head. She also couldn't help but eye him with a new awareness of it now.

What was it like for him? His fangs were only unsheathed when he changed. Where did they go? Up into his jaw apparently, like a cat's retractable claw; to be kept protected and so unbelievably sharp. Did it hurt when they came out? He didn't look as though it did. It seemed an easy and natural shift. Now that she was unstartled by his alternate appearance, he looked like a natural creature. Different to be sure, but not like something monstrous or abnormal.

He brought his finger away from his mouth to reveal two perfect drops of blood there. He'd hardly needed to apply any pressure to produce them, his fangs were so sharp. Now he brought that finger to her throat and lightly rubbed it across the wound there.

It was very sensitive to his touch but she forced herself not to flinch away. Felicity waited expectantly but her skin only felt rather warm as his finger moved across it. She looked up at him as he caressed her wound once more and then took his hand away. His eyes had become blue once again.

She reached out to hold his wrist as he was about to bring the finger to his mouth, presumably to suck and clean away the rest of the blood there. He looked at her a bit strangely, as she stopped him to ask, "What would happen, if my blood met yours? Or if I... drank it? Would that change me?"

He pulled his hand slowly but firmly from her and brought his finger to his mouth to quickly clean it. "Yes and no. You wouldn't become a true vampire. You haven't been drained."

"What would happen? Do you know?" she asked.

She thought perhaps he looked a little ill for a moment. He licked his finger again as a new bead of blood tried to form there. "Unfortunately, yes, I do." He looked at her gravely. "You know... there've been others. Other girls.

I hope that you don't feel threatened by that. It'd be hard to live 340 years and never get close to anyone, to never have loved."

He gently brushed the back of his hand across the side of her face as he gazed into her eyes. She loved when he did that. She spoke to him with a smile. "A girl would have to be crazy not to fall in love with you."

"Well, I don't know about that, but I do know that my love for *you* far outshines the rest."

She held his gaze, wanting to think of him selfishly as only her own for a moment before she asked. "So, what was her name? What happened?"

"Eileen. Young Irish farm girl, back in 1873," he began.

"You've got some head for dates," she observed.

He shrugged. "It helps to keep things from getting all muddled together. Anyway, we tried it. Thought that since her body was still healthy and alive, she might play host to the blood without losing her humanity; to live in some sort of symbiotic relationship with it, gaining its curative properties without… losing anything.

It worked well at first actually. With each small drink from me, she gained some of the more useful vampiric traits. Heightened senses, night vision, she even saw marks. It was rather amazing.

'Twas only little drinks I gave her, and they were few and far between. We thought to only sustain her abilities. We hoped that perhaps she might even gain immortality through me that way.

What we hadn't reckoned with was the tenacity of vampire blood's will to survive. We'd thought that it would be filtered through her system and over time, without a new transfusion it would leave her, wear off, as it were. We were wrong.

We should have waited to see, I suppose. Looked for evidence of its passage from her, lessening of its effects, but she was always a bit too eager for more. It can be quite heady, gaining such powers and abilities unknown before. And if vampire blood is tenacious, Eileen was nothing if not its mirror. Always thought she knew just what she wanted that girl did; and wouldn't rest 'til she had it.

As for the blood, she always wanted just a little more, and saying 'no' to pretty girls has never really been a talent of mine. It's something that I had to learn the hard way. Emotional strength and responsibility are not fun traits to wield, but they are necessary at times.

You once told me that you thought I seemed to feel responsible for all vampires and carry the guilt of all of my kind upon my own shoulders. I really don't though. I've enough guilt of my own, believe me."

"So, what happened?"

"At some point 'just a little more' became too much. She went through some sort of organ failure. The vampire blood decided she didn't need her internal workings any longer, but her body wasn't quite yet ready to agree.

I believe that she was in difficulty long before she ever let on to me. Once it was plain that she was in trouble I offered her a true change, but she wouldn't accept it yet. She wanted to wait. She'd thought it would get better, stabilize. That it was only a period of adjustment.

She went into a coma. I did it then. When it was clear she would not awaken on her own, I drained her and gave to her fully of my blood. I should have just let her go."

"Did she ever wake up? Did it work?"

"It did actually, but she was never the same after that. The combination of the slow change and her time unconscious, all she'd been through... I don't know. She couldn't handle things. Her comprehension of the situation seemed imperfect. She was still a sweet and lovely girl but, forgive me for saying, she was a bit... mentally unstable after that."

"What became of her?"

"She had terrible troubles controlling her thirst, as though it tortured her, before long she simply chose to leave the world rather than face it. She committed suicide."

"How awful! I'm sorry. It must have been hard to deal with."

"I did all that I could to help her. What I really should have done was turned her away before things went too far. Quite a lesson in responsibility.

It made me question my own judgment surely. Had I truly believed that she was strong enough, that she'd a desire and a will to live as I did; or was I only feeling guilt ridden and afraid to lose her? Even if my judgment was sound, who was I to proclaim myself in control of her destiny? Who am I to grant eternal life? I am nothing but a lonely and grief-stricken man. Hardly qualification for such power."

Cain stared at her soberly and Felicity couldn't help but wonder if he might have anticipated her recent ponderings. He spoke to her with a quiet seriousness. "This life of mine is not nearly the exciting and mysterious fight against evil that you may imagine it to be. In all reality, it is darkly treacherous, lonely and hard. I would trade it for yours in a heartbeat... if I had one."

What exactly was he trying to convince her of? She refused to be swayed. Besides, he had brought up new interesting ideas. "Still, if you had stopped before things went too far, she would have been okay, right? If you only gave someone enough blood to give them those abilities that you mentioned... to see marks and stuff. That would be wild!"

"I didn't relay the story to put ideas into your head. I don't play around with stuff like that anymore. The costs are higher than I care to pay. I've enough ruined lives on my conscience." He continued his serious gaze for a moment more and then began to smile. "Well, look at that."

He reached out and gently stroked his finger across her throat. "At least this blood of mine's good for something."

She raised her hand to the spot, but of course, she couldn't tell much by touch. She sat up in the bed. "It worked?"

"It's not perfectly healed. There is still evidence of it, but I believe that it's greatly improved over what it would have been, and in time, it still may fade more. Go and have a look for yourself," he said with a gesture to the bathroom mirror.

She kicked her legs from the covers and jumped out of bed to go and see. When she first looked into the mirror, she almost did think that it was gone. It had faded remarkably. Upon closer inspection, it could still be seen, but what a difference! She kept tilting her head this way and that, trying to see it from different angles. It was practically gone!

Felicity jumped as Cain unexpectedly put his hands to her shoulders. She hadn't seen him come up behind her as she'd studied herself in the mirror. She turned to look at him now and grinned. "Thank you. It's amazing!"

"I know that you'd been affecting that it didn't concern you at all, but just look at how happy you are! I'm glad I could help. When you think back on our time together, that scar really wasn't the memento that I'd wanted to leave you with," he told her.

Felicity couldn't help but lose her smile at his mention of being apart. She had an awful lot of thinking to do over the next two days. She gave a quick glance once more at herself alone in the mirror and the indistinct line of a scar at her throat where her injury used to be. Then she turned back to Cain for another kiss.

He was just folding his arms around her when her stomach rumbled making an embarrassingly loud gurgling noise. She broke off the kiss to look down at the floor with a little self-conscious chuckle.

When she raised her eyes back to Cain, he was smiling as he said, "Being alive can have its drawbacks. I'm guessing it's time for breakfast?"

"Sounds that way, doesn't it?" They moved from the bathroom and Felicity gave a glance towards his little refrigerator behind the bar. It was unlikely to contain anything that she would want. "Guess I'll have to go out huh?"

Cain gave her an apologetic little shrug. "Let's get dressed and venture upstairs to see what sort of day we've outside."

Once they were ready, she followed Cain upstairs. The windows were letting in little light. It seemed a gray and gloomy day. They opened the door to reveal thick and ominous storm clouds moving in. Felicity flinched as a rumble of thunder sounded from over head. "What a rotten day."

Cain looked at her oddly. "No. Actually, this is a good thing. It means I can take you out to breakfast."

Felicity eyed the sky again and then looked back to Cain in worry. "Are you sure? I mean, do you do this kind of thing often? What if it suddenly clears up?"

He smiled. "Why don't you let me worry about that? Paper said there's a big storm front moving in. We're supposed to have weather like this all weekend. We may even see snow before it's through. I wouldn't worry over unexpected sunny skies. It's not likely, besides, we won't be picnicking," he said with a laugh. "We'll go back and get your car. That way if there's a problem, I'll be somewhat protected until you can drive us home. Alright?"

"Okay," she reluctantly agreed.

The sky remained cloudy and dim as promised. They never actually got rain, but thunder did threaten now and then. As she finished up breakfast, Cain urged her to think of something fun for them to do. She professed to be at a loss. He pressed her some more. "There must be something that you can think of. Something whimsical and fun. I don't often do things like that. I want to see you smile and laugh."

An idea popped into her head and he seemed to see it in her eyes, but no, it was silly. It seemed kind of dumb and surely, he wouldn't want to. He nudged her arm from across the table. "Come on, I know you've thought of something. What is it?"

She laughed. "Well, there is something that Deidre and I used to do a lot of, but I don't think it'll be your kind of thing."

"Sounds perfect. Tell me!" he insisted.

"Roller-skating?" she mumbled with a smile. "I know it seems kind of childish but it is a lot of fun once you get the hang of it." He chuckled. "You don't want to, do you?"

"I'm sure you'll be surprised to hear it, but I've actually been on skates before."

"No! *You?*" she asked incredulously.

"Well don't sound so shocked. I did live through roller-disco and all of that. I try to hold myself aloof from such things normally, but there are some fads just impossible to ignore. I'm not very good at it, but I'm willing if you are."

"Well, nobody's clumsier than me. It took a lot of practice, but now at least I can keep from falling on my butt most of the time." He laughed. "I can't even imagine you on skates… or living through the seventies…or the eighties even. Did you wear tight leather pants and a sequin glove on one hand?" she teased with a giggle.

"No," he replied shortly.

"Good, that might have been disturbing," she admitted.

He glanced down at his black leather jacket, t-shirt and jeans with boots. "This is pretty standard attire for the last few decades. My wardrobe is boring but timeless. I don't find myself dressing up for much. And things like crazy patterns and loud colors are not really my style. The seventies were an absolute fashion nightmare for someone like me to live through."

She grinned. "Well, I like your look. Who was it that decided that vampires should wear tuxedos and opera capes anyway?"

"The same person who put them into coffins I'd imagine. Very dramatic, but not anything I'm all that comfortable with, besides, I couldn't very well go skating in a cape, could I? I hope that I remember how."

"I'm sure it'll come back to you. The skates are different now though. Most places use all in-line blades." She laughed at his obvious confusion. "You probably used the old skates that were two wheels in front and two in back. Now they put them all in a line down the middle, like an ice-skate. It takes better balance."

"Well, I'm usually not entirely ungraceful, and it's not as though I'm very worried over breaking anything. I'm sure I'll manage."

She shook her head with a smile. She couldn't believe that this was how they'd spend their day. It would be fun though. "I don't even know where there's a rink around here."

"We'll find one. Come on."

~~~~~~~~~~~~~~~~~~~~~~~~~~~~~~~~~~

They skated, they fell, they laughed and they had a wonderful time. The afternoon flew by. Afterwards they sat on a bench unlacing their skates and carefully surveying the sky through the front windows of the roller-rink.

"Looks as though the weather's holding," Cain observed. "Why don't you drop me off at home so that you can change and get ready for work? Then come back for me and if the sun permits, I'll take you for an early dinner before you have to go in."

"Sounds like a plan." Felicity smiled as Cain finished trading the skates for his boots. "Did you have fun today?"

He beamed back at her. "You know I did. I don't think I'll be strapping wheels to my feet again anytime soon..." Felicity laughed. She had actually turned out to be the better skater. It was so endearing, the way that he had needed to cling to her at first just to keep his feet. "But this has been a day that I will always think back upon with a smile."

Unfortunately, Felicity lost her smile all too easily. Why did he have to go and say things like that? 'Look back upon', as though it were crucial that he build these memories now, because he would never see her again.

She couldn't help it when her eyes filled with tears at the reminder of his plans to leave. He noticed and admonished her for it. "You're not allowed to cry," he said firmly.

"Why not?"

His tone softened. "Because if you do, then you'll go and make me cry, and ruin our fun day."

She bit her lip and blinked to force back the tears.

"Where do you want to go for dinner?"

~~~~~~~~~~~~~~~~~~~~~~~~~~~~~~~~~~

After dinner, she dropped him off at home before she left for work. He promised to meet her at the DownTime later. He had a 'date with a butcher' to attend first.

He arrived just before eight to spend the last two hours of Felicity's shift, reading in the café. Friday nights were fairly busy, and working with Harold left her to feel less inclined to spend her time hanging about the café with Cain instead of at her register.

Things were slowing down now. 9:30, they'd be closing soon. She was just finishing ringing up a customer, when she noticed someone new enter the store.

He wasn't at all remarkable in appearance really. Just another boy. He was almost fifteen maybe, with shoulder length wispy blond hair. He wore jeans and sneakers with a brown and orange camouflage-hunting jacket.

What struck Felicity as strange, was the fact that he didn't go to browse in the bookshelves as most people did. He stood at the front scanning the store as though looking for someone. He had very bright green eyes that seemed to pierce through every person they rested upon. They never paused on Felicity though. After a minute or two, he headed directly for the café.

He seemed to be making his way straight to Cain. Sure enough, he reached Cain's table and stopped before it. When Cain looked up at him, Felicity could swear that the boy actually bowed his head to Cain before speaking. Cain offered him a chair and the boy sat. They treated each other rather formally. Felicity didn't imagine that they might be old friends; it all seemed very business-like. They spent the next twenty minutes or so quietly talking while Felicity tried not to very obviously observe them.

Cain never even glanced in her direction. The boy must have had his full attention. Felicity began straightening her register area and making ready to close as she watched them. She found herself staring hard at the boy. He had to be a vampire. Who else would come to speak to Cain?

It was rather odd that his manner was nothing like the young teenager that he looked to be. She wondered how old he was. Why, he could be a sixty-year-old man for all she knew! How strange and frustrating might it be for him to be forever treated like a kid? Then again, it surely had some advantages as well.

Finally, they stood. She saw the boy hand something to Cain. She couldn't really tell what it was. Something small, like a business card maybe? Very odd.

The boy started in her direction as Cain began gathering his things to leave. As the boy approached the registers on his way to the door, he turned his eyes on Felicity for the first time.

He looked at her as though he knew exactly who she was and she could have sworn that he actually gave her a slight smile. It was not malicious in nature but Felicity found it a bit eerie all the same.

Her mark. Of course, he could see it. He must have known she was there and her relationship to Cain all along. He just hadn't spared her a glance at first because Cain had been his priority.

The boy turned away from her and left the store. She just stood there, watching him walk across the parking lot. She was a bit startled when she looked back at the register and found Cain standing before it. She hadn't noticed his approach.

He smiled at her surprise. "I know you're dying to ask, so I'll save you the trouble. Yes, he was undead. He's a messenger, from Arif. They'll be leaving town. He and his horde will be traveling up to Albany.

I must say, I'm rather relieved. I didn't relish the idea of them hanging about after I've gone."

Felicity looked back out the front windows but the boy was gone. She sighed as she turned her eyes down to the counter before her. She had no idea what to say, and once again, the reality of Cain's leaving was a depressing weight upon her.

He seemed to sense her melancholy thoughts and sought to lighten them. "I've been to the market. I bought some ice cream for later."

She looked up at him hesitantly as he tried to make her smile. "What flavor?"

"They didn't have 'Butter Rum Ripple'. Do you like 'Butter Pecan'?" He smiled as she nodded yes. "I also bought whipped cream, chocolate sauce, butterscotch syrup, sprinkles and cherries."

She laughed. "That's an awful lot of toppings. I thought you didn't even really eat ice cream."

"I don't." He leaned forward conspiratorially and spoke quietly with a sly smile. "I'm planning to decorate *you*."

Her eyes went wide and she surely turned very red in the face as she sought to hide her shocked smile. She tried to gather her composure as he leaned closer and gave her a kiss on the cheek. "Sounds sticky," she whispered.

"We'll shower," he whispered back.

Harold made her jump guiltily as he yelled from the café. "It's ten o'clock."

Cain just smiled. "I'll see you outside."

~~~~~~~~~~~~~~~~~~~~~~~~~~~~~~~

Saturday night found Felicity at her register again, daydreaming over last night and the day past. The evening before had indeed been quite sticky, romantic, a little silly and very memorable. Today had been spent in quiet comfort. Cain had first taken her out through the pouring rain to breakfast once again. Then as the rain eased up, they had spent some time walking along the edge of the stream in the park through the drizzle. It was wet and cold but she'd hardly even noticed. Cain had held a large umbrella over them and they'd watched the ducks playing in the puddles along the bank. All the while, floating through her head was Cain's statement that *she* was his sunshine.

They went home to Cain's, stripped off their wet clothes and made love. Slow, tender and almost surreal. She'd allowed him to drink from her again and it had been one of the most intimate and erotic interludes of their relationship. Just closing her eyes now to think of it could make her head spin.

They'd spent the remainder of the day wrapped in a big fluffy blanket as Cain read her excerpts and recited remembered passages from some of his favorite books and poems.

It was so comfortable and soothing just to lie there with him reading to her. It felt like perfect peace and happiness. How could she even question the desire to spend all of her life just so? What more could she want?

It was wonderful to see him become so animated and excited over ideas and questions posed in the literature they perused. They had lively discussions and wistful imaginings and just... talked. He knew so much! It seemed as though there wasn't an idea or a situation that he hadn't already encountered and formed an opinion on. More than ever before, she found him absolutely fascinating.

Tonight. She would tell him tonight. The decision was made. No more nervous wondering or uncertain hesitation. No more depression and grief over future separation. She wanted to be with him, she did; for always.

What good was humanity without someone as marvelous as Cain to share life with? She would let him drain her and then she would drink of his blood, as much and as many times as he thought necessary until it was done. She would become a vampire.

She knew that he could do it without worry over physical difficulties. He was so meticulous and careful about such things. He had sounded disapproving of his power to change others when they had spoken the other night, but that was only regret over past mistakes and resignation over a decision for the future already made.

He had offered her his blood before, more than once. She had always let him think that it was out of the question. She was sure that his recent disapproval of the deed stemmed from the fact that he was trying to resign himself to the certainty that she did not *want* to be transformed. How happy he would be, to know that she'd changed her mind!

There were certain drawbacks of course, but that was to be expected with any big decision. She was strong. She could handle it. She could get through *anything* with Cain at her side.

She would miss her family, but she could probably still see them once in awhile. In the beginning anyway, before her failure to age became noticeable. She'd just have to be careful, not to let on how she'd changed. She and Cain could get married before them at an evening ceremony, and then he could whisk her away to live elsewhere. She would tell her parents that she'd be moving abroad. Maybe he would even take her to see Herald Manor!

Being a creature of the night wasn't at all what she had originally perceived it to be. So, she would no longer be able to walk in the sunlight, big deal. It's not as though she could never see the sun again, it would just have to be from someplace sheltered and protected. A small price to pay for so many magical abilities!

She could live forever! That was almost as scary as it was exciting. Was this the way she wanted to look for the rest of her life? Never to grow or change in any significant way? No wrinkles, no gray hair, no disease. She would be forever immune and protected from such things.

She would be able to see and do all of the things that Cain could do… in time. He would teach her, to see marks and recognize other vampires.

Other vampires… she would have nothing to fear from them now. Nothing to fear from anyone. She couldn't help but recall Sindy as she had fought her way through the zombies who had attacked her in the bookstore entrance that night. She had been so fearless. Felicity had found it amazing.

Sindy… and other young vampires. Cain felt a duty to teach and protect them. He would want to continue with that. She could help him. He could teach her the way of things and she could work at his side. Helping others and saving people. That certainly seemed like a worthwhile endeavor to commit one's life to.

It would be scary and new and not at all what she had expected for her life, but she would be with Cain. That was a reward even greater than any strange new magical ability.

Why wasn't he here yet? He'd said that he was coming to meet her just as he had the evening before. Perhaps he had gone to see Arif and his men before they left.

Still, he should be here by now. Doubt and worry had just begun to creep into her mind when she felt him. Yes, he was definitely moving closer, coming to the DownTime. He was moving very fast; he must have taken his motorcycle. She breathed a sigh of relief as she felt the comforting and familiar warmth and shivers of his presence approach and surround her.

Finally, she saw him pull into the lot, riding his bike as she'd surmised. He parked it and entered the store. She gave him a broad smile as he came to her. He gave her a little kiss hello over the counter. "I thought you'd be here sooner," she chastised him.

"Sorry, I had some stuff to do." He glanced about the store; it was fairly empty. They'd be closing in less than half an hour. "Do you think you could steal away for a moment?"

She looked over to see Ben cleaning up after his last customers in the café. They were just putting on coats to leave. "Sure, hang on." She came out from behind the register and called to Ben as he began to head back to the counter with a tray of empty cups. "Hey Ben, I'll be right back, okay?"

Ben did not look very happy, but he didn't say anything. The store was empty, it's not like anyone was going to buy anything else. He'd deal. She turned back to Cain. "Is everything all right?"

"Yeah." He nodded. "Come on." He gestured for her to follow him outside. He held the door as Ben's customers left, and then she went out as well. She folded her arms for warmth in the night chill.

The rain had stopped earlier and now it was just a bit windy. The dark clouds overhead made the night seem that much more oppressive and ominous. Certainly, this was the calm before the storm.

"What's up?"

He moved away from the entrance to the store and she followed. Cain turned to her and reached out to put his arms around her waist and pull her in for a kiss before answering.

"I've got to go."

She stared at him uncomprehending for the space of a second. Then she became indignant. "What? Now? Like *this*? I thought we'd have tomorrow. You can't leave *now!*" She couldn't help but move a step back from him in quiet outrage.

He glanced up at the sky. "There's a big cold front moving in. There's even a blizzard warning out. Not exactly motorcycle weather brewing. If I don't leave now, I may get snowed in. And if I were to let myself get snowed in, I might also let myself forget to leave after. I've got to go."

He looked miserable but firm. After her initial shock, she broke into a smile. "No, but see... you don't have to. I've been wanting to tell you something."

He didn't look eagerly expectant as she'd hoped. Perhaps he hadn't guessed. "I want to come with you. I want to do it... let you change me. We can be together, just like you wanted."

First, he looked confused, then very surprised. "But... you don't want to be like me."

"I want to be *with* you."

"It's not the same. You'll have to leave school... your family!"

"I know. I don't care."

He stared at her very closely for a long time. She couldn't tell what he might be thinking. Getting used to the idea she supposed, but he hadn't smiled yet. She was waiting for the broad grin of relief that she had expected. He very slightly shook his head. "You'll lose your *life*."

"I'll have a new life... with you."

"Felicity, you're too young to know what is right for your future."

"No, I'm not!" He was going to argue with her? "Do you even remember what it's like to be young? To know what you want and to have everyone around you believe that they know better? Like your father or your brother did?"

He gave a little laugh. "Yes, but it turned out that my family really *did* know what was best for me. Your parents want you to have an education and the responsibility of a job to help you develop character.

I want you to *live* life before you die. Not to choose something that you don't even really want or understand just because of me. You'd resent me terribly for it."

"No, I won't! I love you! I want to be with you!" She felt desperate to convince him. He had to know that she was resolute.

"I love you too, but you can't even fathom all that you'd be giving up. It's a difficult existence that I lead."

"I'm strong and I'm not afraid to do what I have to."

Cain studied her face for a very long moment. "I know that's true... and it will serve you well." She smiled as he raised his hand to hold the side of her face. He breathed deeply and sighed. "Do you trust me?"

She knew that he wouldn't fail her. He would do it right. "Implicitly."

"Then do you promise to do as I say; follow my exact instructions?"

"I promise," she assured him.

"Good." He smiled at her and stroked his thumb back and forth across her cheek as he held her chin cupped in his hand. "Finish school."

"What?" she asked in confusion.

"Find a career doing something that you enjoy, something that does good in the world."

It suddenly dawned on her what he was saying. "No."

He kept on, though his voice slightly trembled. "Don't be afraid to love again. Keep me locked in a little corner of your heart if you will, but then give your love to another."

Her eyes filled with tears. "No!"

His eyes were tear filled as well, yet he did not waiver. "Choose wisely. Find someone who will recognize the amazing young woman that you are and will love you deeply and truly."

"Cain no!" Tears were spilling down her cheeks in earnest now. He would not do this. He could not leave her here!

"Get married, be happy. Have babies. Lots and lots of them! You'll be a wonderful mother." He was smiling through tears of his own and it reminded her of how he'd looked when speaking of his daughter, so full of love and pride.

But he could not do this. He *did* love her, didn't he? "Cain please!"

"*Live* your life."

"Cain no, please! You can't leave me! I want to come with you!" He took a very deep breath and exhaled it slowly. He gazed into her eyes and then leaned forward for another kiss. He did love her. She knew that he did. His kiss was passionate and true. He would keep her with him. The love in that kiss had to mean that he would. Their kiss was long and loving. She regretfully gave up his lips as he leaned back to look at her again and speak quietly. "No."

There was no air to breathe. She felt as though her vision was blurred and she couldn't see clearly and his voice was thick in her ears. She could not have heard him right. He let her go and walked to his waiting motorcycle. No.

No! He'd said no? That can't be right. He loved her! He wanted to be with her! He mounted the bike.

Her mouth was open and nothing was coming out. Her cheeks were wet and freezing in the wind. Wait! This isn't how it's supposed to end! She couldn't find her voice to say the words.

He quickly started the engine, loud and thundering. "Cain!" Now the sound leapt from her throat to stop him and was lost in the rolling reverberation of the Harley, but he knew. She shook the seeming paralysis that had held her and began to move towards him. He smiled and mouthed her a kiss.

"Wait!"

He didn't.

He turned to speed away even as she ran to him. It was no use. "Cain wait! Please! You can't leave me!" She screamed after him into the roar of the engine as she ran across the empty parking lot. Even *she* had trouble picking out her voice in the din. No one could have heard her, except for maybe him. It didn't matter.

He was gone.

She just stood there in the empty parking lot. He was gone. He'd left her. He left her! He said no and he left.
He said no.
She had no idea how long she stood there. Time stopped when he was lost to view. He was gone. Nothing else mattered. She stood there staring at the empty road. He was gone.

"'Liss?"

"Felicity, what are you doing? I'm waiting for you to close."
Footsteps behind her. She didn't turn. She couldn't speak.
"It's freezing out here. Do you realize that it's snowing?" Ben reached her and put a hand on her shoulder to turn her to face him. She just stared at him vacantly. His eyes took in her tear-streaked face. His annoyance immediately turned to concern. "'Liss what's wrong?"
Her eyes didn't really see him. She just stared into the falling snow. She needed to say something but there were only two things going through her head. "He said no. He said no and he left. He *left* me."
"Ah 'Liss." Now reaction suddenly hit and as Ben used the hand on her shoulder to pull her closer, she began to cry.

She stood in the parking lot and sobbed into his chest as he held her.

She cried and she sobbed and she mumbled things that he couldn't hear. Ben didn't ask her to clarify. He didn't say a word. He just held her as she cried.

He'd left. He had really left.

Didn't he want to be with her? Didn't he love her? Didn't he think she could do it?

She sobbed until nothing would come any longer but dry gasps for air. Finally, Ben held her back a little and gently swiped the wet hair from her face. "We should go in. You're covered in snow and it's freezing out here."

She didn't say anything, but let him lead her inside.

She felt as though she were in a trance. He'd said no.

They entered the store and her eyes fell on the register. Oh yeah. She was supposed to be working. She started towards it but Ben took her by the arm. "No that's okay. I'll do your stuff. Come sit."

He steered her into the café and pulled out a chair. She sat and stared out the window into the falling snow.

"You want some coffee?" She didn't look at him but gently shook her head. "No. Of course you don't want coffee."

He watched her quietly for a moment. "I know what you need. I have just the thing. Hot chocolate. You want some hot chocolate?" She just shrugged as she stared out into the snow. "You like marshmallows or whipped cream?" She didn't answer. "I like whipped cream, with a little powdered cocoa sprinkled on top... I'll be right back."

She hardly noticed as he set the cup down before her a few minutes later. "Careful, it's hot underneath."

He just stood there for a minute, watching her stare out the window. "I've got to go finish closing out the registers." He left.

He left. How could he do that to her? How could Cain just leave? Didn't he love her?

He did. She knew that he did. *That's* why he'd left. He thought it was wrong to take her away from her life. He thought that eventually she would be unhappy and regretful.

He was wrong... wasn't he?

It didn't matter.

He left.

"'Liss? I'm done."

Felicity looked up to find Ben standing there with her coat over his arm and her purse in his hand. He put them down on the empty chair next to her. "You done with that?" he asked, gesturing towards her untouched hot cocoa.

"Yeah." She looked up at him as he took the cup. "Thanks," she added belatedly.

He took it back behind the counter and dumped it out into the sink as she put on her coat. When he came back, he had his own coat on as well. He shut the lights and she followed him to the door. He set the alarm and stood under the overhang looking out into the snow for a minute. "You want me to drive you?"

She glanced at their cars. They were dusted with snow, but it wasn't bad yet. "No. I'm okay."

He walked her to her car. She got in to warm it up and he went to start his own. He came back with a snowbrush to

357

dust off her windows. It was light and fluffy snow. Not really sticking yet. She just sat there behind the wheel watching Ben brush off their cars. What was she supposed to do now? Go back to the dorm? Go to bed? Wake up and resume her life?

Ben came and tapped on her window. "You're good to go. Are you going to be okay?"

"I'm strong." She had said that to Cain. She'd meant strong enough for him to turn her, not strong enough for him to go.

"You want me to hang out for a little?" Ben was watching her carefully.

"No. I'm all right." She knew where she wanted to be. "Thanks."

He smiled and rested his hand on her arm for a minute. She turned away. He left for his own car. She rolled up the window. He waited for her to pull out of the lot first. Damn.

She drove back to the dorm. She sat in the parking lot for a minute just staring at the steering wheel. Then she turned the car around and went to Cain's. She knew that he wouldn't be there, but she couldn't help it.

No motorcycle in the driveway. No telltale shivers of his presence anywhere. The snow was really coming down now. She could hardly see. She wondered how far he'd gotten before he had to stop.

Crazy notions of driving out blind and trying to 'feel' him flitted through her mind. No. She wasn't *that* stupid. Cain could afford to take chances like that. He had assurance of survival that she did not. She shut off the car and mounted his front steps. The key. He'd given her a spare, for the night of the Halloween ball. She kept it in her purse. She dug it out and worked the lock.

It was dark and barren as always. She closed the door behind her and confidently strode across the room to the basement stairs. There she flipped on the stairwell light and made her way down.

Cain's room. She managed to find the bedside lamp without tripping over anything. She turned it on. The room looked just the same. He hadn't taken anything. There was nothing to take. Just the bed, still messed from when last they'd been in it. The pile of books they'd been reading still lay on the floor.

Felicity dropped her things and stripped off her coat and shoes. She climbed under the covers of the bed and buried her face in the pillow. It still smelled lightly of his aftershave. She shut the light, lay there in his bed and cried herself to sleep.

~~~~~~~~~~~~~~~~~~~~~~~~~~~~~~~~~~

It was dark when she woke. It was always dark down here. That was the point. She sat up and found the switch for the lamp next to the bed. Her watch showed the time to be 7:30 a.m.

She just sat there on his bed for a few minutes, surveying the room. She got up feeling almost numb. As though her limbs were heavy and she moved in slow motion. He was gone.

She went to the laundry room. Nothing. He'd taken his clothes and left nothing behind. She went to the bathroom.

The cabinet was bare. She went behind the bar. The refrigerator was empty and clean. No trace of what it had once held. No one could ever guess.

He wasn't coming back. She'd known, but still...

She wandered over to the books by the bed on the floor. She picked a few of his favorites out of the pile. She would keep them. After donning her shoes and coat, she made her way up the stairs with her purse and an armful of books.

When she opened the front door, she was blinded by the brightness of sunlight on snow. The sky was sunny, the world crisp and clean, covered in white. She was lucky to keep her feet on the stairs as she trudged through the snow without a free hand.

She managed to unstick the icy passenger door of her car and dump the books on the seat before they fell into the snow. She reached across to put in the key and start the engine. Once it caught, she straightened back up to stand outside as she let it run and warm up on its own.

She stood gazing out at the ground and the rooftops, blanketed in fresh snowfall. The branches of the trees were encased in ice, making them seem made of glass. It was beautiful. She wondered if Cain could see it at all, from wherever he was. Would it hurt his eyes? He was probably sleeping.

New tears tried to drip down her face once again as she thought of all that she had lost. She forced herself to try and blink them away...to look at all that she had not.

A cardinal was flitting through the branches of the trees nearby; a bright blood red streak and a snippet of song, singing to all the world of how it was good to be alive.

~~~~~~~~~~~~~~~~~~~~~~~~~~~~~~~~~~~~~~

Felicity found it very hard to agree in the first few days that passed, but alive she was; a fact that wasn't going to change anytime soon she'd imagine. Not that she wanted to die. What had she wanted... really? To be with Cain of course, but beyond that? Had her decision been a foolish one? Should she be thankful that he had neglected her wishes? She found it very hard to feel that way... right now. Maybe someday.

The days passed. Life went on, whether she wanted it to or not. She went to class. Partly because she knew that Cain would want her to, but mostly because... what else was there to do? She didn't want to go home. She had spent all day Sunday alone in her room crying, she certainly needed no more of *that* if it could be avoided. Enough regretful and depressing thoughts filled her head when she tried to fall asleep each night.

She found herself lying in her bed and thinking of him before she could fall asleep. He was probably just waking up. Where was he? Did he miss her? She missed him so bad that it hurt.

At least the last time that they had been apart, she had known that he was there. She could feel him and believe that somehow things would work out. Not anymore. He was gone.

She saw no one, not really. She went to class as though sleepwalking, going through the motions. She took to eating lunch in her room. A yogurt, a sandwich, whatever. Nothing really mattered. She called in sick to work; until Thursday morning. She got a phone call from Mr. Penten begging her to come in if she was at all well. He was having coverage problems. Fine. Whatever. She sighed as she hung up the receiver of the pay phone out in the hall. Time for class.

After History class, she went back to the dorm and headed for the kitchen. She opened the fridge for her yogurt when she realized, yesterday she'd eaten the last one. Damn. She had nothing left. She hadn't done very much shopping to begin with. Her eyes searched the refrigerator, as though something with her name on it would suddenly materialize. No such luck.

Everything else was neatly labeled. Regina, Debbie, Bridgette, Penny… The labels and marker were right there in the door. Everyone used them, it discouraged problems. She briefly entertained the notion of just taking something of someone else's. No one would notice.

A sound behind her made her jump. Deborah stood there with arms crossed. "Are you just going to stand there?" Felicity moved out of the way for her and headed for the door. Cafeteria it is.

She was on line with a chef salad when she noticed Ben. He was sitting with a bunch of guys. Some of them were the ones he had introduced her to early last week. He didn't notice her. She didn't bother to try and make eye contact. She paid for her stuff and came out to head for an empty table in the corner. She had just settled everything and sat down when Ben came to her table with his tray. "This seat taken?" he asked.

She just shrugged and gestured for him to sit if he wanted. He smiled and sat as he spoke. "I was beginning to think you had given up eating." She just shrugged again and started on her salad. "I would've called but... I figured you just wanted to be left alone for awhile." He tilted his head to meet her eyes. "It's good to see you. I've had to resort to sittin' with *those* guys," he said as he jerked a thumb in the direction of his former lunch companions.

She begrudgingly smiled. "Allie's not back yet?"

He traded his smile for annoyed concern. "No. How long did she say she'd be gone?"

She thought for a moment. "Two weeks. That's how long she said she took off from work anyway."

Ben was obviously counting days in his head. "It has to *be* two weeks by now! When did she leave, Tuesday?"

"So?" Felicity dropped her fork onto the plate and gave Ben a steady stare of irritation. "Ben, she's in the Pocono's, with the guy that she loves. *She's* happy. I'm sure it's very easy to lose track of time when you're spending it like that." She tried to keep the resentful edge from her voice, but it didn't really work.

Ben just watched her for a moment, and then decided to drop the subject. He began to eat his lunch.

Something suddenly occurred to her. Allie was with Mattie. Mattie knew Cain. They were friends, they kept in touch. Most likely Mattie would know how to find him. She could talk to Allie when she got back... get her to convince Mattie to take Felicity to see Cain. It was a hope...

Felicity looked at Ben again and couldn't help but feel bad. "Waiting to make up with her huh?"

"I just want to get it all over with. Tell her I'm sorry and put it behind us. I don't know what'll happen from there, but waiting around like this sucks."

Ben didn't say any more about it and they ate in silence as cafeteria commotion went on around them.

After a few minutes, Felicity looked back up at him in realization. "Hey, I got a weird phone call this morning. Mr. Penten wanted to know if I'd start taking more hours because Ashley quit!"

Ben went back to eating. "Yeah, I know."

"What's going on?" Felicity asked.

"She's leaving," Ben said quietly.

"Well, I get *that*," she told him.

"No, I mean… school, town, she's *leaving*."

"Why?" Felicity asked.

Ben shrugged. "She's transferring schools."

"In the middle of a semester? That's ridiculous! Why would she do that?"

"What do you think? She got her parents to let her go to sunny California. She's been goin' on about how she was really meant for the west coast, but I know it's because of the ever-present blood-sucking population in this town. She's freaked," Ben stated bluntly.

"I thought she didn't believe you?"

Ben gave her a steady look. "You know, Ashley isn't really as stupid as she pretends to be. She just does that because she thinks guys find it attractive. Which really is stupid, so… there's an oxy-moron for you."

"You never seemed to mind," Felicity replied a bit acidly. He dropped his eyes and looked away. Why was she being mean to him? Her unhappiness wasn't his fault. "When does she leave?" she asked gently.

"She already left. This morning," he explained.

She looked at him sympathetically. "I'm sorry."

He gave a little chuckle. "I'm not. I was ready to break up with her anyway, she was drivin' me nuts." Felicity couldn't help but laugh at his confession. He gave her a little nod and then shrugged. "Long term relationships were never really my thing."

"Why not?" she asked.

He seemed to think about it for a minute and then leaned forward to speak to her confidentially. "I'll let you in on a little secret. When it comes to girls…" He leaned back again and spread his arms as though very impressed with himself. "I can wine 'em and dine 'em, date 'em and dance with 'em. Spend evenings of questionable morality and all of that," he added with a sly smile. Felicity rolled her eyes and looked away momentarily with a smirk. "But when it comes to every day stuff, routine hangin' out, seeing 'em all the time… it never works. Girls always seem to bore me to tears or drive me insane."

Felicity opened her mouth in disbelief and eyed him for a moment in questioning irritation. "Thanks a lot."

Ben rolled his eyes and smiled. "Well not *you*. You and Allie are like the only normal girls I know." She arched her brow. "Alright, *Allie's* questionable."

She laughed and went back to eating her lunch. Ben did too. He spoke again without really looking at her. "Anyway, I think I'm going to fade back from the whole dating scene for a while. 'Remove myself from the market' as it were."

She laughed as he continued. "No really. I'm going to focus on some more important stuff for a while. Save some money, concentrate on my grades. I'm always so busy thinkin' about my plans for the weekend that I never really spend time planning for the future.

I don't really want to live with my dad forever you know," he admitted sheepishly. She giggled. "Dating's fun, but I'm starting to think I should take a break from the impractical fun stuff and concentrate more on what's real. You know, take a break and have a life."

She stared at him over the table for a minute. He just smiled and finished his lunch. She answered him quietly. "Yeah, me too."

He spoke to her as he began preparing to leave for his next class. "It's a little hard to swallow, but at some time or another I figure you gotta take the red pill."

"Huh?"

He looked up from packing up his stuff and stared at her over the table. "Don't even tell me that you've never seen 'The Matrix'."

"Nope. I'm guessing there was a pill involved?"

"Unbelievable." He shook his head in contempt and then looked to give her explanation of his attitude. "I watch a lot of movies; I tend to make references. When Allie's here... she *gets* it, but it's not much fun if you never even know what the hell I'm talking about!"

"Sorry," she offered.

"Fortunately, it's fixable. I am hereby placing myself in charge of your cinema education. What's today, Thursday?"

She looked at him dubiously. "Yeah..."

"Cool. From now on, Thursday is movie night. After work, my house, you bring the popcorn, I've got the movies. You in?"

She looked at him blankly for a moment. "Okay…" she answered hesitantly.

"Great. I've gotta go. I'll see you later."

She was still sitting there, watching him leave when she thought to say 'bye'.

~~~~~~~~~~~~~~~~~~~~~~~~~~~~~~~~~~

Later at work, she finished closing out her register and went to sit at the counter to wait for Ben, wondering how she was going to get out of 'movie night'. Why had she even said she'd go? It wasn't really something she felt up to.

Ben looked up at her from counting his drawer. "So, you know what you wanna watch? I've got just about everything you could think of."

"Oh, you know… I think I'm going to have to pass."

He stopped counting. "How come?"

She looked at him blankly for a minute. "I haven't got any popcorn."

Ben laughed and put down the bills in his hand. He came out from behind the counter and walked to the shelf down in front of the counter to her right. He picked up and handed her a package of 'movie butter microwave popcorn'. "This one's on me."

She rolled her eyes and smiled. "Ben, I'm sorry… I'm just not really in the mood."

He looked disappointed. "Okay. I understand. You probably wanna just sit in your room alone and be depressed… again." She avoided eye contact. "But I wish you'd change your mind and come. *I* haven't got anything else to do." He eyed her hopefully and smiled. "It's just a movie. I promise we won't have *too* much fun."

She sighed. He stood there and wouldn't let her break his gaze until she answered. It would be better than having to endure another '3P Thursday' at the dorm. "All right, I guess."

He just smiled and went to finish closing out. She followed him in her car back to his house. It was a small L-shaped ranch style home. No other cars were in the driveway. He opened the front door with his key and she followed him in.

The house was nice… but a little unkempt. Not very well decorated and definitely in need of a woman's touch. She got the impression that Ben and his dad didn't do very much entertaining.

From the entryway, Felicity could see the dining room; she doubted anyone had eaten in there in the recent past though. The table was piled with what looked like a month's worth of mail and newspapers. The kitchen could also be seen from the entryway. It was nice and fairly clean, but the sink was piled high with dishes.

She glanced around as Ben hung his coat in the hall closet. He reached out to take hers. "Is your dad home?" she asked.

"No, he's away again. He had to go up to Albany for a business meeting."

She walked a little further into the house as Ben hung up her coat. The living room was nice and fairly neat, but every table seemed to have a thin coat of dust over it, as though no one ever even used the room on a regular basis. She took a few more steps in and was about to sit on the couch when Ben stopped her.

"Oh, we're not going to watch the movie out here. My T.V.'s much better." She looked at the old 25" television in the living room and then at Ben, doubtfully. He smiled. "Really. My room's down here," he said with a gesture down the hall.

Was he kidding? Now she outright laughed. "Said the spider to the fly."

He realized her thought and laughed himself. "No, it's not what you think, believe me. If I were trying to be *slick,* I think I could do better than *this.* I'm on a break, remember? In fact, I'll have you know that you are the only girl – well, besides Allie – who has ever been privileged to even *see* my room."

Felicity eyed him skeptically. "Aren't you supposed to have a reputation as some sort of 'ladies man'?"

He looked a little embarrassed but answered her steadily. "I take them to 'the Hilton'."

She raised her eyebrows with a smirk. "Classy," she murmured.

Ben rolled his eyes and shook his head as he started down the hall. "Come on." He opened the door to his room and stepped aside for Felicity to enter.

Whoa.

It was a fairly large bedroom decorated sparsely in various shades of blue. It was impeccably neat, everything clean and organized. It almost looked like an office. This effect was especially heightened by the fact that the entire wall opposite the door was covered with floor to ceiling shelves except for a space in the center that held a huge flat screen T.V.

Most of the shelves were filled with movies; the rest seemed to house plastic sleeved comic books. Felicity walked a few steps further into the room. It looked like a wall from blockbuster, they were even in alphabetical order; and the T.V. was almost too big for the room really. She looked back at Ben. "I'm guessing your dad's not charging you rent."

"Told you my T.V. was better."

"A little *big*, isn't it?" She started to grin. "Isn't that supposed to mean that you're compensating for something?"

He laughed. "Hardly. When I move out of this dump and get my own place it'll be just fine."

She turned to see the rest of the room. The wall to her far right had a window, with his full-size bed in the corner that met the wall the door was on. It was neatly made with a comforter that had a geometric pattern of blue and white.

There was also a desk on that wall with more shelves above it, but these shelves did not hold movies. They were filled with at least two dozen... "You have *toys?*" she asked with a broad smile.

"They're not toys, they're action figures."

"M-hmmm." She went for closer inspection. Comic book personalities she assumed. She recognized Batman and Spiderman of course, but most of them were of characters that she didn't know. She picked up the figure of a very well endowed and scantily clad woman with an arched brow and a smile. "So, what's *her* name?" she asked, bobbing the girl around as though 'playing' with her.

Ben became flustered and walked to retrieve the figure. "Et-dt-dt. Don't *touch* them. All right, please?" Felicity laughed at him as he carefully repositioned the lady in question. "See, this is why I don't let girls in my room."

Felicity giggled some more. "Sorry. Wow, Allie was right. You *do* have an inner-geek."

"I am not a geek! They're collector's items. Graphic novels and comics are cool."

"Well, I don't read comics, but I do like your toys…" She corrected herself as he looked at her warningly, "action figures."

"So, what do you want to watch?" She looked at the wall. It was pretty over-whelming; she had no idea what to pick. "Tell you what, why don't we watch 'The Matrix'?" Ben suggested. "It's pretty intense sci-fi for a beginner, but I'll talk you through it. At least you'll get the 'pill' thing."

She laughed. "Okay."

"Make yourself comfortable." He walked over and took the pillows from the head of the bed. He then placed them against the wall, the length of the bed so that they could sit on it like a couch. "I'll go make the popcorn." He was just leaving when he ducked his head back into the room. "And don't touch my stuff."

~~~~~~~~~~~~~~~~~~~~~~~~~~~~~~~~

He was right, it was a good movie. It was also very sci-fi and a little confusing for someone as uninitiated as her, but Ben helped her get it. The red pill represented reality… at least that was one reference explained. She was probably going to have nightmares about robot spiders and things in her belly button… but he was right, it *was* better than sitting alone in her room depressed… again.

She finished the last of the popcorn as the credits rolled. Ben took a swig of soda and then patted her on the back. "So, you are now one movie wiser. Do it again next week?"

"Next Thursday's Thanksgiving."

"Oh yeah. You going home?"

"Of course, I am; are you kidding? My parents are ready to kill me! They bought me a car for my birthday and I haven't driven home once since. What are you doing? Do you have like an aunt or somebody that you visit, or is it just you and your dad?"

"I don't have any other family around here, and since my mom died, my dad's not much for holidays. He always says he'll be around, and then takes off for some last-minute work emergency. Usually, Allie comes over. She's not a very good cook, but between the two of us we usually manage to concoct something edible."

"That's it? No house full of people, no giant turkey?"

Ben shrugged. "I'm used to it. Thanksgiving's not really a big deal anyway."

"It is at my house." What if Allie didn't come back in time? What if Allie didn't come back *at all?* It wasn't something she wanted to bring up to Ben, but it did seem a distinct possibility. She knew that he worried over it too. "You and your dad should come have dinner with us."

"What? No, that's okay," he assured her uncomfortably.

"Really. Why not?" she asked.

"We're not going to just invite ourselves over your house for a major holiday," he explained.

"I thought you didn't think that Thanksgiving was a big deal?" she asked him factitiously. "You're not inviting yourself; I'm inviting you."

"You should talk to your mom first. She probably doesn't want extra people for such a big dinner."

"I'll ask, but I know she won't care. You should come, ask your dad." He still looked doubtful. Truthfully, she couldn't stand the idea of having to face her family alone. She didn't want to talk about school or answer questions about what she'd been doing. She'd much rather take the focus off of herself.

Besides, she came from a fairly large family. Ben's pathetic descriptions of his anticipations for Thanksgiving were depressing. He should come. "My mom's a great cook. I make the stuffed mushrooms and the sweet potatoes. You like mushrooms?"

"Yeah," he admitted with a little smile.

"I put extra Romano cheese in them. And the sweet potatoes… lots of brown sugar, granola and marshmallows on top. They're really good." He didn't answer but he looked like he might sway towards a yes. "My brother Eddie isn't even coming home I don't think, so there's an extra bed right there. And the sofa in the living room opens up too."

"You have a brother?"

She laughed. "I've got three."

Ben looked at her for a moment, and then he laughed too as he seemed to nod his head to himself. "Now I get it."

"Get what?" she asked.

"Why you're always calling me big brother. You miss them."

She let out a sharp laugh. "Hardly!"

"Older or younger?" he asked.

"One older, two younger. Edmund is a junior over at Syracuse. He's on the football team. 'Go Orangemen'. He and my dad are like totally into it. He hopes to go pro. He's going to dinner at his girlfriends' this year. My mom's depressed."

"A junior? So, he's *my* age," Ben observed.

She looked at him oddly. "Oh yeah... ew."

"Thanks," he replied with a laugh.

"Then there's Robert. He's 16, annoying, obnoxious and smart as hell. Does way better than me at everything school related and loves making me look like an idiot. He'll probably get a full scholarship and then point out to my parents how much money *I'm* costing them for school.

My little brother Richie is 14. He's sweet... for a teenage boy, I guess. Thank God. One Robbie is bad enough," she assured him.

Ben laughed. "I always wished I had brothers."

"Yeah well, come spend the weekend at my house and I guarantee you'll be cured. Ask your dad, okay?"

"Yeah, okay. If you clear it at your house first," he told her.

"No problem." She glanced down at her watch. It was after midnight. "I'd better go; I've got Algebra at 8:15 tomorrow morning."

"Yeah, it's late." He walked her to the front door. "I'm glad you came. I hope the movie was... diverting."

She laughed. "Yeah. Thanks. I think I'll still be trying to figure it out tomorrow."

"It does take a few viewings to soak in," he said with a smile as he helped her to put on her coat.

She couldn't help but wonder if Cain had ever seen it, and what he might think. It didn't really seem like his kind of movie on the surface, but she knew that the questions it posed and the ideas that it explored would be the kind of thing that they could spend all night talking about.

After a week of misery, she had finally spent over two hours not thinking about and missing him... and now here she was back at square one. Damn.

She sighed and looked back up at Ben as he opened the door for her. "Good night."

Chapter 14 - Have faith

Cain

On the road
Midnight, Saturday

Cain slowed around the curve in the road, wondering again if he should stop for the rest of the night. The weather was likely to get worse before it got better, but he needed to put as much distance between himself and Felicity as possible before stopping. He *really* did. He fought to keep himself from turning back for her even now. He wanted there to be no chance that she might feel and be drawn to him in the coming day.

His love for Felicity seemed a dull and throbbing ache in his heart – its only pathetic and fruitless attempt to beat, irony unfair and cruel. He would gladly trade all of his immortal gifts for a beating heart right now, one that could sustain life and love on its own. If only he had a heart that could beat with no need for unnatural agents designed to persuade and subdue others in a quest for blood; a heart that did not force him to keep himself on a path devoid of personal happiness.

Felicity. He tried again unsuccessfully to force her from his thoughts. She'd said that she had changed her mind. She had wanted to come. She had wanted to give up everything. Her family, her friends, her job, her schooling, food, sunlight, her body, her *life*. She was willing to lose it all… for him.

He wasn't worth it.

It had taken every ounce of strength in his body to force himself from her. Oddly enough, it was the vampire within him that had given him the will. It had wanted her. It had wanted to drink from her. It had wanted to drain her. Just being close to her was a struggle now.

The past two nights had been an odd mixture of amazing happiness and torturous temptation. He had drunk from her when she'd allowed, but he had needed to be so careful not to partake beyond the limits. As it was, he was drinking from her far too often to maintain safely for any longer amount of time. The influence of the vampire in him was growing more potent with every drop of human blood that he fed it. He could feel it fighting for dominance within him. He never remembered it being so strong. It was a bit startling.

Most of his life he had been able to ignore the alternate creature within him. He played host to the blood, but he never had to question whether he was in control, while he sustained himself solely on animal blood that is. Human blood seemed to have a more intense effect on his system. It engaged the 'hunting' urges within him. It awoke the predator, and more and more the true vampire was emerging. It was subtle still, as he recognized the warning signs long before an outside eye could observe them, but the vampires' power could grow quickly… he knew.

He was unsure just what made the difference. It was not necessarily the blood itself, but most likely, the act of drinking from a host. He needed to change to drink from a victim. That was a strong determining factor in his control, he was sure. The more he let the vampire out, the more it wanted to be free of his human restraint. There was no need to change his visage when drinking from a cup.

The fact that he was using his venom again fueled the creature within him as well. It gave him territory. It asserted his dominance over other, younger vampires. It gave him a sense of his power.

All of these things contributed to his unsettledness. He was beginning to feel as though his careful hold upon his situation was beginning to slip away. Was it age that strengthened his blood? Perhaps it was the infusions of vampire blood that he had received from Sindy. If some part of it stayed within him as he had speculated, rather than dissipating over time, then blood from Sindy would make a difference. Large or slight he was unsure.

The vampire was strong, but he had to have faith in himself and believe that the man in him was stronger. Drinking from Felicity was so difficult now. He felt as though he needed to bargain with his inner beast. He had to fight to stop, before it went too far. 'Let her go' he would command himself, speaking silently to the vampire within. 'Let her go, or so help me you will never drink again'.

Sometimes it frightened him to address his alter ego as though it had a mind of its own, but at times like this it often helped, better to have an adversary to fight. He was unsure if the perception was valid. It didn't matter, so long as he won in the end.

He had done it. He had left. Felicity would live, assuming her rightful place in the world. He wanted to feel proud of his strength and a sense of accomplishing something good and right. At the moment the only feelings he was aware of, were thirst and despair.

The snow was coming down thickly now. The road before him was lost behind a sheet of white. Time to stop. He tried to think where he would stay. He had hoped to get further than this. Perhaps it would only be a short delay before he could travel on ahead of the dawn.

He pulled to the side of the road as an unsettling but necessary thought came upon him. Sindy. She really was the very last person that he wanted to think of or see right now, but he was leaving. He would not return to this town again; not for a very long time, if ever. He couldn't return, the temptation to visit Felicity would be too great. She needed time to move on, and so did he.

But he couldn't just leave without giving Sindy some sort of clue as to where he might be found in the future. He had thought of this earlier, but hadn't wanted to see Sindy until after everything with Felicity was complete. Now he wished he had just spoken to her days ago and been done with it. He really had no desire to see her tonight, but he couldn't just leave. Vampires are nomads by nature and not easily tracked down once separated by great distance. However much he did not want her with him now… forever was a long time.

He sighed, fought the sick feeling inside him, and set about trying to find a way to bring her to him. Sindy no longer carried his venom within her, so this would not be easy to accomplish quickly. He revealed his trace; although it was doubtful he would just happen to be in her range. He was not in the habit of letting his presence be known, so anyone who wanted to see him would hopefully take notice and come to him now; not something he wanted to rely on though. He could wait all night without her coming into range. He wanted to get this over with and leave.

Perhaps he should try to summon her psychically. He had originally assumed that this was not an option because his venom was gone from her now, but what about blood? He had never allowed her to drink from him; she carried nothing of him now, but what did he have of her? He had drunk from her... many times. Most of her blood should be gone from him by now, but what if some of it *did* stay? There must be some accumulative effect. Otherwise, little drinks over time should not have been so devastating to Eileen, as he had relayed in his story to Felicity. He had even speculated earlier that perhaps some part of Sindy's blood had stayed with him, strengthening the vampire influence already so firmly entrenched in his body.

A blood tie was a thing not easily broken. Perhaps it would give him the connection that he needed to bring her to him now. Nothing to do but to try. He would do his best to summon her and see. The force and turmoil of the emotions within him at the moment certainly should help. His despair over leaving Felicity lent power to his call even as he tried his best not to think of and dwell upon his loss. Even if not well controlled, just the fact that he was uncloaked and the force of his sorrow should be strong enough to draw some notice.

He worried briefly that Felicity might somehow 'pick-up' the summons that he was sending out, but then dismissed it from his mind. He knew that he was not very psychically skilled and Felicity wasn't at all, if not through his venom – which did have a definite and limited range. He was a fair distance from Felicity now.

But Sindy was a vampire, and a very psychically skilled one at that. She did not give herself very much credit for having great range, but Cain thought that she was mistaken in that. He was certain that she had psychic skills far greater than she had yet realized. He had known many vampires, and almost none of them ever realized their potential; but those few who did, truly amazed him. He'd a feeling Sindy was going to enter that category some day, if she didn't get herself killed first. She certainly knew more of summoning skills than he did. He would try his best to attune his summons only to her and hopefully she would receive and acknowledge it.

This was probably going to take a while. He walked his motorcycle to the overpass just ahead and parked underneath it so that he would not continue to be covered in snow. The wait seemed interminable. All the time, he tried to think of Sindy and his need to see her before he left. He tried to convey his impatience and the strength of his desire to accomplish his will and be done. He tried to concentrate on the task at hand, to keep from calling up the image of Felicity to his mind, but his hope to speak with Sindy was poor substitute to cover how badly he felt about abandoning Felicity. Even when he sought to call up Sindy's image for the summons, only Felicity's sweet tear-streaked face came to mind.

She had cried. He'd known she would, but worse than that, she had seemed desperate and betrayed. She had run after him in a display of recklessness resulting from her despair. Somehow, he had remained strong, but to see her so drastically stricken by his decision had broken his heart.

He stood huddled under the overpass, leaning against the warm engine of his bike. He had the sudden strong desire for a cigarette. Not that he had one, but if he did, it might help. He hadn't smoked in years. It was never something that he had been seriously committed to, but had only sampled during grief-stricken periods in his life, or more precisely, times when he had needed to consciously fight against the thirst. It was usually worst after a blood relationship ended. Smoking helped... a little. He didn't find it very pleasant really. It's not as though he were worried for lung cancer or emphysema, he just didn't really care for it; but it was something to do, something to focus on, a diversion. Nicotine was a poison for the vampire blood to withdraw and expel from his body like the alcohol he sometimes drank. He almost imagined it as a device to keep the vampire blood occupied, so that other cravings might go unnoticed.

He would have to pick up a pack of cigarettes the next time he passed a mini mart. Where the hell was Sindy? He really just wanted to get this over with so that he could leave. Although where he would be able to go in this storm, he was unsure. He tried to have patience. He had to trust that she could sense him. He certainly did not relish the idea of having to actually go and seek her out. She had to know he was here waiting for her; she just *had* to feel his call. Even if she did, she was probably delayed by the snow as well. He would wait just a little longer. It's not as though he could get very far until the snow stopped anyway.

He suddenly had the fear that *she* had left without informing him. Perhaps she had left town and was already some great distance away. He hadn't seen Sindy since the night in the gym when Felicity had been attacked. Her cloaking had become flawless, so he had not sensed her since. The vampire she had left with (his name had turned out to be Roger) had kept her company for a while he was sure, but while Cain had felt Roger's presence here and there afterwards, he hadn't been around at all recently, not that Cain had paid much attention to him. Sindy could be with him now someplace far from here, or they might have parted company. He had no way to know, and couldn't say that he cared; except that he was disturbed by the idea that he might never see her again.

He tried to analyze why. He couldn't really convince himself that he cared all that much for her. Things might be easier if he did, but it was Felicity that he loved. No one else would fill that need for him now, but he did care about Sindy as a person. Truthfully, although she would probably never want to admit it, he suspected that she needed him. She had shown some small flicker of desire to change her life. Surprisingly, as far as he knew, she wasn't drinking from humans any more. That was a great accomplishment, worth being proud of.

He had shown her the way, just as he had countless others but she had actually listened. Most other vampires did not follow his advice as he would hope. They might sample butcher-bought blood to appease him, but always found it lacking. The hunt satisfied not only their thirst, but relieved their boredom as well. The most he could accomplish with the majority of those he met, was to teach them not to kill. He would help them to master the art of leaving a victim before drinking them to death, and living off of two or three little drinks a night instead of one kill. It was distasteful to him, but better than the alternative. At least their victims were left alive.

Actually, Sindy had been a vampire that he had been almost convinced that he could not change. He had taught her not to kill, but he'd never dreamed that she would follow his practice of surviving off of purchased animal blood. As strong as she was, if she were to attempt to continue her abstinence from humans, she would probably need some support now and then. He needed to be there for her. She had proven herself to be so much stronger a person than he had ever expected. He did have faith in her ability to change, but he could not just disappear and hope for the best. It would undermine all that he had worked for. He wished she would show up already.

Thoughts of Felicity again tried to creep into his unoccupied mind. He hoped she could be happy. She would be. Of course, she would. Was he so pompous and naïve as to think that she couldn't be happy without him?

But could *he* be happy without *her*?

That didn't matter. That had never mattered. Happiness was not his goal. He was doing the right thing. He was doing what was right for her and he was going back to his own self-appointed duties as well.

He would find those in need of help and he would guide them; that in itself should be fulfilling. It did bestow some small happiness to know that he was making a difference. He was doing good in the world. He was doing the right thing. He should just forget Felicity now, but somehow, he knew that although he might travel the globe… Though he might meet and change the lives of many others that he would encounter… No one would make him happy the way that she did. All of the grand sights and experiences of the world would not compare to time spent snuggled next to her, sharing whispered secrets and laughter under the covers in his bed. She saw him differently than others did. She seemed to see through everything… his power, his age, his venom, his guilt, his sins… she looked right through it and saw the man inside.

A sad little smile came to his face before he could try to reprimand himself and hide his feelings away again. She loved him. *Him.*

Irrelevant. It was good that he was leaving. It was good for her. She thought that she knew what she wanted, but she had such limited perspective. To live for eternity as a vampire, giving up her human life… He could not let her make such a decision based on young love and naiveté. It would be irresponsible and selfish on his part. She was unready.

But maybe… someday…

He tried to squash the thought even as it came upon him, but it was too late. The seed of the idea was already there within him.

Give her time. Let her *live*. She should have a chance to experience life on her own as he had intended, and she would.

But that did not mean that he should *never* see her again.

What if he did come back? Not to visit really, but just to *see* her. To see that she was alright. That she was getting along well in the world as he had hoped she would.

Not right away of course. Even *he* could not inflict such torture upon himself, but at some point in the future, he could come back. To see what she was doing with her life. To see that she was happy.

Just to… look in on her from time to time. Once she was older. Once she knew more about what the world really had to offer… what if she *wasn't* happy? What if she really did wish that he had chosen otherwise? Well, things might be different *then*, might they not?

"You called?"

Sindy's voice seemed to cut through the blustering wind like a sultry whisper in his ear. He barely managed to steel himself not to jump with a guilty start.

He turned, expecting to see her in one of her revealing little dresses. Although vampires could feel the cold, it didn't trouble them much. Most younger ones didn't bother to dress for it. Stupid give away on their part. Any human would have found the lack of a coat very inappropriate out here in the snow. Sindy was smart; she must have come to the same conclusion. She was covered in a very long and sumptuous black fur coat. The thing looked inordinately garish on her in his eyes.

She smiled at him as she clutched it closed at the top near her throat against the wind. He got the impression that she liked the feel of the fur in her fingers more than she truly held it against the weather. "What are you pullin' me all the way out here for? Would it have killed you to get a room first?"

He looked away from her into the snow as his despair tried to return. How could he have ever believed that he could spend his time with *her* and be satisfied? But that was unfair. Those had been the thoughts in his mind before he had ever laid eyes upon or let himself get close to Felicity. He had not really seen Sindy that way in a long time. The feeling showed no signs of returning at the moment. He looked back upon her face.

At least his call had worked. She was obviously pleased to be summoned by him, no matter how she might complain or pretend to be annoyed. His unhappiness was not her fault. She was just a young girl trying to find her way; however misguided she may have been in the past. It was his duty to teach and help her just as he did for others like her.

"So, you just gonna stand there and look at me? Not that I mind, but if you want, I could give you a little more to see." She gave him a sly smile and seemed to threaten that she would open her coat. Just what was she wearing under there anyway?

He shook his head at her lightly. He glanced about to see how she might have arrived, but the night held no clue. "You here alone?"

"Yeah. I like to have you all to myself."

He let out a small breath of a laugh. "And Roger?"

"Oh, I lost him nights ago. Too wishy-washy. Turns out he was just lookin' for someone new to follow. You know, someone to give him orders and tell him what to do with his life."

"Sounds like you were a perfect match."

She chuckled. "Yeah, you'd think, but it's getting' old. I told him if he was lookin' for a leader, he should pay Arif a call. I'm outta the biz. Turns out I prefer a man who already knows where he's goin'."

He dropped his eyes to see the tips of her toes just poking out from beneath the hem of her fur coat in the snow. Hadn't she bothered to don shoes? "I'm leaving."

He definitely caught her interest with that news. It took a moment for her to realize the implication. Then the artifice left her features and she looked at him with honest interest. "Is that right?" She gave him a small but hopeful smile. "Want some company?"

"No. I really don't."

He felt cruel as her face fell. She quickly composed herself again into the confident seductress she liked to portray. He spoke again before she even had the chance to try and tempt him with some indecent proposition or lewd remark. "*Right now*, I just want to be alone in the world." He sighed. "But the world is a big place. It's all too easy to lose someone. Unfortunately, losing *myself* to anonymity is a luxury that I haven't got at the moment. Right now, I have others who count on me. Perhaps you're one of them." He felt himself getting tangled up in words. He stopped speaking and stared out into the night to clear his mind. Keep it simple. He reached into his pocket and drew out the paper he had written earlier. He handed it over to Sindy who looked at it rather oddly.

The gesture very much reminded him of Arif's man Kieran, giving him the card with a cell phone number printed on it. A direct line to Arif's coven, should he ever again wish contact. He wondered by the look on Sindy's face if Arif had treated her to the same information. She looked as though she were experiencing déjà vu.

His note did not hold a cell phone number though. He never carried electronic devices. Silly as it seemed, recent technologies rather scared him. It was too much, too fast. Looking into store windows filled with computers, i-Pod's, and fax machines made him feel so alien and disconnected from society. He had a basic understanding of their purpose, but shied away from such things when possible. He had no desire to understand that aspect of the world. His habit of reading the newspaper to scan for evidence of vampire activity kept him current enough. Leave the technology to those who wished it. He had no need for such 'modern conveniences'.

Sindy studied the scrap of paper as he spoke to explain it. "It's a house address. I own it. As much as I would prefer to go into seclusion for a while, I'll have to be there for a bit. I'm meeting someone. Something tells me that I may be called upon to play the mentor for a while longer. If you'd like, you can join us.

Make no mistake; it's an invitation for knowledge and camaraderie… nothing more. I won't be there until December. I do need *some* time for myself, but after that, I'll be playing teacher again. You should stop by. I have a feeling you might find it very… interesting.

Or don't. I can't say how long we'll stay. Not more than a month or two, I'd imagine. Still… if you come, I can give you an idea as to where I might be found in the future. If you ever need help... or if you just want to talk. I don't know, perhaps you would rather I just be lost." He lowered his eyes, unsure what else to say. It's not as though he were offering her much. Actually, it probably sounded rather arrogant and rude considering...

"Thanks. You'll see me again. Not that I *need* anything... but maybe *you* need someone. I'm not gonna pretend I'm a very good listener but... I could be there for you, if you want. Who knows, maybe there's a thing or two that *I* could teach *you*."

He had a hard time meeting her eyes. He didn't want to think about the future. The present was bad enough. "I've gotta go."

He didn't really wait for a response. He got on the Harley and started up the engine. The snow seemed to be drifting off now and it looked as though he would be able to continue riding until the dawn.

He still didn't really know where he was going, just away. He would drive until the dawn forced him to seek shelter and then he would continue the journey tomorrow night. He would travel and spend his time clearing his head, preparing to move on. He would be 'the wanderer' until the time came to go and meet Mattie and he was forced to deal with the world again.

He revved the engine and looked back to see Sindy standing there watching him silently. It was only then, that he thought to wonder again where she had come from. How had she gotten here? He'd called her out onto this desolate road that led out of town into nowhere. She was just standing there clutching her fur coat and looking stark and black against the white snow. "You need a ride?"

She just stared at him for a minute, her lips pursed and her expression contemplative. She looked like she was trying to figure him out. A little smirk came upon her face. Perhaps she already had, and found him amusing in some way. "No."

She turned and walked off into the night, her long black fur coat making a little sweeping arc, and then a trail in the snow. He watched her progress towards town until he could no longer pick out her black form, swallowed by the darkness.

He turned to face his own path forward. The road before him looked very dim and unpromising, but he had faced such roads before in his life. He never knew where they would lead… but he had faith. This was his path, chosen for him with a higher purpose. However difficult it was to accept, he had to believe that everything happens for a reason.

He would make every effort to do what he felt was right, and pray that he would have the strength to do it again tomorrow.

Chapter 15 - Things change

Felicity

Felicity's dorm room
11:30, Monday night

Felicity lay in bed trying to fall asleep. She'd actually come to bed over an hour ago, but sleep wouldn't come. It was the same every night. All she could think of was Cain.

Where was he now? Nine nights he'd been gone. Nine whole nights. He could be almost anywhere by now. Someplace far, far away. Did he think about her? Did he miss her even half as much as she missed him?

It was getting better. Not that she really *wanted* to let him go, but everyday life was getting a little easier. She was going to class, going to work, keeping busy and forgetting to be depressed for a while, but night-time… night-time sucked. She would lay awake in bed and that's when her heart would ache. Somewhere he was waking up, getting dressed and getting ready to head out into the night. Where was he going? Who was he with? Was he alone? She didn't want him to be unhappy, but she really hoped that he was alone. Was that cruel?

Maybe she should be hoping that he had someone else. A friend. Someone to talk to, to take his mind off of things and help him go on, but she knew him. He didn't have things in his life to divert him the way that she did. He isolated himself from others, on purpose. The only friend she knew he had was Mattie, and obviously *he* was still off with Alyson. Eventually Cain would look for other vampires who might need his help, but right now, she was almost certain that he was alone. Her tragic and tortured hero... that was what he seemed in her mind.

Of course, every time she came to this conclusion and convinced herself that he was sitting alone somewhere, depressed and missing her, another darker thought tried to intrude. Sindy.

Those first few nights after Cain had left, she could think of nothing but the heartache and unfairness of losing him, but soon after, she had begun to wonder where all of the other vampires had gone. She knew that Arif and his followers had left. Cain had told her so, but were there others? Would she ever see another vampire?

She was still marked; she would be for a while, so she really hadn't anything to worry about on that level. She'd certainly gotten quite a bit of venom into her system before Cain had left. Her mark shouldn't fade until... mid-December probably. She still had the vial as well. So come the time that her mark did fade, she could always start wearing the vial again. There was no one left who should be interested in her anyway.

But what about Sindy? She wouldn't have gone with Arif. She had seemed very angry with him over the whole 'Chris thing'. She had left the gymnasium with another vampire. Where were they now? Were they still hanging around here? As unsettling as that might seem, she almost hoped that they were. She wished she would spot them somewhere, just so that she would know, because if they weren't here, then there was a chance that they had gone off to follow Cain.

Felicity knew that Sindy wanted him. No matter who else she was with, Sindy wanted Cain. Even if only to prove that she could get him to want her back, and then move on. It's not that Felicity never wanted Cain to ever look at another woman... well, okay, she didn't really want him to, but she knew that eventually he would. She could grudgingly accept that... but *Sindy*?

Then again, what if Sindy wasn't following Cain? What if she was hanging around here? Felicity would be happy to know that they weren't together, but having her here would not really be such a good thing either. What if now that Cain was out of the way, Sindy decided that she wanted to renew her quest to turn Ben? Or what if she went after Felicity, just for spite?

No. She couldn't think that way. Sindy didn't want to risk Cain's disapproval. She wasn't here anyway. Felicity would have seen her. If there were any other vampires in the area at the moment, they were keeping themselves well hidden. That was just fine with her.

Cain's friendship with Mattie came to mind again. How close were they? Did they see each other regularly? Probably not often, but Cain did say that they kept in touch.

After Allie got back, maybe Felicity could even meet Mattie. She could talk to him and convince him that she needed to see Cain again. She could have another chance.

A chance for what? For Cain to tell her no again?

What if he didn't? What if seeing her again after being apart was enough to wear him down, enough for him to agree to change her? What then? Was that really what she wanted? Cain had said no for a reason. He had really felt that he was doing the right thing. Shouldn't she trust his judgment... even though it hurt?

One thing at a time. She didn't even know if she would get to see Mattie. What if she didn't? What if Allie wouldn't take her to meet him? What if Allie didn't come back at all?

That made her think of Ben. Poor Ben, waiting all this time to fix things between him and Allie. What if she didn't come back? He'd be devastated. It was his own stupid fault for being so stubborn and not talking to her before she left, but Felicity knew that in a way it was only because he cared so much, that he'd been angry with Allie in the first place. She hoped Allie came back.

In the meantime, she would have to convince Ben that he and his dad should have Thanksgiving at her house. Allie didn't seem likely to return in time and Felicity couldn't stand the thought of Ben having Thanksgiving dinner alone with his dad. They didn't seem to have a very close relationship and Alyson's absence would stand out that much more, making things so hard on him.

Besides, she had spoken to her mother on the phone about it the other night. Her mom was fine with having guests. In fact, she was very happy to have something else to focus on, since her brother Eddie wasn't coming home for the holiday weekend.

Felicity would be very happy to give her parents someone else to focus on as well. It had been hard enough getting out of having to come home this weekend. Her parents were getting suspicious that she had been totally avoiding them. Maybe Felicity should have just gone home, but she really didn't want to have to deal with questions about what she'd been so busy doing these past weeks. The scar on her throat was much improved – thank you Cain! – but you could still see it if you really looked. If she waited until Thanksgiving, her aunt and uncle would be there with her cousins for added distraction and things would be too busy for anyone to notice. She didn't want anyone to try to really sit her down for serious questioning. If she brought home guests to take some of the spotlight, so much the better.

She'd have to speak to Ben about it at lunch tomorrow. She hadn't seen him today; he had an extra physics lab every other Monday.

These thoughts buzzed around her head and before she realized it, Felicity had fallen asleep. For the first time since he had left, she had fallen asleep without tears in her eyes over Cain.

~~~~~~~~~~~~~~~~~~~~~~~~~~~~~~~~~~

Felicity woke up in a fairly good mood. She attended her English class and somehow managed to do very well on a pop quiz, leaving the class in reasonably good spirits. Then she got to History class. She took one look at the board and wished she could leave.

They were beginning a new topic. 'England in the 17th Century: The Struggle between King and Parliament'. It didn't really sound like anything she would be all that interested in, but that was not the problem.

17th Century England. How was she going to study that and not think of Cain? He was born there, that was the start of his life! He had sat and had discussions at his dinner table with his father and brother over the very topic! It was why his father hadn't wanted him to leave England. Not only was this going to be difficult and frustrating, she couldn't help but wish that they could have studied it earlier. Then she could have just asked him what had happened and been done with it! This was not going to be a class to look forward to.

When the professor finally let them go, her mind was hopelessly muddled with thoughts of Cain again. 'What was the social climate of England at that time? What do you think the common man thought of such controversies? How about Nobles and Lords? And how did religious beliefs come into play?' Thanks a lot, teach.

Ben had already gotten them a table when she arrived at the cafeteria. She dumped her stuff with barely a word and got on line.

She came back with her sandwich tray and sat down with a thud.

Ben just watched her for a moment. When she started to unwrap her sandwich and it was obvious that she wasn't planning to exchange pleasantries, he decided to go first. "Hi!"

"Hi," she replied with barely a glance.

"How ya' doin'?" he asked.

"Fine," she answered shortly.

He stared at her for a minute while she started eating her lunch. "What's new?" he asked with a humorous little lilt to his voice. He was teasing her for her clipped response. She didn't answer, she just gave him an annoyed look and took a sip from her water bottle. "Not much for conversation these days are ya'?" She just shrugged and took another bite of her sandwich. "That's okay. It's still better than sittin' with *them*," Ben said, jerking his thumb towards his friends at another table across the room.

They looked like they were laughing and having fun. She felt bad that Ben felt obligated to sit here and try to cheer her up instead. "Sorry. I'm just having a rough morning. You probably would be happier sitting with them," she said, as she looked away and took another bite from her sandwich.

"Na, spoil my lunch. You're much easier on the eyes."

She tried to smile but it didn't really work with a mouth full of chicken salad. She knew he was just trying to distract her; to make her feel better and take her mind off things. She resolved to let him. After she swallowed, she looked up and gave him a real smile. He seemed relieved to have pulled her out of her funk. He gave her a smile back, and then went on with a new conversation... business as usual.

"So, remember when you first got your car, you asked me if I'd help you fix it up?"

"Oh yeah. You don't have to, it's okay. I'll probably just ding it up anyway. The parking here is impossible."

He laughed with a little cringe. "Remind me to never lend you *my* car. I was thinkin'… I know it's minor but, what kind of stereo have you got?"

She shrugged. What kind? "I don't know."

"CD?" he inquired.

"Tape deck," she clarified.

He nodded as he ate his sandwich. "Well, I got a new one a little while back. You want my old one?"

She shook her head a little, as she finished a gulp from her water bottle. "That's okay."

"I could put it in for you. You might as well take it; it's got a CD player and it's just sittin' on a shelf in my garage. There's nothin' wrong with it."

"So, why'd you get a new one?" she asked.

"Multi-disc," he explained.

She grinned. "Was that before or after you decided to start saving money and concentrating on important stuff?"

He responded to her little smirk with a steady gaze and a little smile of his own. "Before. You want it? I'll put it in for you."

"Okay. If you want. Thanks." With her mind off of history, she suddenly remembered what she had been waiting to tell him. "I talked to my mom last night, about Thanksgiving. She's fine with it."

Ben immediately seemed to avoid her eyes and concentrate a little too intently on his food. "Oh, yeah...I don't know."

"Did you ask your dad?" she asked.

"I mentioned it," he told her vaguely.

Her shoulders slumped. "He's not cool with it, huh?"

"Are you kidding? He was relieved. See if I have another offer, then he doesn't even have to pretend to feel guilty when something comes up at the last minute and he has to skip out."

"On *Thanksgiving?*" she asked incredulously.

"He does that. It's no big deal. It's just Thanksgiving. Some people don't even see it as a real holiday."

She stared at him across the table. "People *I* know do."

He looked back at her with a derisive little laugh. "You know people who were *at* the first Thanksgiving."

"Funny. You're off by a couple of decades, but nice try. So, are you coming?" she nudged.

He went back to trying to be evasive and very interested in his lunch. "I don't know. I might just hang around here."

"What for? If your dad's not even going to be around…" He wouldn't look at her. She changed to a softer tone and tried to get him to meet her eyes. "You're still hopin' Allie'll show, aren't you?"

He finally did look up at her. He seemed very sadly hopeful, like a little kid asking if there really was a Santa Claus. "I know she's late, but she's got to come back for Thanksgiving, right? We *always* spend it together, it's like a tradition." Oh, wow. He almost looked as though he were holding back rising tears. "We make stupid stuff like chicken fingers and macaroni and cheese."

Felicity couldn't help but laugh a little at the thought, but was quickly sobered again by his forlorn and hopeful look. "I don't know."

Ben began to really look upset. "I went to Tommy's after work last night. Allie quit."

400

"She came back?" Felicity asked anxiously.

"No, over the phone. She wouldn't even tell him anything. She just said 'it was time to move on'. What does that even mean?"

"I don't know," she admitted quietly.

He sat up a little straighter and seemed to pull it together. "Her rent's paid up for the next two months, and all of her stuff is still there… I have a key." Felicity just sat looking at the table. Did that really mean anything? Ben continued, looking for reassurance. "So, she's gotta come back, right?" Felicity shrugged. What could she say? Ben gazed at her, desperately serious as he asked, "Would *you* have?"

She couldn't look at him. She thought of the night Cain had left. Ben had found her out in the parking lot and tried to comfort her. What had she told him? She could barely remember the words. She knew she had been hysterical. She had told Ben that Cain had left. What else had she said? She was pretty sure that in her daze she had told Ben that 'he said no'. Would Ben even remember or know what that meant? Probably. He was pretty savvy.

As he looked at her now, he seemed shaken. "Let me guess, you don't know."

They sat in awkward silence for a moment as she avoided his eyes. There was no point in saying any more on the subject. There was nothing to say. She forced herself to start eating again, instead of giving over to tears as she'd like. Thinking of that night had made her eyes go all watery and brought a lump to her throat. She stared at the table until her vision cleared and wouldn't look at Ben until he continued with his lunch as well.

After a few minutes, she went back to the original question as though uninterrupted. "I doubt my mom would be keen on chicken fingers, but I can make macaroni and cheese if you want." She finally lifted her eyes to meet his. He didn't seem to want to accept her attempt to lighten things. "You've got to come to my house for Thanksgiving Ben."

"Why? Because you feel bad for me, sittin' alone in my empty house waitin' for somebody who might not even show?"

"No. I do… but that's not why I want you to come."

He just sat there looking at her for a second. "It's not? Then why?"

"Because, Thanksgiving is supposed to be for spending time with people that you care about. And if you don't have other obligations, then I'd like you to come."

"Really?"

"Well, sure. I know I haven't been very good company lately. I've been kind of moody. I hardly talk to you these days and when I do, I'm either distant or I snap at you. I'm surprised you take it."

"I've had a lot of practice… I'm friends with Allie," he reminded her.

They both laughed. "Well, you're a good friend. If it means anything, you'll notice that you're the only person that I actually *sit* with while I eat my lunch in a bad mood and ignore everyone."

He nodded. "I was kind of hoping that counted for something."

"It counts for a lot. Thanks… for understanding… and being my friend." She thought again, of how he'd tried to comfort her after Cain had left. He was sweet. She was lucky to have such a good friend. He'd never even asked her to talk about it. "Although I must say… there *is* something that's been kind of bothering me."

"What?" he asked.

"Well, about Cain… I've been waiting for you to say '*I told ya' so.*' It's been hanging over my head. Makes me very 'on edge'. You should just say it and get it over with."

He gave a little laugh at her abrupt tone. He looked at her quietly for a moment before answering. "I wasn't going to. You'd think I'd like to… but to be honest I just feel really bad that it's been so hard on you. Kinda sucks the fun out of it." She shook her head with a little laugh. "So… you can consider yourself 'off edge'."

She gave him a tentative smile. "Well, that's a relief," she said jokingly. "So, I have to leave tomorrow night. You coming?"

"I have to work; I'm closing with the new girl," he told her.

"Oh yeah. Have you met her?"

"Yeah. Her name's Candy… or Brandy… something like that."

Felicity giggled. "Mr. Penten said it's Mandy. Lucy trained her, so if she screws up don't blame me." Ben chuckled. "What's she like?"

He just shrugged. "She's okay, I guess. Anyway, I don't know if you want to get such a late start tomorrow night. Maybe you should just go without me."

"Trust me; I'm not all that eager. A late start sounds just fine. Unless you really don't *want* to come."

Ben thought about it for a minute. "All right. Mr. Penten's going to have to do some schedule shifting, but if you really want me to, I'll come."

She grinned. "Good. Ask your dad again too. Maybe he'll surprise you."

"Yeah, I doubt it. Where do you live anyway, is it far?"

"A little under two hours."

"We're talkin' farm country, right?"

She smiled. "A little... but we're on kind of a steep mountain, so it's mostly woods."

"Dirt roads?" he inquired.

She laughed and looked at him oddly that he should ask. "A few."

"Yeah okay, let's take *your* car."

She laughed. "Okay but if you want to listen to decent music, you'll have to put the stereo in tonight."

"I can't I'm closing with you, remember? That's okay. I guess I can suffer through two hours of actually having to talk, as long as you promise not to be all moody."

She smiled and nodded. "Promise".

~~~~~~~~~~~~~~~~~~~~~~~~~~~~~~

Ben was right, his dad wouldn't come. He'd said that since Ben had other plans, he was going to spend the long weekend in the city and get some extra work done. That's what Ben told her anyway. Felicity never actually met him. According to Ben, his dad had a little apartment there. He worked late hours, so he did overnights a lot. Felicity couldn't imagine why anyone would want to commute all the way to New York City from here anyway.

So, it was just she and Ben. He insisted that they stop at Allie's before they left so that he could tape a note to her door with Felicity's phone number on it. He said he'd taped one to his door at home and his window as well. That sounded kind of odd, but he assured her that if Allie came around, *that* was the note she'd see. She usually came over late and she never went to the door. She'd been climbing in his window for years.

By the time they got home to Felicity's house, it was almost eleven-thirty. After introductions, Felicity was able to set Ben up in her brother's unused room and then go right to bed.

The next day was busy as expected. Her aunt and uncle arrived with her cousins, 9-year-old twins John and Jenna and 6-year-old Kevin, turning the house into happy chaos. Felicity was given cooking tasks to help her mom and aunt with, so Ben was left to socialize with the guys. They had the football game on. She felt a little bad for Ben; he said he liked football, but she knew he wasn't *that* into it. She hoped he wasn't bored.

Her dad was such a sports fanatic. When they'd arrived last night, he'd asked Ben what sort of team he was on at school. Felicity had tried to cover any awkwardness for him. "Dad, not everyone is a sports nut."

Ben had seemed unfazed though. He'd just answered 'the debate team', with a smile. Now her dad and her uncle were parked in front of the TV watching football games as her brother Richie tried to teach her cousins how to play a card game on the floor. From the kitchen, Felicity could see that Ben had resorted to talking to *Robbie*.

After a while, Ben came into the kitchen to see if they needed any help. Her mom had given him a big smile and told him they were just fine and he should go relax. Felicity caught his arm to whisper to him before he left, "Unless you're lookin' for something to do. I hope you're not too bored."

"Not at all. I've been talking to Robbie. We're getting along great."

Felicity looked at him dubiously and she noticed that her mom seemed a little surprised as well. Robert usually had to be forced to be social with guests. In fact, even her mom would admit that he was often rather rude. "Really? What are you talking about?"

"His criminal justice class. He's a smart kid," he answered, and then returned to the living room to finish their discussion.

Felicity gave a pained look to her mom and aunt. "Oh no. He's been turned."

Her aunt laughed. "Maybe it's the other way around. Maybe your friend Ben has found a way to tame the beast."

Her mom laughed as well. "I'd say that makes him a keeper."

Felicity just rolled her eyes and shook her head. Both her mom and aunt knew very well that she and Ben were just friends.

Dinner went well, with easy conversation and delicious food. Felicity couldn't help but be delighted by Ben's grin when she brought out macaroni and cheese along with the other side dishes she had made.

The next morning at breakfast, her mom began asking questions. She wanted to know how Felicity was doing in school and remarked that she hoped all of the extra studying she had been doing would reflect in her grades. Felicity quietly murmured that she hoped so too. Although for her grades to reflect the number of times she had used studying as an excuse not to come home would take a miracle. Ben tried to soften things for her. "The first semester is always the hardest. I know she's got some tough professors."

Then her mom remarked to Ben that Mr. Penten must be pretty tough as well... demanding such long hours every weekend. Felicity had tried to cover Ben's confused look. "Yeah, the store's been kind of shorthanded."

Felicity stood and looked to Ben who seemed done with his breakfast. "You finished?" He nodded and she took his plate and brought it to the sink.

Her mom seemed to know that she was trying to avoid any more conversation. "You kids have plans for today?"

"Yes, actually we do."

Ben looked understandably confused. "We do?"

"Uh-huh. Come on."

He looked at her questioningly as they left the kitchen. She smiled. "You owe me a Monopoly rematch."

Ben laughed as she led him to the upstairs hall game closet. She stood before it with her hands on her hips in annoyance. "It should be in here. I know we have it."

"That's okay. We can play something else."

Just then, Robert came up the stairs and began to head towards his room when Felicity stopped him. "Robbie, don't we have Monopoly?"

He stopped to give her an irritated look as though she were keeping him from something. "Yeah."

"It's not in here," she told him.

"Do I care?" he asked facetiously. Felicity gave him a withering look. Robbie glanced at Ben and then back to Felicity. "What do you want it for anyway?"

"For to play it."

"Yeah right. Pretty flimsy cover. Why don't you just go make out in your room like normal people?"

He turned and stalked down the hall to his bedroom as Felicity felt her face quickly turning red. She spoke quietly to Ben without really looking at him. "Okay, let's pretend like that wasn't at all embarrassing."

Before Ben could answer, Richie approached. Felicity was grateful for the distraction. "Richie, do you know where the Monopoly game is?"

"Yeah, it's in my room. You want it?" he asked.

"Please."

Richie brought the game out to them and then looked very surprised when they asked if he wanted to play, as though he didn't think that they would want to include him. Felicity assured him that it was fine, and the three of them played together. It took the better part of the afternoon but they had a good time.

Actually, it was Richie who won. Felicity suspected that Ben had let him, but he wouldn't admit it. She lost miserably… again. Something Ben had fun teasing her over. She pointed out that *he* hadn't won either, but he said that the important thing was that he hadn't lost *to her*. Men.

Come Saturday afternoon, they were watching TV when the phone rang. Felicity's mom called into the living room that it was for her. Over the course of the weekend, Felicity had noticed that Ben always seemed to freeze at the sound of the telephone. He was waiting to hear from Allie. Now he looked at her with hopeful expectancy as she picked up the phone.

"Hello? Oh... Hi Deidre." She gave Ben an apologetic little shrug and he sat back down by the TV as she took the call. Deidre was determined that they get together tonight. When Felicity explained that Ben was there, Deidre became very excited at the prospect of Felicity having a new boyfriend. Although she was disappointed that they probably wouldn't want her tagging along if they went out tonight.

Felicity explained that she and Ben weren't romantically involved and Deidre became excited again. They should all go out together, for pizza or something! It would be good to get out of the house. Felicity agreed to talk to Ben about it and call her back. Ben had told her that he was up for anything she wanted... so pizza it was.

Later, when they picked Deidre up, Felicity was happy to see that her friend had toned down the eye shadow a bit from the last time they had seen each other. Her sweater was rather tight; with a very low-cut v-neck, but actually, Deidre looked very pretty tonight. She was obviously quite impressed with Ben. She proceeded to flirt with him madly over the entire course of the evening.

At first Felicity wasn't really sure what Ben thought of her friend. He was very friendly to her and didn't seem to mind the attention, so Felicity tried to fade back a bit and give them more of a chance to talk; Ben kept pulling her back into the conversation though.

Before long it became clear to Felicity that Ben was just being nice to Deidre, he really wasn't interested. Unfortunately, Deidre didn't seem to get the message. Felicity discreetly tried to get her friend to tone it down but Deidre refused to acknowledge her.

At one point, Deidre actually *asked* Ben if he had a girlfriend. She then went on before Ben could answer. "Obviously you don't or you wouldn't be coming home with *Felicity* for Thanksgiving, but still…" She sucked in a little hiss of breath and gave Ben her best seductive smile. "You're a really good-lookin' guy Ben. You're a Junior, right? Freshman girls must be positively falling all over themselves for you."

Ben looked down with a humble little smile. Felicity answered sarcastically for him, "Yeah. It's a wonder no one's been injured." She gave Deidre a little warning glare to cut it out and then rolled her eyes as Ben laughed.

Deidre went on as though she hadn't noticed Felicity's ire. "So how is it that a hottie like you isn't already taken?"

"I had a girlfriend. We broke up."

Deidre was instantly all sympathy. "Oh, how come?"

"She moved."

"Her loss."

Felicity shook her head with a weary sigh, by the end of the night she felt terribly embarrassed and was very grateful that the evening was over. She pulled into Deidre's driveway to drop her off and they said their goodbyes. Deidre was in the front, which put Ben in the back. Deidre turned to

Felicity and gave her a quick hug. "We really have to keep in better touch. Call me."

Then Deidre turned to Ben in the back seat and gave him a hopeful smile. "You too Ben. Call me sometime. Have Felicity give you my number." Felicity could have died. She didn't turn around to see Ben's face and was afraid to try and meet his eyes in the rearview mirror, although she did wonder what he thought of the offer. He didn't say anything. He must have smiled though. Deidre didn't seem disappointed by his lack of response. She turned to smile at Felicity again and then left the car to go into the house.

Felicity just sat there with her cheeks burning. Deidre was always far more outgoing than she was. Usually, it left Felicity feeling as though she were too shy. She had always been glad in the past that Deidre had been brave enough to talk to guys and try to get them double dates when Felicity didn't dare, but somehow, between this year and last, it struck her differently than before. For some reason Deidre's behavior came off as immature, brash and far too forward. Maybe it was just Felicity's perspective that had changed.

She was a little startled when the passenger door opened again. It was Ben. She hadn't even realized that he'd gotten out to switch seats. He settled himself next to her and put on his seatbelt. She turned to look at him with a small smile of apology. "I am so sorry about tonight."

He actually looked like he didn't know what she was talking about. "Why? I had fun."

She put the car into gear and began driving them home. Maybe she had read things wrong. Maybe Deidre's outgoing and 'in his face' approach *was* the way to get a guy's interest.

Felicity was certainly no expert. "You want Deidre's number?"

Ben looked at her very strangely indeed and then he laughed. No, she hadn't read him wrong. "No, thanks."

Felicity gave a little laugh of her own. "Not exactly subtle, is she?"

"It's okay. She's cute. I'm just not lookin'."

Something about the way he said 'cute' made her realize that Ben was almost three years older than she and Deidre. She had thought about that once or twice before, like when he'd mentioned being the same age as her older brother. Was it odd that they had gotten to be such good friends? Did he think of her as being *younger*? "Cute like *a kid*?"

He gave her that strange look again. "No." He shrugged. "You know... just cute."

She nodded with a little smirk. "Oh. Cute like one night at the Hilton and then she'd drive you insane, cute."

He actually looked shocked. "I don't do one-night stands."

"You *don't*?"

"*No*. I may not have mastered the 'long term' relationship but it's not like I wake up next to a girl and run the other way! Besides, I'm not doing that sort of thing anymore, remember?"

"Oh right, because of the whole 'get serious and concentrate on real life' thing." He laughed and nodded. "So, this new responsible life of yours involves celibacy?"

Again, he looked shocked. Felicity was a little shocked at herself. She never would have spoken to a guy about such things... but talking to Ben was different. She felt like she knew him so well. She could tease him about things she wouldn't dare utter to any other guy. He laughed. "No. I'm just going to be a little more... discriminating."

"M-hmmm. According to Allie you're already *way* too picky when it comes to girls."

He nodded with a smile. "Yeah, I am, but there's a big difference between being picky about a girl you want to spend a lot of *real* time with... and being picky about a girl you just want to take to the Hilton a few times."

She tried not to be embarrassed by his candor. She smiled and chuckled, shaking her head a bit. "Oh. I get it."

He turned to look at her steadily for a moment as she drove. "Do you?"

She laughed. "Yeah. You're *waiting*... to fall in love."

He gave a little chuckle and then looked back out the window with a sigh as they pulled into the driveway. "Not really.

~~~~~~~~~~~~~~~~~~~~~~~~~~~~~~~~

And so, the weekend passed. Felicity was very relieved that no one had noticed the faint scar at her throat. In private, Ben had even remarked that it was miraculously faded. She hadn't told him what Cain had done. She'd just smiled and agreed that she was glad it looked so much better.

The time came to go back to school and Felicity promised her parents that she would try to make it home more often. They said goodbye and assured Ben that he was welcome to come back anytime.

Life goes on. It's funny how quickly 'routine' can set in and take over when you're not looking. School, work, regular everyday stuff. At one point Felicity was actually shocked to realize that whole days had gone by without her thinking of Cain even once. At first, she felt horribly guilty, but that passed. What did she plan to do, mourn his leaving her forever?

Her plans of begging Mattie to take her back to Cain were fading. Not that she wouldn't, but it didn't seem likely that she would ever have the chance. It was the first week of December, a whole month since Allie had left, and she was nowhere to be found.

Ben put the CD player in her car for her and they resumed their Thursday night movies. It was pretty much the only 'social' thing she did. Karen was always busy with Jack, so she didn't see her all that much. At one point, she thought that maybe she would attempt to get closer with Bridgette and Regina from her dorm, but they only regaled her with questions about Cain.

The new girl at work was nice, but didn't seem very interested in ever getting together socially. She was twenty-one and liked to go dancing at Venus. She was never rude, but Felicity got the impression that she thought going out with a 'minor' would cramp her style.

Mandy was also absolutely beautiful and single. She probably didn't want Felicity hanging around when she was out meeting guys. Honestly, Felicity was a bit surprised that Ben wasn't at all interested in her. He must really be serious about the whole 'taking a break thing'. Mandy was pretty friendly to him, but from what Felicity could see, Ben totally ignored her.

So, humdrum life carried on. Weeks went by and they weren't exciting or mysterious. She didn't save anyone's life or fight the forces of evil. She had no night vision or special psychic abilities. In fact, she found she was rather afraid of the dark these days. *This* is what Cain had been loath to take her away from? For *this* she should be grateful?

Thursday night again and it was snowing, hard. Third time this week. They were sure to have a white Christmas. Felicity sat in the car waiting for Ben to leave the parking lot before her. He'd freak if he thought she didn't let it warm up enough first. Men.

She followed him home past houses decorated with cheery Christmas lights and parked behind him in the driveway. His house was dark and unadorned. No other car outside. His dad must be away… again. He hadn't been home last Thursday either, so she still hadn't met him. Ben said he usually only bothered to come home for the weekends these days.

He popped the popcorn as she studied the 'movie wall'. She pulled out an older tape as he came back into the room. "Ooh, how about this?"

"You've never seen 'Romancing the Stone'?" he asked.

"Bits and pieces, but I never got to see it all the way through. I always miss the end." Ben sighed. "Come on, you picked the last two. After 'The Matrix' and 'Predator' I think you could humor me with something *human* for a change. You don't like it? It's *your* movie."

"No, it's a good one. Go ahead, put it in."

So, they sat and watched Kathleen Turner cry as she wrote romance novels and Michael Douglas fight an Alligator for a jewel. It was great; until they neared the end. Kathleen Turner's character was struggling with the villain of the film when the man shoved her to the ground, climbed atop her and tried to slit her throat with a knife. Felicity had been sitting back and casually hugging her knees as she sat on the bed, but now she found herself shrinking down behind her legs and unwittingly guarding her throat with her hands. She watched in horror as chills ran down her back and phantom stinging sensations regaled her throat where Chris had tried to kill her in the very same way.

Ben must have noticed her distress. He didn't say anything, but moved closer and put his arm around her. She gratefully leaned into him and watched in cringing fascination as their heroin fought the man off. When it was finally over, she breathed a great sigh of relief and even gave a small smile to Ben as she realized just how rigidly tense she had been throughout the scene.

He looked down at her in apology. "Sorry. I totally forgot about that part."

"I'm okay." She sat up straighter to watch the rest of the movie and Ben removed his arm. He seemed to look over at her once or twice more, but he didn't say anything else. She kept her eyes on the screen, enthralled with the story and wondering how it would end. The conclusion was so terribly romantic that Felicity found herself crying almost uncontrollably. She knew Ben probably thought she was being silly, but she couldn't help it. It was so melodramatic;

something in it just struck a very personal emotional chord in her.

What was wrong with her? Movies never affected her this way, but she was in a pretty fragile emotional state these days. She looked up to see Ben smiling at her, and realized that she must look like a sentimental fool. "I thought it was mostly an action movie," she said with a sniffle. "I hadn't realized it was such a *romance*."

"It's called '*Romancing* the Stone', 'Liss."

"Oh yeah," she mumbled sheepishly as she tried to wipe her eyes with her sleeve.

Ben smiled as he got her a tissue from the box on his dresser, and then sat back down next to her on the bed. "You do realize that it was a happy ending?" he teased.

She took the tissue with another sniffle as the credits rolled on a sailboat heading down the New York City streets. "I know, but it was just so romantic. The way he came back at the end..." 'Why do they always do that in movies?' she thought. Guys don't pleasantly surprise you in real life. It never happens that way. Love just swooping in to save the day when you least expect it.

"You're crying all over my bed."

She quickly tried to use the tissue again, but it was already soaked. She crumpled it up in her hand and leaned to place it on his nightstand. She looked up in apology. "Sorry."

He laughed at her a little. He'd only been teasing. "It's okay." He quickly leaned forward and before she knew what he meant to do, he had touched her cheek, under the corner of her eye with his lips, kissing a tear away.

It was almost exactly what he had done after saving her from Chris. She'd been crying in fear and he'd leaned over her, crying in relief that she was alive. He had leaned down and kissed her tear away in just the same motion, but this was different. This was not a life-or-death moment. It was just a movie. And here in his room, it felt a little different. A little *too* familiar...intimate. He knew it too.

He slowly leaned back and stared at her in awkward silence. He looked almost desperate to explain himself. In a poor attempt at humor to cover any embarrassment, he licked his lips and tried to smile. "Salty," he offered weakly.

She just sat there and stared at him, Ben. Her best friend. He had saved her life, more than once. He had made her laugh when she was sad and made her argue with him until she wanted to smack him. He had been there through it all. He'd tried to warn her about losing her heart to Cain and he had held her as she cried when he left. Through everything and even now, he had been her best friend; and he seemed perfectly willing to let things go on that way, indefinitely, but was it possible that he wished they were... *more?*

He sat perfectly still. It was almost as though he was aware that she was seeing him differently for the first time... and he was terrified to ruin it. He sat frozen and gazed at her, awaiting her response. Looking for some small sign of her acceptance. Waiting to follow her lead as to what he should do. She had no doubt that if she laughed and then went on with regular conversation, he would accept that. It would be like nothing had ever happened. *Was* that what she wanted to do? She tried to analyze the moment as she watched him watching her.

The wait must have seemed interminable. She sat there and studied his face and looked at him with new eyes. Her heart began to pound as she sat up a little straighter and then leaned ever so slightly closer to him.

He didn't move. She almost would have laughed if watching from another perspective. He held himself still like a man afraid to spook a hesitant horse. After another moment, she raised her lips to his for a kiss.

Tentative and sweet, her lips touched his. It only took that first touch for her to know that she wanted more. She moved closer still, to kiss him again. It was thrills and butterflies and excitement that she had thought forever lost.

But although her heart was racing, she didn't entirely give herself over yet. She ended the kiss and leaned back to see his reaction. He grinned. "It's about time."

She leaned back in open-mouthed awe at his audacity. "You are *so* arrogant!" she said in amused disbelief.

He was unfazed. He spoke quietly and seductively as he leaned in for another kiss. "Yeah… I know." She didn't pull away, but she didn't quite kiss him back either… although she wanted to. He moved to meet her eyes again. "But you have to admit, I've been *very* patient. That's not usually my strong suit."

He smiled at her and then leaned forward to kiss away a tear on the other side of her face. He kissed another further down her cheek and then his lips chased a tear that had slid down the side of her throat.

Before she could help it, Felicity had jerked back from him. It was *that* spot. *Cain's* spot.

Ben looked at her oddly. "Take it easy. I don't bite."

For a moment she was upset by the obvious reference, but after searching his face she wondered if he had really meant it that way, or if it had just been an unfortunate choice of words. He seemed to realize his mistake. He didn't say anything else, but he obviously hadn't meant it maliciously. Slowly, he gave her a tentative little smile.

It touched her to see the ever confident and self-assured Ben that she knew, looking so hopeful and vulnerable. She couldn't resist coming back to his lips again for another kiss. She kissed him and let him wrap his arms around her lower back. He gently teased her lips with his tongue until she permitted it to enter her mouth.

Wow. He was a *really* good kisser. Her head was spinning. She found herself almost amazed that he hadn't venom of his own. After a few minutes though, he pulled back from her as though uncertain about something. "Wait, 'Liss… maybe this isn't such a good idea." She looked at him in disbelief. *Now* he was having second thoughts? He saw the look on her face and sought to reassure her. "I want to, believe me. I *really* want to, but… are you sure you're ready? To move on I mean. It's just… I don't want to be the 'rebound guy'."

She began to smile as she studied his face. He meant it. He really cared about her; she *knew* he did. And she was more than a little surprised to realize just how much she cared back. When did this happen? She gave him a reassuring smile, full of new and slightly bewildered comprehension. "You're not. *You're* the guy I should have been kissing all along."

Now Ben smiled too. "Well, *I* could have told you that."

She laughed as he took her back into his arms to resume their kiss. What had started out as so hesitant and exploratory quickly became passionately urgent. She kissed him with heated fervor that he returned with equal passion if not more.

It seemed almost amazing to her that this was Ben. Her best friend these past months that she had grown to know so well, and yet this was a part of him that she had never known before. The way that he anxiously drew kisses from her lips was surprising and exciting, and yet even while discovering this new part of him, he seemed so familiar and comfortable that it just felt right somehow. Even more amazing to her than the fact that he seemed eager for her kisses, was the fact that she so desperately wanted his. Once given over to it, the feelings he brought out in her were so strong that they astonished her. Restraint was like trying to hold back an avalanche.

She found herself wanting to feel his skin. It was an irrational desire, but she just had to feel her hands on his skin. She pressed her palms against his chest as they kissed and then slid them down until she found the hem of his shirt. Without a moment's hesitation, she slid them up underneath. Her hands ran up the ridged plane of his stomach and onto his smooth broad chest under his shirt. His skin felt so hot it was like he was burning with fever. Some disconnected part of her mind came to realize that she had expected him to feel like Cain. Although Cain had never felt cold to her, Ben's body was noticeably hot to the touch in comparison.

Ben's body was warm and pulsing, brimming with life. His heart pounded in his chest every bit as fast as hers and his skin felt so warm and inviting to her caresses. His chest rose and fell with ever quickening gasps for breath in his growing excitement over her. Little details that she might not have even noticed before, but now... they spurred her own excitement that much more.

He leaned back from her and pulled his shirt off over his head. That startled her for a moment. She hadn't really been suggesting for him to do that, but she *had* wanted to feel his skin. She looked at his bared chest and wondered just *what* she wanted.

She couldn't help but feel the sexual tension build within her as she gazed at him. For someone who wasn't into sports, he certainly had the body of an athlete. Her eyes lingered for a moment on the slight scar just below the very center of his breastbone. Then she ran her eyes over his broad pecs, took in the few little wisps of hair that framed his nipples, and the toned muscles of his arms. He wasn't terribly muscular, but fairly filled out and well defined. Fighting off vampires must be good exercise, she thought to herself with a smile.

He was about to lean in to kiss her again, when she lifted her own arms above her head in invitation. He looked at her a bit uncertainly, but she only waited patiently for him to remove her shirt as well. He took it off of her and threw it onto the floor next to his own, revealing her bra underneath. He went back to kissing her then, as his hands caressed the newly bared skin of her back.

His hands wandered over her bra strap once or twice, but he never paused to unhook it. Maybe he was unsure if she would want him to. She reached back and undid the clasp herself, impatient at the fabric between them. She wanted to feel his skin pressed up against her.

As she unhooked the back, he stopped kissing her to meet her eyes. He seemed very surprised at her. Not disappointed of course, but surprised. She didn't care. She wanted him to hold her, skin to skin, so that she could feel the warmth of his embrace. He watched as she brought her hands up to the straps at her shoulders, poised to slide them down to remove her bra and reveal her breasts beneath.

He didn't let her. He covered her hands with his own on her shoulders to stop the motion. He kissed her fervently and then, to her great astonishment he used his hands on her shoulders to give her a playful shove down to the bed. As her head hit the pillow, she gasped in surprise at his forcefulness. Truthfully, she found it thrilling. It ignited her desire for him in a way that she wouldn't have expected. She raised her eyebrows and gave a surprised little laugh. He smiled at her acceptance of the act.

Ben looked at her with such undisguised longing, but it seemed with agonizing slowness that he brought himself down to her. She eagerly wrapped her arms around him, feeling the warm closeness that she had longed for. It felt better than she had even imagined it would, even with her bra still between them.

He kissed her again as he lay atop her lightly. This time it was not only his kiss that excited her. He held himself from pressing against her very strongly, but the bulge in his jeans was becoming impossible to ignore. She was amazed that he found her so alluring; his arousal over her was clearly evident. His lips left hers to anoint her jaw line with little kisses that traveled to her ear. She almost forgot to breathe as he tickled her with his tongue and gently sucked upon her lobe.

His kisses moved downward... and then paused. She knew that he had been about to kiss her neck, but was afraid of her reaction. No, this would not do. She had always enjoyed having her throat kissed and she could not let it become a memory that was only of Cain. If she was going to move on, then she should do it right. She needed to feel that she could give herself over fully; otherwise, it would become a barrier between her and Ben. It was best broken now, swiftly. She would have to get past it.

She ran her fingers through the hair at the back of his head and then gently pressed him downward; permission to go on. He continued, letting his kisses trail down her throat, but they did not linger. He moved them to the center of her chest, where he placed a tender kiss between her breasts, just above the fabric of her bra. He looked up at her with a fond smile and she returned it with her own.

He raised himself from her a bit and eyed her bra. He slipped his hand beneath the strap at one shoulder and slid it down without yet revealing her breast. He was obviously savoring the moment. He removed his hand from the strap and slowly slipped it inside the bra, closing his eyes and caressing her with a gentle squeeze. He held her cupped in his hand as he slowly grazed his thumb over her hardening nipple. Finally, he opened his eyes and lifted her breast free of her bra as though he were unwrapping a greatly anticipated prize.

He dipped his head down to meet her skin and took her nipple into his mouth. She could not help but let a small moan escape her and he looked up at her with a slight smile in his eyes as he suckled her gently. After a moment, he repeated his actions almost identically for the other breast as she played her fingers over his shoulders and held him close.

Finally, he left her breasts to remove her bra and toss it onto the floor. He came back to kiss her tenderly. Their kiss grew in intensity and her desire for him swelled until she wondered how it was possible that she hadn't longed for this from him before.

Ben left her lips to place kisses down the center of her torso, until he reached the rim of her jeans. She closed her eyes in anticipation and waited to see what he would do. He tickled the top of her belly with licks and kisses, making her again meet his eyes. He looked up at her playfully, but after a moment, his expression grew serious. "Do you think that we're going too fast?" 'Oh God, don't stop now.' She didn't say that of course, but that's what went through her mind.

Was that wrong? Did he think less of her, that she had become so uninhibited? She looked at him questioningly. "Do *you?*"

He laughed that she should even ask. "*I've* been fantasizing about this for months. *You're* the one who's just getting used to the idea."

She sat up a little to see him better. "Months?" He lowered his eyes a bit sheepishly. She grinned. "You've been fantasizing about me?"

He actually looked almost bashful as he met her eyes again. He smiled. "Don't let it go to your head."

She gave a little laugh. He dipped down to place another kiss on her abdomen and then silently looked askance of her. What the hell. She gave a little nod towards the waistband of her jeans. "Go on," she whispered. He looked a little undecided. He obviously wanted to, but was afraid to push her too far too fast. He was so sweet. She gave him a nod of reassurance. "Really. I want you to."

He smiled and crinkled his nose at her dubiously. "You sure?"

She laughed and wiggled her hips against his chest. "Yes."

Ben grinned. He took the edge of the denim just over the buttonhole into his teeth. He then gently tugged upwards and then down again, pulling it free of the button. She watched in amazement as he used his tongue to flip up the tab of her zipper. He then took the material into his teeth again and yanked it sideways, causing the zipper tab to slide down and open fully. She laughed at him in surprise. "Show off."

He gave her a sly grin and then grasped her jeans in his hands at each hip and tugged them down. She lifted herself to let him pull them free. He brought them down to her ankles, removed her shoes and socks and then her jeans. They landed on the floor next to their shirts.

She wore plain cotton bikini panties. He didn't even look at them really. He paused to take off his own sneakers. She had thought he might remove his jeans as well, but instead he brought himself back to lay with her for more kisses.

Once again, he let his lips travel down her body. He smothered her belly in kisses, and then placed one firm kiss upon the little cotton triangle of her panties. Rather than continue there, he sat up, parting her thighs and positioning himself on the bed between them.

He ran his hands down her left leg to under her knee and then to her ankle as he lifted it from the bed. He had her leg raised high as she pointed her toe like a dancer. He gently caused her to bend and flex her leg at the knee as he held her ankle in one hand. He ran his other hand down her leg, pausing to kiss and admire the contours and shapeliness of it.

He rested her foot on his shoulder as he kneaded the full meat of her calf and thigh with almost as much attention as he had given each of her breasts, his caresses alternated with gentle, pulling little kisses. She had never thought of her legs as all that appealing, but she found his obvious appreciation of every inch of her body incredibly sexy. He let her bring her left leg to rest only to turn and fondle the right. His attention to detail was almost maddening.

Just when she thought she couldn't wait any longer, he came back to kiss her again. He lay down beside her as his fingers caressed the inside of her thigh and then came up to slip down beneath the cotton of her panties. They seemed to leave a trail of fire on her skin beneath them as they slid between her legs. There he found clear evidence of her eager anticipation of him. Even as he began to stroke and massage her, Felicity found her own hand groping blindly to find the button of his jeans.

He paused in his attentions to slightly inch away from her reach. Her fingertips brushed the denim that restrained him but she couldn't maneuver to free his body for her. "Take it easy," he teased. "*I've* waited this long; *you* can show a little patience."

She looked at him in confusion. "Why?"

He smiled and wrinkled his nose at her again. "I'm shy," he whispered teasingly.

She looked at him in odd amusement, but before she could comment or question him further, his attentions to her body were strongly renewed. His fingers moved against her and within her until she was absolutely mad with desire. She could barely even think. His motions brought her so close to climax that she had to arch away from him lest she become carried away.

"Ben!" With only his name, she demanded that he stop so that he might undress and attend to her properly. He understood perfectly. He gave a little laugh and leaned down for another kiss before he let her go.

He left the bed to approach his tall dresser across the room. He opened the top drawer and fumbled through it for a moment as she waited impatiently. Finally, he found what he was looking for... and he didn't look happy. "Oh shit."

"What?" she asked.

"Shit!" he repeated.

She sat up to look at him. "What?"

"This... being with you, it was kind of unexpected." As he spoke, he raised his hand for her to see. He held a box of condoms. The bold print across the front proclaimed them to be Magnum X-tra Large.

She stifled a laugh. How many guys bought them just for the prestige of the title on the box? It seemed a ridiculously blatant display. That couldn't be what Ben was showing her could it? "So?"

"So... I'm not exactly... prepared." He shook the box a little and she realized that it was open on its side... and nothing was falling out.

"Oh." He looked so disappointed it was almost funny. She smiled. "It's okay."

"No. It's not," he insisted in somber defeat.

"I'm on the pill," she informed him.

Ben looked at her in hopeful amazement. "*You're* on birth control?"

She smirked at him a little. "Well, it wasn't originally *for* that, but yeah, I am."

He looked as though he wouldn't quite dare to believe that he shouldn't be deprived of enjoying her body. He eyed her doubtfully. "Still, I always use a condom. *Always.*"

She thought for a moment and then sat up a little more in confidence. "Well good. Then we know you haven't got anything. And the only guy that I have ever been with is *incapable* of carrying disease. So, there's no problem."

Ben looked annoyed and ill. "You're right. Now we really don't need one, 'cause boy did *that* just kill the mood."

She sat up fully to stare at him. "Well, it's not like you didn't know."

"That you were sleeping with a *dead guy?* Yeah, I guess I mentally blocked it out."

"Ben! It's not like I was with one of those zombie things! Cain's body is just like any other guys'."

"Does he have a *heartbeat?*" he asked her almost viciously.

She dropped her eyes to the floor. "Well, he didn't *seem* dead," she mumbled.

"I guess you had to *be* there," he said factitiously.

Her face crumpled and she felt like she would cry. Why was he doing this? He was ruining everything! She grabbed the end of the comforter and pulled it up to cover herself. "You're such a jerk!"

How could she have opened herself to him? How could she have let herself believe that it would be a good thing? She was so emotionally charged it seemed almost instantly that she'd been drawn from one extreme to the other. She huddled under the blanket and cried. She heard him come closer but she didn't look.

"You're right." He sat down on the bed next to her. "I *am* being a jerk."

He put a hand on her shoulder but she shrugged him off without looking. "Don't touch me," she mumbled from under the blanket.

"I am so sorry 'Liss. It's just that… you have no idea how hard it's been. To see you with *him* and to know that he was kissing you and loving you…"

She looked up at him accusingly. "Just because he's a vampire?"

"A little, but mostly… because he wasn't *me.*"

That made her pause. Had he really wanted to be with her all of this time? She had thought that maybe he had begun thinking about her when Cain had left, but she'd had no idea that *all along*… She thought back again over all of the time that she'd known him. That first night that Ben had told her that Cain was a vampire, it seemed so long ago… he had come to her room and asked her to go to the movies with him. He'd tried to make it seem very casual and non-chalant, but… Had he been attempting to get closer to her even then? She thought of other times, little things that should have shown her how he felt about her. The necklace that he'd bought her for her birthday, the way that he had danced with her at Homecoming, his concern over her on Halloween… had he really been waiting all this time?

She looked up to study his face again, but he wasn't looking at her. He sat on the edge of the bed in only his jeans and put his head down into his hands with his elbows on his knees as he spoke. "This is all wrong. Why'd I start this now? It *is* too soon, and now I've gone and messed it all up. I'm sorry.

Please don't hate me 'Liss. I don't blame you for being upset, but... you *have* to forgive me." He looked up at her in atonement. "I know you're prob'ly thinkin' this was all a big mistake. Nothing else matters to me now as much as your friendship, I don't want this to mess that up. How can I make this right?" She lowered her eyes in contemplation.

He kept on. "I have to know that when I see you tomorrow, at work or at school... I have to know that we're okay. It can't be all awkward and weird. You have to let me fix it."

She still didn't say anything. "I'm sorry 'Liss. Please, forgive me?" He watched her for a moment and then put his head back down into his hands. "I wish I could just take it all back."

She thought of the way he had savored the moment before removing her clothing and how she had felt when he'd kissed and caressed her. He turned his head to look at her, his eyes pleading forgiveness. She sat up again. "You don't really want to take back *all* of it... do you?"

He just looked incredibly relieved that she was going to talk to him. Then he seemed to realize what she had said. "Were there some parts that you wanted to keep?" he asked hesitantly.

She grinned and leaned a little closer to him. "Yeah." She moved to kiss him and as her lips touched his, she felt their passion reignited. *"Oh yeah."* She kissed him again. He found his way beneath the blanket to wrap his arms around her.

After the kiss ended, he looked at her with serious concern in his eyes. "Are you sure it's not too soon? I could wait. It might kill me, but I could try."

"No." She laughed and kissed him again. "It's right. Just do me a favor? Try not to say anything else stupid, okay?"

"Maybe you'd better just shut me up." He laid her back on the bed as they began to kiss again. They were all tangled in the blanket and his jeans were rough against her hips. After a few moments, she could tell that he was having a very hard time keeping from rubbing himself strongly against her. She pressed herself firmly against him as well. This was unbearable. "Ben, you know... If you're really uncomfortable, about not using a condom... Well, we could make each other happy in *other* ways."

He leaned back to eye her with a grin. "Yeah?"

"I know I sure wouldn't mind some more of that *special attention* you were givin' me before," she admitted.

He gave her a sly smile. "You liked that huh?"

As though he had to ask. She smiled. "And um... *I* can give special attention too." She licked her lips suggestively and he looked as though he couldn't believe her boldness.

"Are you really on the pill?" he asked incredulously.

She nodded. "Uh-huh."

He gave her a last brazen kiss before he disengaged himself from the blanket to leave the bed. He stood back a few steps and then began to take off his pants. She watched him with a silent smile as he pulled them from his legs. As he bent to take his socks off, her eyes were illicitly drawn to his underwear. The bulge hidden there looked awfully large. As Felicity lay there, half covered by the blanket she stared harder at him. He straightened and then removed his underwear to reveal his body to her.

Felicity's eyes widened as she saw him. He was *huge*. She had thought that Cain was a well-made man, but this was something entirely different. "Oh my God."

She hadn't meant to actually say that *out loud*, but it seemed to spring from her lips uncontrollably. Ben looked as though he couldn't believe she had said it out loud either. "Thanks. Now I'm not at all self-conscious or uncomfortable."

She gave him a look of apology. "I meant that in a good way," she said, trying to cover her shock.

"Uh-huh," he muttered.

She peeked up at him with a little smile. "I'm sorry, but Ben... *oh my god,*" she repeated in a little whisper.

He rolled his eyes at her. "Sorry. It's a birth defect."

She felt terrible. "Come here."

He came and sat down next to her on the bed. She tried very hard not to stare. She was certainly not an experienced judge, but this was obviously beyond normal. He was just *so* big. Any desire she had felt had immediately fled. She knew that women were supposed to want size in a man, but to her he seemed absolutely terrifying. She hoped it wasn't too obvious.

"You're gettin' all intimidated on me now, aren't you?" he asked. He said it with a playful edge, but it was true. He didn't seem too surprised though. She couldn't be the only girl to have had this reaction. He smiled at her and leaned down to give her a little kiss on her cheek and whisper in her ear. "I know it's a bit *much*. We can stick with the *special attention* plan if you want." He started kissing her ear again, and she couldn't help but snuggle closer against him. "It's okay..." he whispered breathlessly between kisses. "Really, it's your call." He leaned back to look at her again. "But you have to know, that I would *never* hurt you."

She froze for a moment. He couldn't know of course, but that was almost exactly what Cain had said to her... just before the first time that he'd drunk her blood. She found herself gazing into Ben's eyes. "I know you wouldn't." She gave him a little kiss. "I want to."

He didn't say another word. He kissed her passionately and then moved down to take off her panties. He kissed the inside of her thighs until she couldn't help but try to hold her legs more open to him. His kisses traveled up between them until the heat of his breath and the teasing licks of his tongue made her squirm.

She was so ready and eager with anticipation that it seemed torture to have to wait any longer, but when he came back to lie over her, she felt the broad tip of his penis press against her gently and she couldn't help but tense. "Ben, wait. I..." she struggled to find words to voice her concern. She didn't *want* to be frightened of him but... "I don't think it'll fit."

He started laughing. It didn't make her feel bad though. It was a comfortable and loving little laugh. He bent to kiss her again before he whispered, "Don't worry, I'll fit. It just takes a little... coaxing. I'll be gentle, I swear. Do you trust me?"

"Uh-huh." He kissed her and tried to bring her back into the moment as he pressed against her again. Passion returned with his kisses and her body was undeniably eager for him. Her lips moved down the side of his throat, and as he began to enter her, she couldn't help but close her teeth lightly on his shoulder. She gripped him with a force like iron, but he was ever gentle as promised. It was like slow, passionate torture.

Back and forth, slowly he made his way further as her doubts fled before the promise of gratification. He straightened his arms to hold himself up from her, to give himself better leverage and she was forced to let him go. As she lay back on the bed, he felt so far away. She wanted to feel him lying down on her, to wrap her arms around him and share more kisses, but he seemed afraid to let himself press down on her too strongly as he whispered, "Don't let me hurt you. You tell me."

"Uh-huh." She looked up at him but he had closed his eyes. He seemed so hesitant and afraid to harm her that he was in pleasurable torment. Each slight motion from him drew a moan from her that voiced her delight even as it pleaded with him to come back to her lips. She needed him close, she needed his kiss, she needed more…

He pressed slightly deeper within her and she moaned louder. He instantly looked down in concern. "'Liss, you okay?"

She quickly nodded her head against is fears, but this was not working. She couldn't let him go on with this affection that was like interminable agony. To feel so close to satisfaction and yet be kept from truly being with him… "Ben?"

He withdrew in concern. "I'm sorry." Wow, he was so worried for her, how could he even enjoy it?

"No, I'm fine. It's just… Do you think that maybe… *I* could be on top?" she asked hesitantly.

He looked very amazed and aroused that she would ask, but then he grew doubtful. "You might have kind of a hard time."

She grinned and gripped his shoulders as she brought herself up to him for a kiss. Then she startled him by turning and pushing him down on his back roughly to the bed. She smiled at him with a sparkle in her eye, thinking of the excitement that *she* had felt when he had pushed *her* down before in almost the same way. She sat astride his belly and leaned down over him, smiling playfully. "No… I won't."

He had seemed very aroused by her actions, but was a bit sobered by her words. "Had a lot of practice, have you?"

She looked down at him in annoyance, but before she said anything harsh, she realized that it was just a defense mechanism. He was feeling inadequate – odd as that might sound for a man of his proportions. She looked down at him sternly and refused to be baited. "Shut up."

She kissed him before he could respond and he didn't fight it. Now she was the one to let her kisses travel down *his* body. She placed a small very deliberate kiss on the scar on his chest, and then moved downward over his stomach.

She had originally thought to savor and show appreciation for his body in the way that he had for hers, but in practice… she just hadn't the patience. She moved herself down between his legs and took his penis into her hand. She was very aware not to hesitate in the least. Her kisses moved down his stomach and followed the light line of hair there, to the smooth skin surrounded by downy curls below.

Felicity caressed and kissed him gently in her hand with a care that she hoped would make him feel that his body was something she treasured, and was not afraid of. Then she took him into her mouth briefly, though he barely fit. The rumbling moans that emerged from deep within his chest begged her for more as she covered him with licks and velvet kisses. She was sure to leave him good and wet for herself.

He looked at her through a haze of ecstasy as she came up to set herself astride him. She positioned herself carefully and began to let her weight down upon him, but the angle wasn't quite right and she quickly lifted herself with a hiss.

"'Liss stop. You don't have to, really."

She lifted her hips upwards away from him, and then lay down flat upon his belly and chest as she brought her mouth to his lips for a kiss. "I thought I told you to shut-up," she whispered teasingly. She kissed him and then used her hand to help position him between her legs where she lay.

She gently moved herself down onto him and drew in another hiss of air as he began to enter her body, before Ben could protest, she took his lips again with her own. This was good, this was right. He was so warm and close against her as she moved her hips to take him further.

She had to end their kiss for a gulp of air. She couldn't help but cry out as her body stretched to accommodate him fully, but it was so good to feel him deep within. *This* is what she had been wanting when his hesitant motions before had teased her so. Her gasps for breath came in time to her movements down upon him until the hollow ache inside of her was entirely filled with him. A missing piece to make her complete.

She looked into his eyes to see such wonder and affection in them as he gazed back at her. She smiled and cupped the side of his face with her hand as she kissed him again. He was such a mixture of boldly headstrong confidence and quiet vulnerability. So stubborn and willful and yet now he gave himself over fully to her control.

How could she have known him so well, and yet never *known*? His kisses held such loving desire for her and she drank up his passions as though she'd been starved without them. It fit so perfectly that her best friend should be her lover as well.

She was amazed at how acutely aware she was of each new sensation. In being with *Cain*, the venom had certainly held its pleasures, but she'd never realized how much it also must have clouded her mind. *Now* with Ben, each slight bit of friction, every touch seemed so raw and intense.

She began to build her movements faster upon him and it seemed to drive him wild. He began kissing any part of her that he could reach with his lips. She arched her body upwards until he found her left breast. He took her into his mouth and sucked strongly upon her in time to the rhythm of her pulsating hips.

She thrust herself down upon him mercilessly as a wave of ecstasy caused her to lose control. He released the nipple of her breast to cry out as climax overcame him and she clenched her muscles tight around him as she was carried on that wave to the same perfect fruition.

Felicity held him tightly until she lost all strength and collapsed upon his chest gasping for air. She lay and gave him tender kisses on his throat and shoulder until finally, she began to lift herself from him. She sucked in a long deep hiss of breath as he left her body and then she collapsed once more, rolling to the side of him onto her back.

They lay there in recuperative silence for a moment, and then Ben propped himself up on one elbow to face her. She smiled up at him as he gazed upon her with such blatant adoration. The strange thing was… she'd seen him look at her that way before. Maybe not the *exact* same expression, but so similar that she must have been blind not to see it for what it was earlier. Odd times, here and there during conversation or just sitting quietly at lunch. How had she never recognized it before?

He leaned down to kiss her. She pursed her lips but it was the corner of her eye that he kissed. Once… twice, and then lots of little pecks all over her cheek and her eye. She laughed. "No more tears."

"Good." He smiled at her and then dipped down to give a little lick between her breasts. She had to laugh at the absurdity of it. "Still salty though."

She cringed and shook her head with a grin. Of course, her body was covered with a thin sheen of sweat from their exertions. "I work hard for my rewards," she responded in justification.

Ben gave her a sly smile. "I noticed." He lay back on the bed next to her as though completely exhausted. "Oh my

God 'Liss." He looked over at her again in concern. "Are you okay?"

She giggled. "I'm fine." Actually, she *was* a bit sore, but she certainly wasn't going to tell him that, besides, it was worth it.

"I have never been with a girl like that."

She lay there looking up at the ceiling in confusion. It seemed kind of an odd thing for him to say. "What do mean?"

"I've never been with a girl who likes to be in charge. I mean, not that the position's new, but usually it doesn't really work out... on account of my *birth defect*."

She rolled her eyes and gave him a little shove. "Stop calling it that."

"No really. Most girls seem to find me pretty intimidating. They're never assertive like that. They always seem to want to follow my lead, like I wouldn't ever want to let them take charge of things."

Felicity smiled. "Well, you are kind of bossy."

He laughed a little and shook his head. "*Thanks*, but I always end up having to kind of... hold back. I mean let's face it, if I ever really *came down* on a girl the way I'd like to... I'm always afraid I'd hurt them. So, it's good, but it's always kind of... restrained."

He leaned up again on his elbow to look at her. It seemed odd to be having this conversation with him about other girls, but as his *friend,* she felt like he needed to get it off of his chest. It was like a confession that he'd needed to talk out... but who could he ever really talk about it with? Allie?

Maybe... but it didn't sound like it. She lay quiet and still, afraid to say the wrong thing to make him feel ill at ease.

She looked up to see him gazing down at her with that adoring look again. He moved her hair aside, gently stroked her cheek, and then smiled with widened eyes. "But with *you*... That was unbelievable! So honest and real. That was *no holding back*. It was absolutely *amazing*." He paused in gently stroking the side of her face to smile at her again tenderly. "You know *why* it was so amazing?"

She eyed him dubiously. "Because I have good rhythm?" she offered with a grin.

He broke out into laughter. "No! Well... *yes*, but no. It's because it was *you*. You're my 'Liss. You *know* me. I don't intimidate you... not really. You're not afraid to stand up to me and you don't take my shit. You're there for me when I need someone to set me straight.

Even just *every day*, I enjoy being with you and you're fun and you're beautiful and you're smart and... and I love you," he looked at her with sudden concern. "You *know* that right? I love you."

She gazed up at him with wide eyes. "I am so stupid."

"Okay, not really the response I was hoping for."

"I *am* stupid," she repeated.

"No, you're not," he insisted in confusion.

"Don't argue with me, ask me *why* I'm stupid."

"Okay..." he began hesitantly. "Why are you stupid?"

"Because I love you too."

He looked at her oddly that *that* should make her stupid. "I don't know if I like where this is going."

"I mean, why didn't I see it before?" she asked.

"You were kind of...distracted."

"Yeah, I guess I was, but I *do* love you. Part of me has loved you all along. Even when you were arguing with me and driving me crazy. I've always felt close to you. It's just... I never realized that it could be...like *this*. What is wrong with me?"

Ben smiled. "You're a teenage girl." She laughed and he gave her a soft, sweet kiss. "I love you."

"I love you too."

"Now *that's* what I was hopin' to hear." He grinned from ear to ear and kissed her again. "I am so in love with you!"

She giggled. "I think you may have mentioned that."

"I know. I can't stop saying it. It feels good. I love you Felicity Snow."

"I love you too Benjamin Everheart. I really do."

~~~~~~~~~~~~~~~~~~~~~~~~~~~~~~~~~~~~

Felicity was pulled from sleep by a noise. She opened her eyes to see what was making that faint 'whirring' sound. Oh, the man on TV was trying to sell a blender.

Ben was still sleeping. She snuggled closer to him and watched with heavy lidded eyes as the man on the infomercial shoved in various vegetables to make an oddly colored, 'nutritious' concoction.

Then she heard another noise. It didn't come from the television, but from the window that shared the wall with the headboard of the bed. That's what had woken her. Her pulse began to race in alarm as she watched the glass slide slowly upwards.

She was about to wake Ben, when she heard someone talking outside. The voice was familiar. She cautiously sat up in bed. They weren't even talking to her, but to someone else outside in the dark...seeming completely unconcerned with anyone in the room at the moment. "I know. You don't have to. I won't take long."

The covers slipped from Felicity as she moved, and she realized that she was still nude. Her eyes quickly searched the floor and found Ben's tee shirt. She grabbed it and quickly put it on as she tried to see the face that belonged to the arm on the windowsill. "Allie?"

Alyson turned to face her through the window as Ben sharply sat up, nearly knocking Felicity from the bed. "Allie!"

Allie's eyes widened as she took in the occupants of the room and their state of undress. "Oh my God, *you guys*..." She was grinning broadly. "Is this a bad time? You want I should leave?"

Ben sat up further and Felicity shoved the sheet into his lap, as he seemed completely oblivious to his nudity. "Alyson Freeman, don't you dare! You get your ass in here right now!"

Allie grinned and climbed in the window with a laugh as Ben continued to reprimand her. "Where have you been? I've been worried sick about you!"

Allie had barely finished climbing in the window when Ben began to climb from the bed to meet her for a hug. Allie briefly eyed him up and down and then turned away slightly with a little smirk. "Jeez, Ben. Put some clothes on."

Ben realized his nakedness and grabbed the sheet to cover himself in annoyance as his eyes searched the floor for his pants. They were across the room. He turned instead to rifle through the drawer of the nightstand.

Felicity got up with a smile and went to give Allie a hug hello. She was glad Ben was tall, his tee shirt hung down far enough on her to preserve modesty. Allie whispered in her ear. "When did *this* happen?"

Felicity grinned shyly at the floor. "Just tonight."

Allie made her look up and met her eyes after a glance at Ben and a smile. "You guys are gonna be great."

Allie turned back to Ben who was finishing putting on some boxer shorts he'd dug up. She spoke louder for him to hear too. "Sorry to barge in. I climb through Ben's window all the time, but I've never interrupted something before. What… was the Hilton booked?" she asked with a sly smile.

Ben came over and grabbed her for an embrace. He hugged Allie's tiny frame so strongly that Felicity was surprised he didn't crack her ribs. "Thank God you're back. What'd you go and quit Tommy's for? You scared me to death."

Allie shrugged as he loosened his hold. "Time for somethin' new."

Ben held her by the shoulders and beamed, that she was really there. "I'm so glad you came back. I'm sorry about everything. It's not fair that I'm always tryin' to tell you what to do. You know I love you… no matter what. Still friends?"

"Of course."

He hugged her again tightly. "You're back," he said again with a smile.

She leaned back to make him let go. "I can't stay," she said quietly.

The happy relief on Ben's faced turned to confusion. "What? Why not? Of course, you can. *It's okay.* You can see whoever you want. I won't say a word, I swear. It's going to be hard but... you don't have to go."

Allie smiled at him sadly. "I love ya' Benji, but yes... I do." Ben began to protest again but she just shushed him and grabbed his hand. She made him open it flat as she pressed it to her slight chest.

That's when Felicity realized.

It was freezing outside... there was still snow on the ground. Yet Allie wore only a thin 'Judas Priest' concert shirt.

Ben stood there in confusion with his hand on her chest. He was about to speak again when something in Allie's eyes stopped him. That's when it hit him. Felicity watched in silence as his eyes went wide and his face drained of color. He pressed his hand strongly to her chest and moved it over a little... searching. He tried again desperately, but Felicity knew... he wouldn't find a heartbeat.

She watched him as the look on his face turned to horror and he silently mouthed the word 'no' a few times before he found his voice. When he did, it was quiet and trembling. "What did you do? *What did you do?* Oh my God Allie, no! What did you do!?" His voice became raised with a mix of hysteria and tears. "You are so stupid! Oh my God Allie! You are so stupid! What did you do?!"

He took his hands off of her and held them before her as though pleading for the obvious not to be true. "Your whole life! This is your whole life! Why? Why would you do this?! Oh my God, no! Allie!" He closed his eyes and then covered his face with his hands for a moment. The way he was gasping for air, Felicity was afraid that he might hyperventilate. Allie just stood there and watched him.

Suddenly he looked up in new distress. "You let me hold you; you let me think you were... Oh my God, you *tricked* me. You got me to invite you into my house! Into my room!"

Allie looked confused and then moved forward to put a hand on his shoulder in reassurance. "Ben, it's still me."

Ben smacked down her hand and backed away. "No! You're not..." He looked as though he couldn't figure out what to believe.

Felicity moved to go to him, to say something, but Allie looked up at her and slightly shook her head no. This was between her and Ben. It was obvious to Felicity that Allie's spiritual essence was unchanged even if her body was not quite the same, but Allie wanted Ben to come to his own conclusion.

Ben started to cry. He just looked at Allie and cried. After a moment, Allie tried again to hold him, but as she neared. Ben's sorrow turned to rage. "Don't touch me! Oh my God... *you fucking demon! Get out!* Get out of my room! *Get out!*" As Ben yelled the last, he turned away from her. He looked like he wanted to punch and break something, but nothing was in reach but Felicity. He grabbed her in a crushing hug and cried.

Even as he did, Felicity's attention was drawn to Allie. Ben didn't see it, but as his last words rang through the air, Allie stumbled as though physically struck. She was shoved back against the windowsill with only the force of Ben's words and his rescinded invitation.

The look on her face was a mixture of shocked distress and hurt betrayal. She opened her mouth as though in pain and unable to breathe. Felicity tried to take a step to go to her, but Ben held her tight as he faced the other way.

Allie reached backwards blindly to grab the edge of the window frame against which she'd been thrown. She hopped herself up onto the sill and ducked her head to lean a bit outside. Once there she was obviously much relieved. It only took her a second to compose herself. She took a deep shuddering breath to help restore calm, and looked back to Ben and Felicity again.

Felicity's gaze met Allie's as Ben still hugged her tight with eyes shut, unwilling to face his childhood friend. Allie was fighting back tears as she tried to smile. She knew him. She had to have known that he wouldn't be able to accept it. Felicity felt like she wanted to shake him, yell at him and make him see that Allie was okay.

Alyson seemed to read her mind. She gave her head a little shake and blinked back her tears. She spoke so quietly that Felicity could only just pick out her words over Ben's quiet sobbing at her shoulder. "It's okay. Take care of him for me."

Felicity tried to smile and nodded as Allie blew her a little kiss and turned to hop down out of the window onto the lawn outside. Felicity stared at her as she did... comprehension of Allie's new vampire state still just sinking in. Was she really...

Another thought came to mind as well. *That could have been me.* She wasn't sure how she felt about that.

Allie turned back for one last look. She was crying now. Her face seemed to crumple as she met Felicity's eyes, and then she just turned and ran. As Felicity's eyes followed her outside, she saw someone else standing out on the grass. For one unreasonable second her heart stopped as she searched the face for recognition... but no. She didn't know him. A young man stood outside waiting. He looked as though he wanted to catch and hold Allie but she wouldn't let him.

As she ran past, the young man turned and looked through the window. Even from out on the lawn, too far away for real clarity, Felicity could feel his eyes meet hers.

It was Mattie. It had to be. He looked disappointed and resentful. He stood there and watched her holding Ben for what was probably only a second, although it seemed like an eternity.

Half a dozen haphazard thoughts seemed to rush through Felicity's mind in the space of that second.

She wanted to run out and assure him that Ben was only temporarily blinded with grief.

She wanted to make Ben see that his grief was unnecessary. Allie would be happy now. This was what she wanted.

She wanted to make Ben turn and face his lost friend. To reconcile them somehow. To make what seemed to Ben an awful tragedy, somehow change into a reunion... something good.

She wanted to go and comfort Allie.

She wanted to find Allie and hug her and talk to her and ask her what it was like. Was she happy?

The last thing that flashed through her mind almost made her feel numb. It was Mattie! She had been waiting, hoping to see him! She could go to him. He could take her to Cain. And if he wouldn't, surely Allie could convince him.

In fact, if she worried that Cain would turn her away for guilt... she could take the matter from his hands. Allie was one of them now. *She could do it.* If that was what Felicity really wanted.

Obviously, Mattie was capable. He and Allie could do what was necessary. She could come to Cain already changed... At that point, he would never turn her away. This was the chance she'd been waiting for.

Mattie only met her eyes for a moment. Then he turned and began to walk away.

She let him go.

Ben gasped at her shoulder like a drowning man coming up for air. Something in him suddenly realized that Allie was really gone. "Allie!"

He turned to face the rest of the room, but of course, she was no longer there. "Allie!" His eyes found the window and he rushed to look out into the night. His eyes must not have found them. "Allie!" They were gone.

Ben turned to Felicity with a look of wild desperation. "She's gone! Oh my God, she's gone! She left! I made her leave... and I didn't get to say goodbye! She's gone! She thinks I hate her. She left and I didn't get to say goodbye." He started to break down again and Felicity went to hold him. The realization of it all was just too much. "'Liss, I yelled and said awful things. She thinks I hate her and she's gone."

"It's okay. It's okay Ben... she knows. She knows you didn't mean it. She knows."

"But she's gone. She's not even... Oh my God 'Liss. Her *life* is gone! I didn't even get to say goodbye. At school... we argued and she left and now she's..." He had no more tears but just a desperate sort of hysteria that shook him with dry sobs.

Felicity tried to speak with a voice of calm authority. She made him meet her eyes. "Ben, she's okay. She really is. She's happy now. It's what she wanted. She's okay."

Ben looked like he wanted so desperately to believe her, but was having a very hard time reconciling her words with his conjectures of the past. His old perceptions and opinions of things were hard to let go. He needed time. He stared at her with the frightened and unseeing look of a deer in headlights.

"Ben, it's okay. You've got me."

He finally focused on her face. Recognition seemed to seep in as his anguish slowly drained away. He looked so grateful for her presence, her steadfast support... for her love. He loved her, and he needed her, he really did. He drew her into his arms. Not a blind grasping hold to reality as before, but a tender, loving embrace.

How had *she* turned into someone that others looked to for confidence? How had she become the calm voice of reason and the pillar of strength in the midst of emotional turmoil? Wasn't she Felicity Snow... the quiet little mouse, afraid of her own shadow and always with a stomach full of butterflies?

A vision came back to her. A memory of her and Cain, outside eating ice cream on a warm September night. She could see him clearly and almost *hear* his words to her then.

'Things change and we're all of us just struggling to keep up, but sometimes… change can be good — when you least expect it.'

"I love you, Felicity." It was Ben, holding her close and kissing the side of her face.

Maybe things really do happen for a reason. "I love you too."

Epilogue

Felicity

Ben's bedroom
Friday morning

Felicity awoke to a cardinal singing outside the window in the early morning sunlight. She opened her eyes to see that Ben was already awake. He gave her a little smile and snuggled closer to her in the bed. "Morning."

"Morning."

He lay there quiet for a few minutes. She could almost see all of last night's happenings going through his head. He took a deep breath and sighed. "I feel like I spent last night on an emotional roller coaster."

She shook her head with a little chuckle. "The ride started back in September for me."

"I hate roller coasters. They always make me sick." He gave her a weary, hopeful sort of look. "Think the ride's over?"

"Are you kiddin'? We're just switchin' tracks," she answered with a laugh. She lay there playing her eyes over his face for a minute. Yeah, she loved him. She really did. "I'll try not to make you throw up."

He laughed. "I appreciate it." He seemed to make a conscious decision to carry on, past it all. He gazed at her and smiled.

She returned his smile with her own, happy to concentrate on new beginnings.

Ben rolled over for some space and rubbed the sleep from his eyes. They still looked a bit bloodshot from last night. She scootched up closer to him and kissed his cheek up near his eye, as he had done to her the night before. He grinned at her a bit weakly. "There has been entirely too much crying going on in this room."

"I thoroughly agree," she said with a smile.

"Well then... new rule. Crying is no longer allowed."

"Really?" she asked in amusement.

"So sayeth King Ben."

"*King* Ben?" she asked with a raised eyebrow.

"My room, my rules," he clarified.

She sat up and thought about that for a moment. "I think you should know...I'm not a big fan of absolute monarchy."

"No?" She wrinkled her nose at him and shook her head. He nodded. "I can accept that. How about an equal partnership?"

She grinned. "Equal?"

"Absolutely. Except..." he leaned forward and whispered to her conspiratorially. "You can still boss me around during sex if you want. I kind of liked it."

She laughed. "I'll try to keep that in mind."

"Speaking of which... how you doin'?" he asked her tentatively.

She smiled at his concern. "I'm fine."

He looked unconvinced. "It's *me* you're talkin' to here 'Liss. Come on." He lowered his voice again although there was no one else to hear. "I know you've gotta be sore."

She shrugged. "Maybe a little."

"Sorry," he offered quietly.

"I'm not," she said with a sly grin.

"Well just so you know, you don't always have to do that. I mean, I know it's a lot to ask. It's okay if sometimes you're not up to it. I'll understand." He gave a little laugh. "Besides, you give good *special attention.*" She laughed as she felt her cheeks turning red. He watched her with a grin of his own. "I love to make you smile."

She'd been about to comment on his own adeptness and special attention skills when she was startled by the noise of a door slamming from somewhere else within the house. "What was that?"

Ben listened for a moment before answering, but seemed unconcerned. "My dad's home." Felicity froze as though caught in the midst of an indecent act. Ben noticed and quietly laughed. "It's okay that you're here." He became very thoughtful for a moment. "In fact...I'd like you to meet him."

Felicity sat up further in alarm. *"Now?"*

Ben laughed again. "You can get dressed first. Then I'll make us breakfast, introduce you... my *girlfriend.*" He seemed kind of tickled by the word. "When he takes Friday off it usually means he's had a rough week. He'll probably just say hello and then leave to go sleep all day."

Felicity still couldn't help but feel a bit uncomfortable, but Ben seemed insistent. He'd already met all of her family. Maybe he just felt that this was the next step. He did seem to be positively glowing over her. It was kind of nice that he wanted to introduce her as his girlfriend. She got dressed and he led her to the bathroom to freshen up before they joined his dad, who seemed to be in the kitchen. The smell of fresh coffee was drifting down the hall.

As Felicity brushed out her hair before the mirror, she couldn't help but wonder what Ben's dad might be like. Truthfully, she hadn't a very complimentary mental picture of him. All she'd ever heard about him from Ben was that he was never home, drank far too much and seemed to live only for his work. He was some sort of stock trader or something.

She rejoined Ben and followed him hesitantly into the kitchen. Ben's dad was sitting at the table with a cup of coffee reading the paper. He looked nothing like Felicity had pictured at all.

He was a very good-looking older man. He looked a lot like Ben really, but with a swath of gray streaked through his hair at the temples on each side, and careworn little crinkles about his eyes. He looked quite distinguished and handsome. He wore a smoky gray turtleneck sweater with a black pair of slacks. She saw that a black and gray sports coat lay draped over the empty chair next to him.

He didn't even look up as Ben entered the kitchen with Felicity just a bit behind him. "Morning dad."

"You're up early. Classes?"

"Not yet. Dad, I'd like you to meet someone." Now he did look up as Ben took Felicity's arm to guide her more fully into the room. "This is Felicity."

Ben's father looked up at her and seemed to narrow his eyes a bit. Felicity was instantly uncomfortable. It was as though he were looking right through her. After a moment though, he smiled.

He looked up at Ben with a rather sly smirk. "I had a feeling you weren't in there alone." Ben shifted a little in embarrassment for Felicity as his father stood to approach them.

He stood before Felicity and gave her a warm grin. "Do you know that you are the first girl that Benjamin has ever *introduced* to me? So, with his twenty-first birthday quickly approaching, I must presume that either my son is incredibly socially awkward… or *you* are a very special young lady.

And judging by the number of times I have been awakened by the comings and goings of the opposite sex through his bedroom window at night… I would venture to guess that it's the latter."

Ben rolled his eyes and shook his head in annoyance. "Dad, you know that's only Alyson."

"Has she had a sex change that I'm unaware of?" Ben just glared at him. Ben's father seemed completely unconcerned with his son's ire. He smiled and took one of Felicity's hands into both of his own. "It is a pleasure to meet you, Felicity."

Felicity tried to smile and keep herself from shyly averting her eyes. After a moment, he dropped her hands and went to take his place back at the table.

Ben spoke to Felicity as he turned to the refrigerator. "How does bacon and eggs sound?"

She was just nodding her head as Ben's father answered. "That sounds wonderful. I'm starved."

Ben looked very surprised and gave Felicity an apologetic look that his dad was planning to join them. She just smiled and shrugged. Rather than go sit, she stood by the counter with Ben as he got things started.

Ben's father spoke from the table. "So, Felicity, are you a student?"

She answered a bit timidly. "Yes sir."

He raised his eyes from his paper to train them on her for a moment. "A *college* student?"

Ben sighed in exasperation. "Yes dad. She's legal."

'Barely', Felicity thought uncomfortably as she averted her gaze. She began to fiercely hope that Ben's father would decide against breakfast and retire to the bedroom as expected.

The sound of the telephone rang from down the hall, drawing Ben's attention. "Oh, that's mine. 'Liss, would you watch the bacon?"

"Sure."

It seemed the moment that Ben left the room, his father's eyes left his paper again to study her. "How are you?" he asked. He seemed very direct and sincerely concerned for her.

She shifted awkwardly. "I'm fine." She looked down the hall after Ben and resolved to be confident. Ben *loved* her. That was all that mattered... right? She turned back to his father with new confidence. "Great actually," she said with a smile.

He smiled in return. "I'm glad that my son makes you happy, but if ever you need to talk… If there's a *problem* that you'd like to share…"

She looked at him oddly. "Problem?"

He stood and moved a bit closer to her. "If I'm not mistaken, it was a few weeks back." He gestured to her throat as he approached.

Her eyes went wide and she self-consciously raised her hand to the light scar there. "Oh this? It's nothing."

"Actually, I was referring to the *other* side." She froze. He could only be referencing the slight marks left by Cain, but they were barely visible! How could he have noticed them?

He seemed to misread her distress. "Never fear dear. It's no reflection on you. One never knows when or where those beasts will strike."

"But how…" she began in bewilderment.

"Their bite leaves an aura about the victim. A 'mark', if you will. I'm rather skilled at reading them. And judging by yours, I'd say you're very lucky indeed to have escaped with your life. You were attacked by a *very* old and powerful creature."

Felicity just stood there with her mouth open in shock. He went on. "Not to worry. It's nearly faded, so if he hasn't returned by now, I shouldn't think you'll see him again. These creatures seldom linger in such rural areas, but should you ever be in need of assistance, don't hesitate to ask."

He seemed to realize her disquieted astonishment at his words. "Let me introduce myself properly." He took back her hand in both of his own, as he had held it before. "Bernard Everheart – Vampire Hunter," he said with a little nod, "at

458

your service. Just...be a dear and don't mention it to Benjamin. I've been very fortunate in keeping him shielded from this sort of thing. I'm afraid it would be a bit of a shock."

She stood staring at him in open-mouthed awe. He dropped her hand and retreated to the table as Ben re-entered the room.

"'Liss? The bacon's burnin'."

~~~~~~

THE SAGA CONTINUES

IN

ALMOST HUMAN

❧ THE SECOND TRILOGY ❧

VOLUME 1

BORN TO BLOOD

~~~~~~

If you enjoyed this book, please take a moment to leave a review online, on your favorite book review website!

You can join author/reader discussions about the series, and get updates on upcoming book releases for this series on the author's web site at:
www.MelanieNowak.com

Made in the USA
Columbia, SC
11 August 2023

21516805R00261